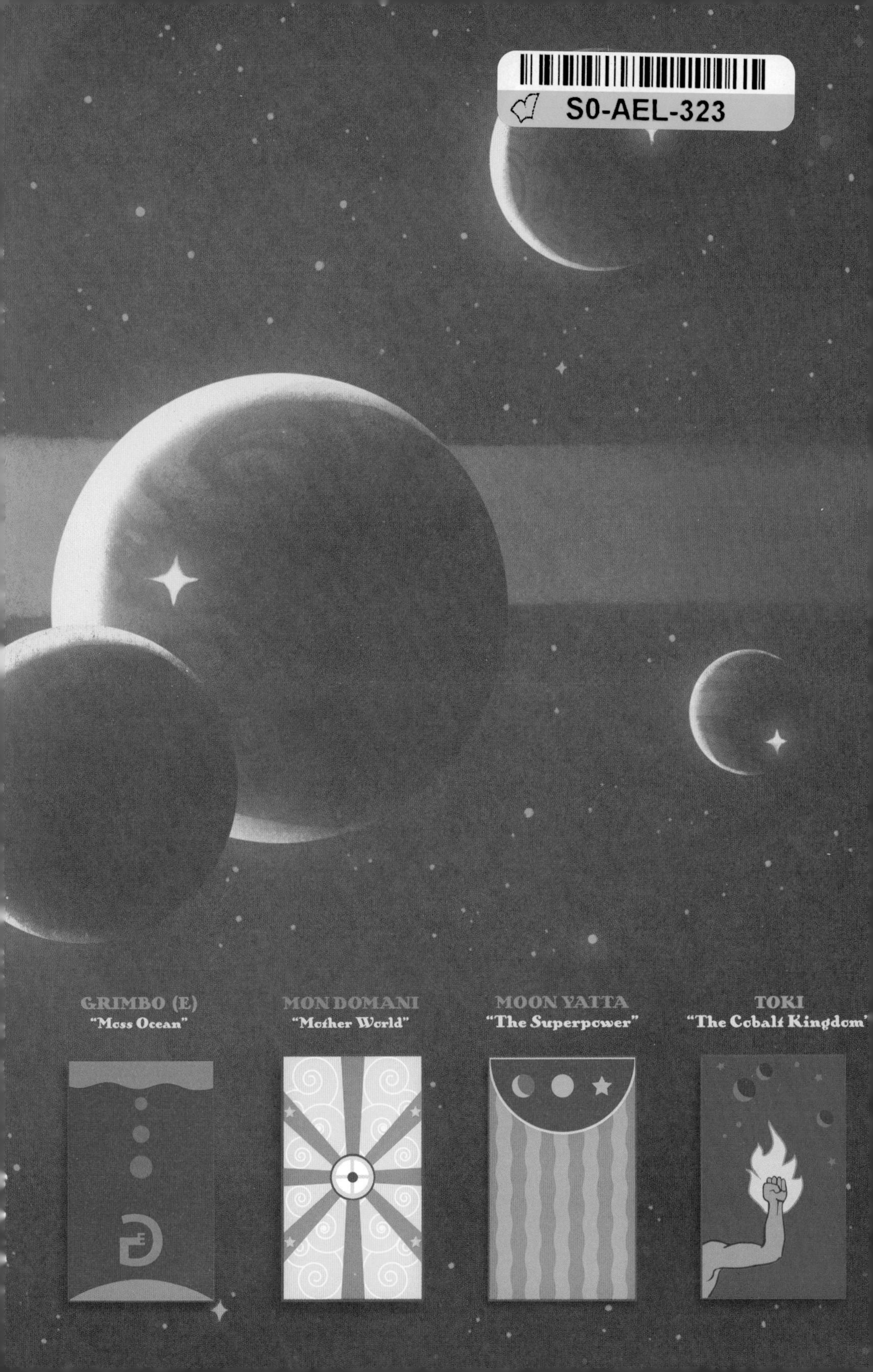
GRIMBO (E)
"Moss Ocean"
MON DOMANI
"Mother World"
MOON YATTA
"The Superpower"
TOKI
"The Cobalt Kingdom"

The Praise for 5 Worlds Is Out of This World!

A New York Public Library Top Ten Best Books for Kids Selection

A *Publishers Weekly* Best Summer Book

An NPR Great Read of the Year

A Junior Library Guild Selection

"Cinematic beauty."
—*The New York Times Book Review*

"For kids who love fantasy and other-world adventures, and for any fans of graphic novels, this book is a must-read."
—R. J. Palacio, #1 *New York Times* bestselling author of *Wonder*

★ "Sensitive writing, gorgeous artwork, and riveting plot, this is a series to keep an eye on."
—*Booklist,* Starred Review

★ "A dazzling interplanetary fantasy . . . that will easily appeal to fans of *Naruto* or *Avatar: The Last Airbender.*"
—*Publishers Weekly,* Starred Review

"This stellar team has created a gorgeous and entrancing world like no other!"
—Noelle Stevenson,
New York Times bestselling author of *Nimona*

"Epic action, adventure, and mystery will draw you in, but the heartfelt characters and their seemingly impossible journey will keep you turning the pages."
—Lisa Yee, author of the DC Super Hero Girls™ series

"Plenty of adventure as truths are uncovered. . . .
Give to fans of Judd Winick's Hilo or Kazu Kibuishi's Amulet series."
—*School Library Journal*

"The beautiful illustrations will have young readers flying through the pages."
—*Deseret News*

"The adventure continues, growing grander of scale
and if possible even more lavish in visual detail."
—*Kirkus Reviews*

"Ends triumphantly and tantalizingly."
—*The Horn Book Magazine*

"Distinctly unique. . . . It oozes with imagination and creativity."
—*Bam! Smack! Pow!*

"An intriguing beginning to what is sure to be a fascinating series."
—*BookRiot*

"I dare you not to get immediately caught up in Oona's epic tale!"
—*MuggleNet*

"Beautiful, with a vast array of characters and creatures from the various worlds."
—*GeekDad*

"A magical adventure full of wisdom, humor, and enough girl power
to make you root for Oona in her quest to light the beacon."
—**Abigail, age 10**

"This book is great! I usually don't like graphic novels,
but this book changed my mind."
—**Lucius, age 9**

5Worlds

BOOK 4

THE AMBER ANTHEM

Mark
SIEGEL

Alexis
SIEGEL

Xanthe
BOUMA

Boya
SUN

Matt
ROCKEFELLER

Random House New York

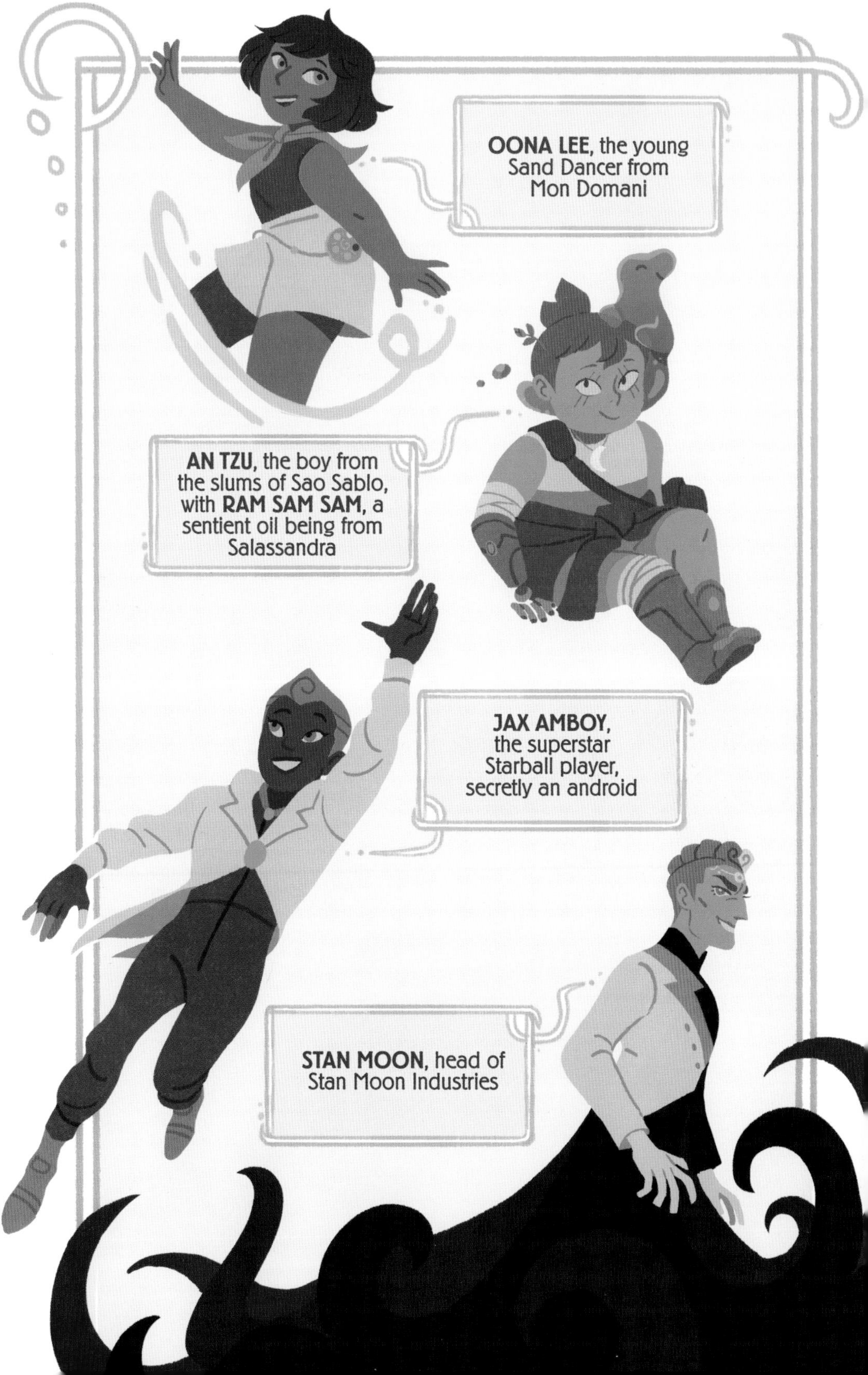
OONA LEE, the young Sand Dancer from Mon Domani
AN TZU, the boy from the slums of Sao Sablo, with **RAM SAM SAM,** a sentient oil being from Salassandra
JAX AMBOY, the superstar Starball player, secretly an android
STAN MOON, head of Stan Moon Industries

THE STORY SO FAR...

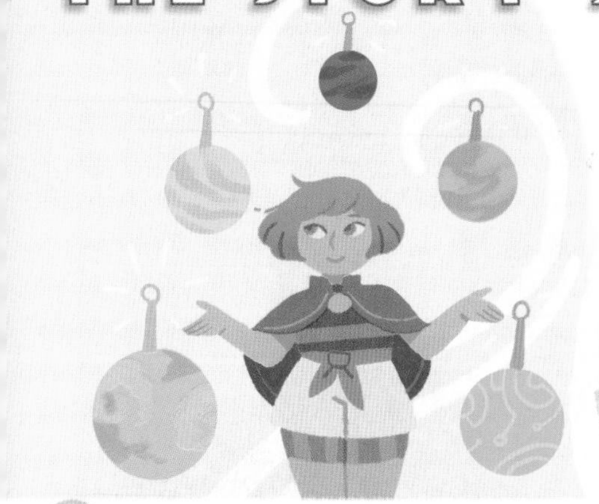

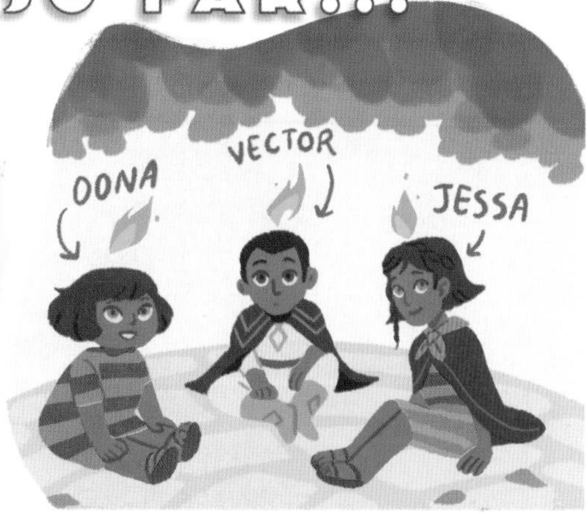
VECTOR
OONA
JESSA

To save the **FIVE WORLDS** from dying out, **OONA** and her friends must light all five ancient beacons: white, red, blue, yellow, and green.

For centuries, **the Living Fire** that lights beacons was the stuff of legend—until three children produced it on the blue world of **Toki.**

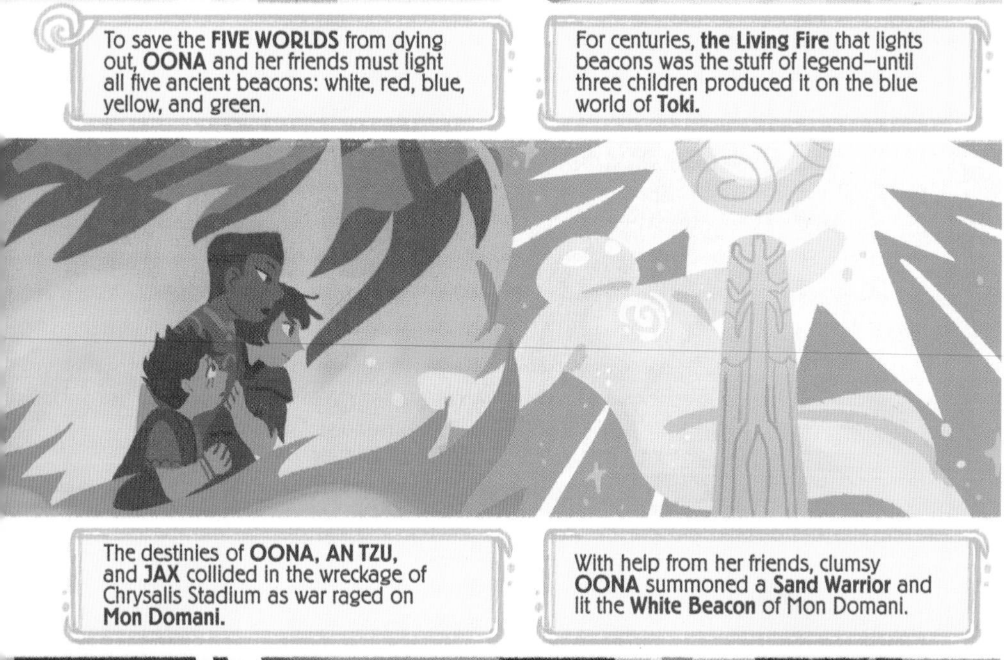

The destinies of **OONA, AN TZU,** and **JAX** collided in the wreckage of Chrysalis Stadium as war raged on **Mon Domani.**

With help from her friends, clumsy **OONA** summoned a **Sand Warrior** and lit the **White Beacon** of Mon Domani.

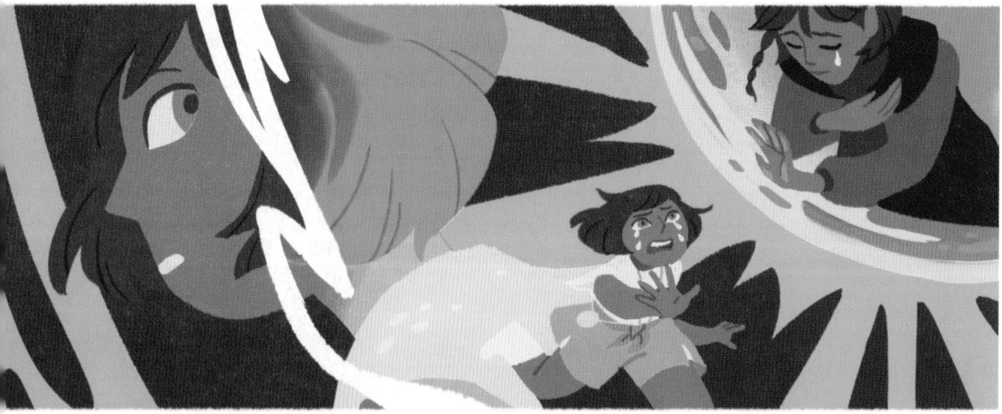

On Toki, **OONA** fought against an evil prince and discovered the truth of her heritage—that she was born on the blue planet.

The battle against the **Cobalt Prince,** and the evil **MIMIC** controlling him, was won, but at great cost: **OONA**'s sister **JESSA** sacrificed herself.

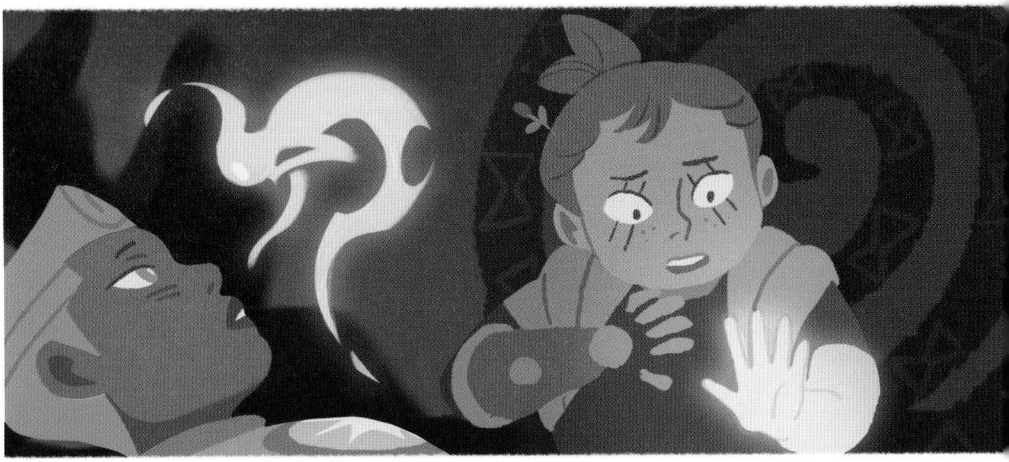

On **Salassandra, JAX** merged with a Salassi spirit known as a **DEVOTI** to become human.

AN TZU suffers from a mysterious **Vanishing Illness** and is beginning to fade away. He uses prosthetics to help maintain his physical form.

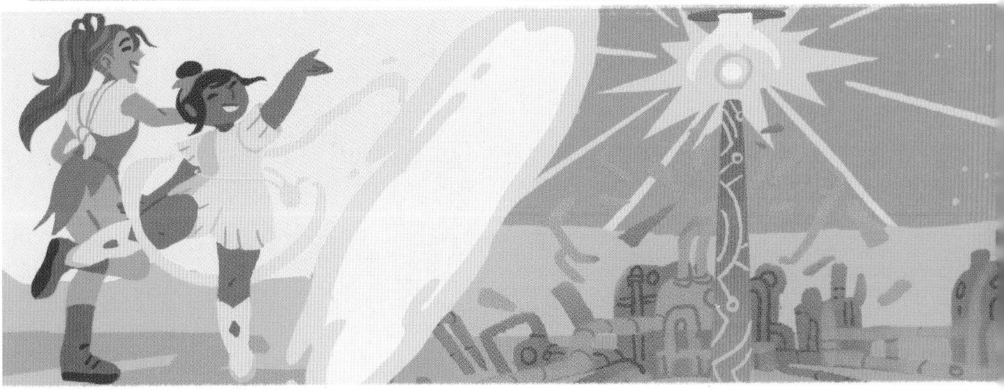

On **Moon Yatta, OONA** trained with **MASTER ZELLE,** who taught her how to create **portals** to defeat the **Red Maze.**

Using a portal, **OONA** lit the **Red Beacon.** Immediately afterward, **VECTOR SANDERSON,** now the new Prince of Toki, lit the **Blue Beacon.**

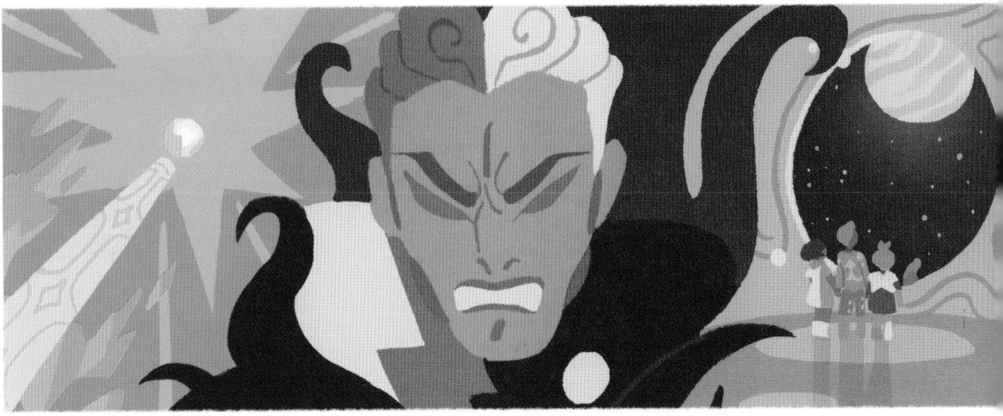

STAN MOON, possessed by the evil **MIMIC,** was elected head of Moon Yatta. He has vowed to hunt down **OONA** and her friends.

OONA, JAX, and **AN TZU** are now traveling aboard the **Flitori,** heading toward Salassandra and the **Yellow Beacon....**

I see moonbeams in your smile!
I hear sunbeams in your voice!
I see starlight in your eyes!
—CASCADELLE, "THE TOKI GIRL FROM MON DOMANI"

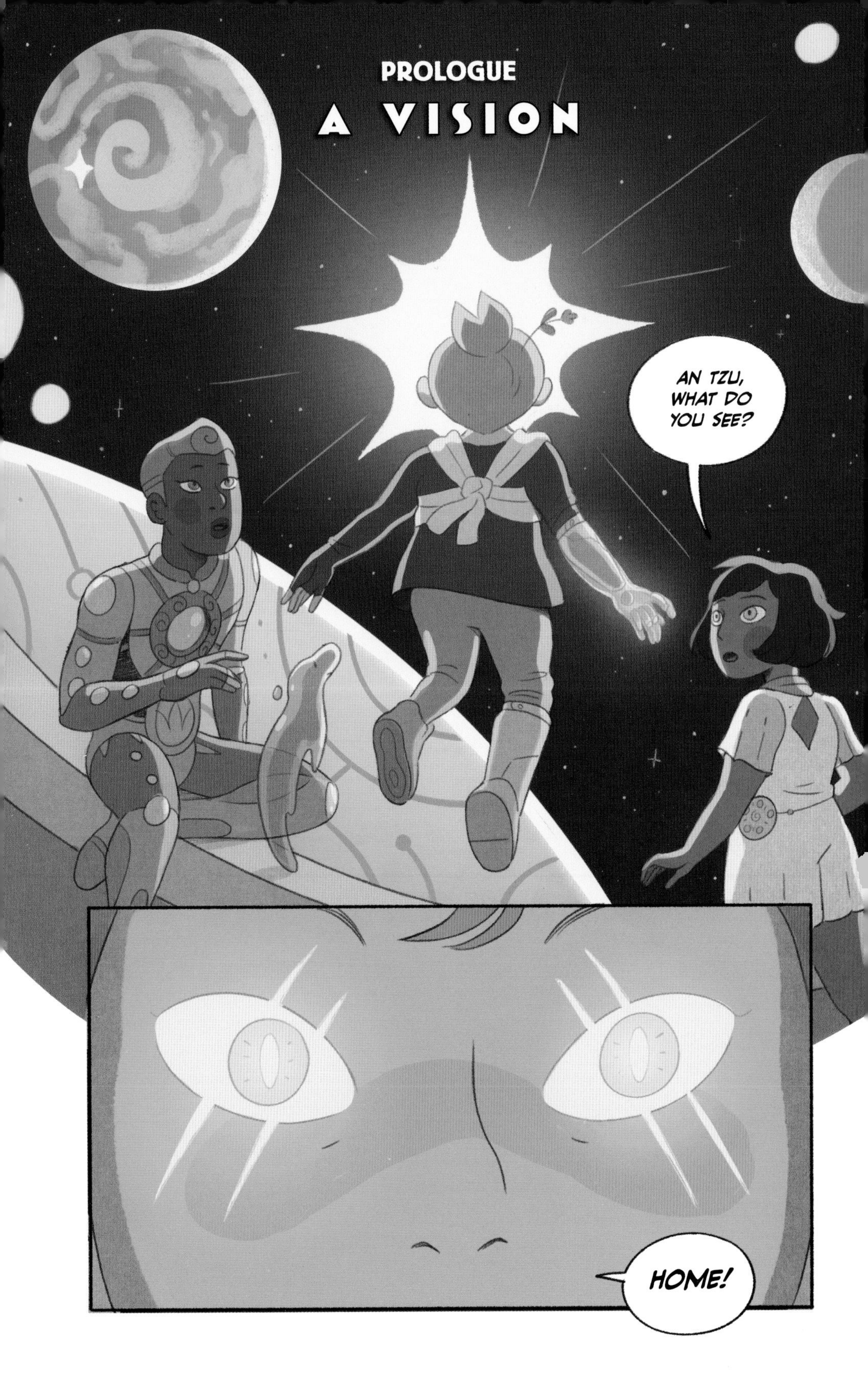
PROLOGUE
A VISION
AN TZU, WHAT DO YOU SEE?
HOME!

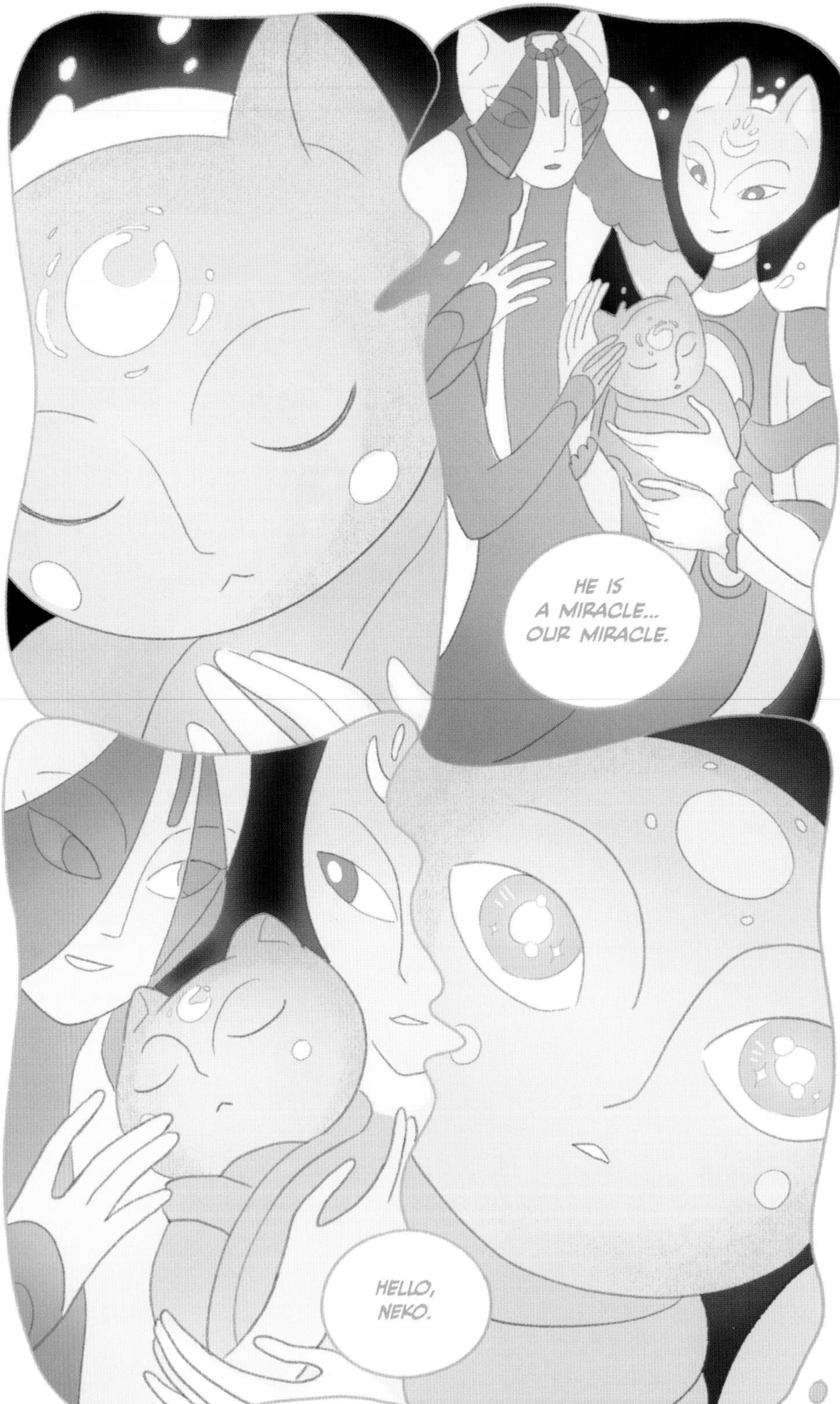
HE IS
A MIRACLE...
OUR MIRACLE.
HELLO,
NEKO.

I WAS LOOKING AT THE SUN AND SAW *THE FELID GODS*... FROM LONG AGO...

BUT WHY? WHAT HAVE THEY GOT TO DO WITH YOU?

I DON'T KNOW!

WHAT DID YOU MEAN, "HOME"? THAT'S A *SUN.*

HOW CAN HOME BE ON A SUN?

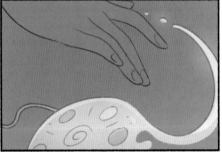

NOT *ON* A SUN. *IN* A SUN!

THE *COBALT PRINCE* SAID THE SUN ISN'T HOW WE THINK. RIGHT HERE, *INSIDE* THE FIERY BALL, IS A COOL WORLD!

THE TOKI PRINCE? WASN'T HE *LYING* HALF THE TIME?

I BELIEVE *THAT PART* WAS TRUE.

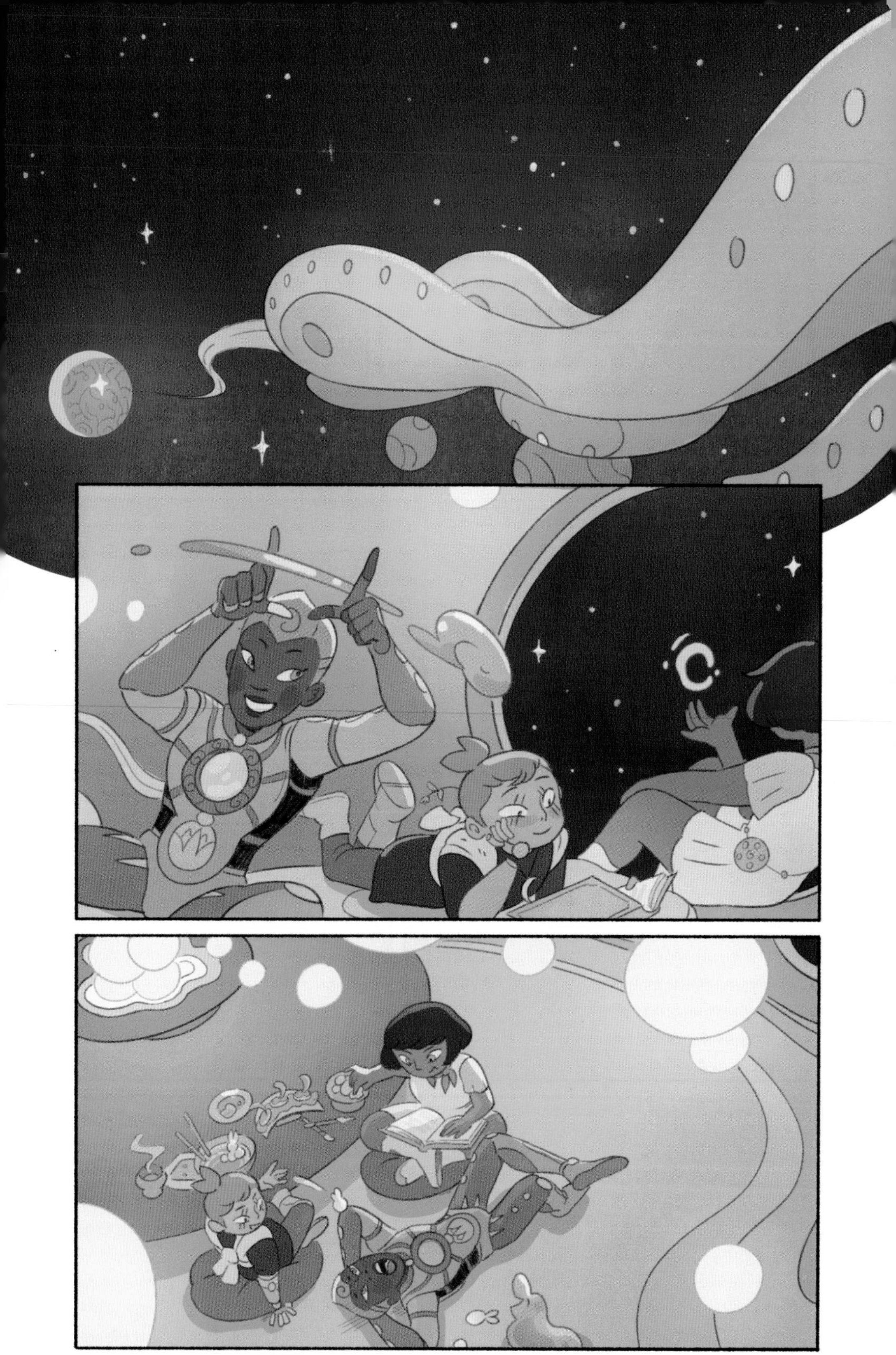

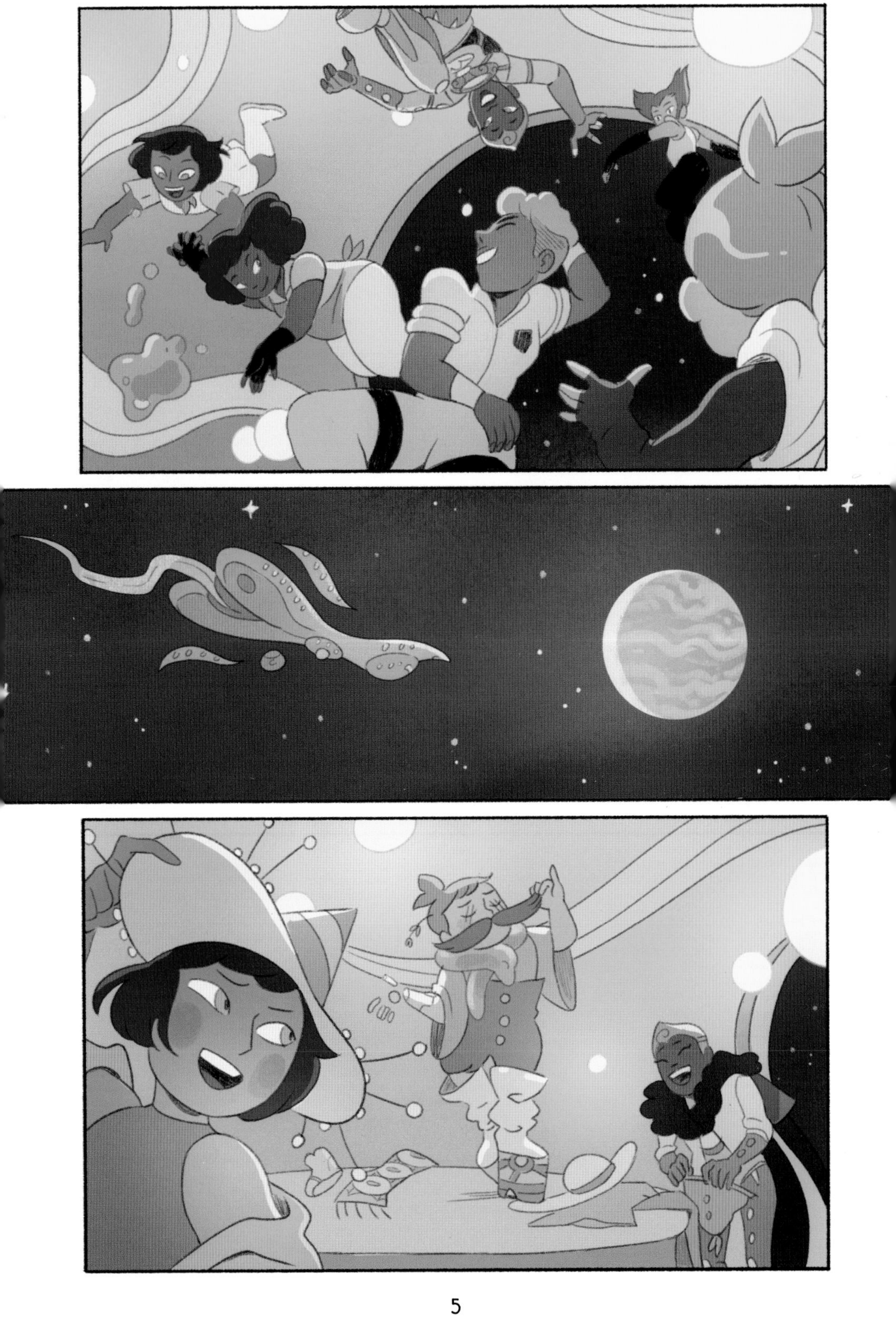

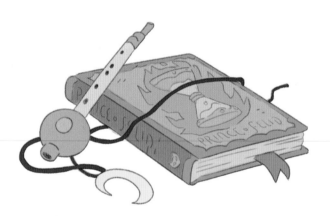

CHAPTER 1
THE GOLDEN GLYPHS

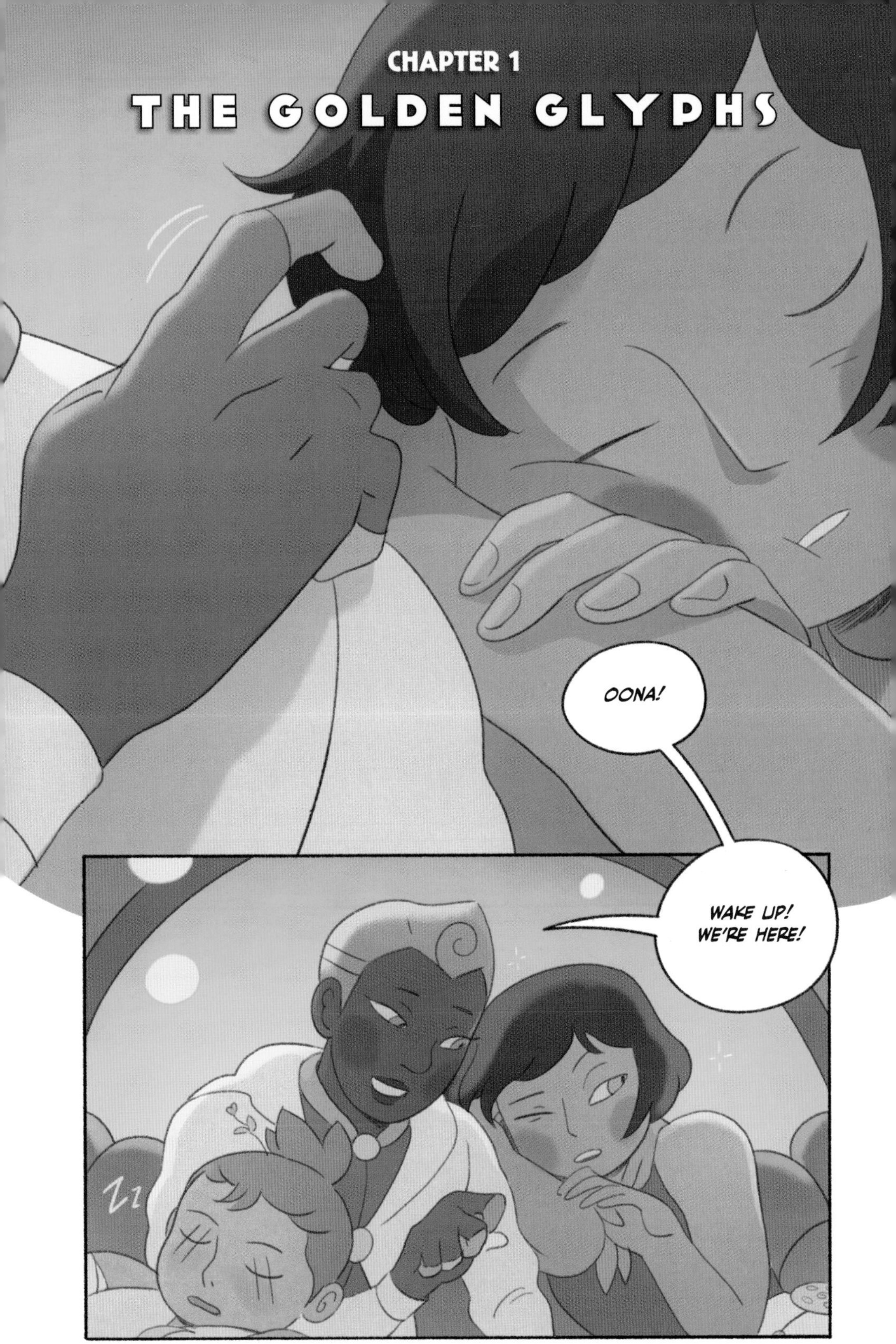
OONA!
WAKE UP! WE'RE HERE!
ZZ

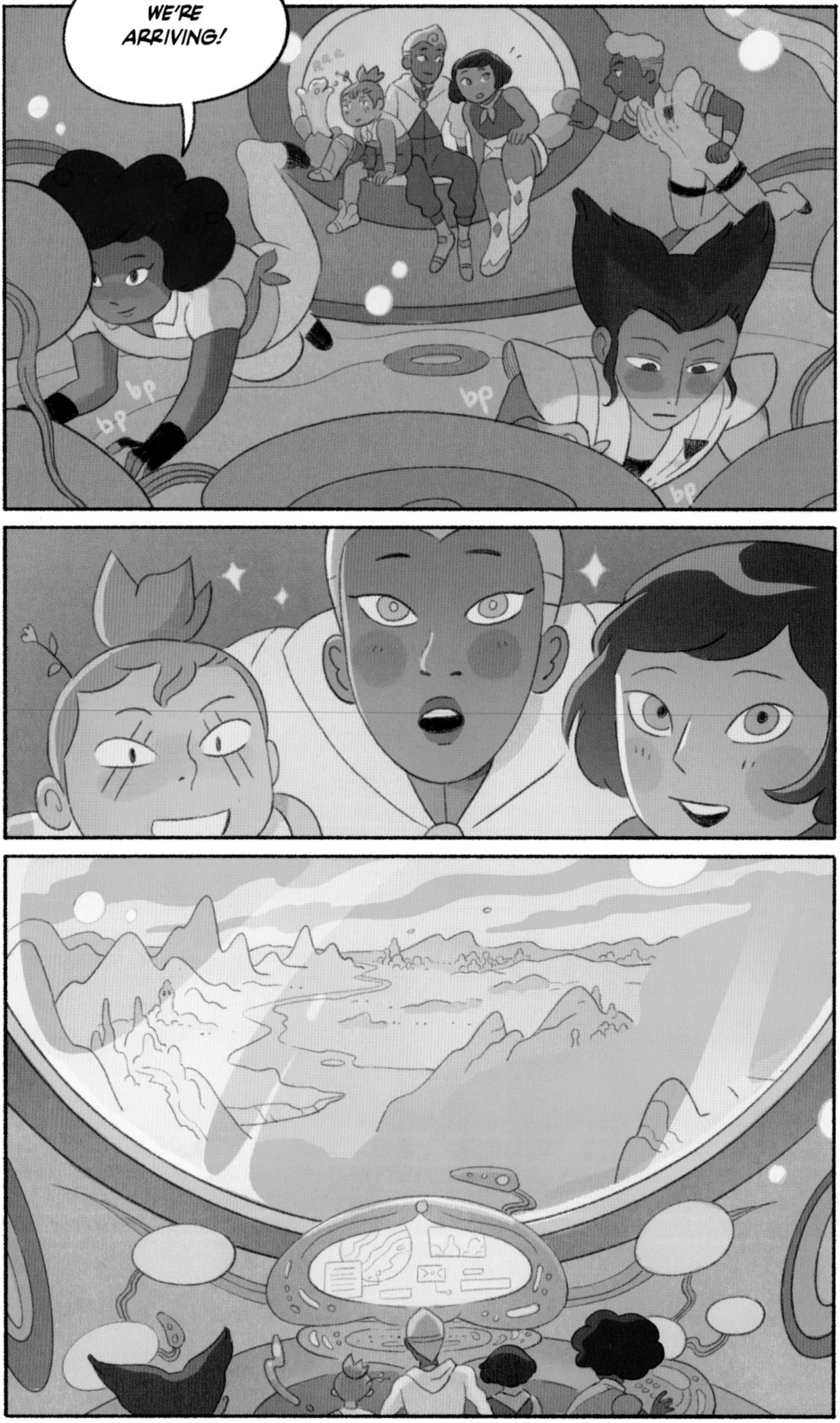
WE'RE ARRIVING!
bp bp
bp
bp

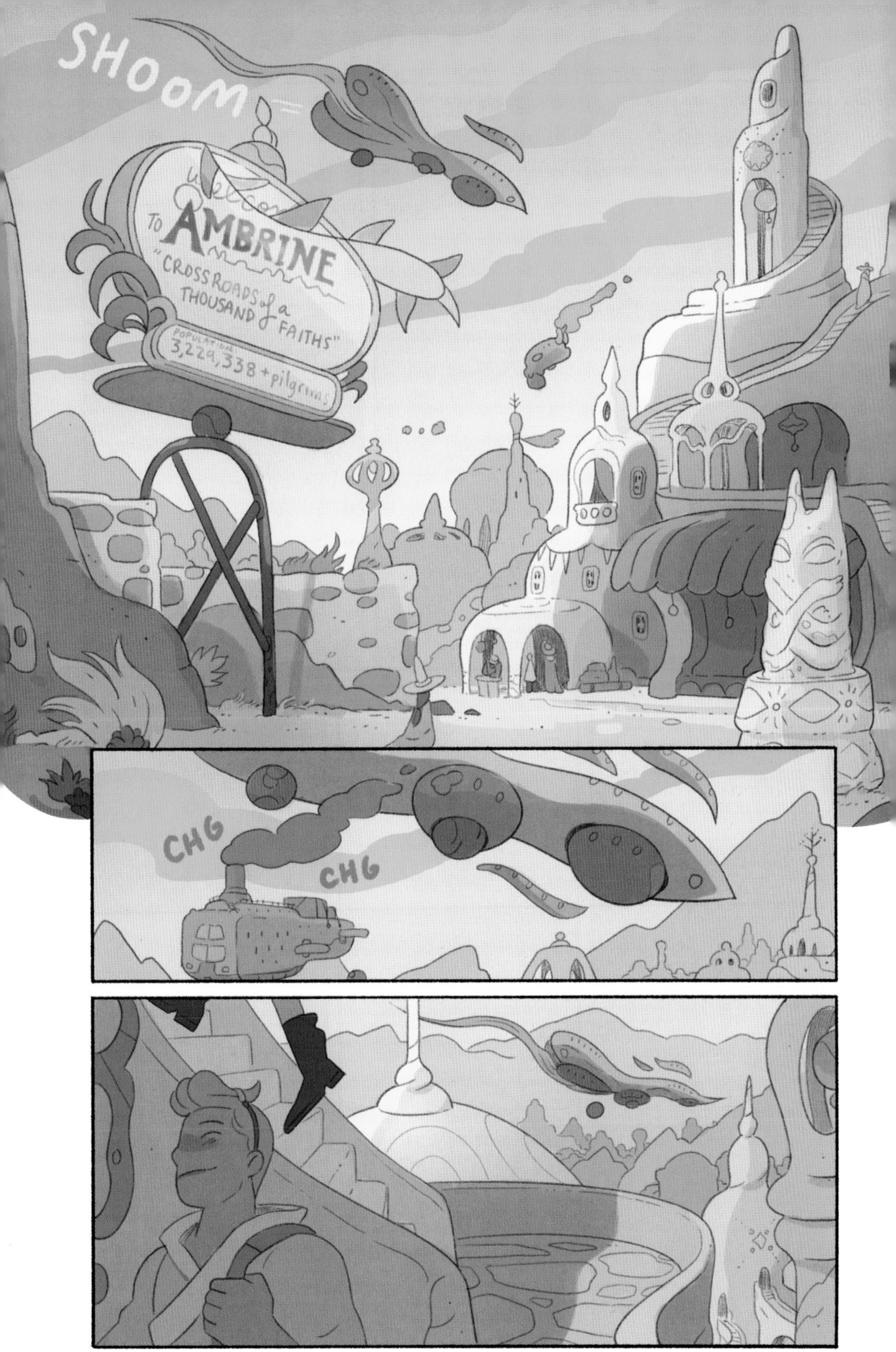
SHOOM
TO AMBRINE
"CROSSROADS of a THOUSAND FAITHS"
POPULATION 3,229,338 + pilgrims
CHG
CHG

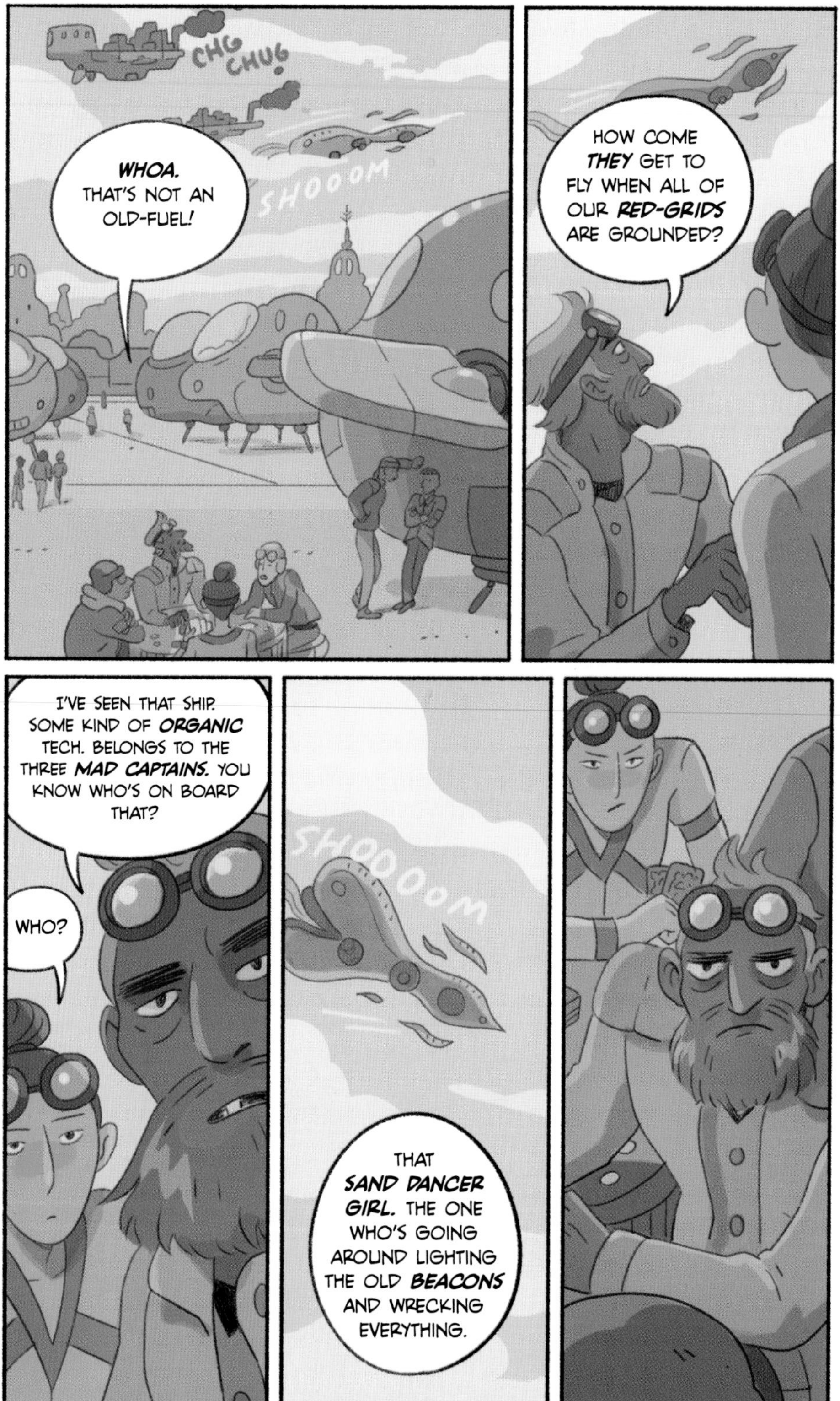
CHG CHUG
SHOOOM
WHOA. THAT'S NOT AN OLD-FUEL!
HOW COME THEY GET TO FLY WHEN ALL OF OUR RED-GRIDS ARE GROUNDED?
I'VE SEEN THAT SHIP. SOME KIND OF ORGANIC TECH. BELONGS TO THE THREE MAD CAPTAINS. YOU KNOW WHO'S ON BOARD THAT?
WHO?
SHOOOOM
THAT SAND DANCER GIRL. THE ONE WHO'S GOING AROUND LIGHTING THE OLD BEACONS AND WRECKING EVERYTHING.

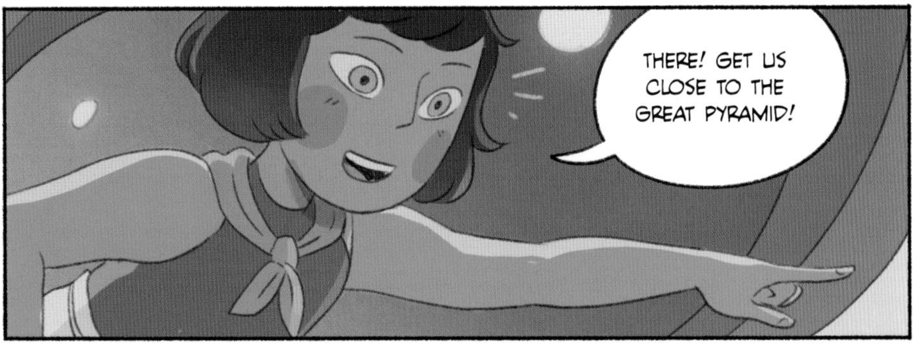
THERE! GET US CLOSE TO THE GREAT PYRAMID!

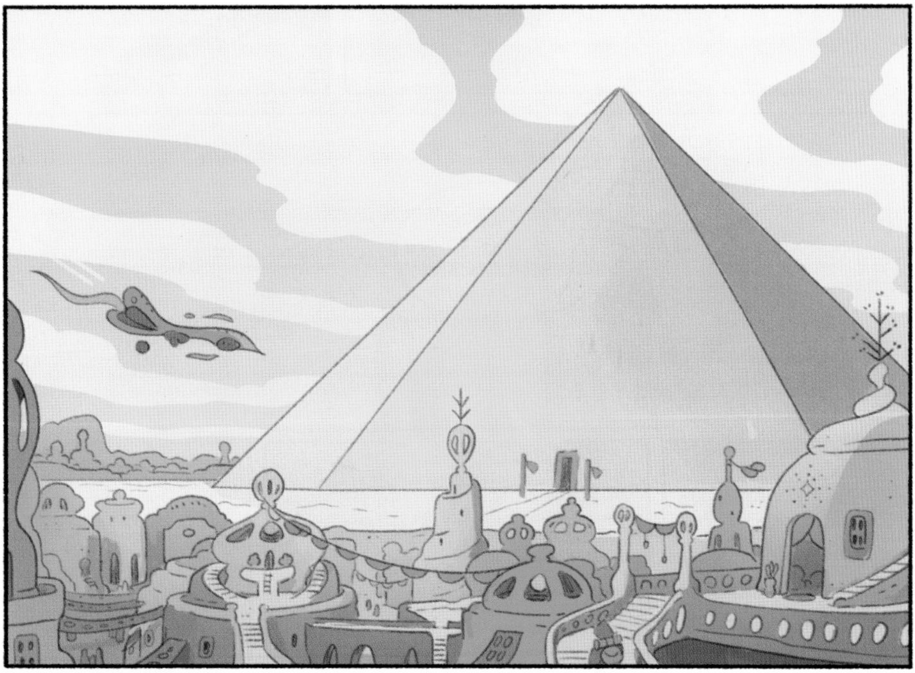

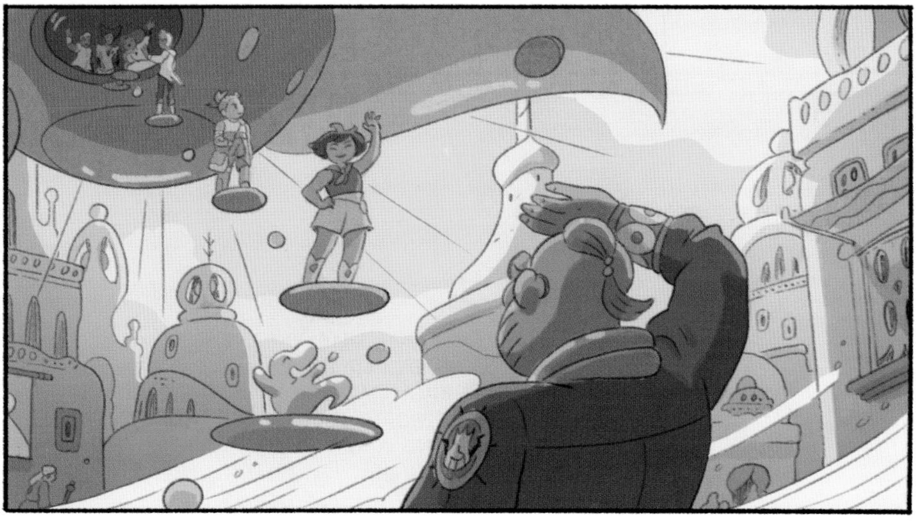

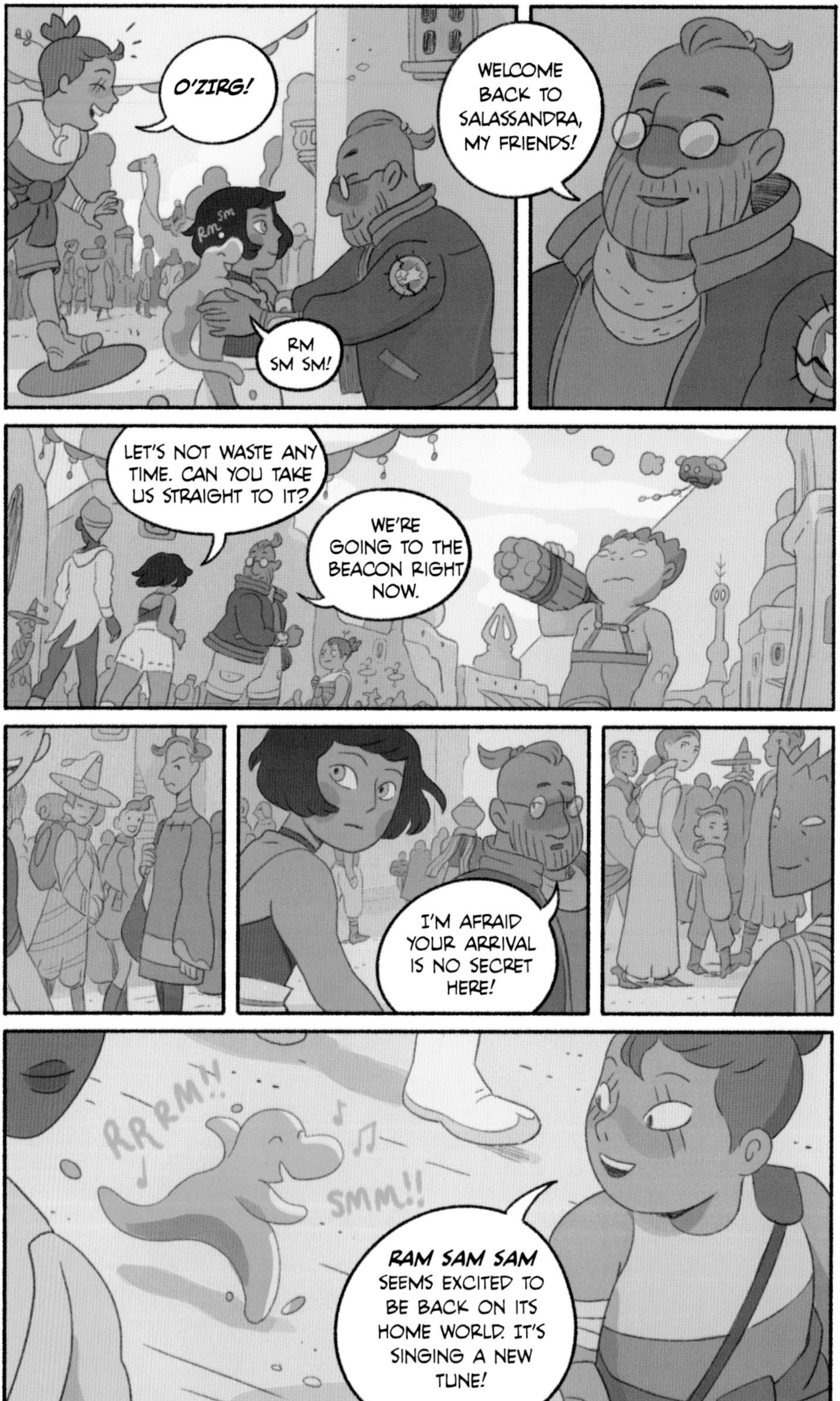
O'ZIRG!
RM SM
RM SM SM!
WELCOME BACK TO SALASSANDRA, MY FRIENDS!
LET'S NOT WASTE ANY TIME. CAN YOU TAKE US STRAIGHT TO IT?
WE'RE GOING TO THE BEACON RIGHT NOW.
I'M AFRAID YOUR ARRIVAL IS NO SECRET HERE!
RRRM!!
SMM!!
RAM SAM SAM SEEMS EXCITED TO BE BACK ON ITS HOME WORLD. IT'S SINGING A NEW TUNE!

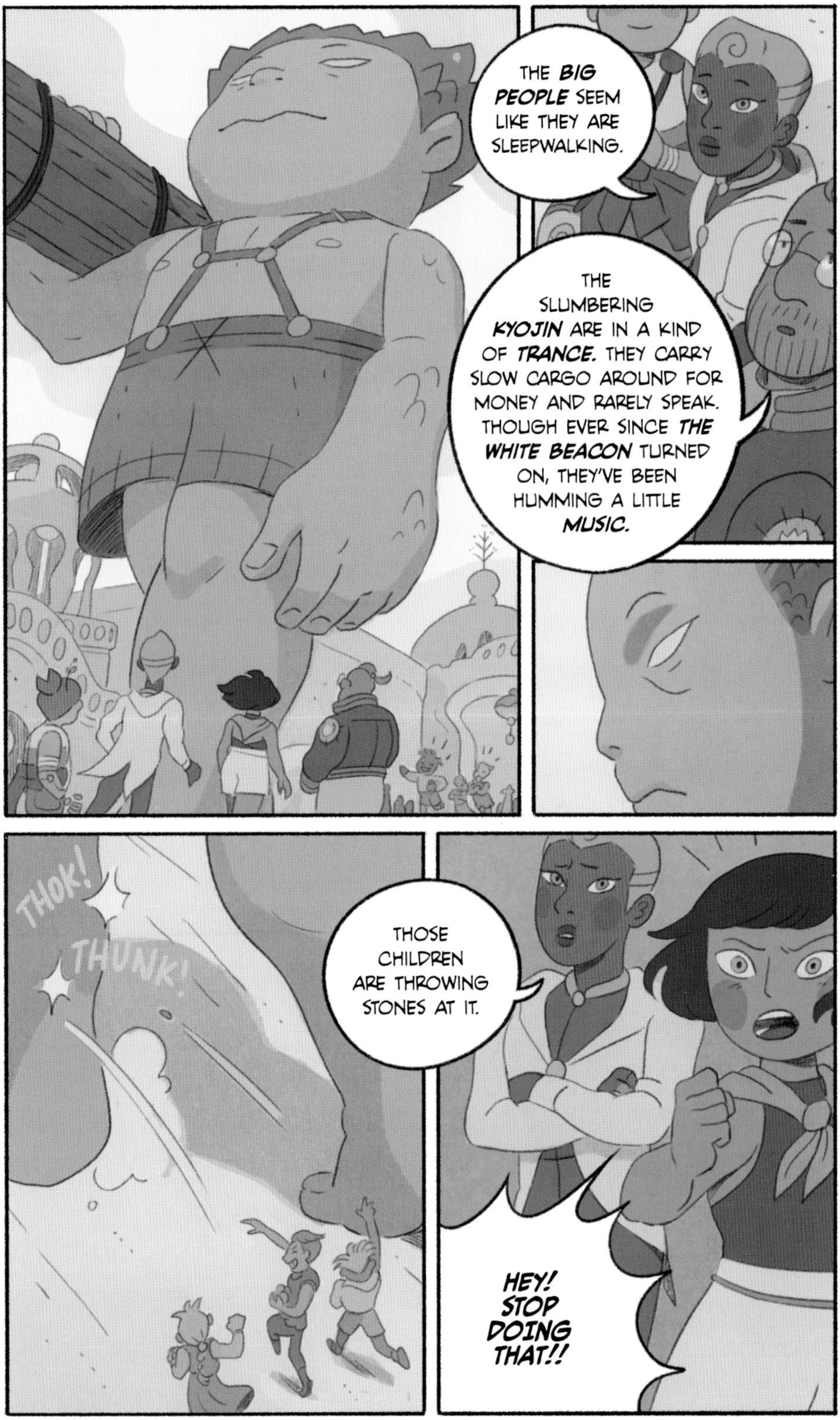
THE BIG PEOPLE SEEM LIKE THEY ARE SLEEPWALKING.
THE SLUMBERING KYOJIN ARE IN A KIND OF TRANCE. THEY CARRY SLOW CARGO AROUND FOR MONEY AND RARELY SPEAK. THOUGH EVER SINCE THE WHITE BEACON TURNED ON, THEY'VE BEEN HUMMING A LITTLE MUSIC.
THOK!
THUNK!
THOSE CHILDREN ARE THROWING STONES AT IT.
HEY! STOP DOING THAT!!

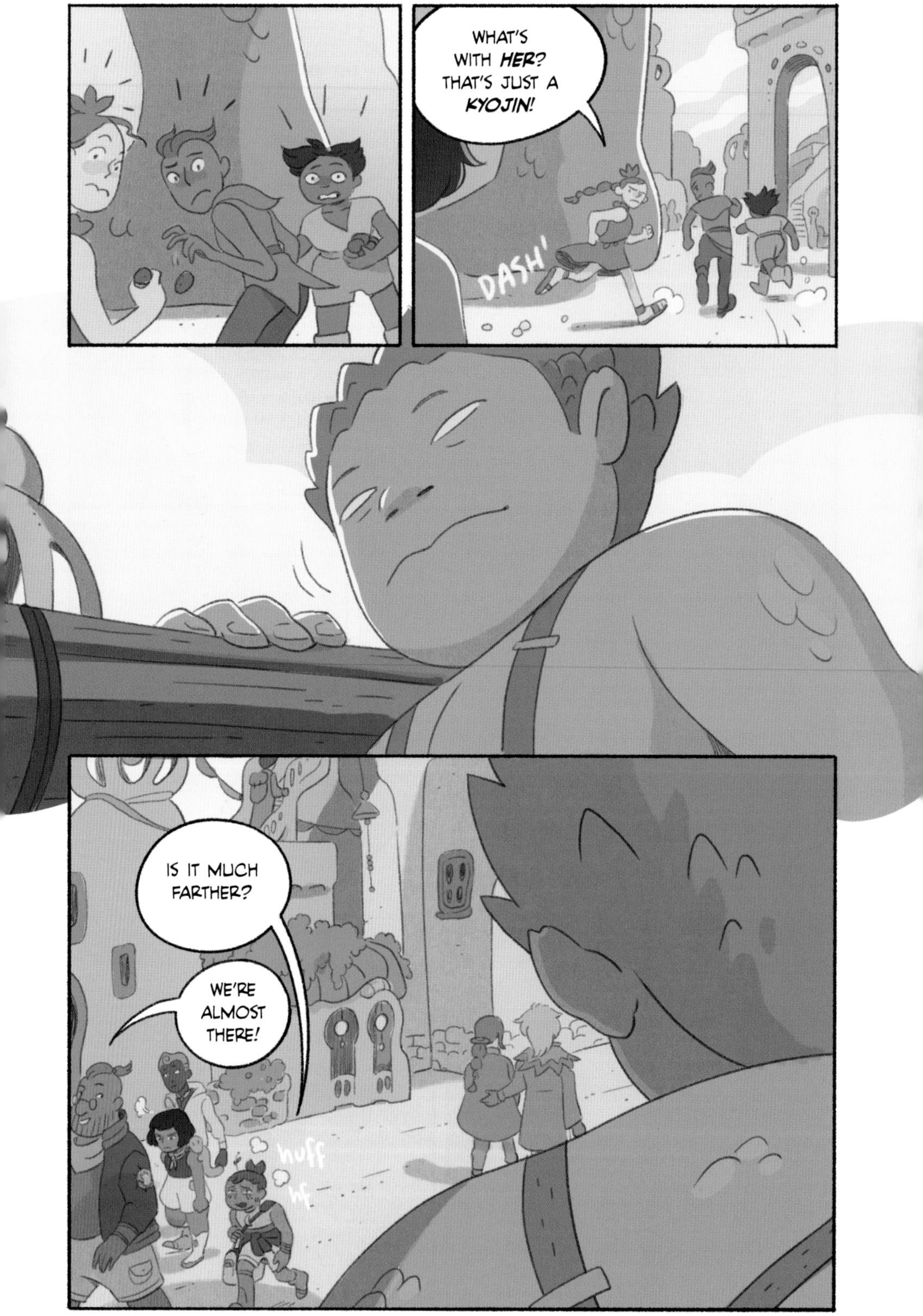
WHAT'S WITH HER? THAT'S JUST A KYOJIN!
DASH'
IS IT MUCH FARTHER?
WE'RE ALMOST THERE!
huff
hf

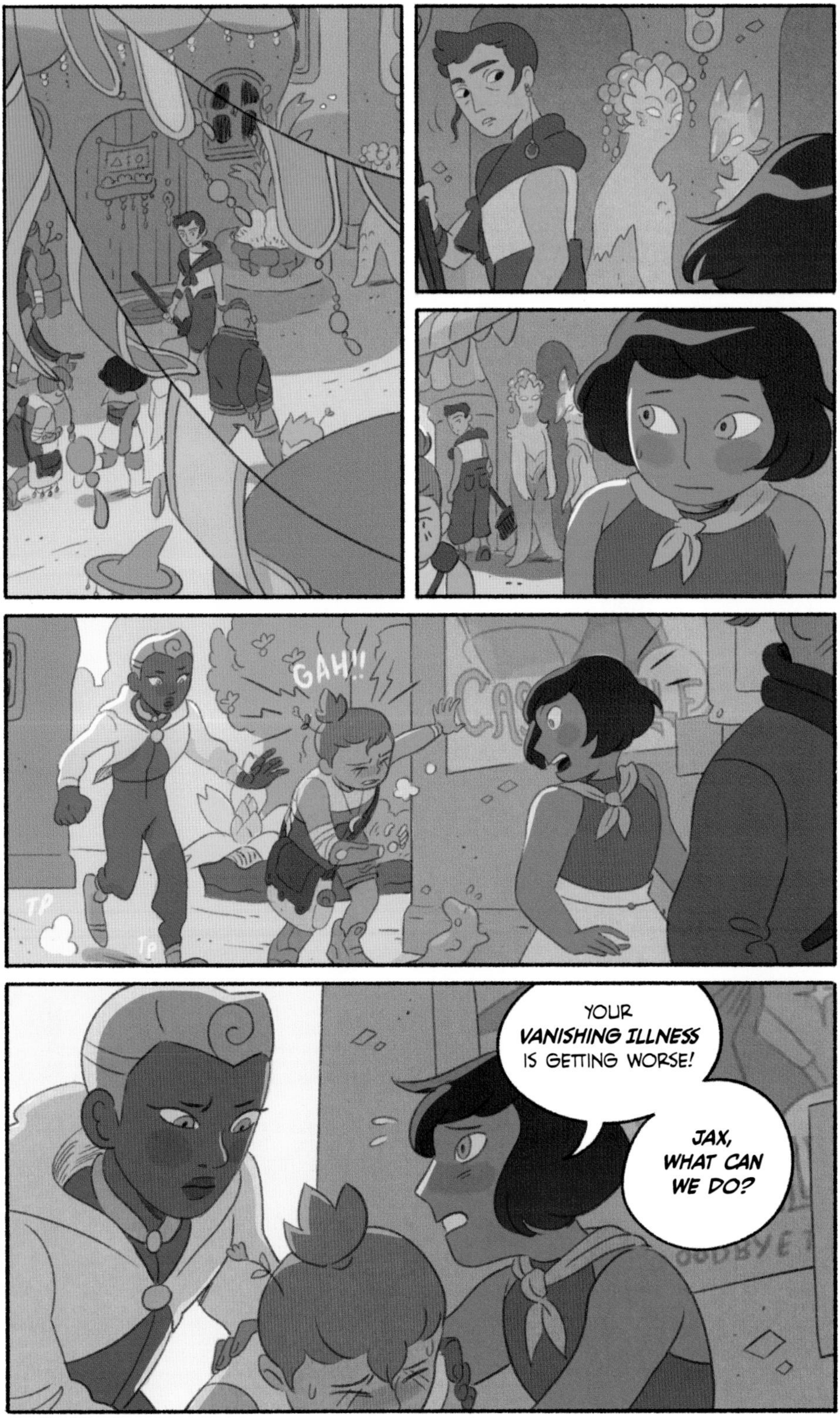
GAH!!
TP
TP
YOUR VANISHING ILLNESS IS GETTING WORSE!
JAX, WHAT CAN WE DO?

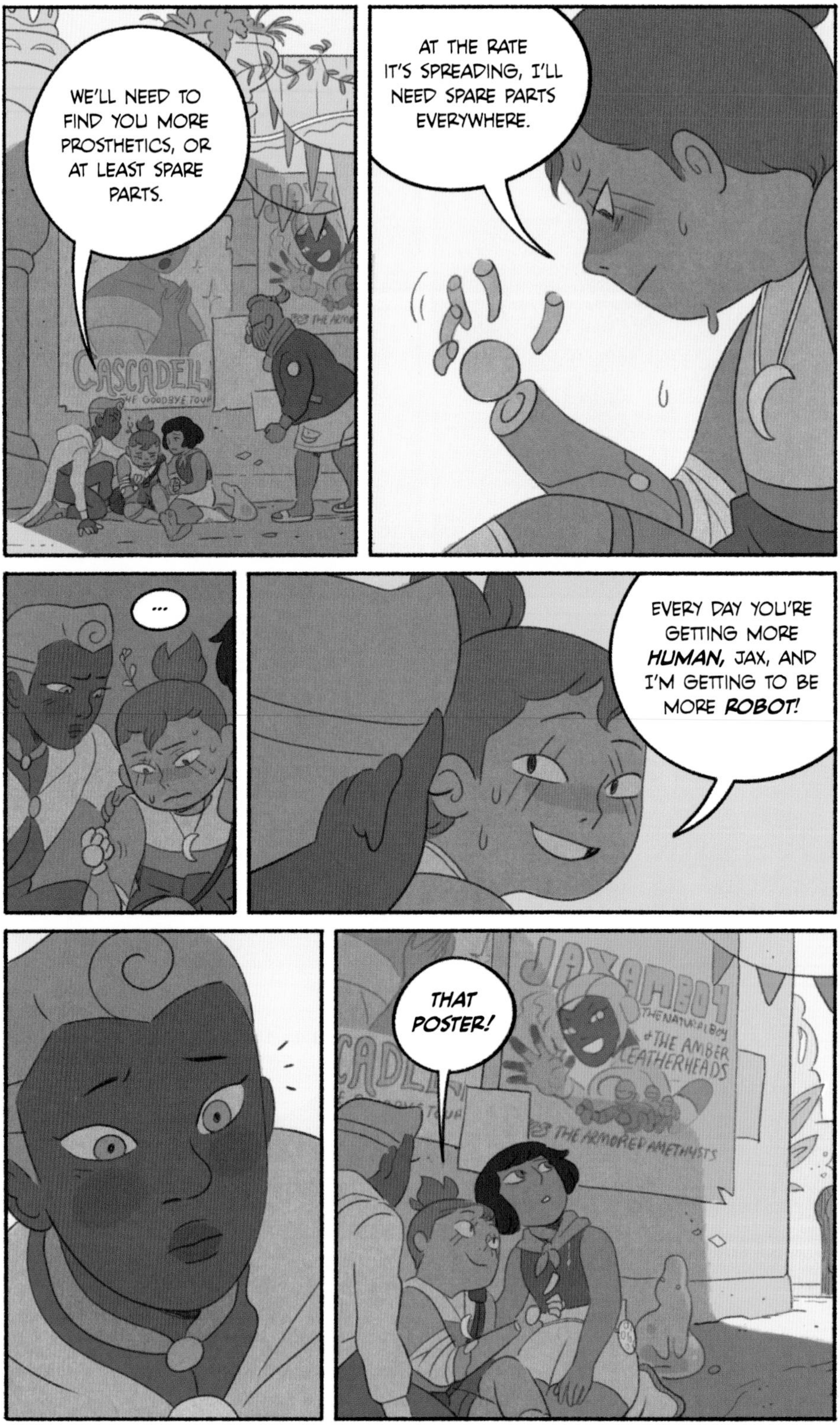
WE'LL NEED TO FIND YOU MORE PROSTHETICS, OR AT LEAST SPARE PARTS.
CASCADELL
THE GOODBYE TOUR
AT THE RATE IT'S SPREADING, I'LL NEED SPARE PARTS EVERYWHERE.
...
EVERY DAY YOU'RE GETTING MORE HUMAN, JAX, AND I'M GETTING TO BE MORE ROBOT!
THAT POSTER!
JAXAMBOY
THE NATURAL BOY
& THE AMBER LEATHERHEADS
THE ARMORED AMETHYSTS

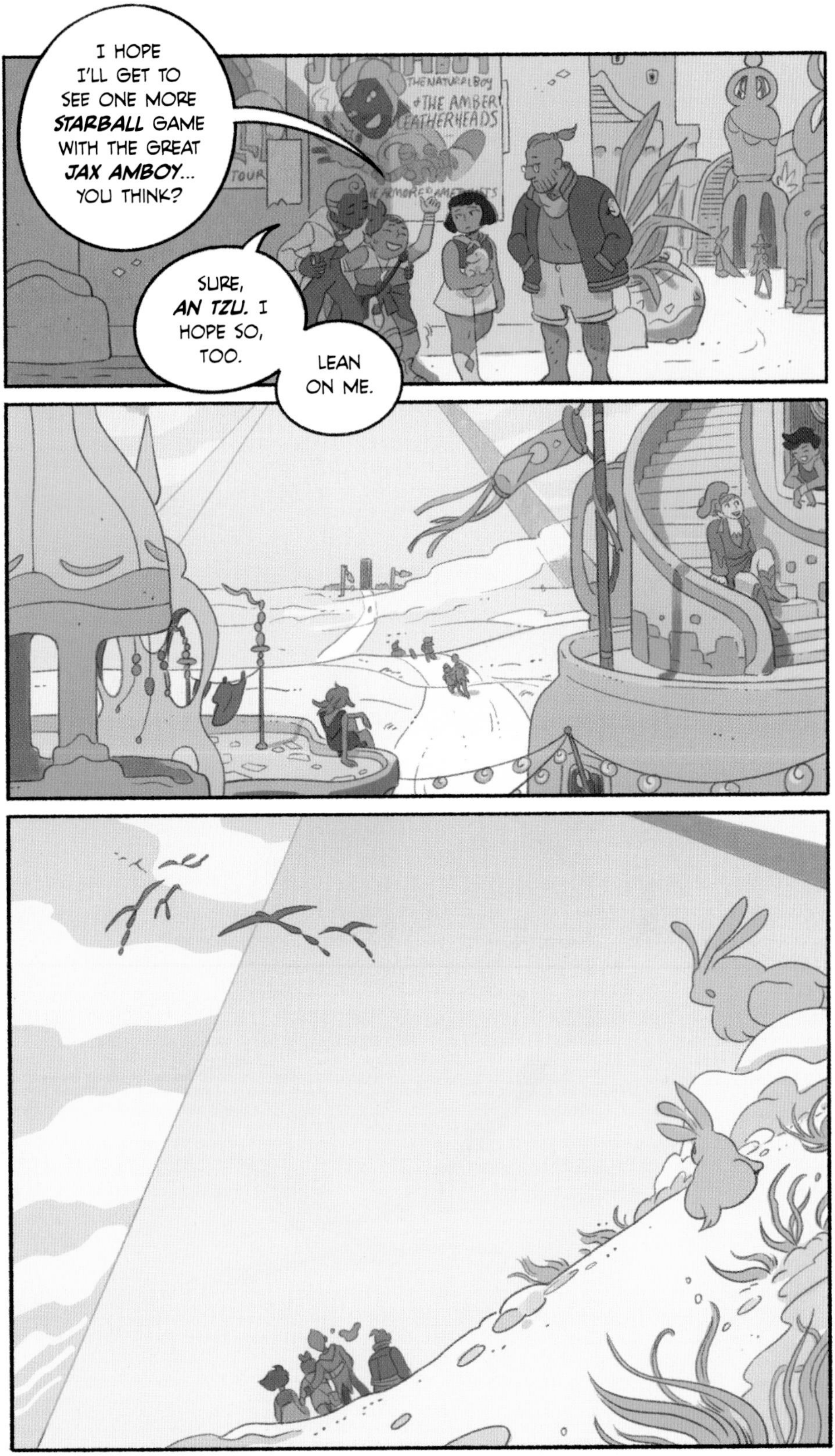
THE NATURAL BOY
& THE AMBER LEATHERHEADS
I HOPE I'LL GET TO SEE ONE MORE **STARBALL** GAME WITH THE GREAT ***JAX AMBOY***... YOU THINK?
SURE, ***AN TZU.*** I HOPE SO, TOO.
LEAN ON ME.

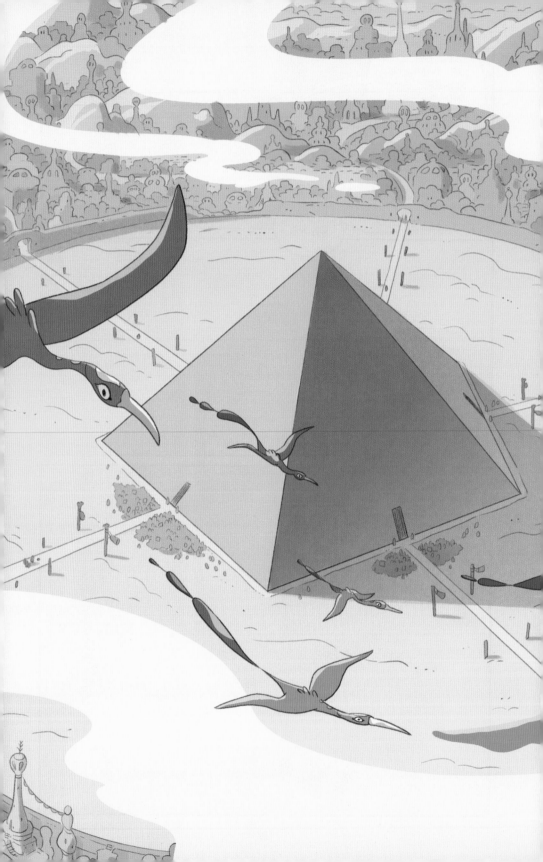

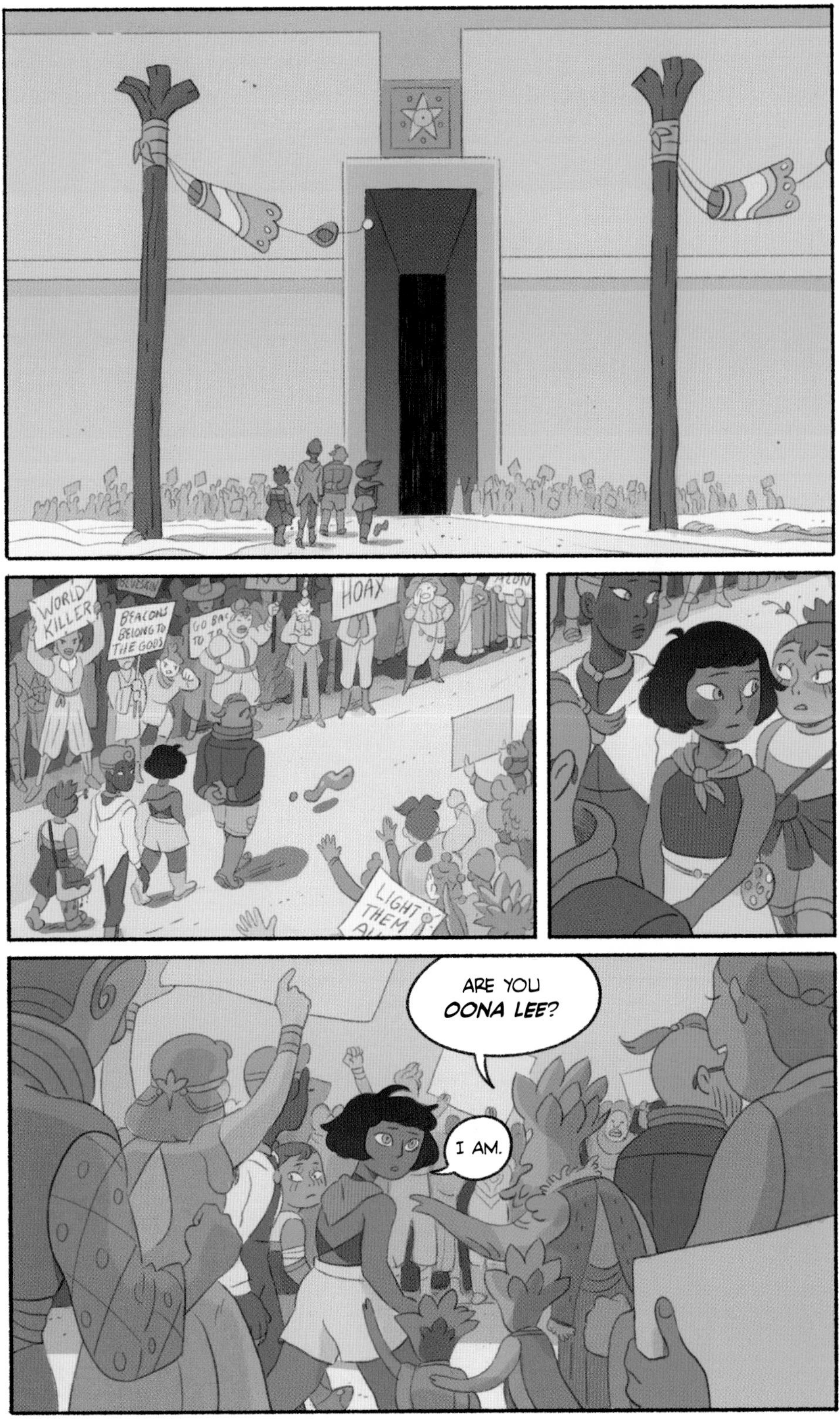
WORLD KILLER
BEACONS BELONG TO THE GODS
HOAX
LIGHT THEM
ARE YOU **OONA LEE?**
I AM.

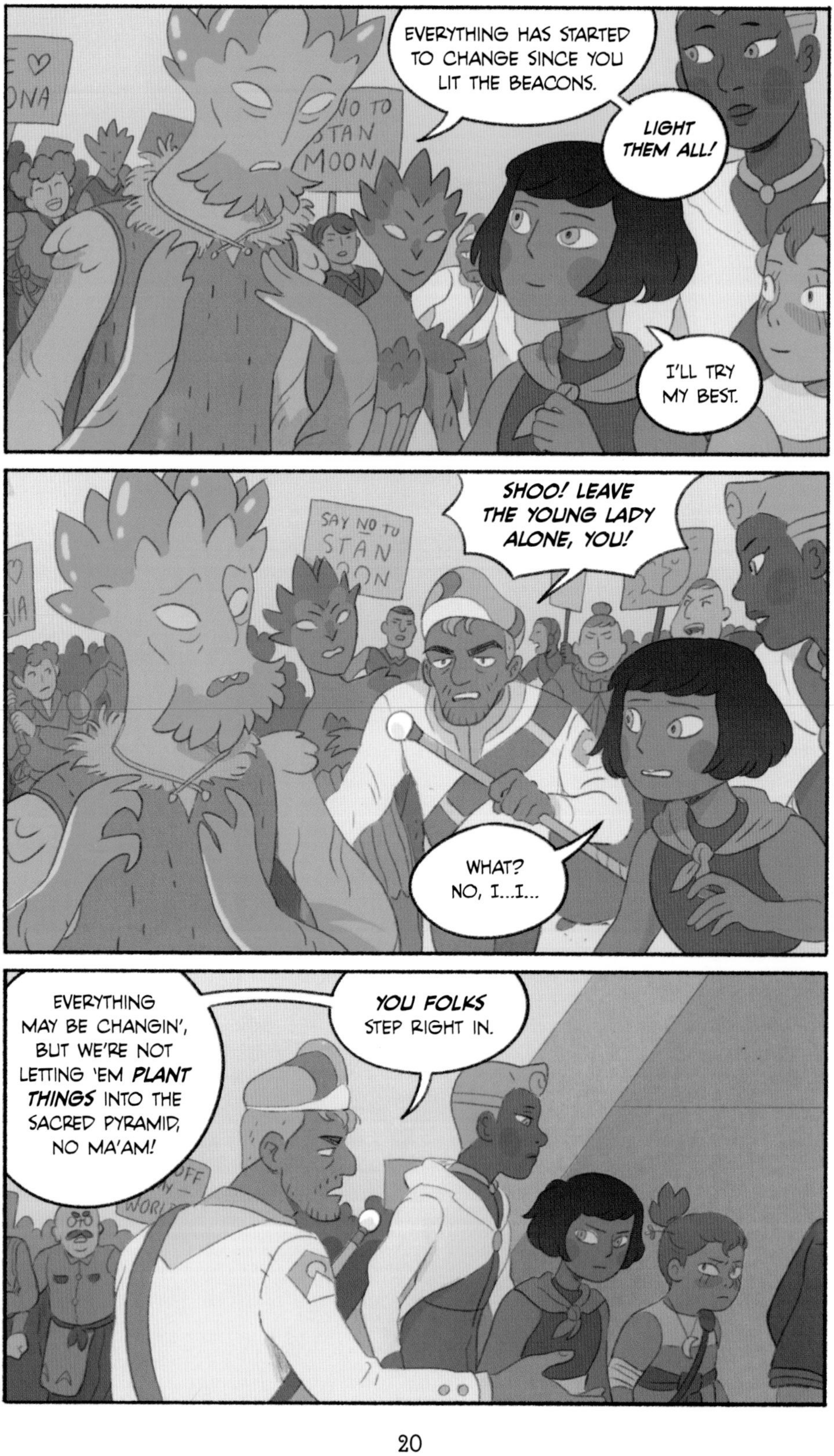
EVERYTHING HAS STARTED TO CHANGE SINCE YOU LIT THE BEACONS.
LIGHT THEM ALL!
I'LL TRY MY BEST.
SHOO! LEAVE THE YOUNG LADY ALONE, YOU!
WHAT? NO, I...I...
EVERYTHING MAY BE CHANGIN', BUT WE'RE NOT LETTING 'EM PLANT THINGS INTO THE SACRED PYRAMID, NO MA'AM!
YOU FOLKS STEP RIGHT IN.

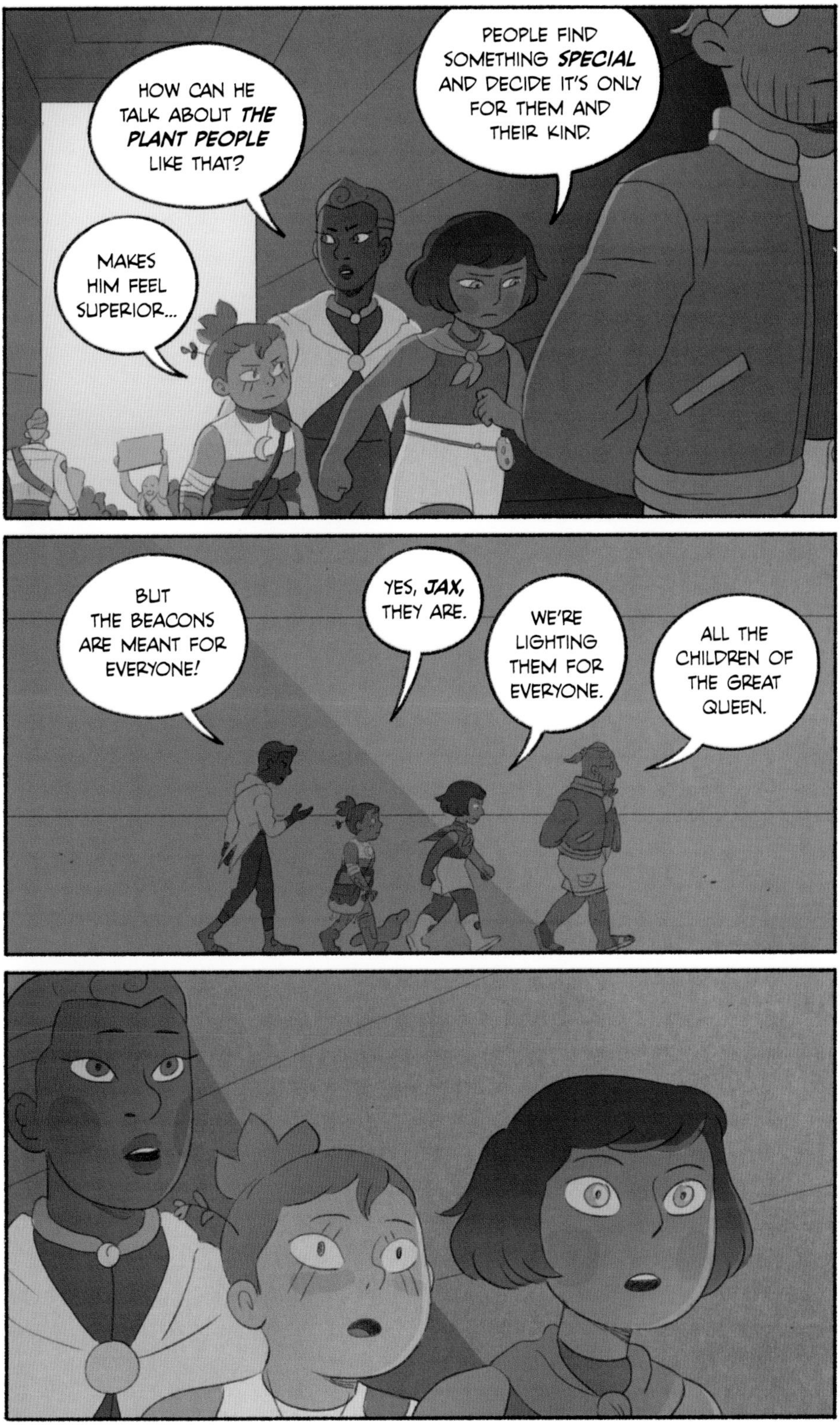
HOW CAN HE TALK ABOUT *THE PLANT PEOPLE* LIKE THAT?
MAKES HIM FEEL SUPERIOR...
PEOPLE FIND SOMETHING *SPECIAL* AND DECIDE IT'S ONLY FOR THEM AND THEIR KIND.
BUT THE BEACONS ARE MEANT FOR EVERYONE!
YES, *JAX,* THEY ARE.
WE'RE LIGHTING THEM FOR EVERYONE.
ALL THE CHILDREN OF THE GREAT QUEEN.

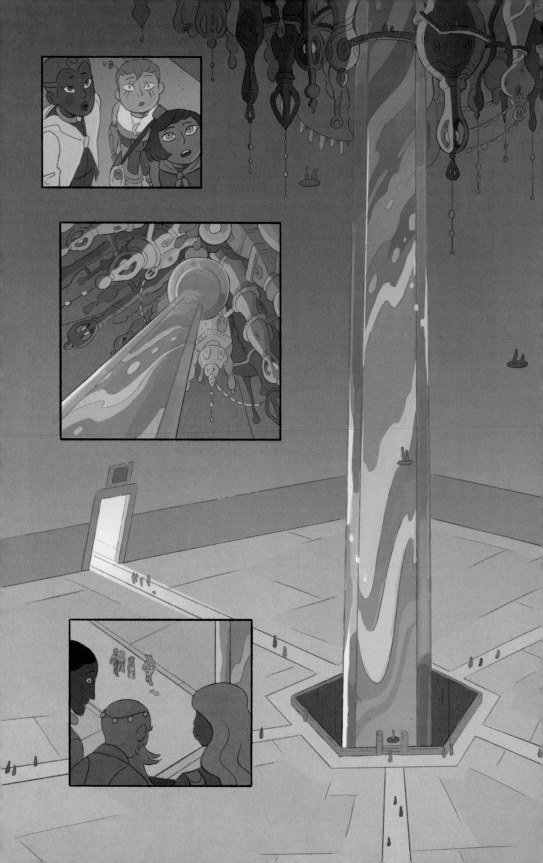

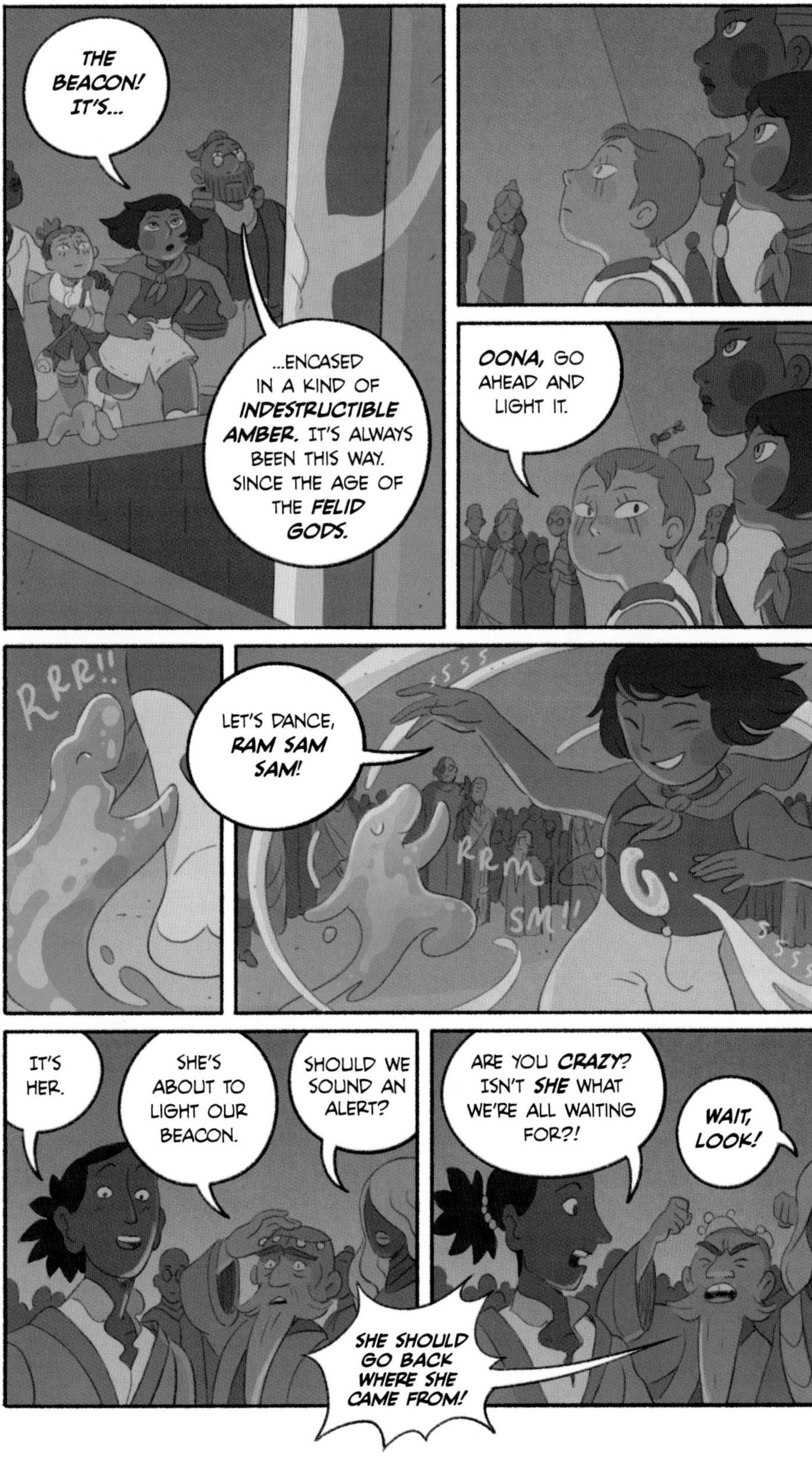
THE BEACON! IT'S...
...ENCASED IN A KIND OF INDESTRUCTIBLE AMBER. IT'S ALWAYS BEEN THIS WAY. SINCE THE AGE OF THE FELID GODS.
OONA, GO AHEAD AND LIGHT IT.
RRR!!
LET'S DANCE, RAM SAM SAM!
RRM
SM!!
IT'S HER.
SHE'S ABOUT TO LIGHT OUR BEACON.
SHOULD WE SOUND AN ALERT?
ARE YOU CRAZY? ISN'T SHE WHAT WE'RE ALL WAITING FOR?!
WAIT, LOOK!
SHE SHOULD GO BACK WHERE SHE CAME FROM!

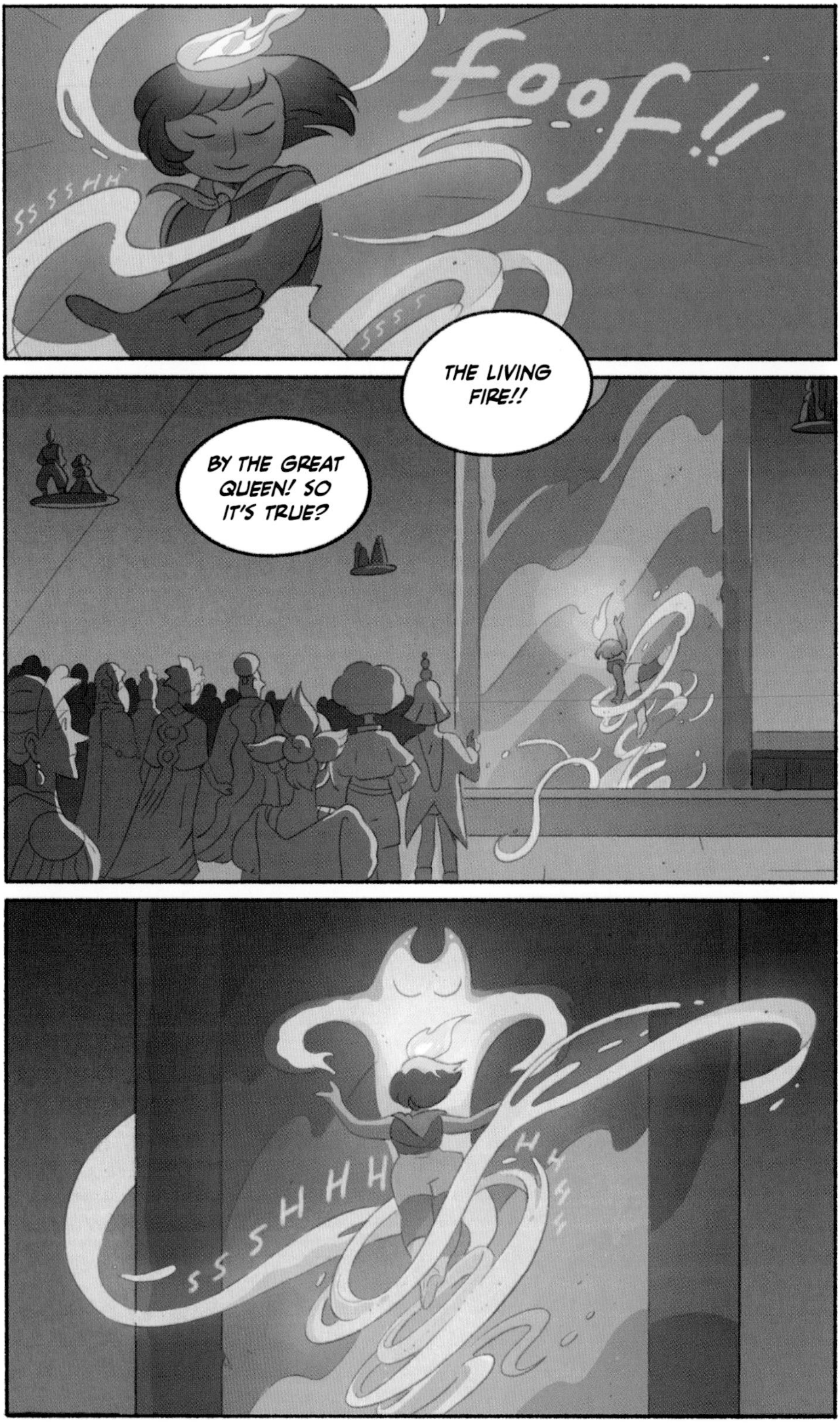
FOOF!!
SSSSHH
SSSS
THE LIVING FIRE!!
BY THE GREAT QUEEN! SO IT'S TRUE?
SSSHHH
HHHH

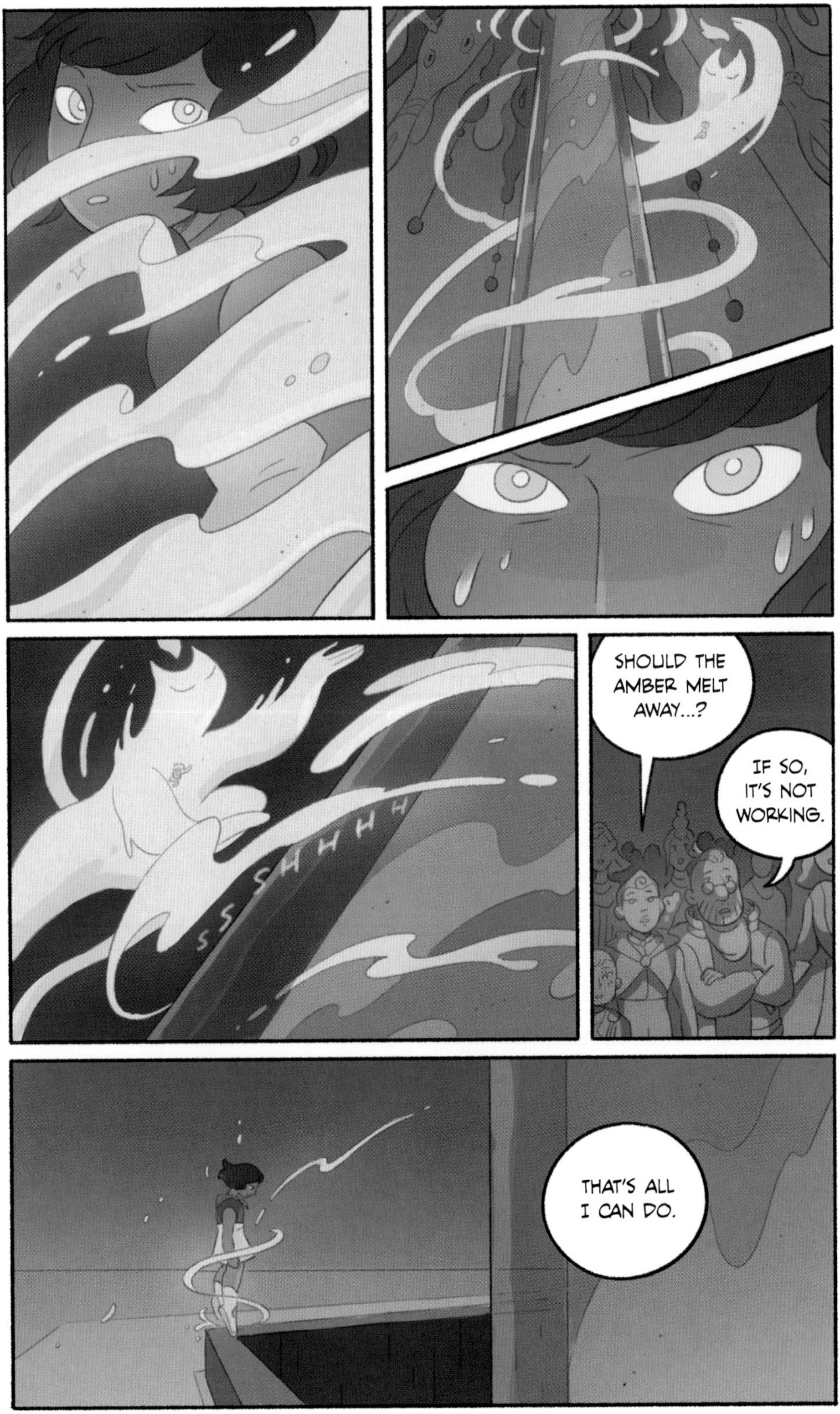
SSSHHHH
SHOULD THE AMBER MELT AWAY...?
IF SO, IT'S NOT WORKING.
THAT'S ALL I CAN DO.

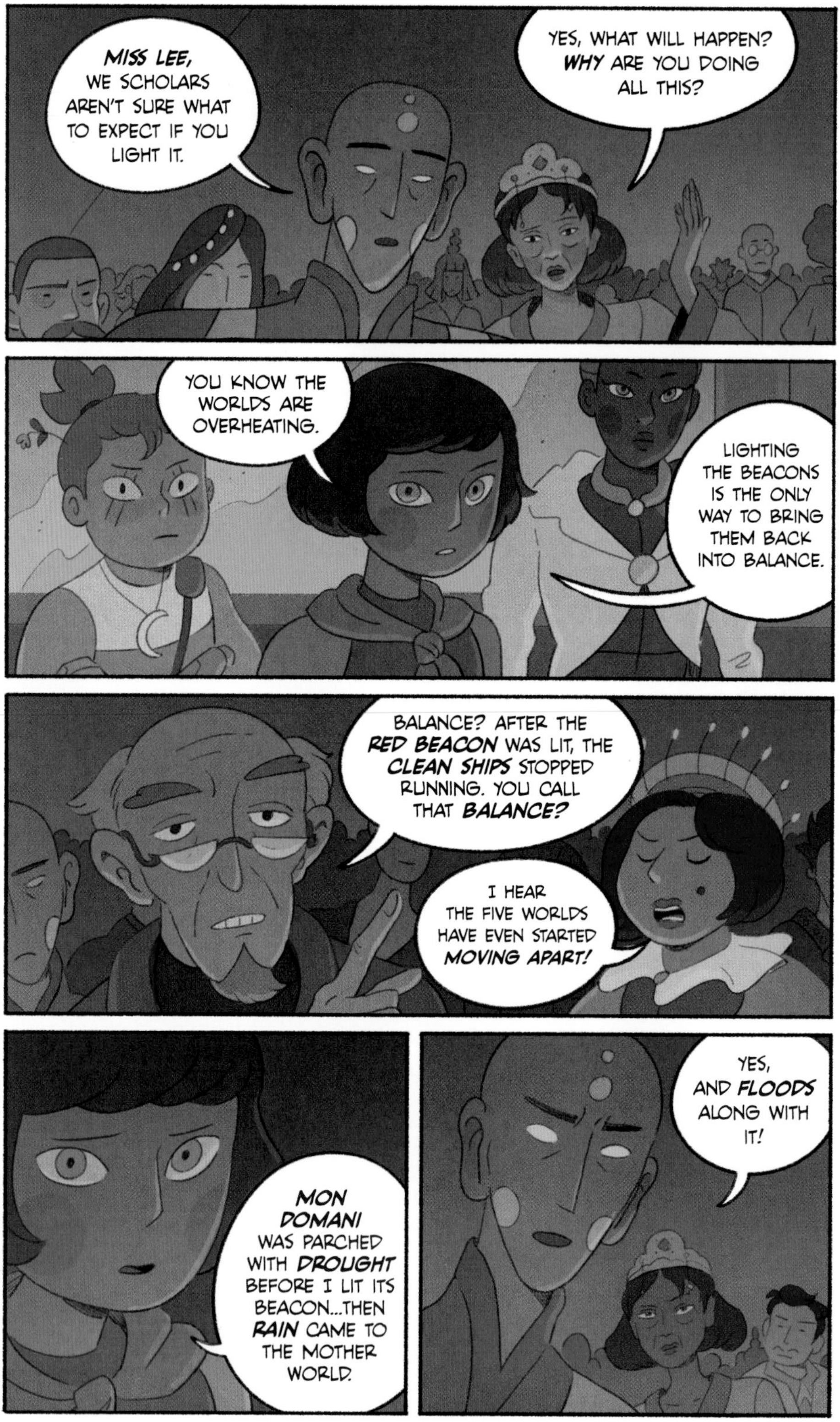

MISS LEE, WE SCHOLARS AREN'T SURE WHAT TO EXPECT IF YOU LIGHT IT.
YES, WHAT WILL HAPPEN? WHY ARE YOU DOING ALL THIS?
YOU KNOW THE WORLDS ARE OVERHEATING.
LIGHTING THE BEACONS IS THE ONLY WAY TO BRING THEM BACK INTO BALANCE.
BALANCE? AFTER THE RED BEACON WAS LIT, THE CLEAN SHIPS STOPPED RUNNING. YOU CALL THAT BALANCE?
I HEAR THE FIVE WORLDS HAVE EVEN STARTED MOVING APART!
MON DOMANI WAS PARCHED WITH DROUGHT BEFORE I LIT ITS BEACON...THEN RAIN CAME TO THE MOTHER WORLD.
YES, AND FLOODS ALONG WITH IT!

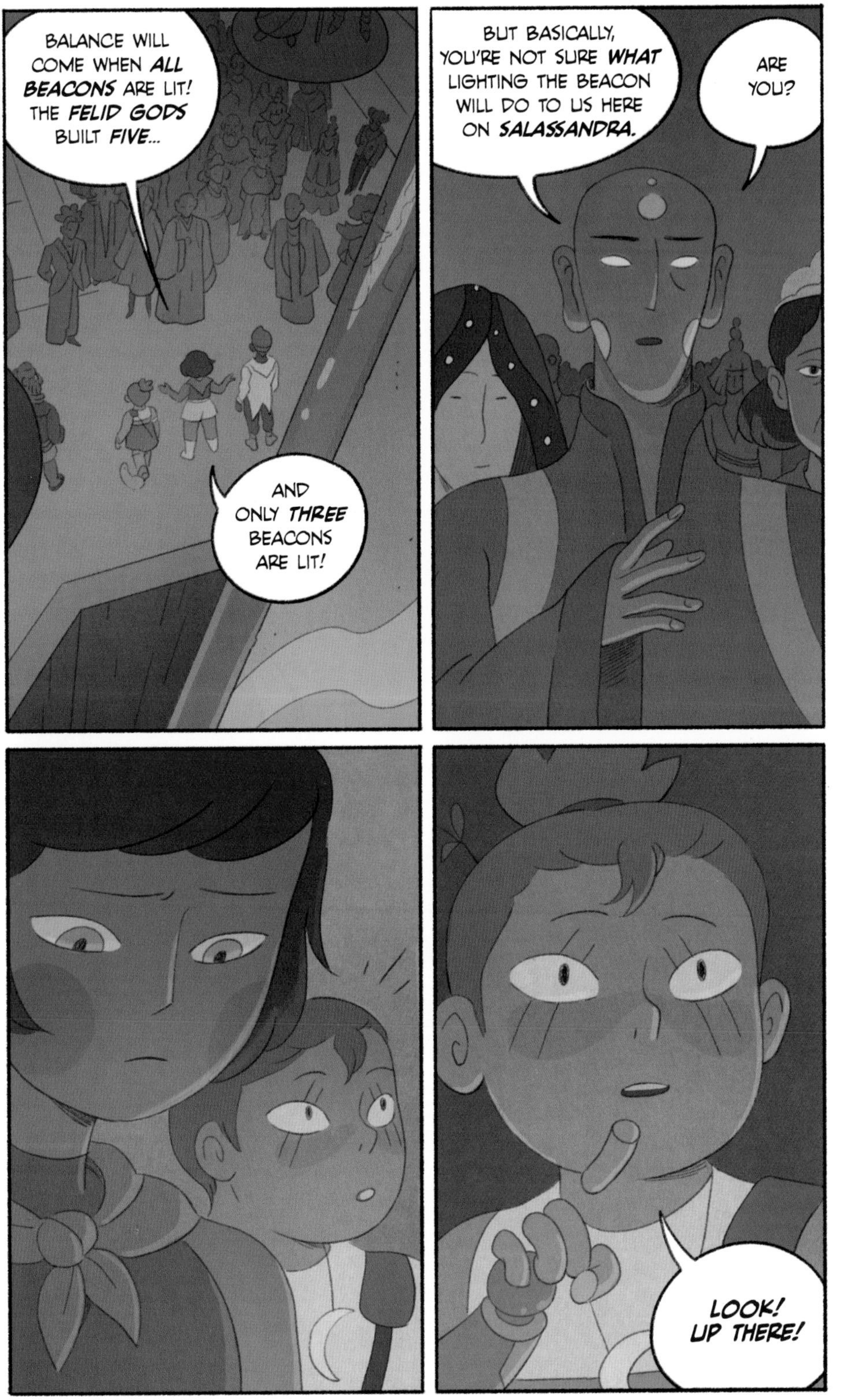
BALANCE WILL COME WHEN ALL BEACONS ARE LIT! THE FELID GODS BUILT FIVE...
AND ONLY THREE BEACONS ARE LIT!
BUT BASICALLY, YOU'RE NOT SURE WHAT LIGHTING THE BEACON WILL DO TO US HERE ON SALASSANDRA.
ARE YOU?
LOOK! UP THERE!

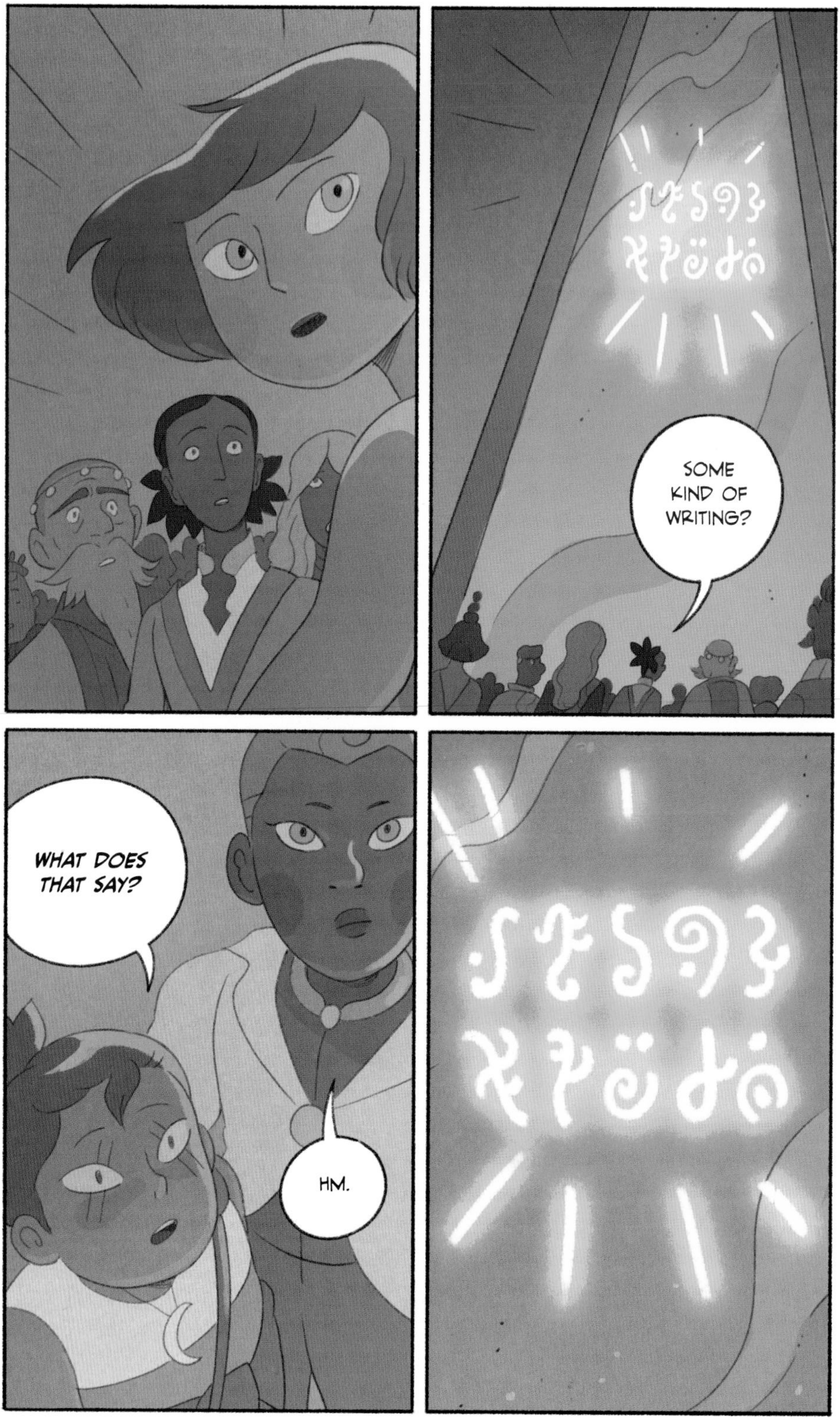
SOME KIND OF WRITING?
WHAT DOES THAT SAY?
HM.

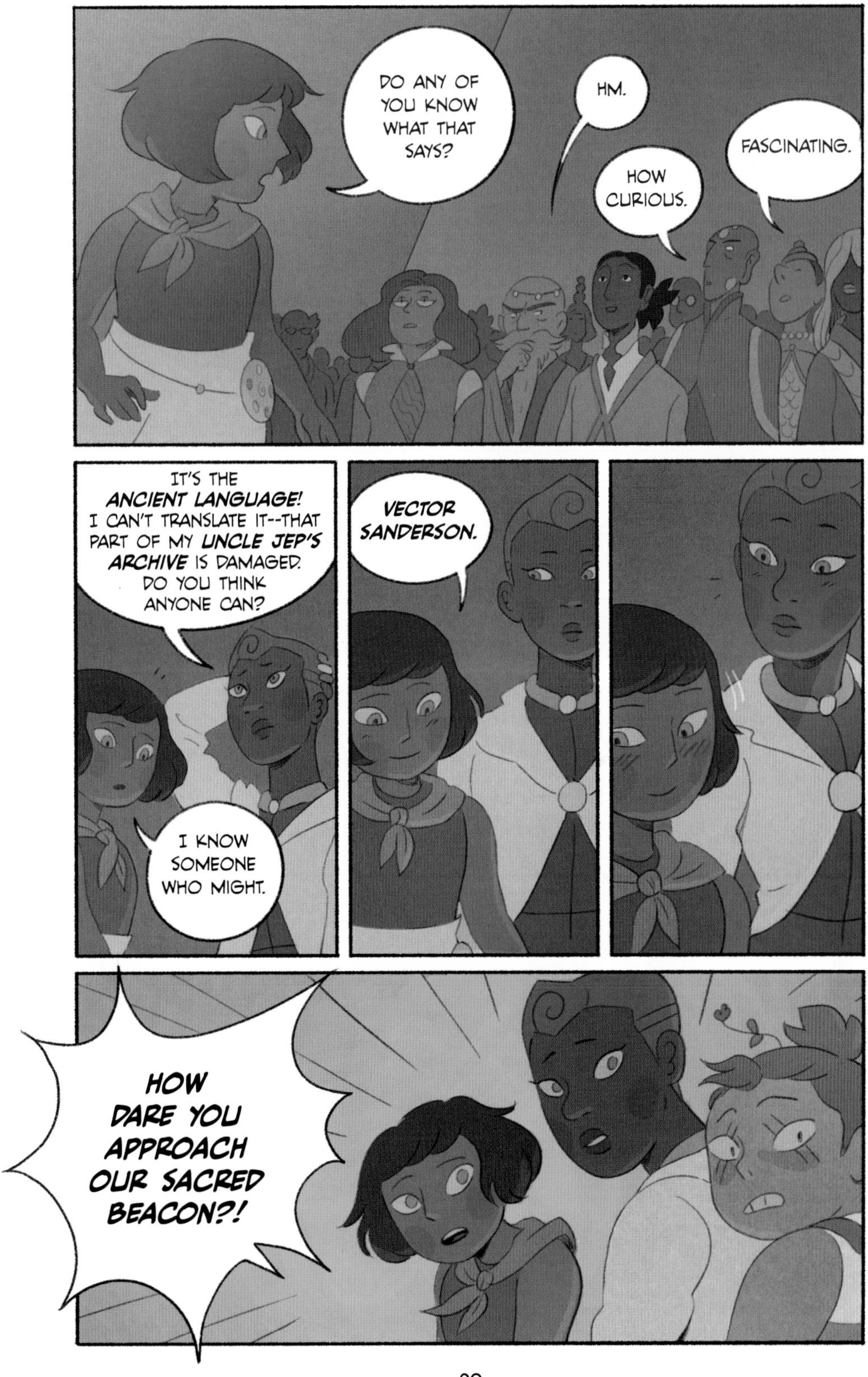
DO ANY OF YOU KNOW WHAT THAT SAYS?
HM.
HOW CURIOUS.
FASCINATING.
IT'S THE *ANCIENT LANGUAGE!* I CAN'T TRANSLATE IT--THAT PART OF MY *UNCLE JEP'S ARCHIVE* IS DAMAGED. DO YOU THINK ANYONE CAN?
I KNOW SOMEONE WHO MIGHT.
VECTOR SANDERSON.
HOW DARE YOU APPROACH OUR SACRED BEACON?!

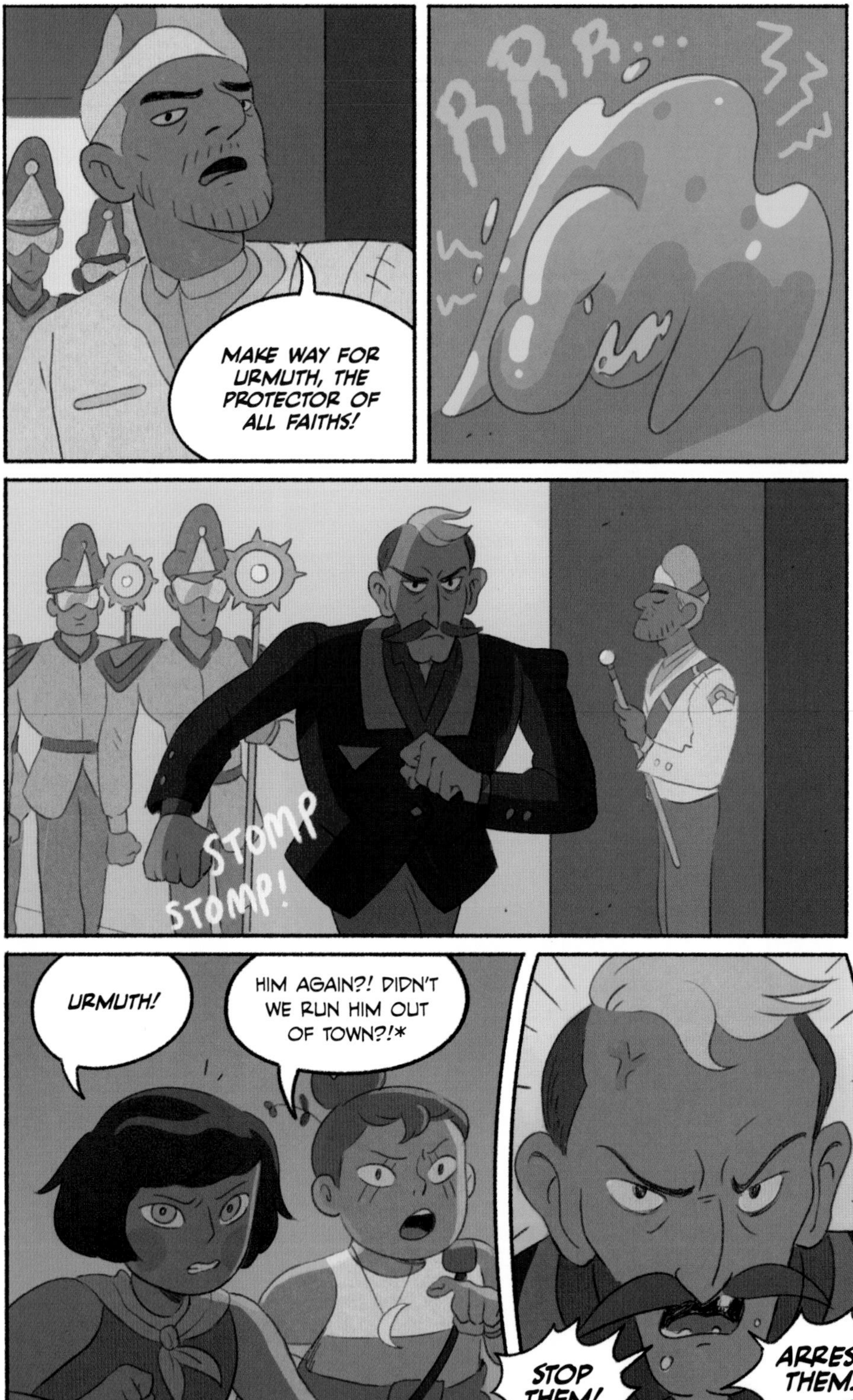
MAKE WAY FOR URMUTH, THE PROTECTOR OF ALL FAITHS!
RRR...
STOMP
STOMP!
URMUTH!
HIM AGAIN?! DIDN'T WE RUN HIM OUT OF TOWN?!*
STOP THEM!
ARREST THEM!

* SEE 5W2: *THE COBALT PRINCE*

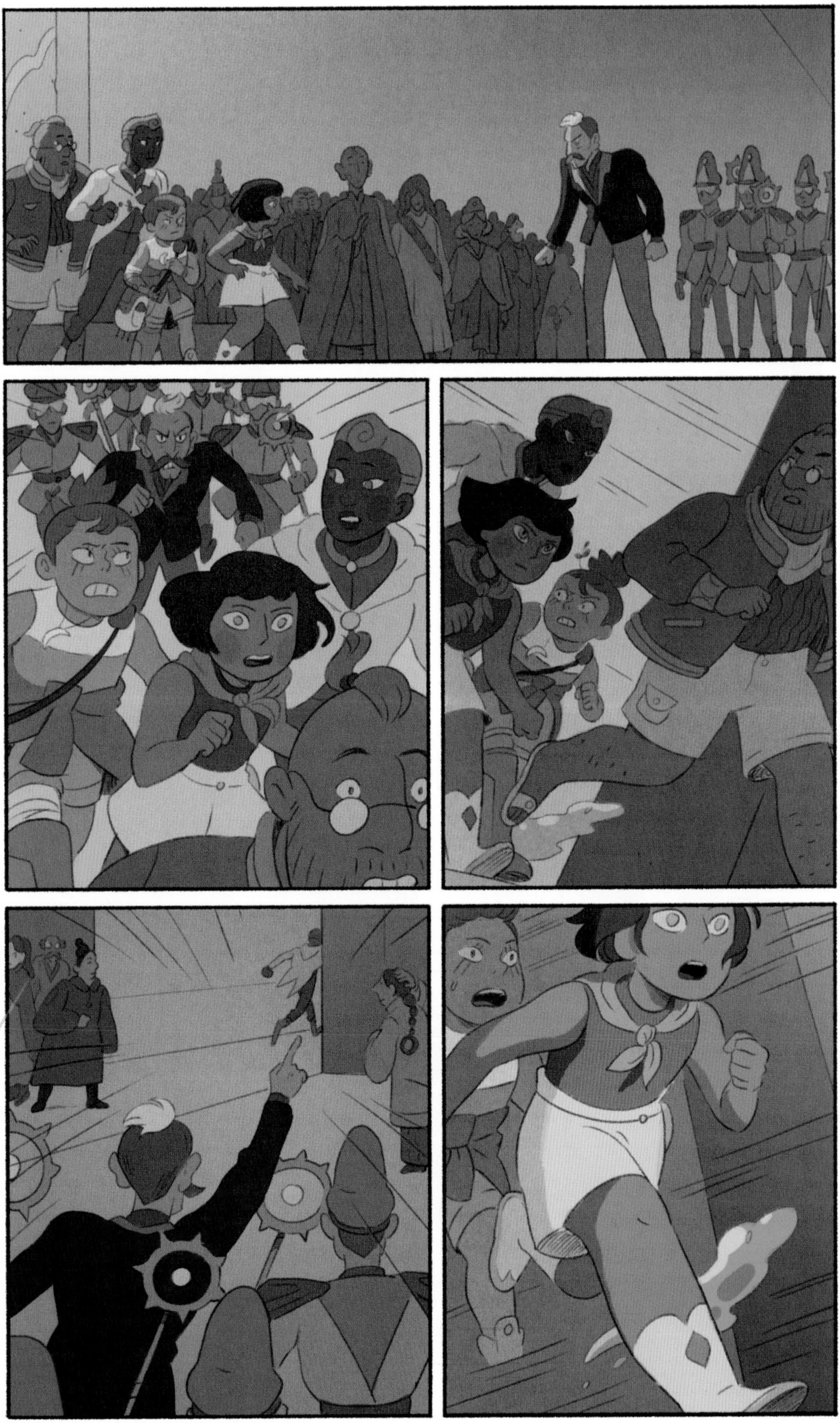

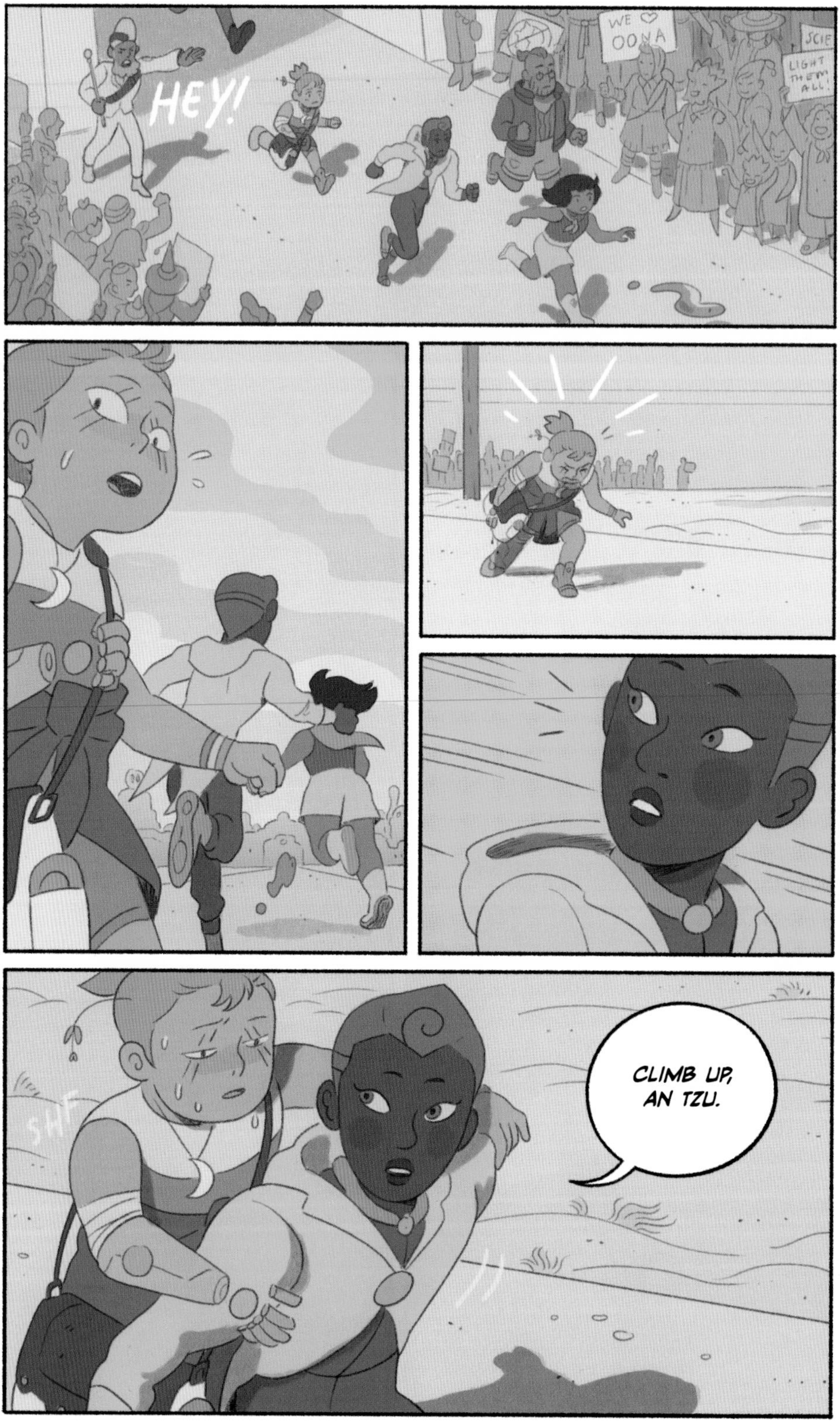
HEY!
WE ♡ OONA
LIGHT THEM ALL!
SHF
CLIMB UP, AN TZU.

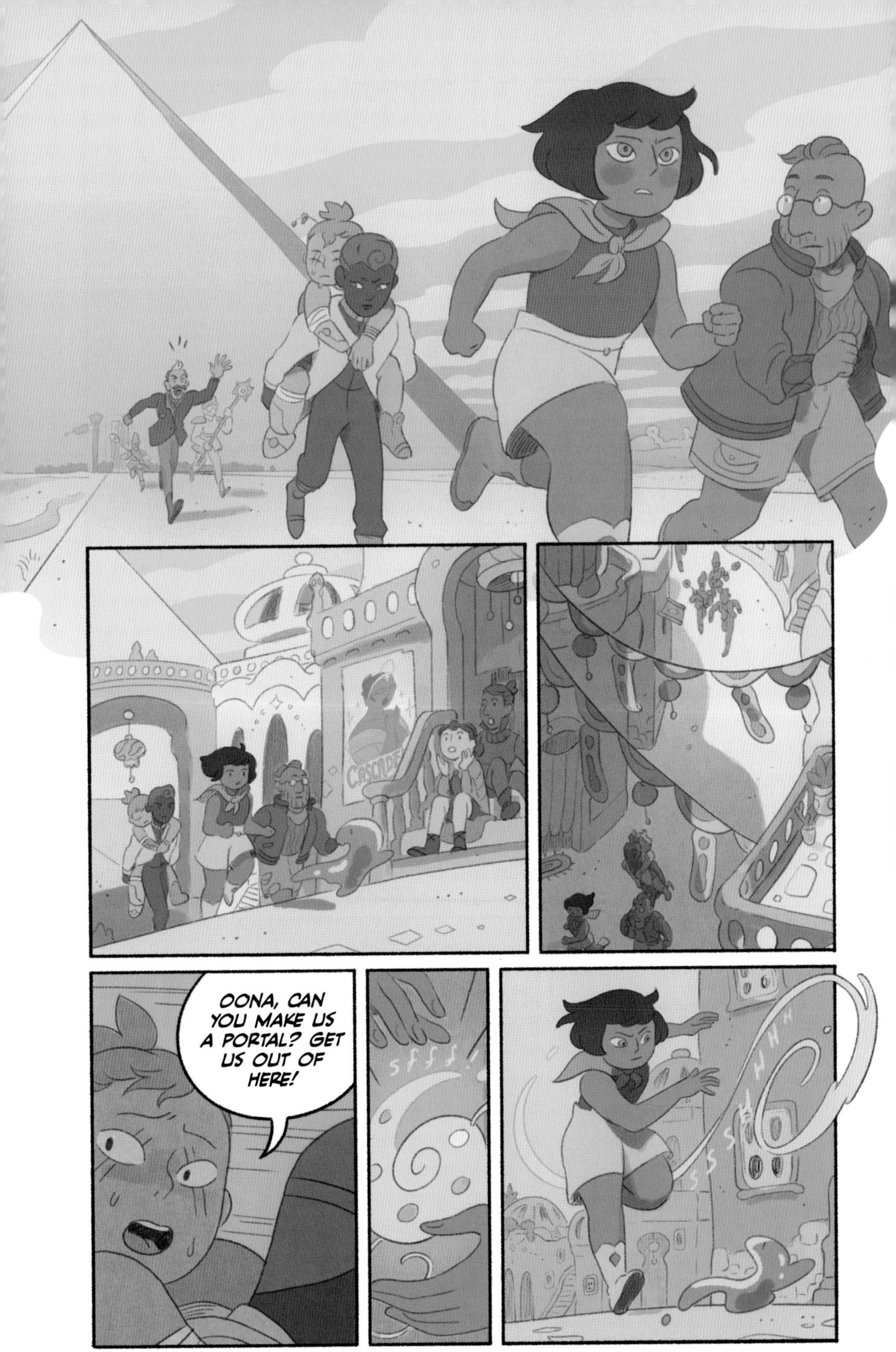
CASCADE
OONA, CAN YOU MAKE US A PORTAL? GET US OUT OF HERE!
SFFF!
SSSHHHH

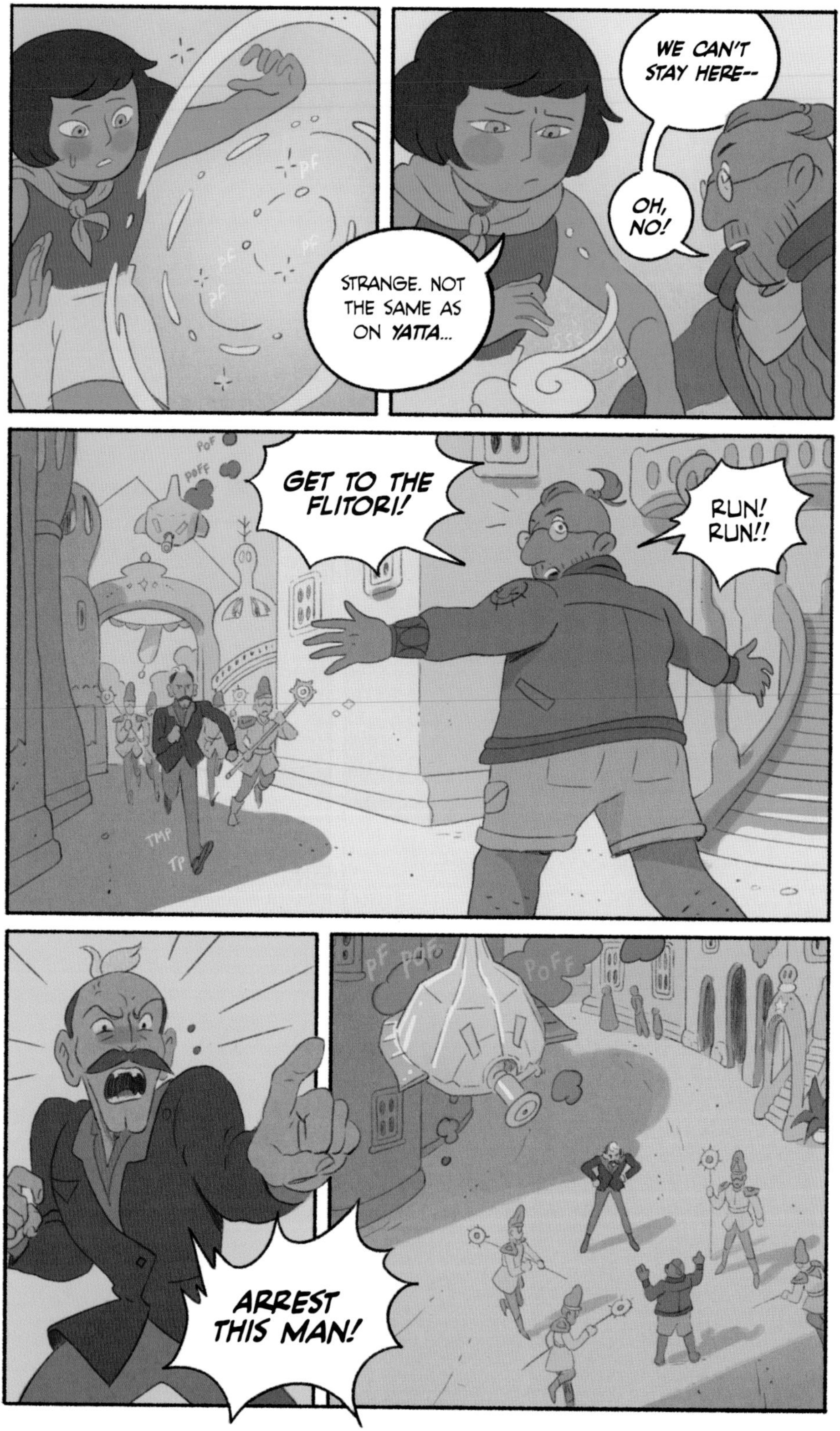

STRANGE. NOT THE SAME AS ON YATTA...
WE CAN'T STAY HERE--
OH, NO!
GET TO THE FLITORI!
RUN! RUN!!
ARREST THIS MAN!

Chapter 2

LIVE FROM SALASSANDRA!

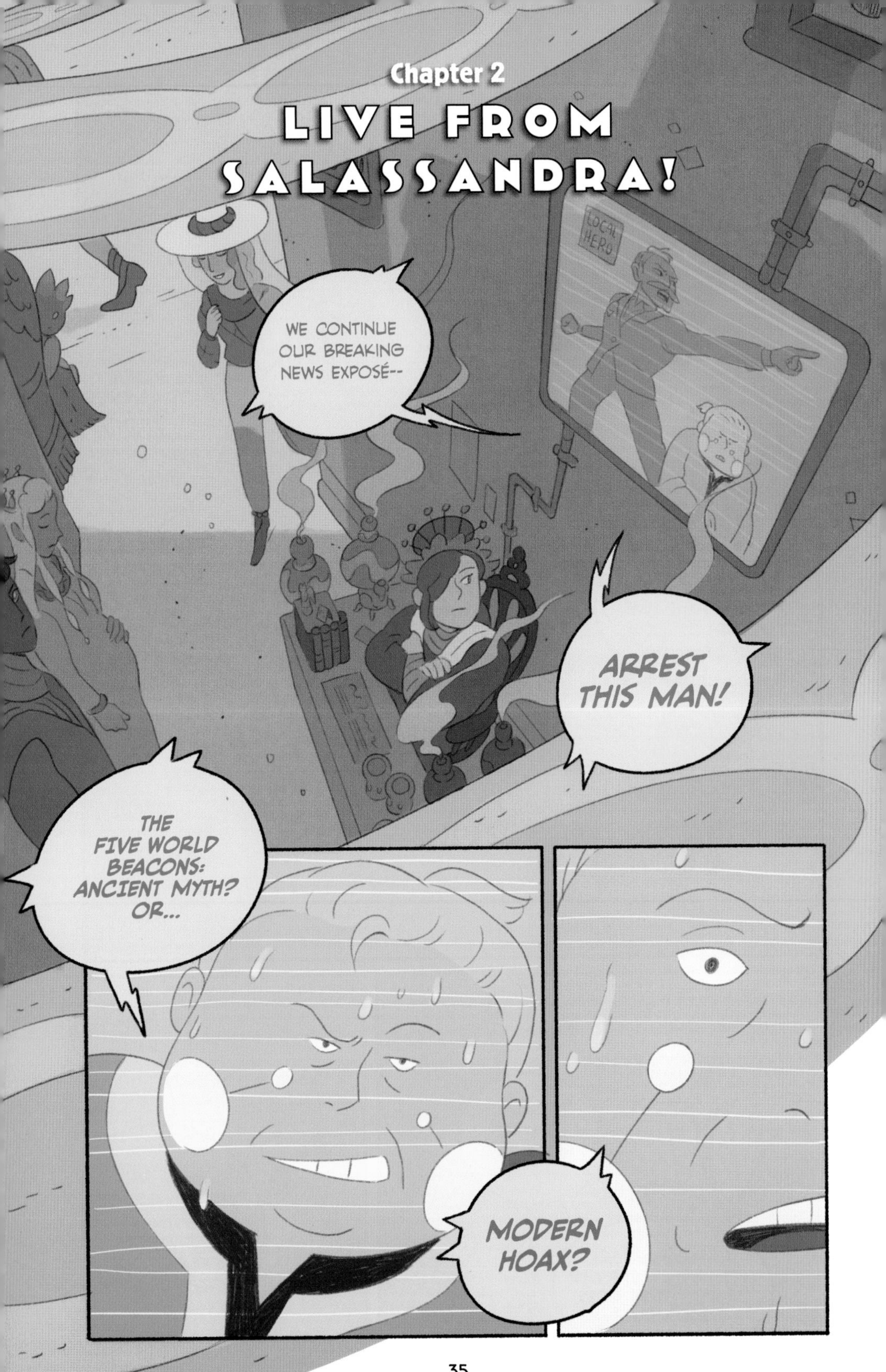
WE CONTINUE OUR BREAKING NEWS EXPOSÉ--
LOCAL HERO
ARREST THIS MAN!
THE FIVE WORLD BEACONS: ANCIENT MYTH? OR...
MODERN HOAX?

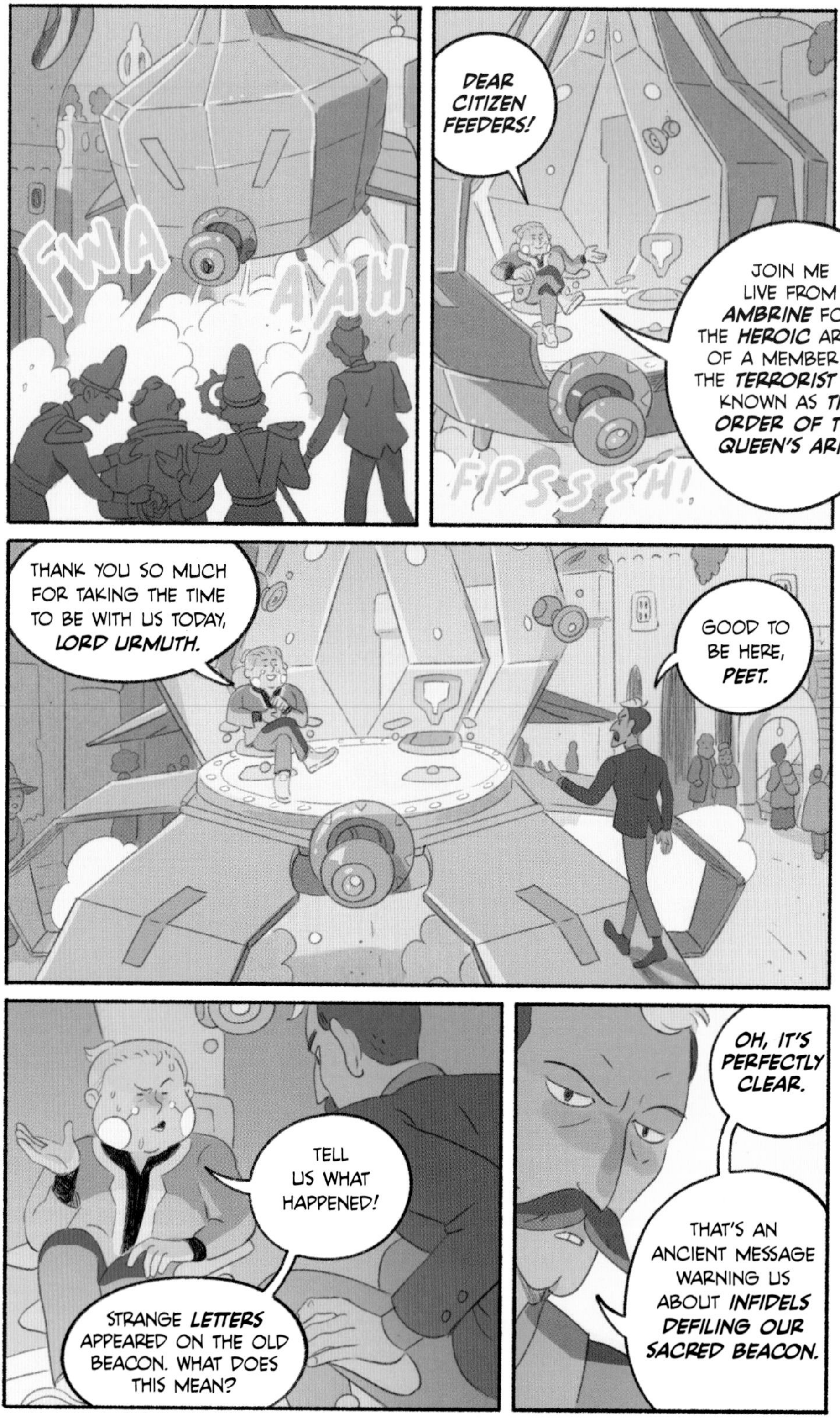
FWA AAH
DEAR CITIZEN FEEDERS!
JOIN ME LIVE FROM AMBRINE FOR THE HEROIC ARREST OF A MEMBER OF THE TERRORIST CELL KNOWN AS THE ORDER OF THE QUEEN'S ARM!
FPSSSSH!
THANK YOU SO MUCH FOR TAKING THE TIME TO BE WITH US TODAY, LORD URMUTH.
GOOD TO BE HERE, PEET.
TELL US WHAT HAPPENED!
STRANGE LETTERS APPEARED ON THE OLD BEACON. WHAT DOES THIS MEAN?
OH, IT'S PERFECTLY CLEAR.
THAT'S AN ANCIENT MESSAGE WARNING US ABOUT INFIDELS DEFILING OUR SACRED BEACON.

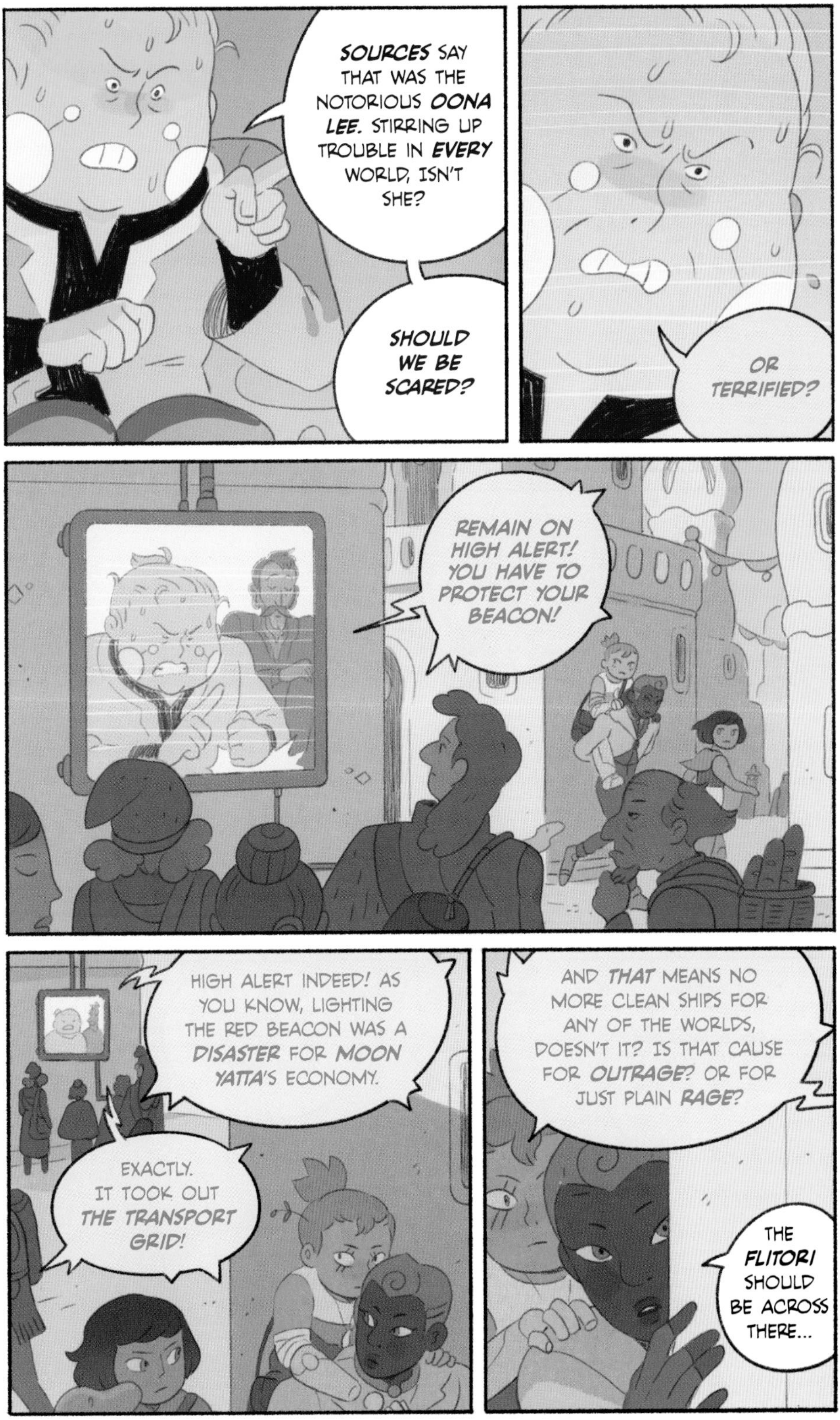
SOURCES SAY THAT WAS THE NOTORIOUS OONA LEE. STIRRING UP TROUBLE IN EVERY WORLD, ISN'T SHE?
SHOULD WE BE SCARED?
OR TERRIFIED?
REMAIN ON HIGH ALERT! YOU HAVE TO PROTECT YOUR BEACON!
HIGH ALERT INDEED! AS YOU KNOW, LIGHTING THE RED BEACON WAS A DISASTER FOR MOON YATTA'S ECONOMY.
EXACTLY. IT TOOK OUT THE TRANSPORT GRID!
AND THAT MEANS NO MORE CLEAN SHIPS FOR ANY OF THE WORLDS, DOESN'T IT? IS THAT CAUSE FOR OUTRAGE? OR FOR JUST PLAIN RAGE?
THE FLITORI SHOULD BE ACROSS THERE...

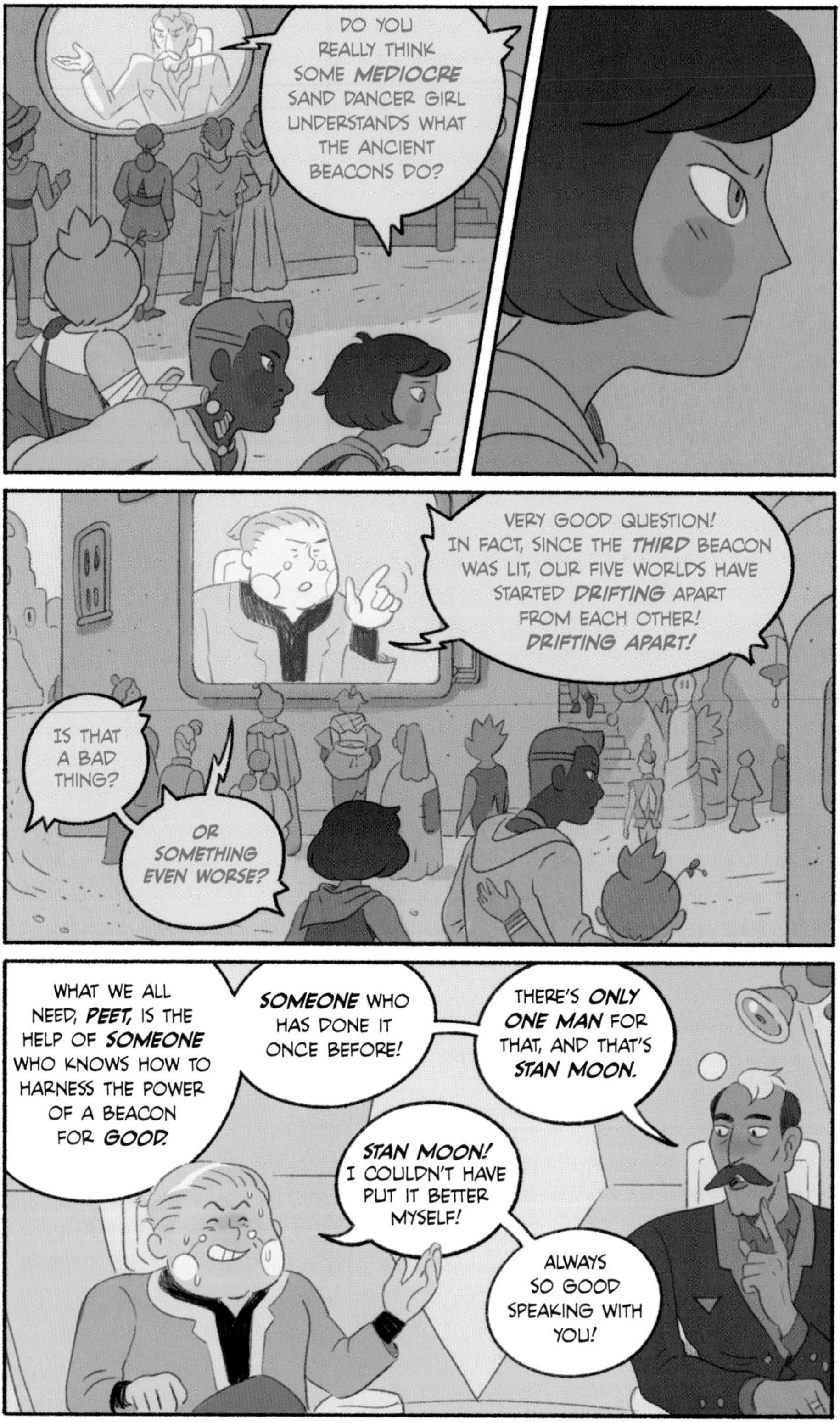
DO YOU REALLY THINK SOME MEDIOCRE SAND DANCER GIRL UNDERSTANDS WHAT THE ANCIENT BEACONS DO?
VERY GOOD QUESTION! IN FACT, SINCE THE THIRD BEACON WAS LIT, OUR FIVE WORLDS HAVE STARTED DRIFTING APART FROM EACH OTHER! DRIFTING APART!
IS THAT A BAD THING?
OR SOMETHING EVEN WORSE?
WHAT WE ALL NEED, PEET, IS THE HELP OF SOMEONE WHO KNOWS HOW TO HARNESS THE POWER OF A BEACON FOR GOOD.
SOMEONE WHO HAS DONE IT ONCE BEFORE!
THERE'S ONLY ONE MAN FOR THAT, AND THAT'S STAN MOON.
STAN MOON! I COULDN'T HAVE PUT IT BETTER MYSELF!
ALWAYS SO GOOD SPEAKING WITH YOU!

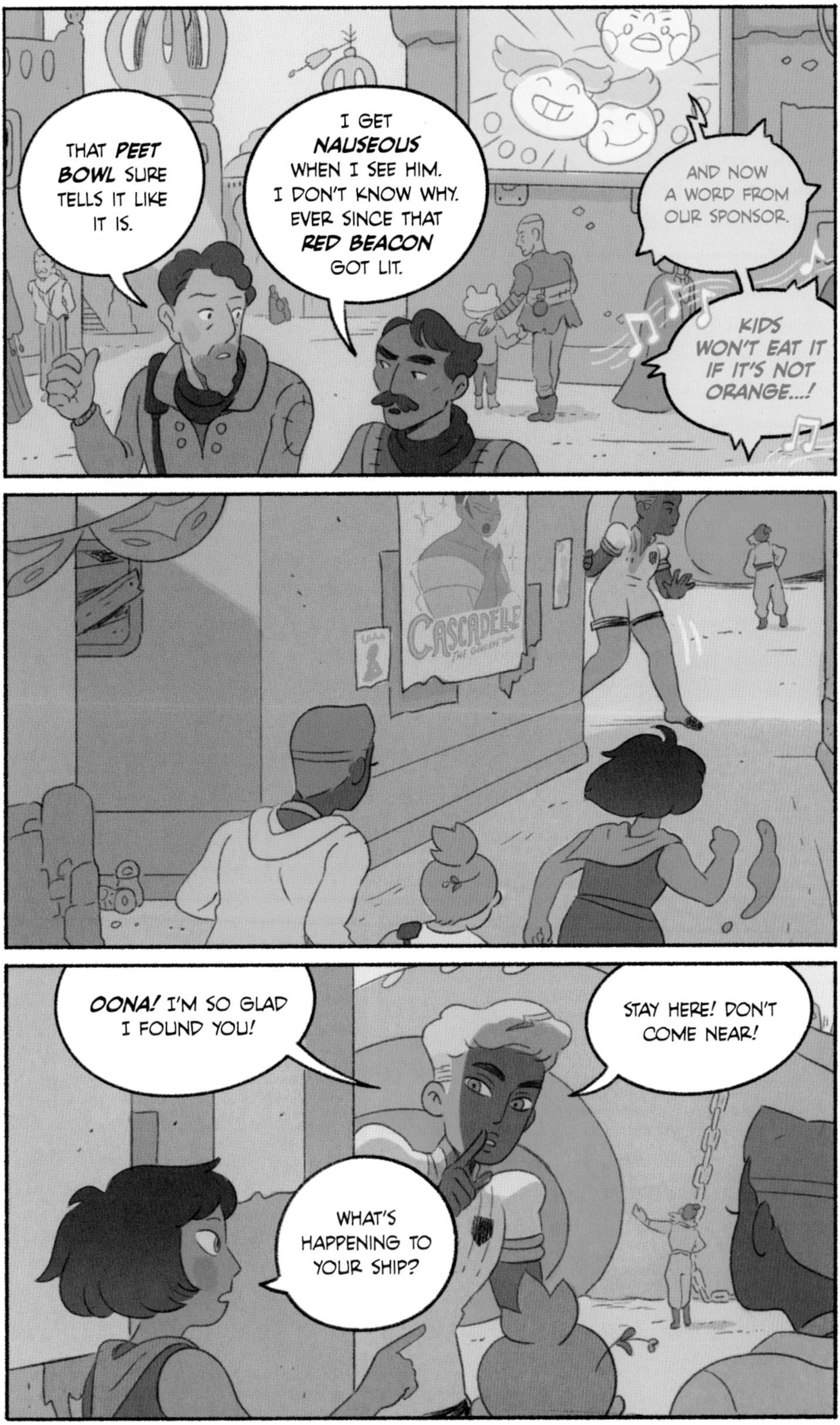
THAT PEET BOWL SURE TELLS IT LIKE IT IS.
I GET NAUSEOUS WHEN I SEE HIM. I DON'T KNOW WHY. EVER SINCE THAT RED BEACON GOT LIT.
AND NOW A WORD FROM OUR SPONSOR.
KIDS WON'T EAT IT IF IT'S NOT ORANGE...!
CASCADELLE
OONA! I'M SO GLAD I FOUND YOU!
STAY HERE! DON'T COME NEAR!
WHAT'S HAPPENING TO YOUR SHIP?

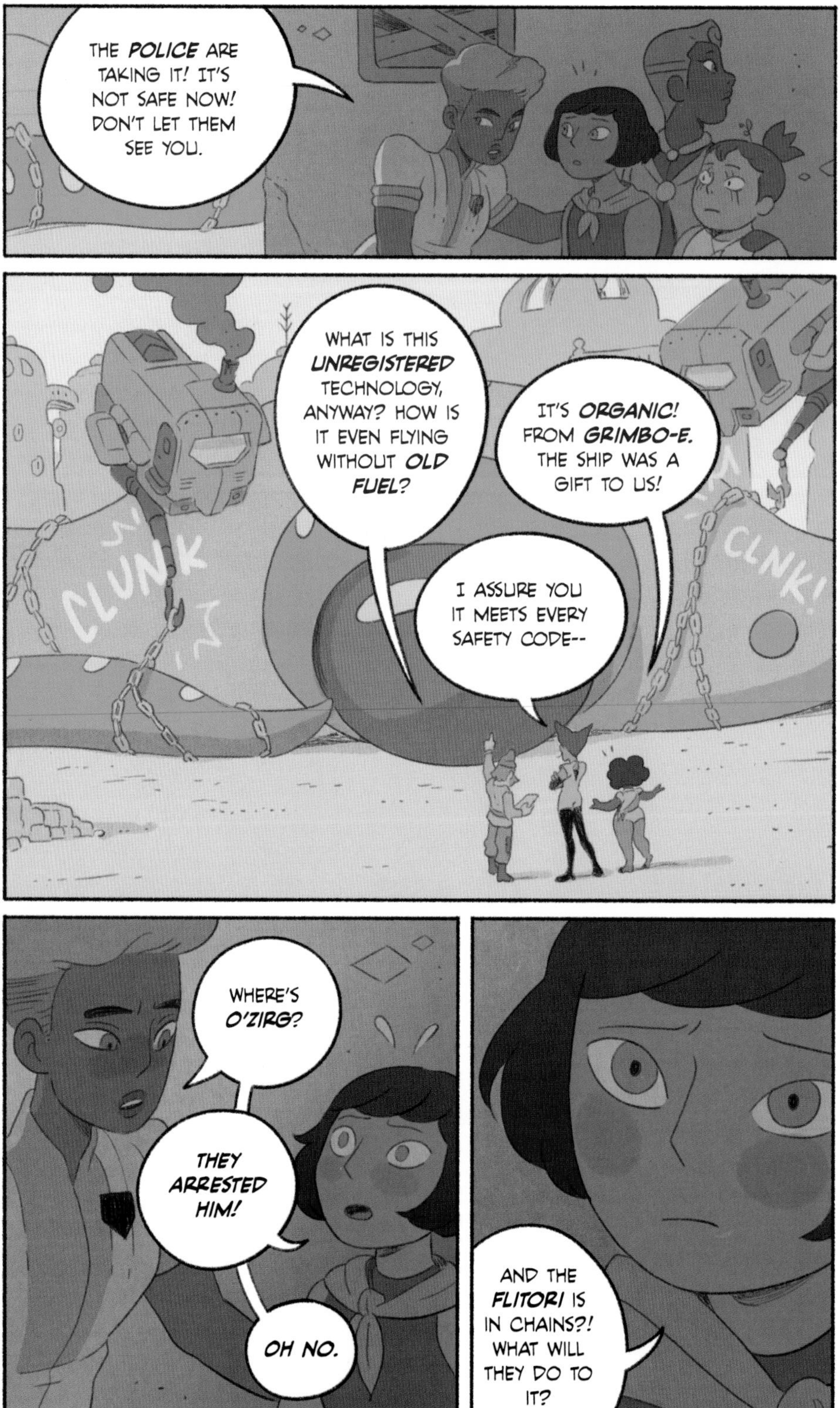
THE POLICE ARE TAKING IT! IT'S NOT SAFE NOW! DON'T LET THEM SEE YOU.
WHAT IS THIS UNREGISTERED TECHNOLOGY, ANYWAY? HOW IS IT EVEN FLYING WITHOUT OLD FUEL?
IT'S ORGANIC! FROM GRIMBO-E. THE SHIP WAS A GIFT TO US!
I ASSURE YOU IT MEETS EVERY SAFETY CODE--
CLUNK
CLNK!
WHERE'S O'ZIRG?
THEY ARRESTED HIM!
OH NO.
AND THE FLITORI IS IN CHAINS?! WHAT WILL THEY DO TO IT?

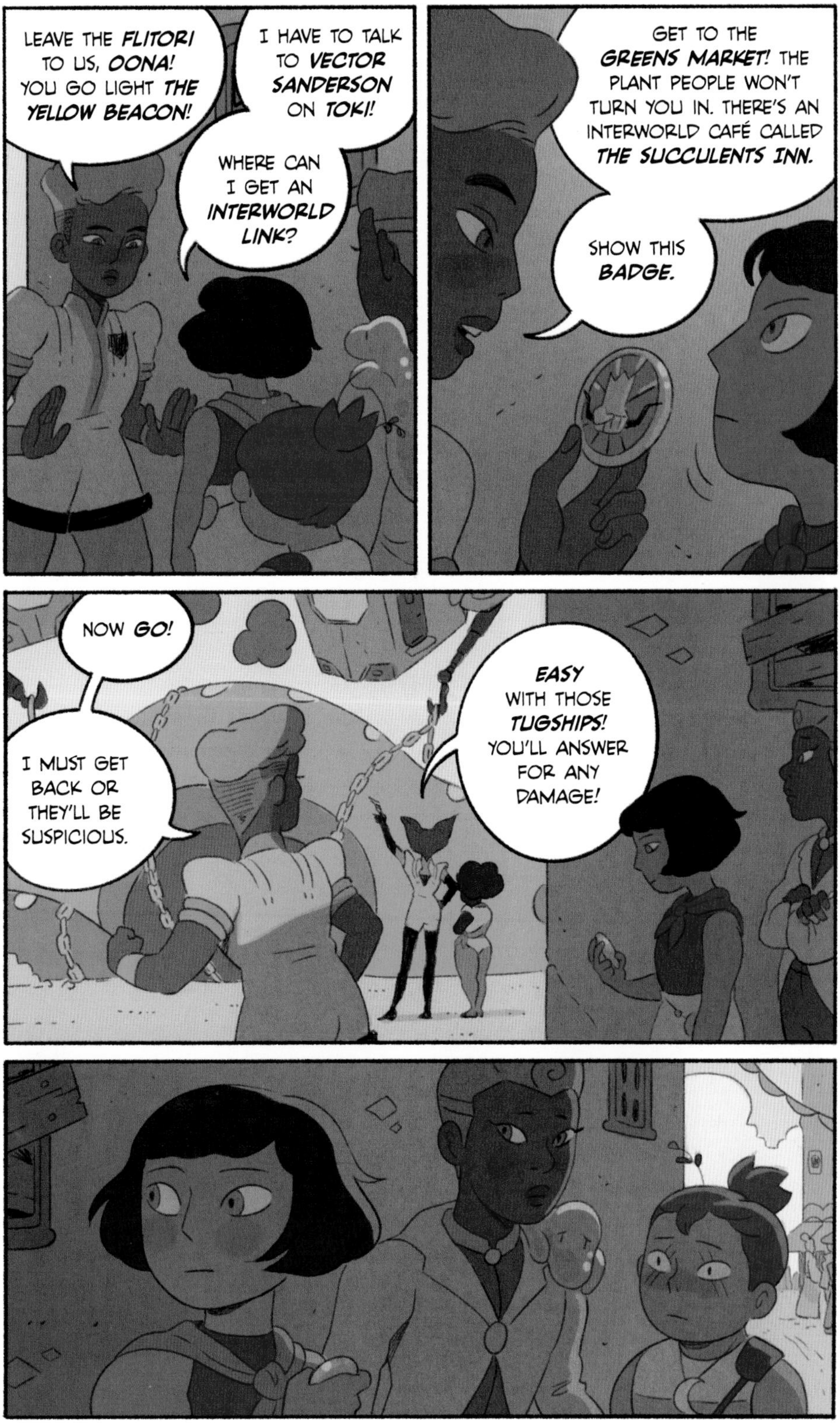
LEAVE THE FLITORI TO US, OONA! YOU GO LIGHT THE YELLOW BEACON!
I HAVE TO TALK TO VECTOR SANDERSON ON TOKI!
WHERE CAN I GET AN INTERWORLD LINK?
GET TO THE GREENS MARKET! THE PLANT PEOPLE WON'T TURN YOU IN. THERE'S AN INTERWORLD CAFÉ CALLED THE SUCCULENTS INN.
SHOW THIS BADGE.
NOW GO!
I MUST GET BACK OR THEY'LL BE SUSPICIOUS.
EASY WITH THOSE TUGSHIPS! YOU'LL ANSWER FOR ANY DAMAGE!

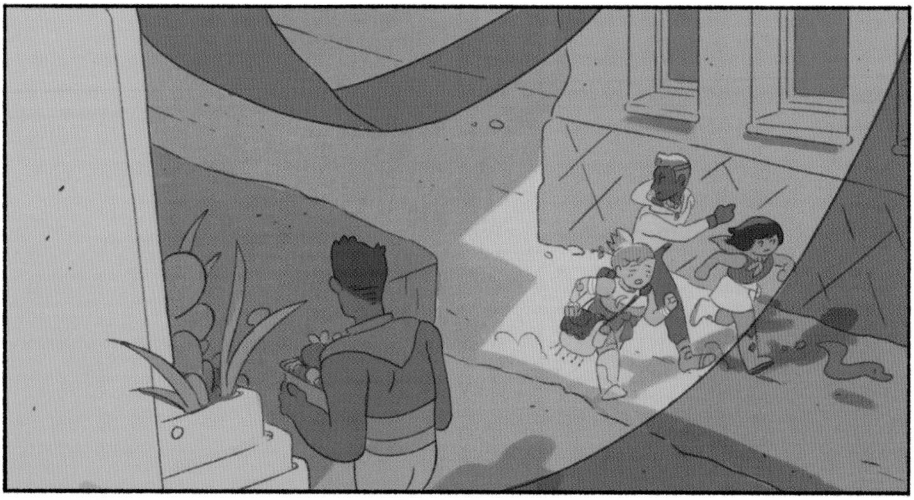

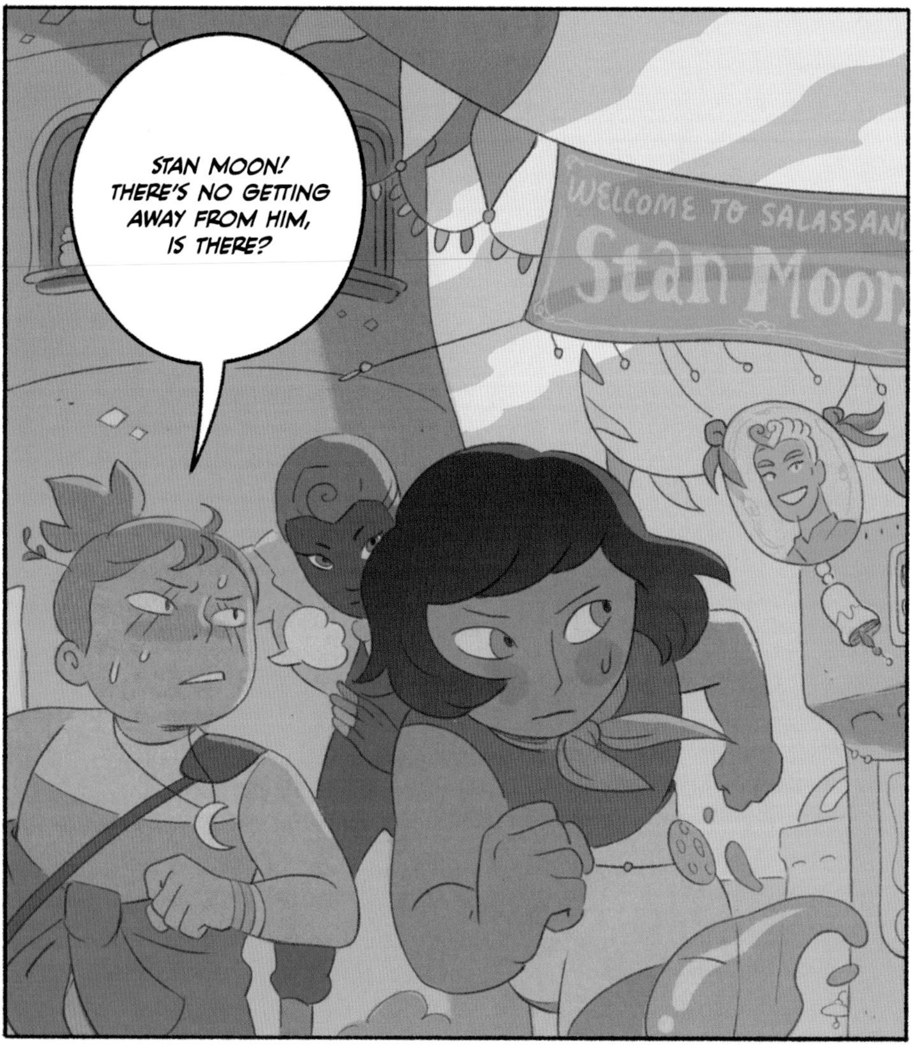
STAN MOON! THERE'S NO GETTING AWAY FROM HIM, IS THERE?
WELCOME TO SALASSAN
Stan Moon

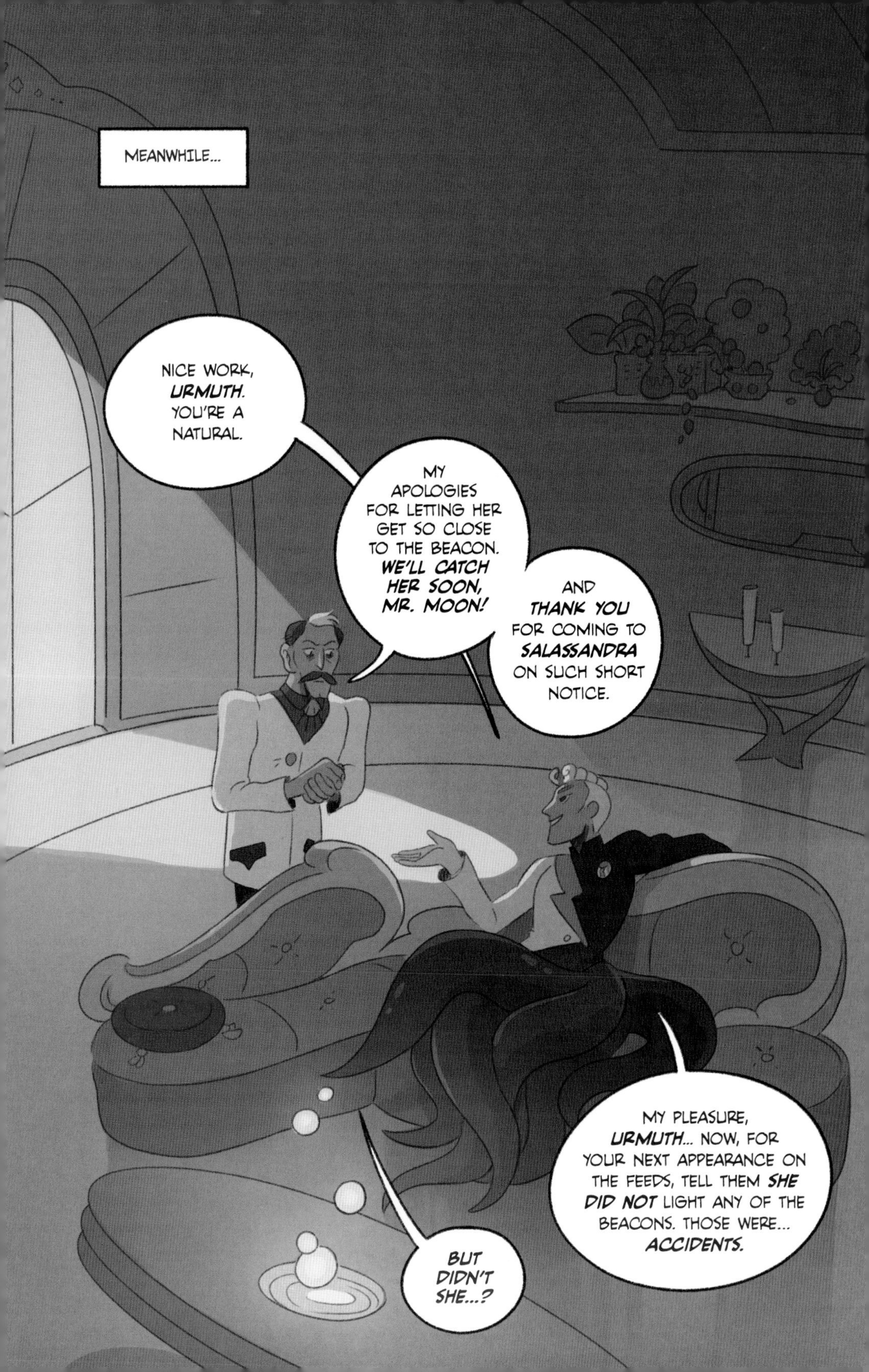
MEANWHILE...
NICE WORK, URMUTH. YOU'RE A NATURAL.
MY APOLOGIES FOR LETTING HER GET SO CLOSE TO THE BEACON. WE'LL CATCH HER SOON, MR. MOON!
AND THANK YOU FOR COMING TO SALASSANDRA ON SUCH SHORT NOTICE.
MY PLEASURE, URMUTH... NOW, FOR YOUR NEXT APPEARANCE ON THE FEEDS, TELL THEM SHE DID NOT LIGHT ANY OF THE BEACONS. THOSE WERE... ACCIDENTS.
BUT DIDN'T SHE...?

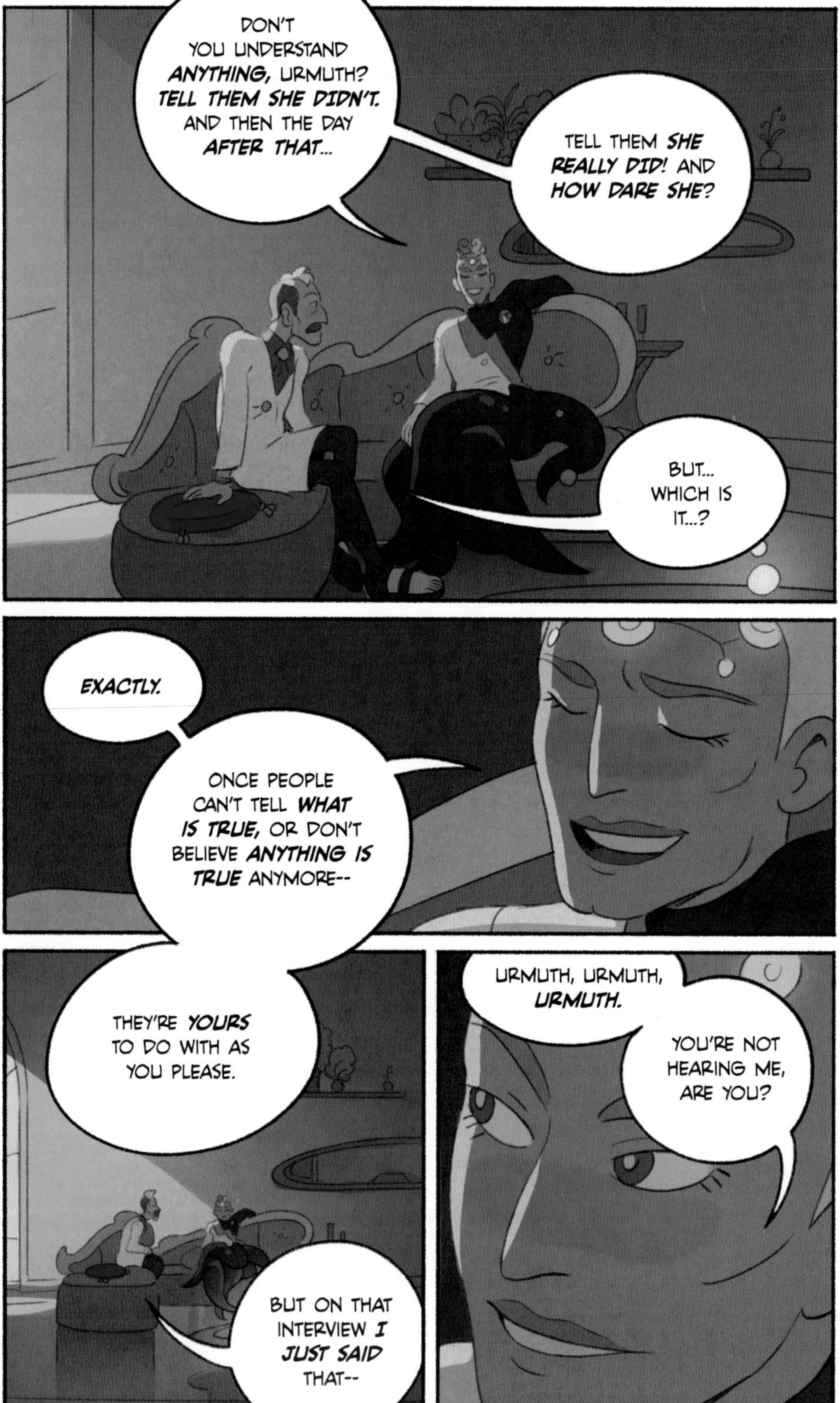
DON'T YOU UNDERSTAND ANYTHING, URMUTH? TELL THEM SHE DIDN'T. AND THEN THE DAY AFTER THAT...
TELL THEM SHE REALLY DID! AND HOW DARE SHE?
BUT... WHICH IS IT...?
EXACTLY.
ONCE PEOPLE CAN'T TELL WHAT IS TRUE, OR DON'T BELIEVE ANYTHING IS TRUE ANYMORE--
THEY'RE YOURS TO DO WITH AS YOU PLEASE.
BUT ON THAT INTERVIEW I JUST SAID THAT--
URMUTH, URMUTH, URMUTH.
YOU'RE NOT HEARING ME, ARE YOU?

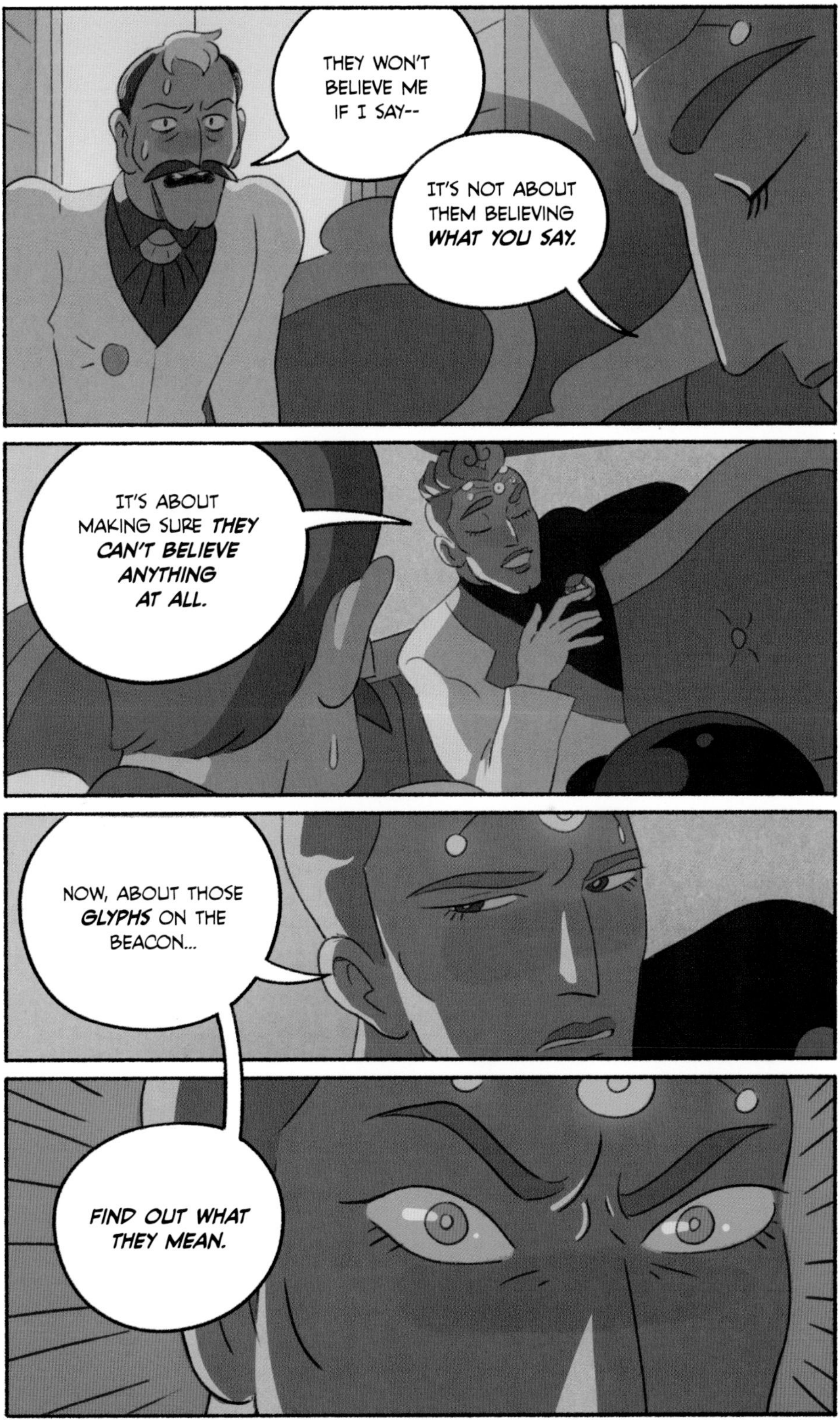
THEY WON'T BELIEVE ME IF I SAY--
IT'S NOT ABOUT THEM BELIEVING *WHAT YOU SAY.*
IT'S ABOUT MAKING SURE *THEY CAN'T BELIEVE ANYTHING AT ALL.*
NOW, ABOUT THOSE *GLYPHS* ON THE BEACON...
FIND OUT WHAT THEY MEAN.

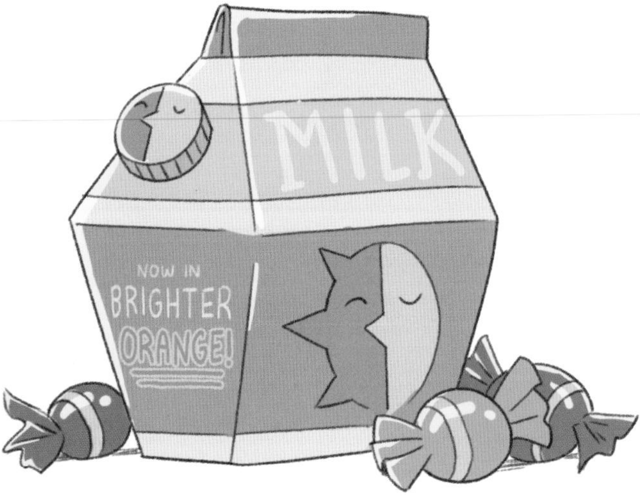
MILK
NOW IN
BRIGHTER
ORANGE!

Chapter 3

TEN THOUSAND VOICES

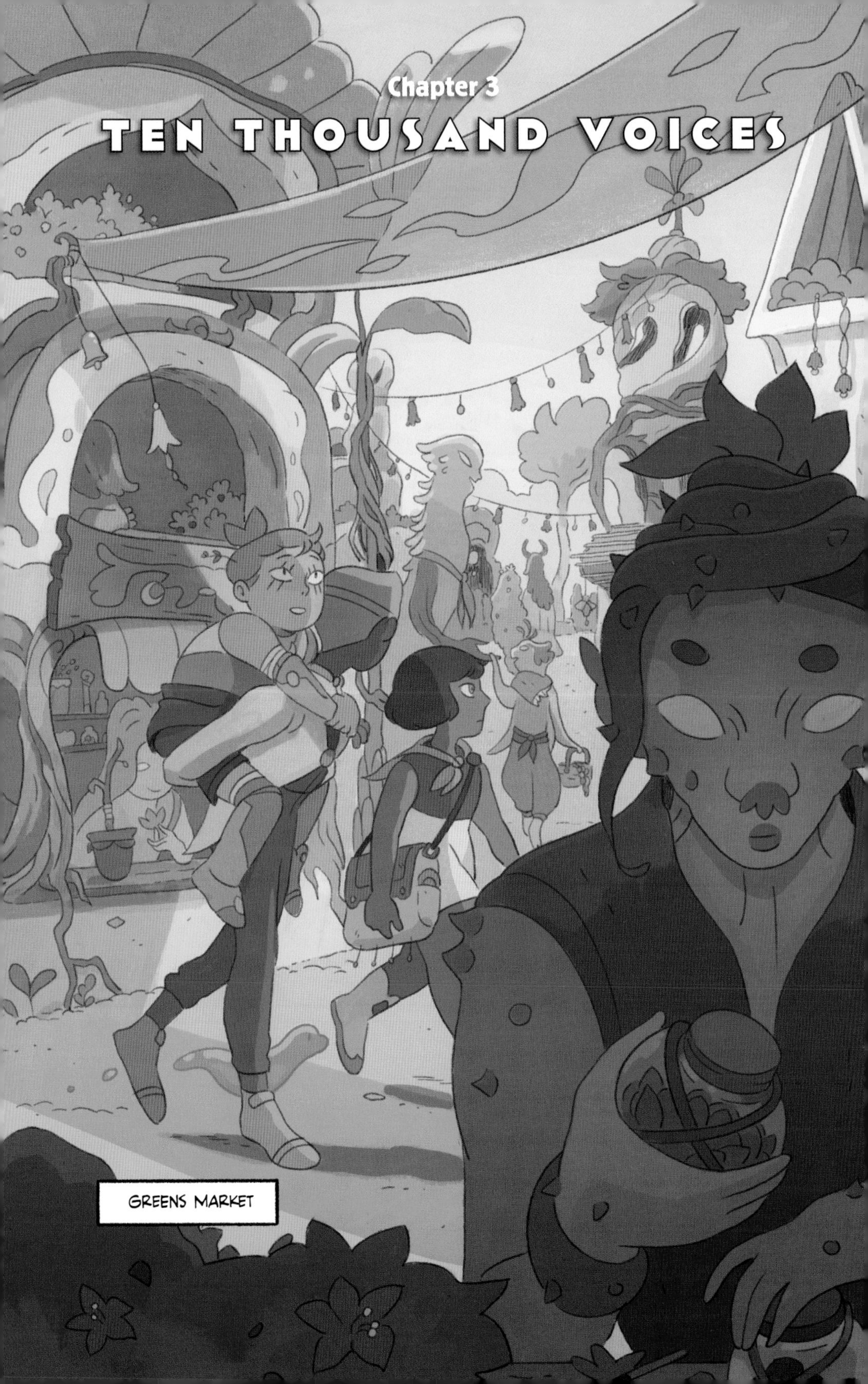
GREENS MARKET

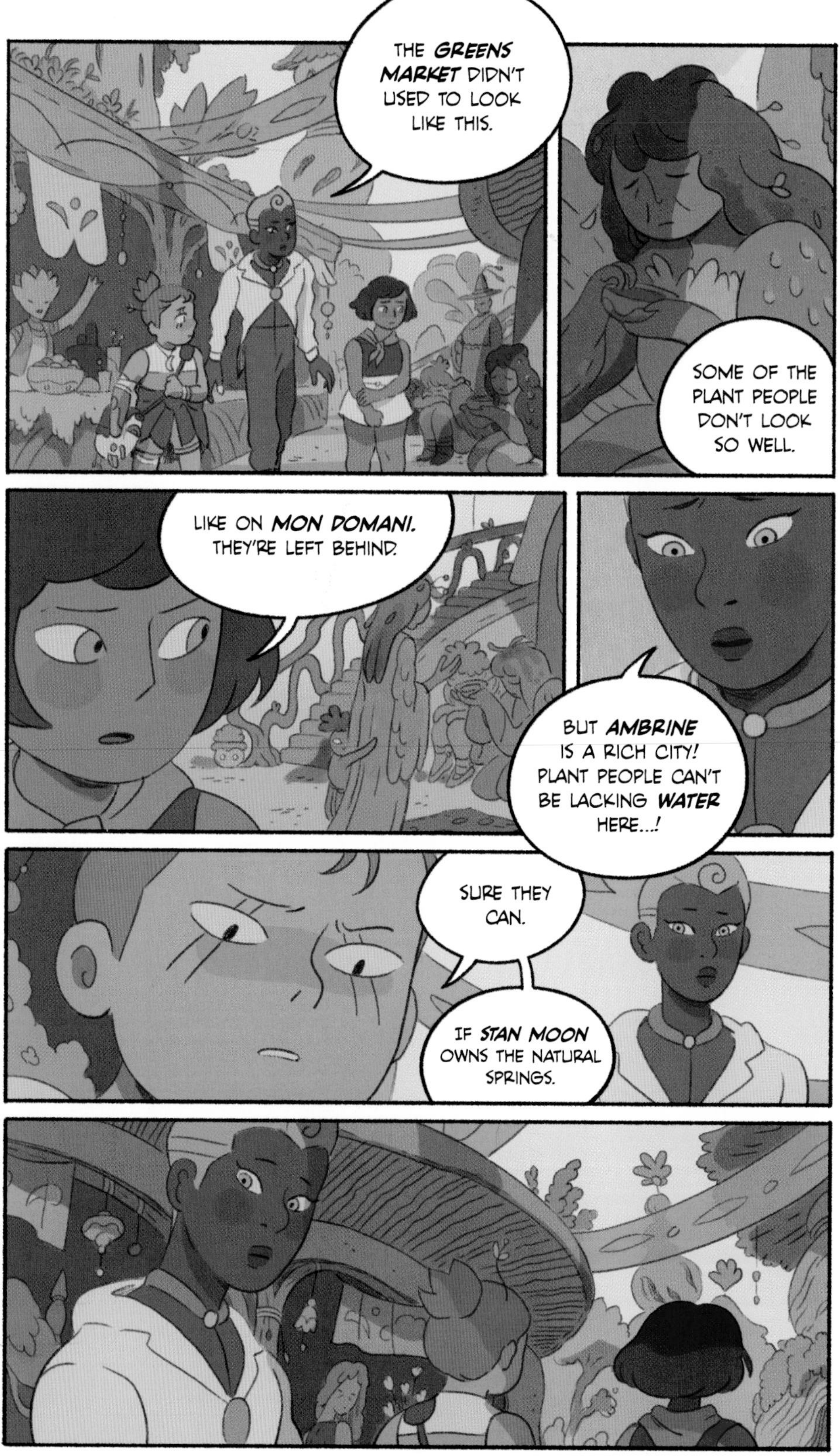
THE GREENS MARKET DIDN'T USED TO LOOK LIKE THIS.
SOME OF THE PLANT PEOPLE DON'T LOOK SO WELL.
LIKE ON MON DOMANI. THEY'RE LEFT BEHIND.
BUT AMBRINE IS A RICH CITY! PLANT PEOPLE CAN'T BE LACKING WATER HERE...!
SURE THEY CAN.
IF STAN MOON OWNS THE NATURAL SPRINGS.

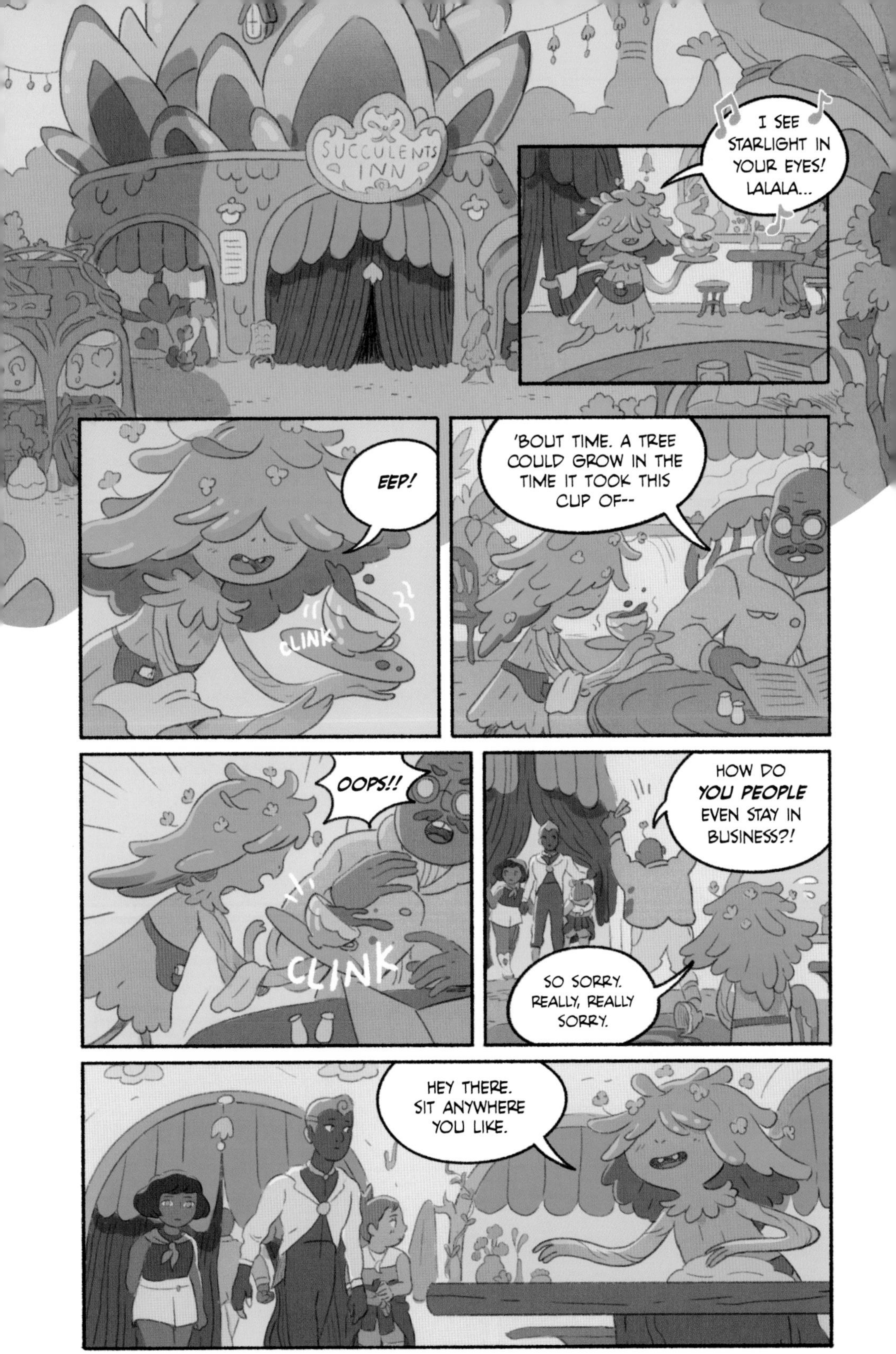
SUCCULENTS INN
I SEE STARLIGHT IN YOUR EYES! LALALA...
EEP!
CLINK
'BOUT TIME. A TREE COULD GROW IN THE TIME IT TOOK THIS CUP OF--
OOPS!!
CLINK
HOW DO *YOU PEOPLE* EVEN STAY IN BUSINESS?!
SO SORRY. REALLY, REALLY SORRY.
HEY THERE. SIT ANYWHERE YOU LIKE.

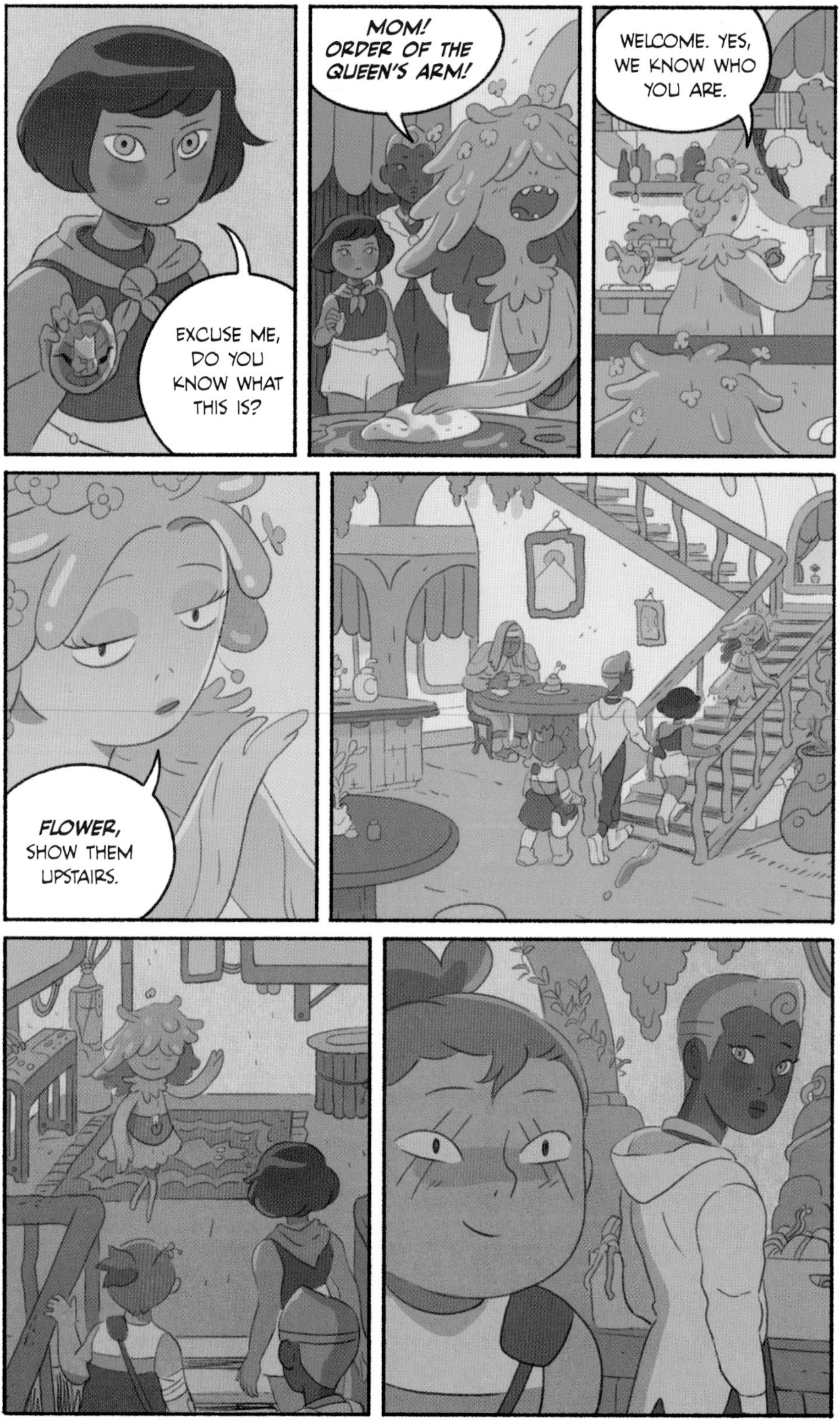
EXCUSE ME, DO YOU KNOW WHAT THIS IS?
MOM! ORDER OF THE QUEEN'S ARM!
WELCOME. YES, WE KNOW WHO YOU ARE.
FLOWER, SHOW THEM UPSTAIRS.

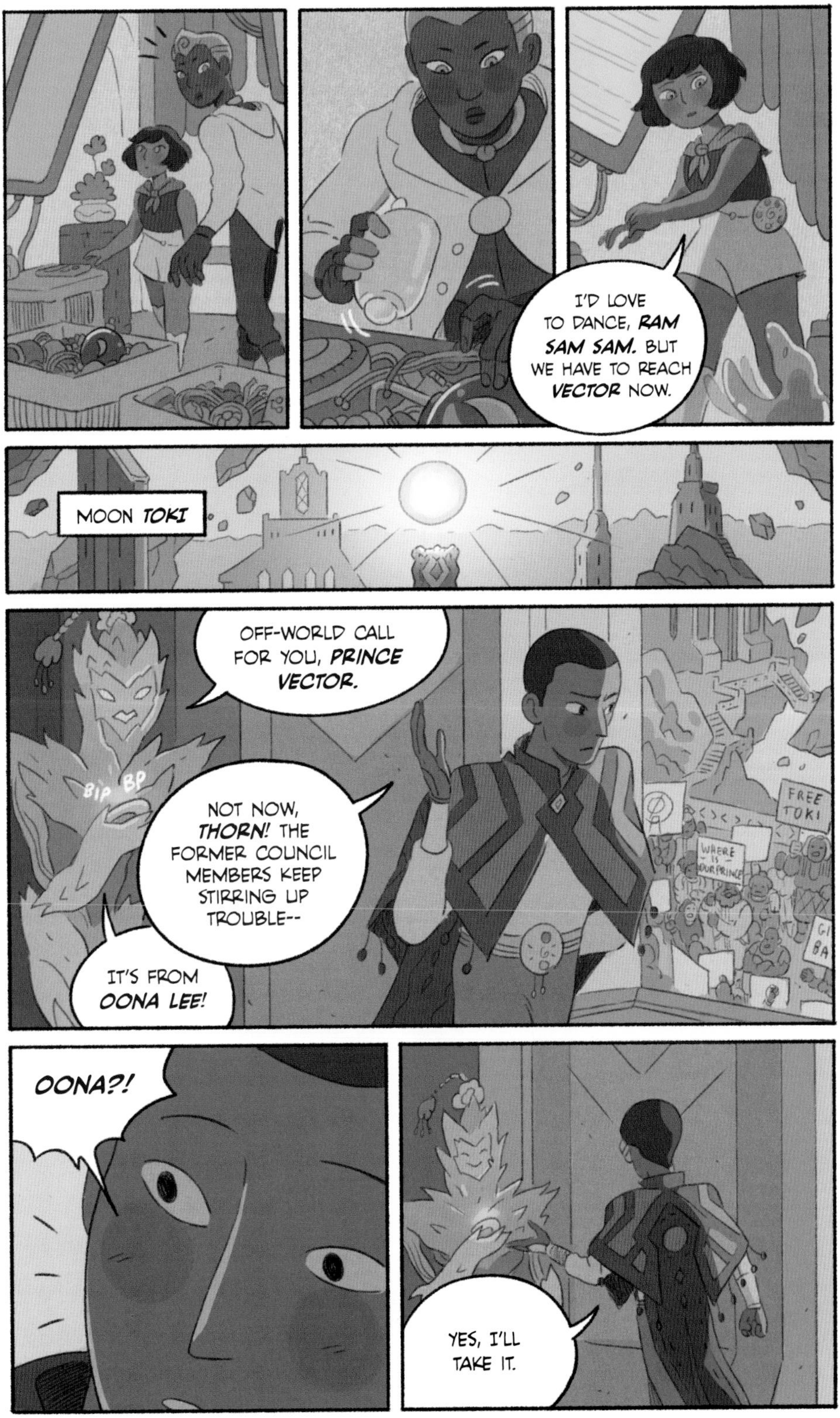
I'D LOVE TO DANCE, **RAM SAM SAM.** BUT WE HAVE TO REACH **VECTOR** NOW.
MOON **TOKI**
OFF-WORLD CALL FOR YOU, **PRINCE VECTOR.**
BIP BP
NOT NOW, **THORN!** THE FORMER COUNCIL MEMBERS KEEP STIRRING UP TROUBLE--
FREE TOKI
WHERE IS OUR PRINCE
IT'S FROM **OONA LEE!**
OONA?!
YES, I'LL TAKE IT.

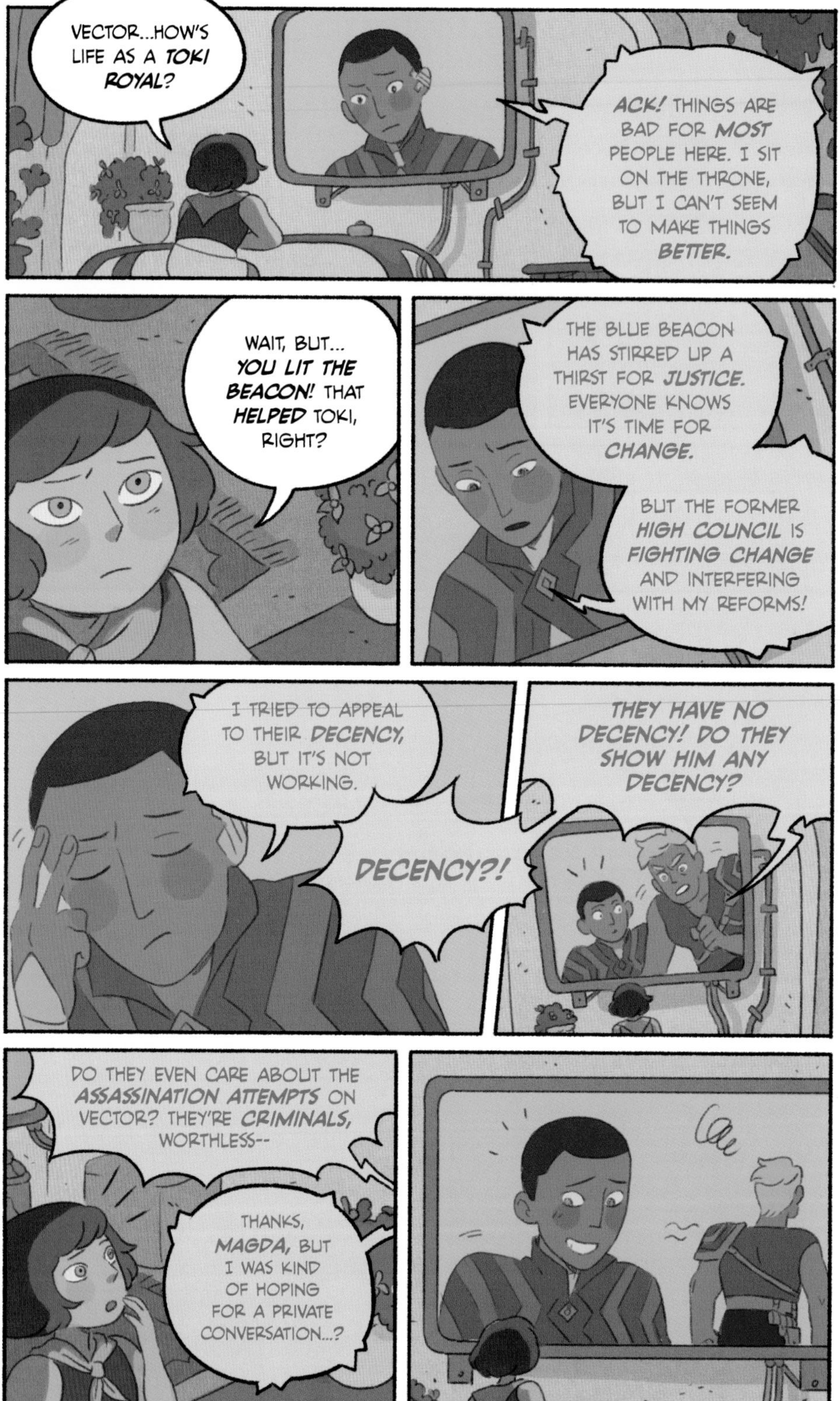
VECTOR...HOW'S LIFE AS A *TOKI ROYAL*?
ACK! THINGS ARE BAD FOR *MOST* PEOPLE HERE. I SIT ON THE THRONE, BUT I CAN'T SEEM TO MAKE THINGS *BETTER*.
WAIT, BUT... *YOU LIT THE BEACON!* THAT *HELPED* TOKI, RIGHT?
THE BLUE BEACON HAS STIRRED UP A THIRST FOR *JUSTICE*. EVERYONE KNOWS IT'S TIME FOR *CHANGE*.
BUT THE FORMER *HIGH COUNCIL* IS *FIGHTING CHANGE* AND INTERFERING WITH MY REFORMS!
I TRIED TO APPEAL TO THEIR *DECENCY*, BUT IT'S NOT WORKING.
DECENCY?!
THEY HAVE NO DECENCY! DO THEY SHOW HIM ANY DECENCY?
DO THEY EVEN CARE ABOUT THE *ASSASSINATION ATTEMPTS* ON VECTOR? THEY'RE *CRIMINALS*, WORTHLESS--
THANKS, *MAGDA*, BUT I WAS KIND OF HOPING FOR A PRIVATE CONVERSATION...?

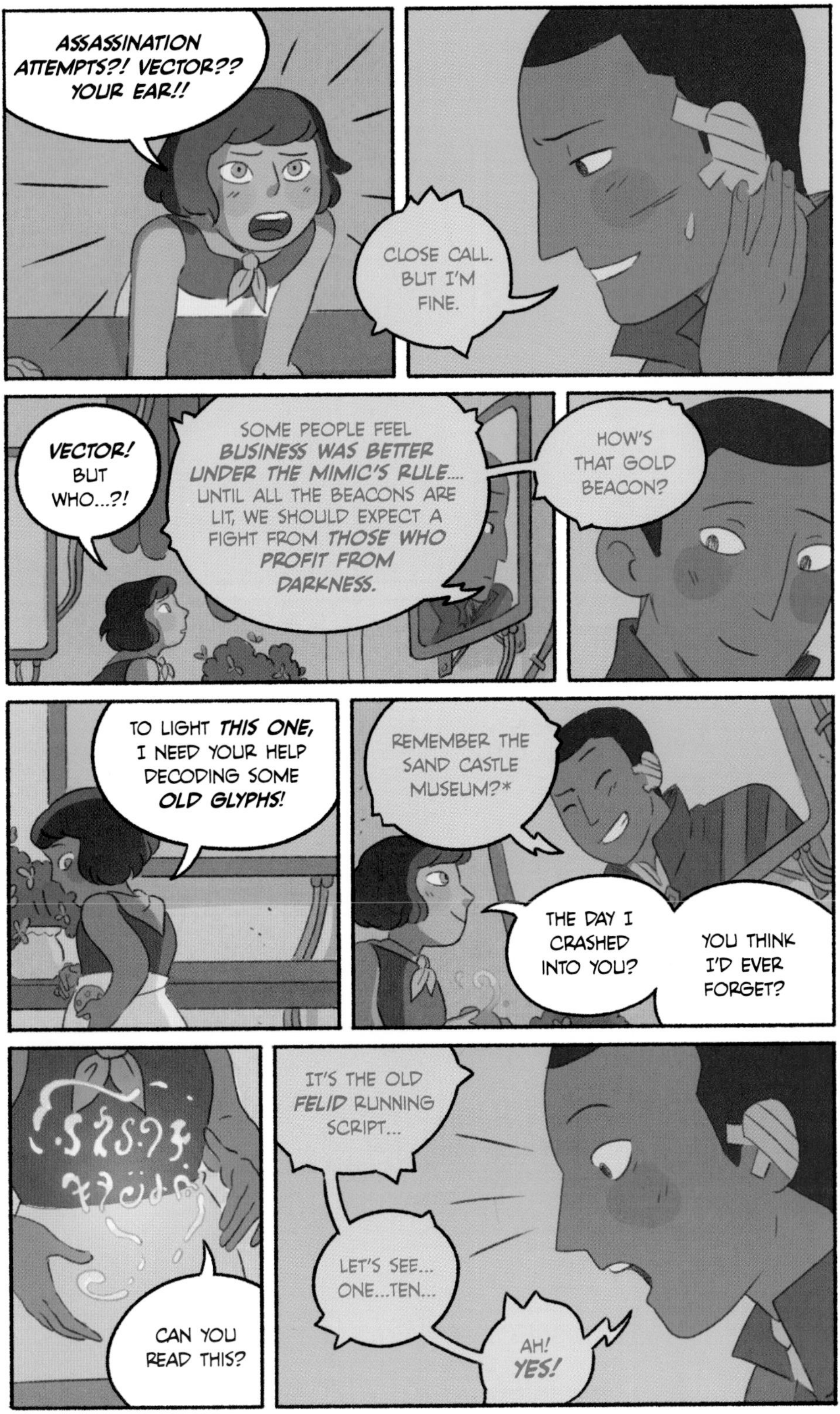
ASSASSINATION ATTEMPTS?! VECTOR?? YOUR EAR!!
CLOSE CALL. BUT I'M FINE.
VECTOR! BUT WHO...?!
SOME PEOPLE FEEL BUSINESS WAS BETTER UNDER THE MIMIC'S RULE.... UNTIL ALL THE BEACONS ARE LIT, WE SHOULD EXPECT A FIGHT FROM THOSE WHO PROFIT FROM DARKNESS.
HOW'S THAT GOLD BEACON?
TO LIGHT THIS ONE, I NEED YOUR HELP DECODING SOME OLD GLYPHS!
REMEMBER THE SAND CASTLE MUSEUM?*
THE DAY I CRASHED INTO YOU?
YOU THINK I'D EVER FORGET?
CAN YOU READ THIS?
IT'S THE OLD FELID RUNNING SCRIPT...
LET'S SEE... ONE...TEN...
AH! YES!

* SEE 5W1: *THE SAND WARRIOR*

"WHEN TEN THOUSAND VOICES IN ONE THE AMBER ANTHEM INTONE...

YE SUMMON WHAT LIES BELOW STONE AND THE WAY TO THE BEACON IS WON."

TEN THOUSAND VOICES...

OONA, I HAVE TO RUN. THERE'S SOME KIND OF COMMOTION AT THE GATES.

I...

I BELIEVE IN YOU.

BZZZT—

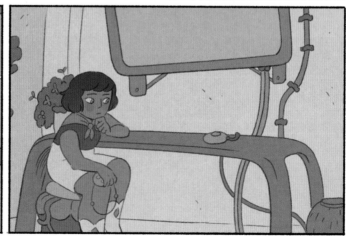

Chapter 4

STRANGE DREAMS

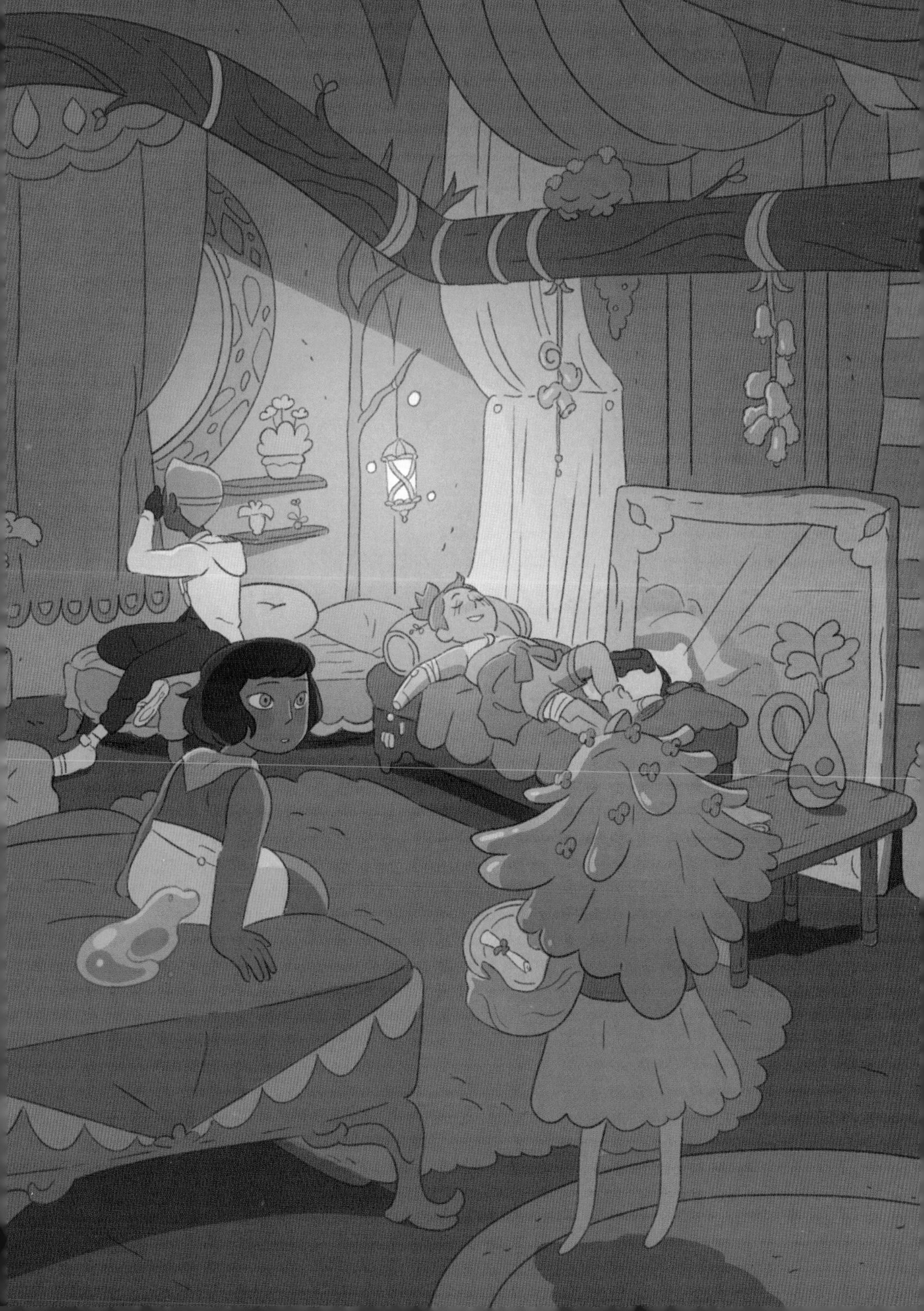

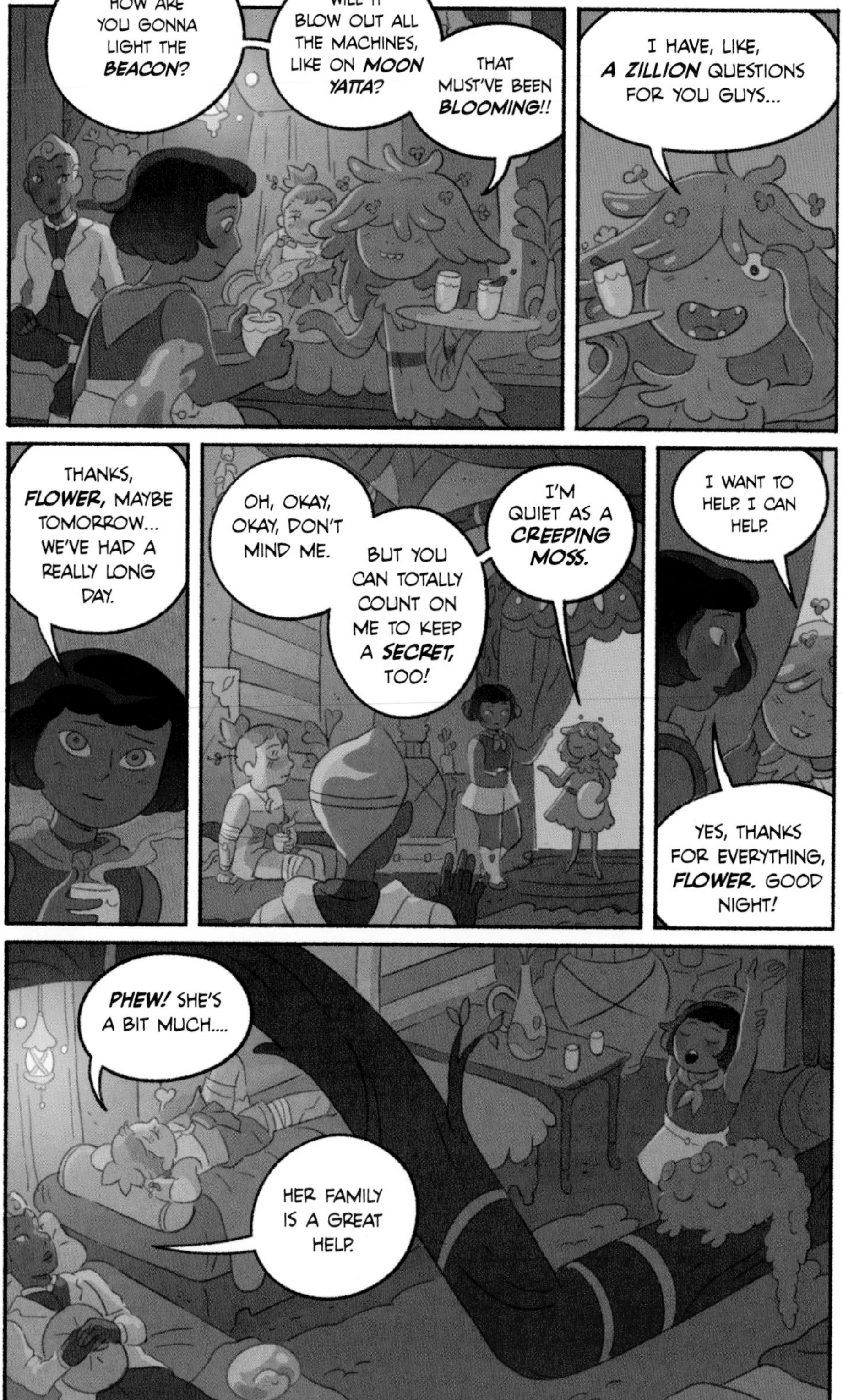
HOW ARE YOU GONNA LIGHT THE BEACON?
WILL IT BLOW OUT ALL THE MACHINES, LIKE ON MOON YATTA?
THAT MUST'VE BEEN BLOOMING!!
I HAVE, LIKE, A ZILLION QUESTIONS FOR YOU GUYS...
THANKS, FLOWER, MAYBE TOMORROW... WE'VE HAD A REALLY LONG DAY.
OH, OKAY, OKAY, DON'T MIND ME.
BUT YOU CAN TOTALLY COUNT ON ME TO KEEP A SECRET, TOO!
I'M QUIET AS A CREEPING MOSS.
I WANT TO HELP. I CAN HELP.
YES, THANKS FOR EVERYTHING, FLOWER. GOOD NIGHT!
PHEW! SHE'S A BIT MUCH....
HER FAMILY IS A GREAT HELP.

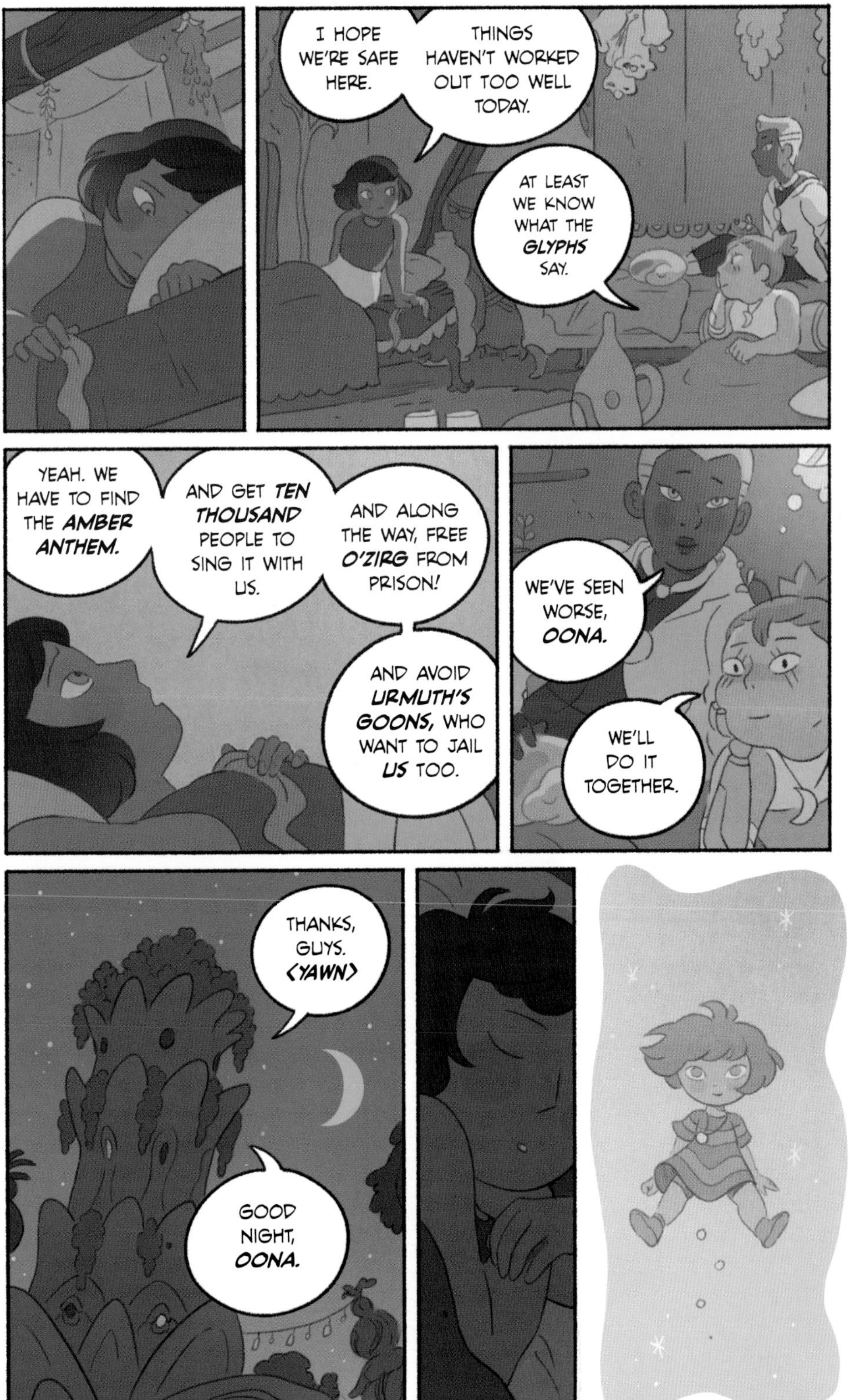
I HOPE WE'RE SAFE HERE.
THINGS HAVEN'T WORKED OUT TOO WELL TODAY.
AT LEAST WE KNOW WHAT THE GLYPHS SAY.
YEAH. WE HAVE TO FIND THE AMBER ANTHEM.
AND GET TEN THOUSAND PEOPLE TO SING IT WITH US.
AND ALONG THE WAY, FREE O'ZIRG FROM PRISON!
AND AVOID URMUTH'S GOONS, WHO WANT TO JAIL US TOO.
WE'VE SEEN WORSE, OONA.
WE'LL DO IT TOGETHER.
THANKS, GUYS. <YAWN>
GOOD NIGHT, OONA.

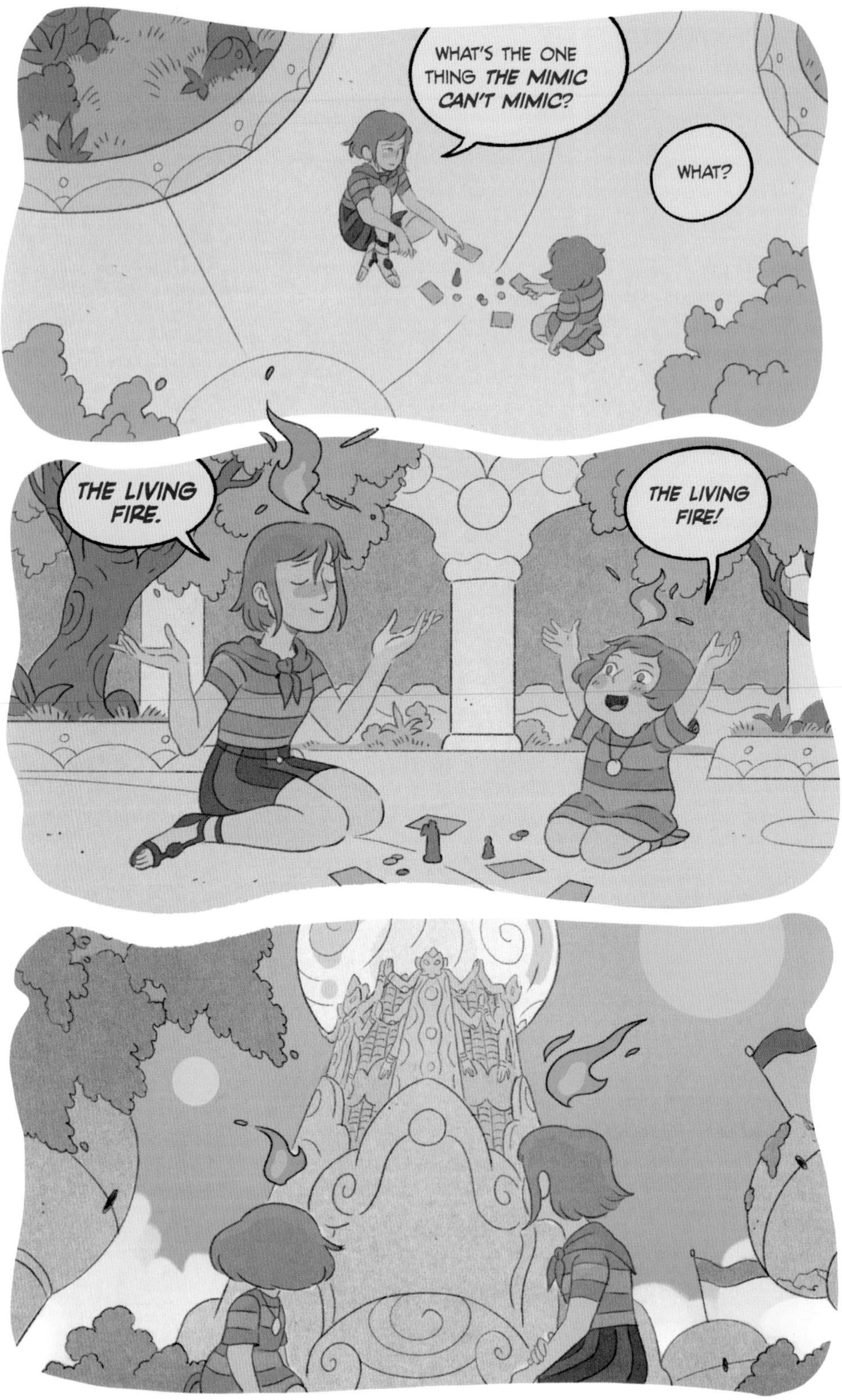
WHAT'S THE ONE THING *THE MIMIC CAN'T MIMIC?*
WHAT?
THE LIVING FIRE.
THE LIVING FIRE!

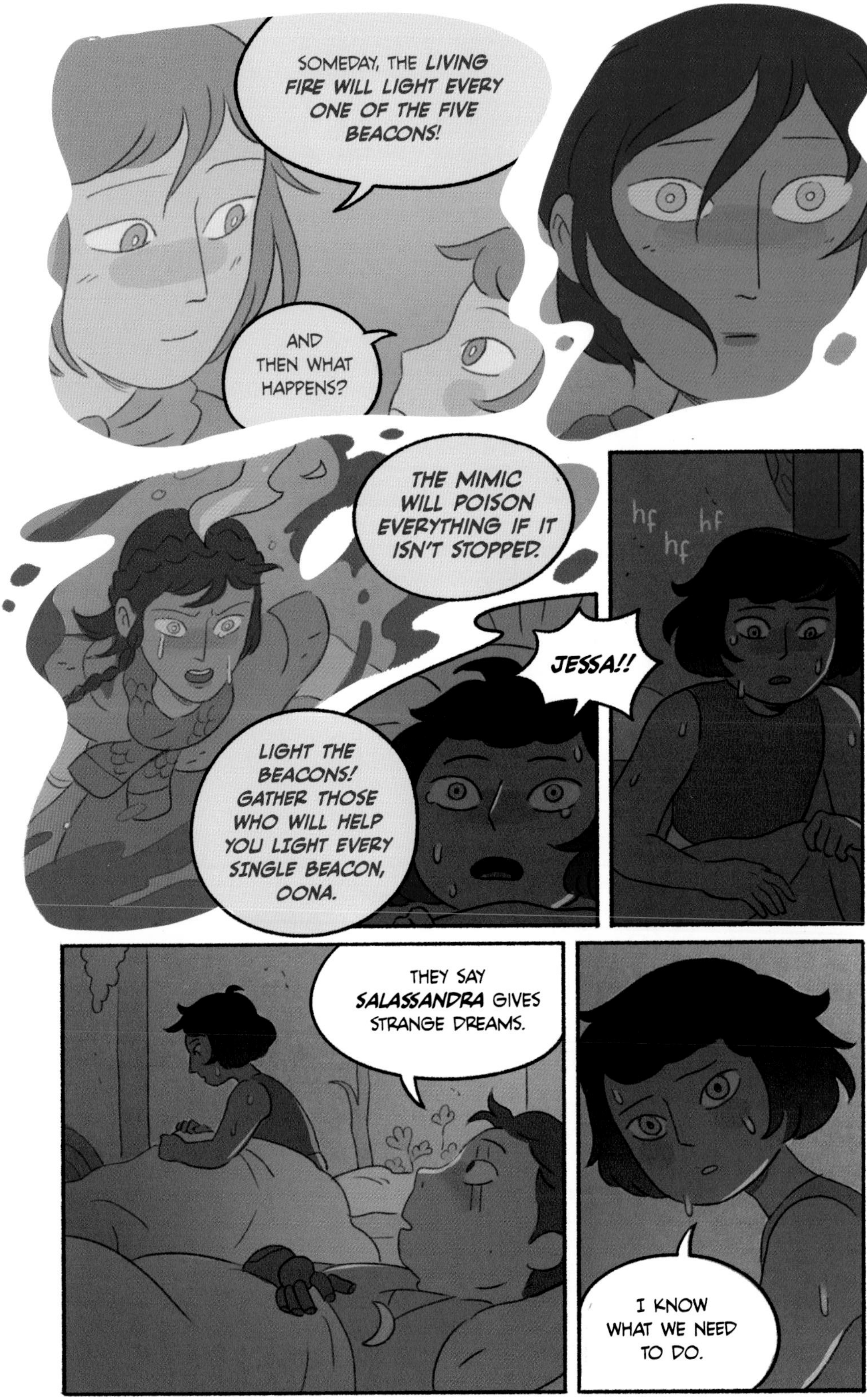
SOMEDAY, THE LIVING FIRE WILL LIGHT EVERY ONE OF THE FIVE BEACONS!
AND THEN WHAT HAPPENS?
THE MIMIC WILL POISON EVERYTHING IF IT ISN'T STOPPED.
LIGHT THE BEACONS! GATHER THOSE WHO WILL HELP YOU LIGHT EVERY SINGLE BEACON, OONA.
JESSA!!
hf hf hf
THEY SAY SALASSANDRA GIVES STRANGE DREAMS.
I KNOW WHAT WE NEED TO DO.

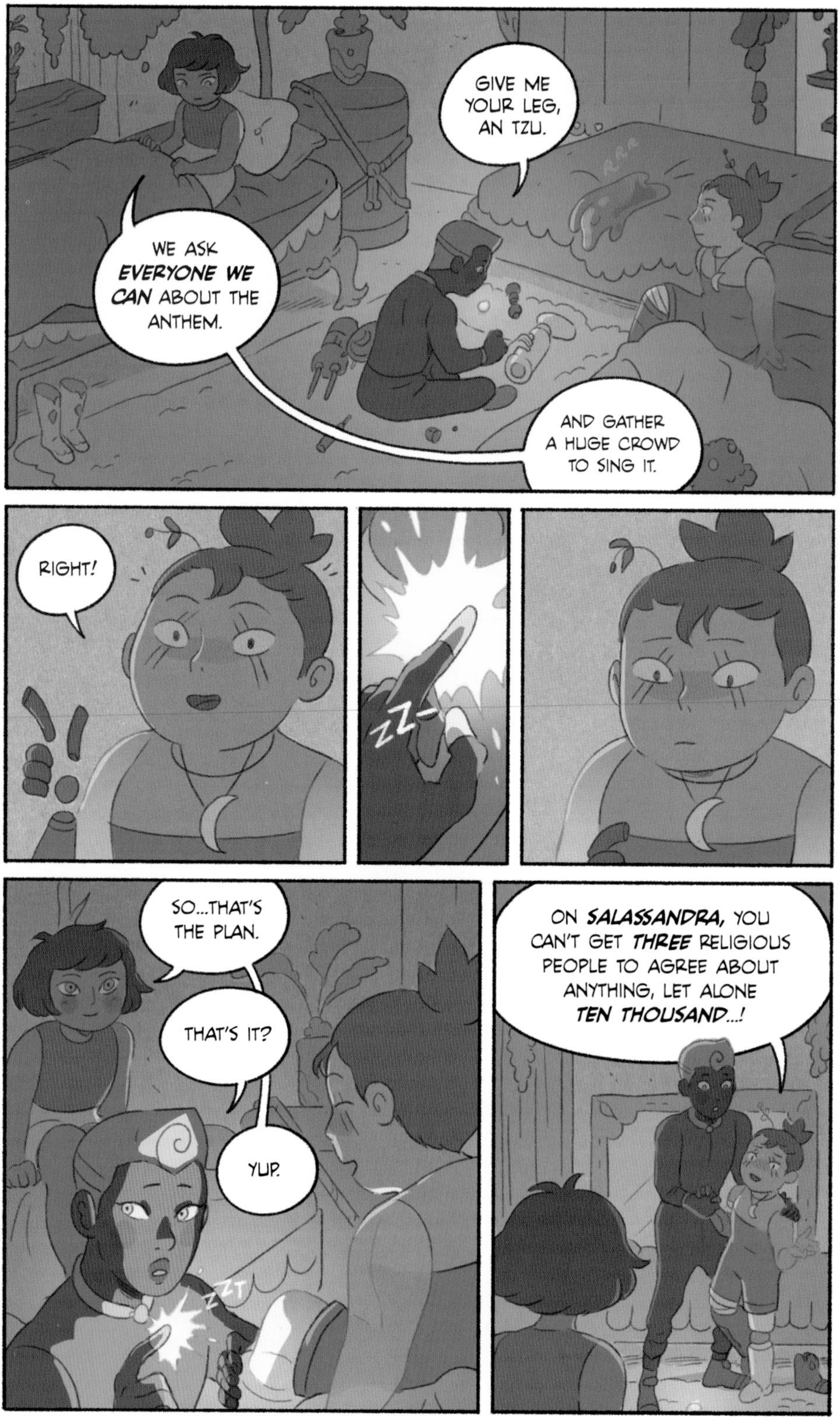
GIVE ME YOUR LEG, AN TZU.
WE ASK EVERYONE WE CAN ABOUT THE ANTHEM.
AND GATHER A HUGE CROWD TO SING IT.
RIGHT!
ZZ-
SO...THAT'S THE PLAN.
THAT'S IT?
YUP.
ZZT
ON SALASSANDRA, YOU CAN'T GET THREE RELIGIOUS PEOPLE TO AGREE ABOUT ANYTHING, LET ALONE TEN THOUSAND...!

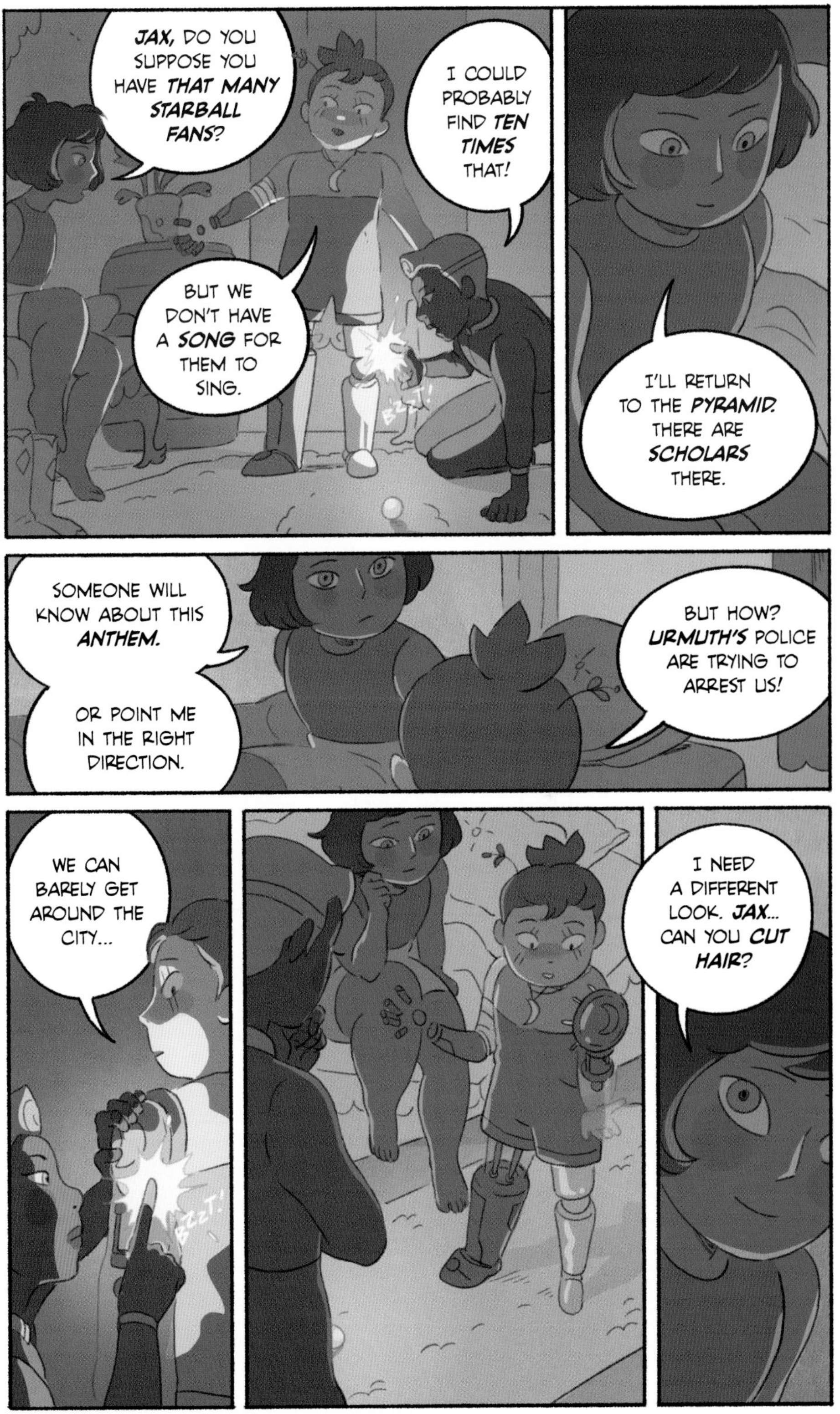
JAX, DO YOU SUPPOSE YOU HAVE THAT MANY STARBALL FANS?
I COULD PROBABLY FIND TEN TIMES THAT!
BUT WE DON'T HAVE A SONG FOR THEM TO SING.
BZZT!
I'LL RETURN TO THE PYRAMID. THERE ARE SCHOLARS THERE.
SOMEONE WILL KNOW ABOUT THIS ANTHEM.
OR POINT ME IN THE RIGHT DIRECTION.
BUT HOW? URMUTH'S POLICE ARE TRYING TO ARREST US!
WE CAN BARELY GET AROUND THE CITY...
BZZT!
I NEED A DIFFERENT LOOK. JAX... CAN YOU CUT HAIR?

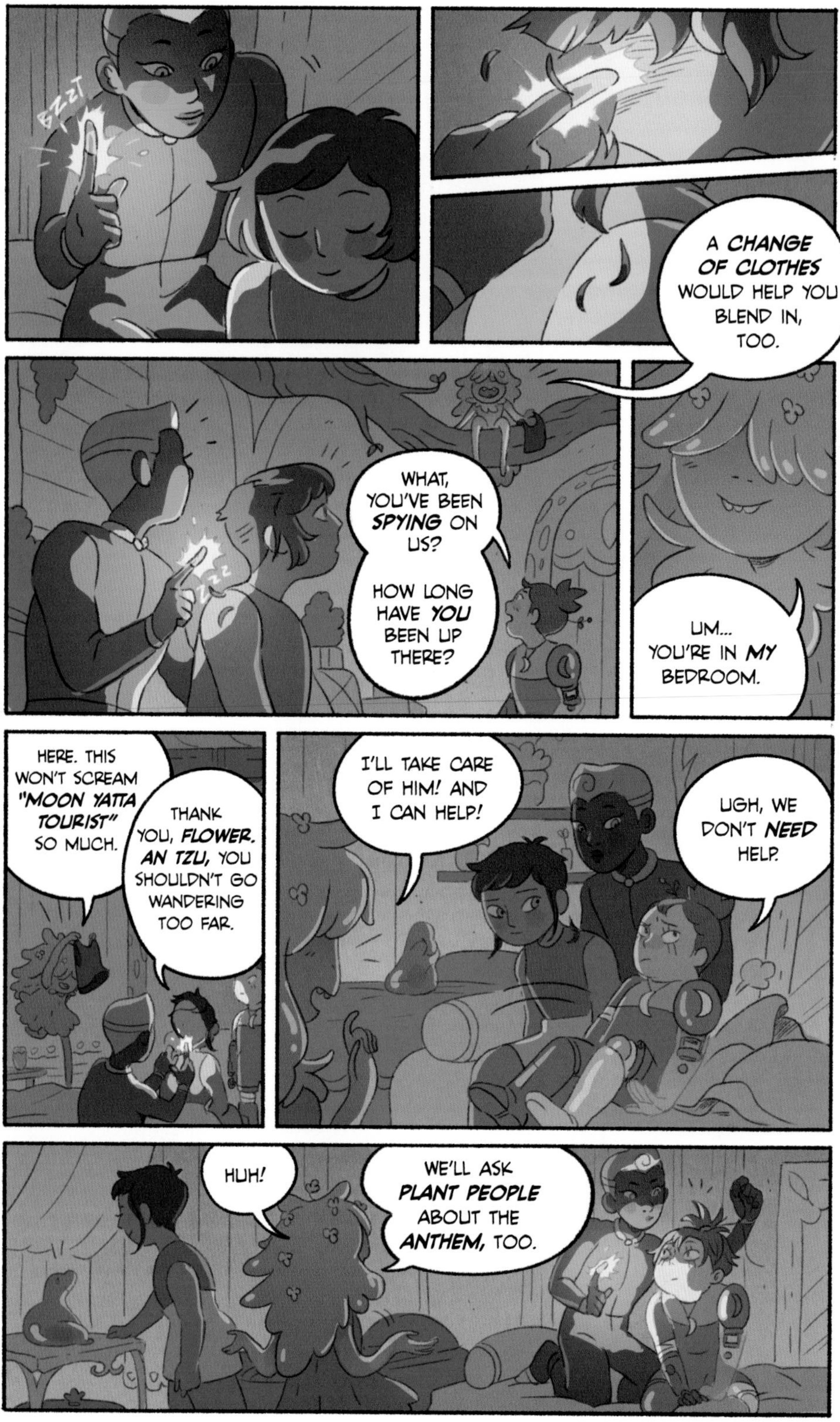
BZZT
A CHANGE OF CLOTHES WOULD HELP YOU BLEND IN, TOO.
WHAT, YOU'VE BEEN SPYING ON US?
HOW LONG HAVE YOU BEEN UP THERE?
UM... YOU'RE IN MY BEDROOM.
HERE. THIS WON'T SCREAM "MOON YATTA TOURIST" SO MUCH.
THANK YOU, FLOWER. AN TZU, YOU SHOULDN'T GO WANDERING TOO FAR.
I'LL TAKE CARE OF HIM! AND I CAN HELP!
UGH, WE DON'T NEED HELP.
HUH!
WE'LL ASK PLANT PEOPLE ABOUT THE ANTHEM, TOO.

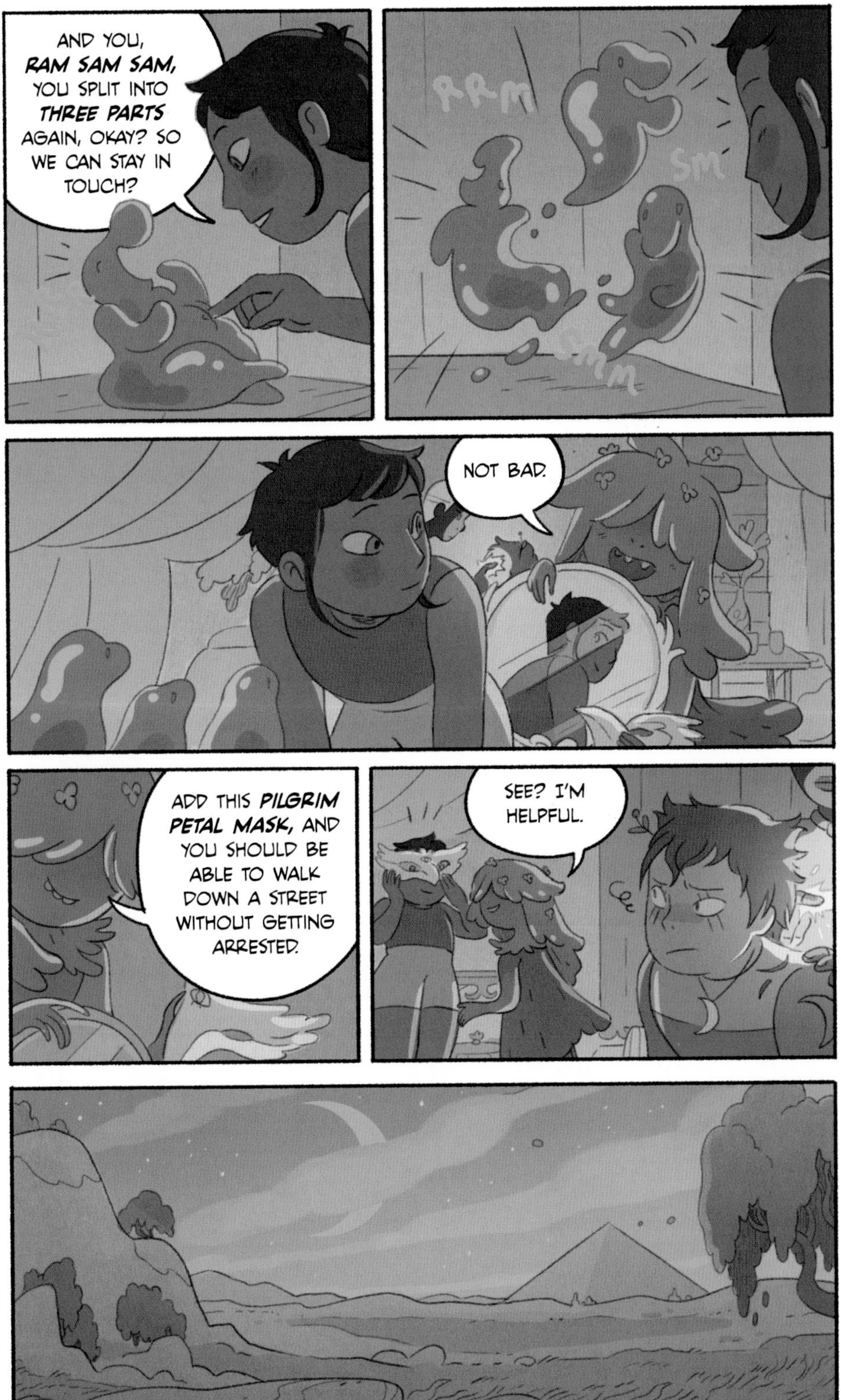
AND YOU, **RAM SAM SAM,** YOU SPLIT INTO **THREE PARTS** AGAIN, OKAY? SO WE CAN STAY IN TOUCH?
RRM
SM
SMM
NOT BAD.
ADD THIS **PILGRIM PETAL MASK,** AND YOU SHOULD BE ABLE TO WALK DOWN A STREET WITHOUT GETTING ARRESTED.
SEE? I'M HELPFUL.

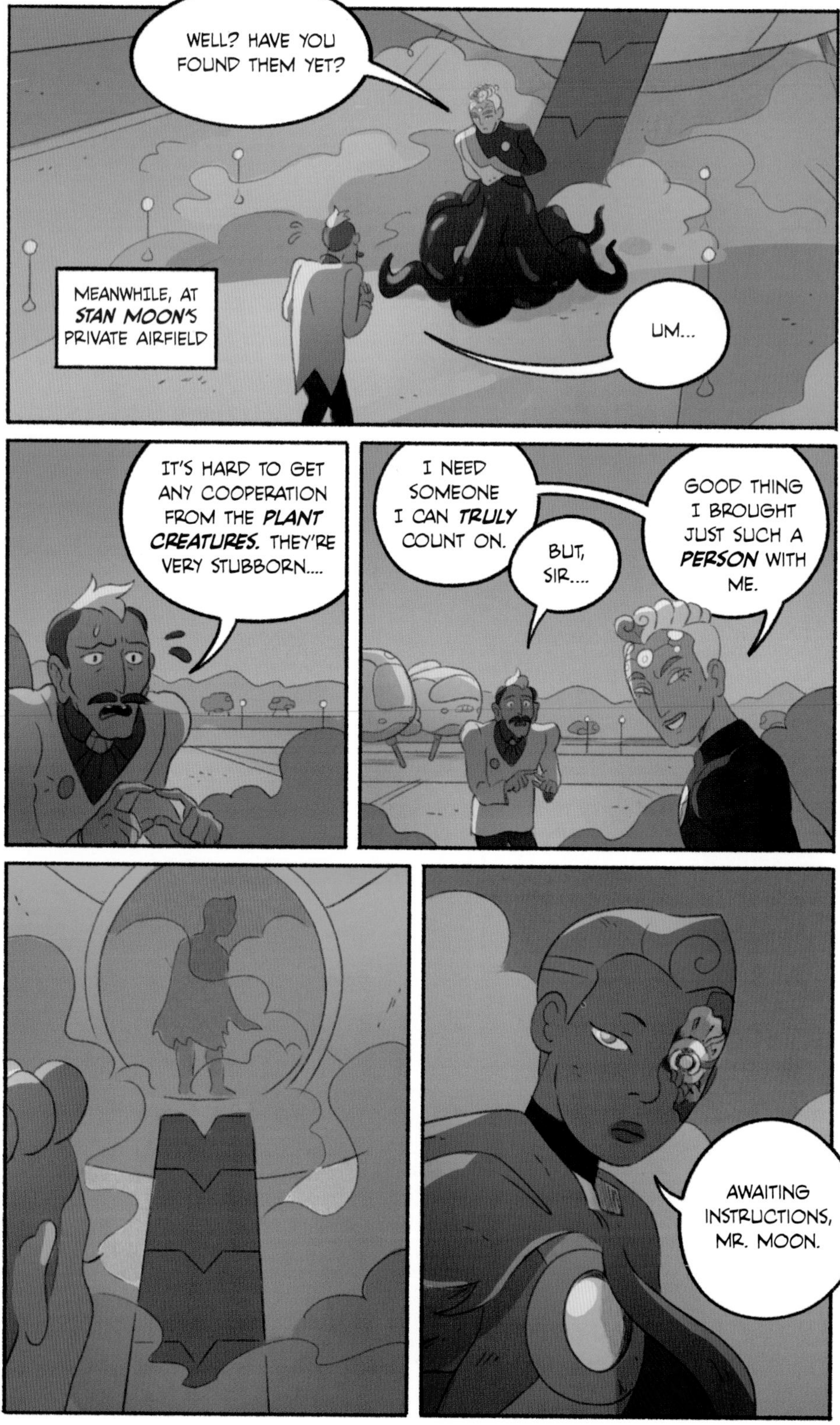
WELL? HAVE YOU FOUND THEM YET?
MEANWHILE, AT STAN MOON'S PRIVATE AIRFIELD
UM...
IT'S HARD TO GET ANY COOPERATION FROM THE PLANT CREATURES. THEY'RE VERY STUBBORN....
I NEED SOMEONE I CAN TRULY COUNT ON.
BUT, SIR....
GOOD THING I BROUGHT JUST SUCH A PERSON WITH ME.
AWAITING INSTRUCTIONS, MR. MOON.

Chapter 5

THE AVIARY

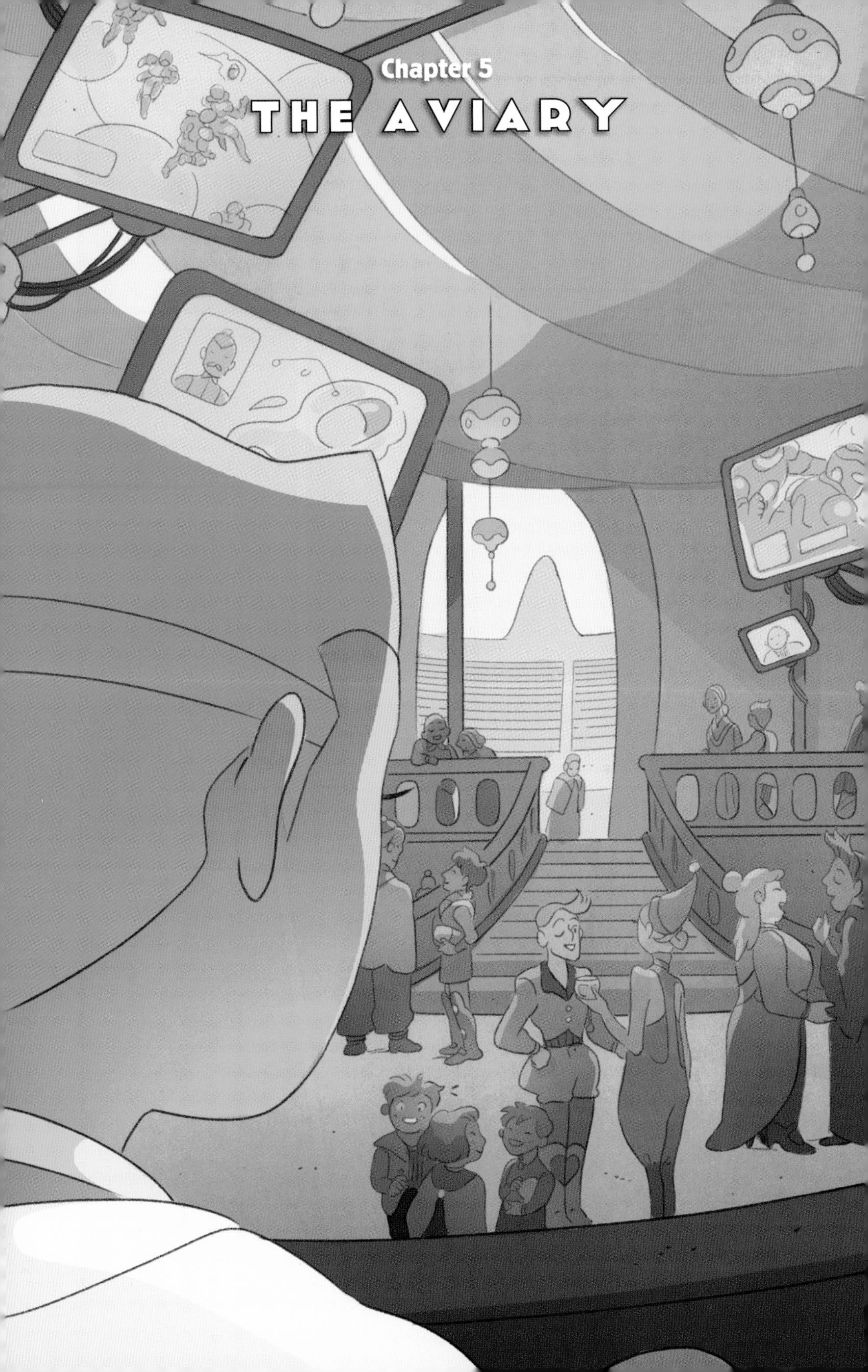

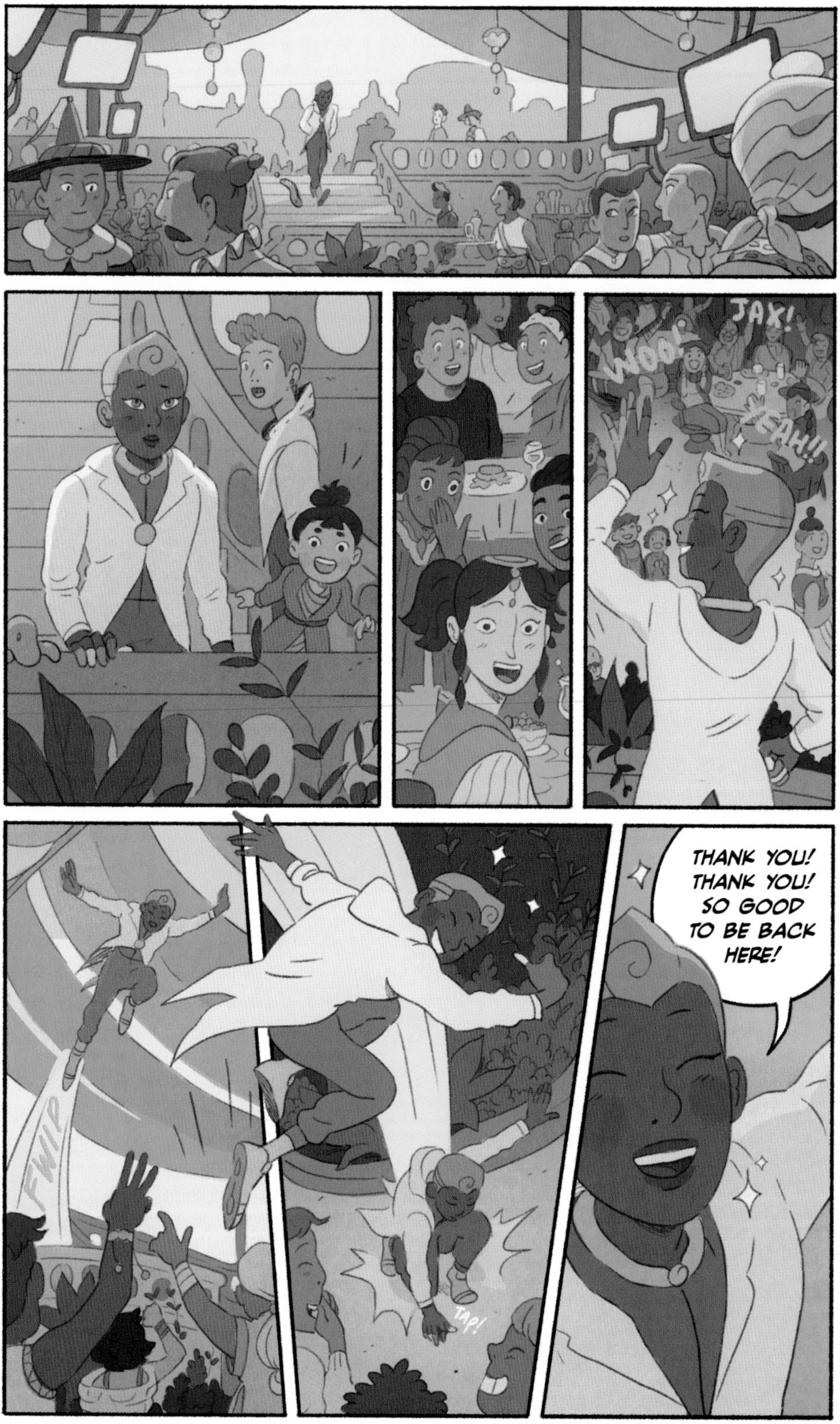
JAX!
WOO!
YEAH!!
THANK YOU! THANK YOU! SO GOOD TO BE BACK HERE!
FWIP
TAP!

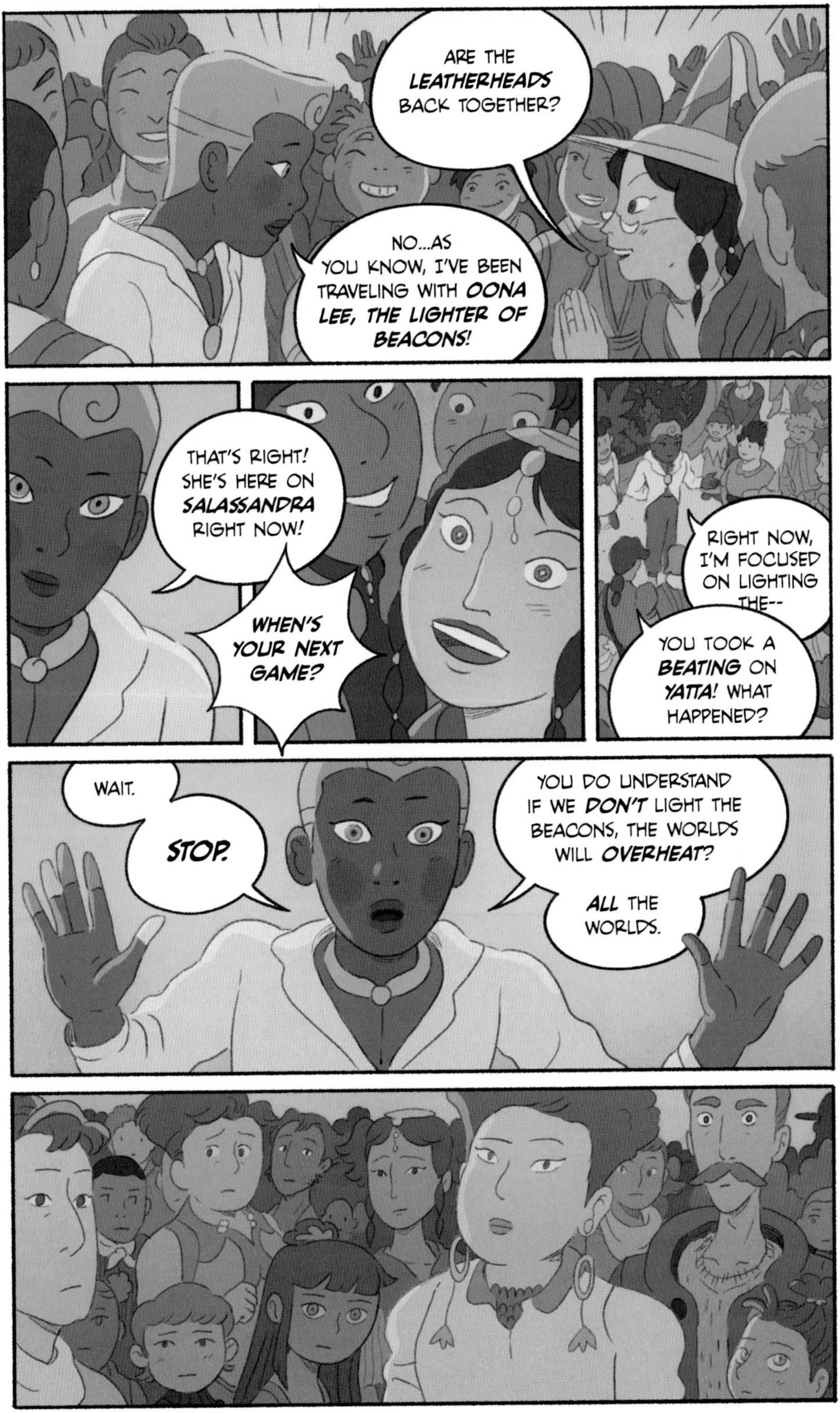
ARE THE LEATHERHEADS BACK TOGETHER?
NO...AS YOU KNOW, I'VE BEEN TRAVELING WITH OONA LEE, THE LIGHTER OF BEACONS!
THAT'S RIGHT! SHE'S HERE ON SALASSANDRA RIGHT NOW!
WHEN'S YOUR NEXT GAME?
RIGHT NOW, I'M FOCUSED ON LIGHTING THE--
YOU TOOK A BEATING ON YATTA! WHAT HAPPENED?
WAIT.
STOP.
YOU DO UNDERSTAND IF WE DON'T LIGHT THE BEACONS, THE WORLDS WILL OVERHEAT?
ALL THE WORLDS.

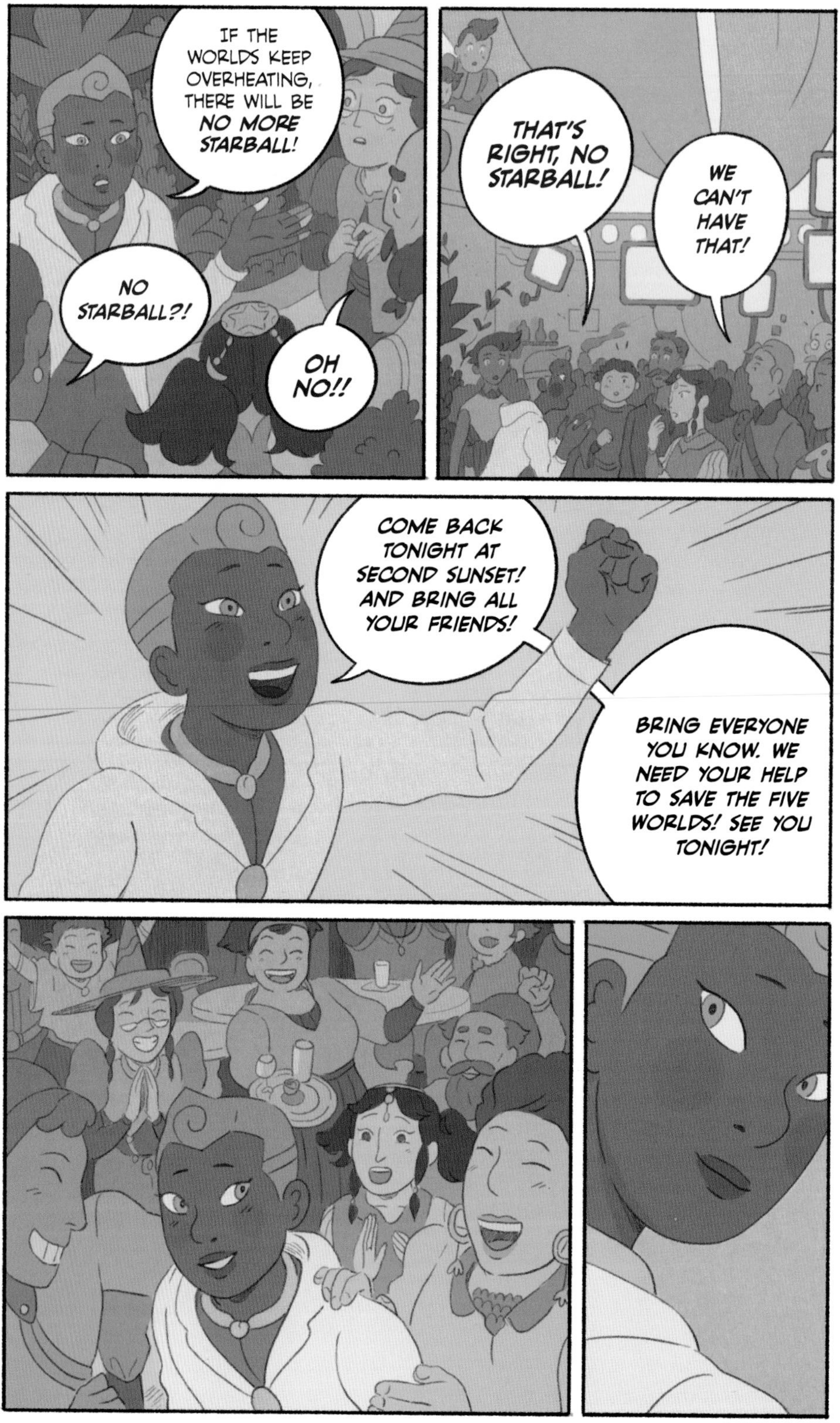
IF THE WORLDS KEEP OVERHEATING, THERE WILL BE NO MORE STARBALL!
NO STARBALL?!
OH NO!!
THAT'S RIGHT, NO STARBALL!
WE CAN'T HAVE THAT!
COME BACK TONIGHT AT SECOND SUNSET! AND BRING ALL YOUR FRIENDS!
BRING EVERYONE YOU KNOW. WE NEED YOUR HELP TO SAVE THE FIVE WORLDS! SEE YOU TONIGHT!

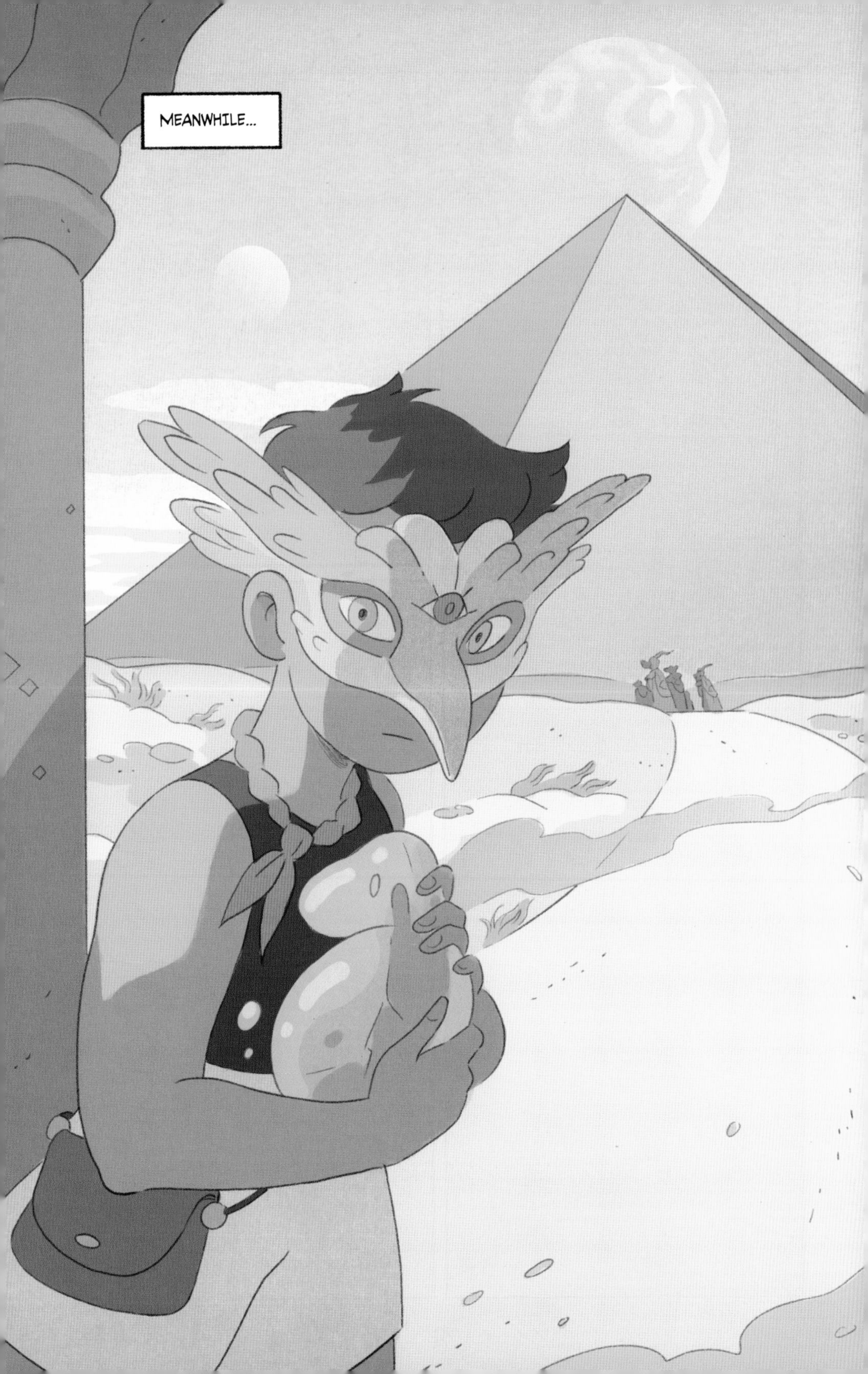
MEANWHILE...

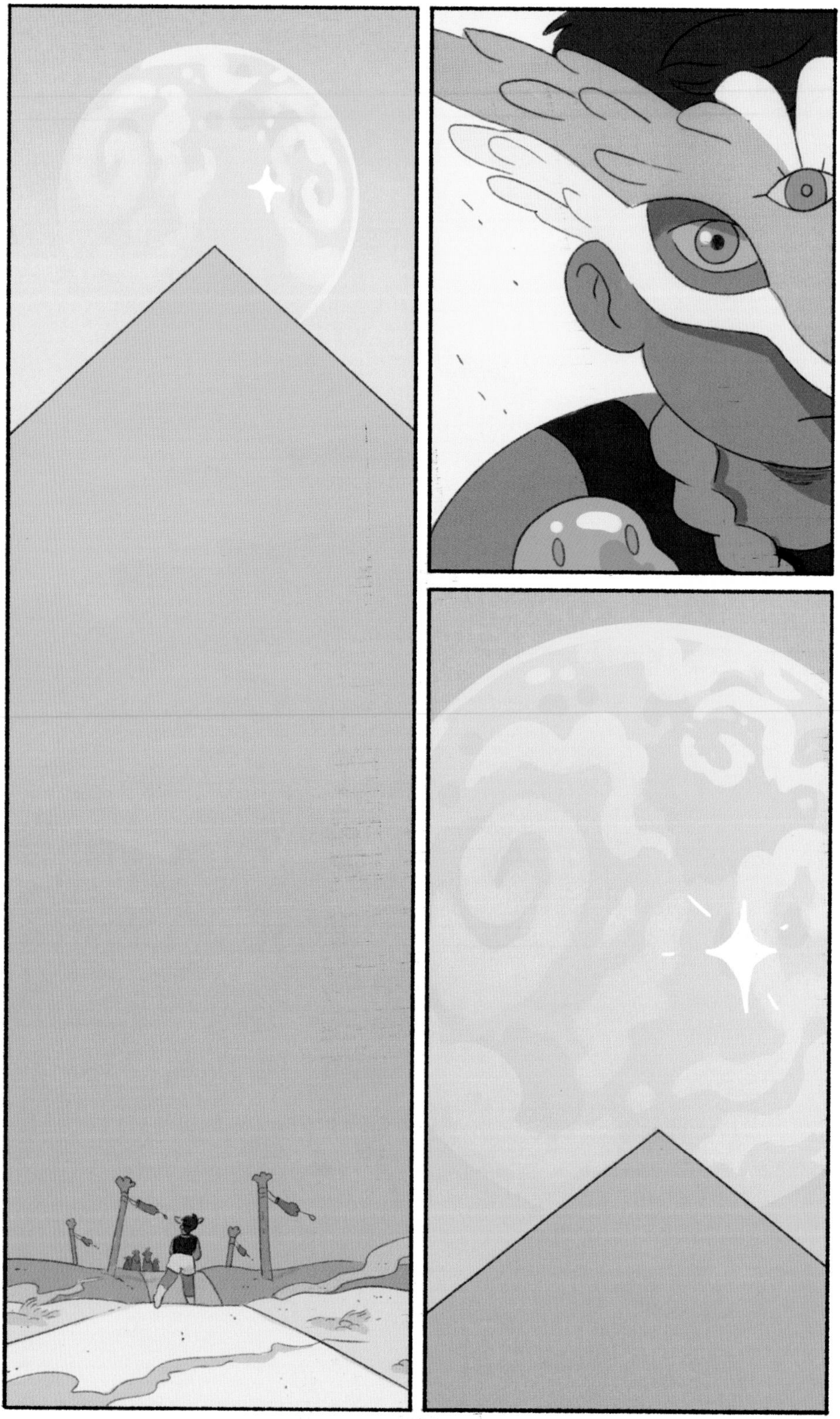

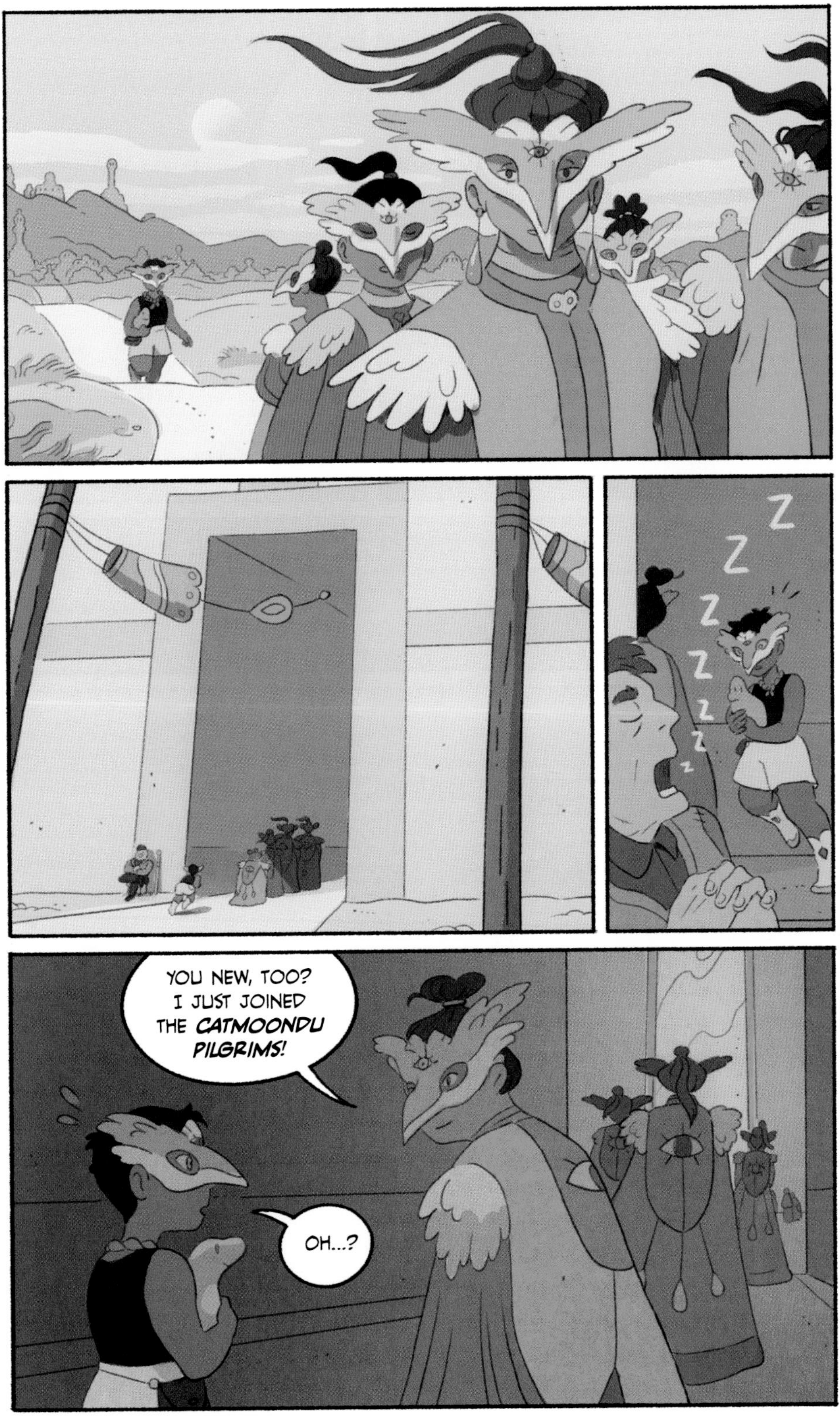
Z Z Z Z Z Z Z
YOU NEW, TOO? I JUST JOINED THE CATMOONDU PILGRIMS!
OH...?

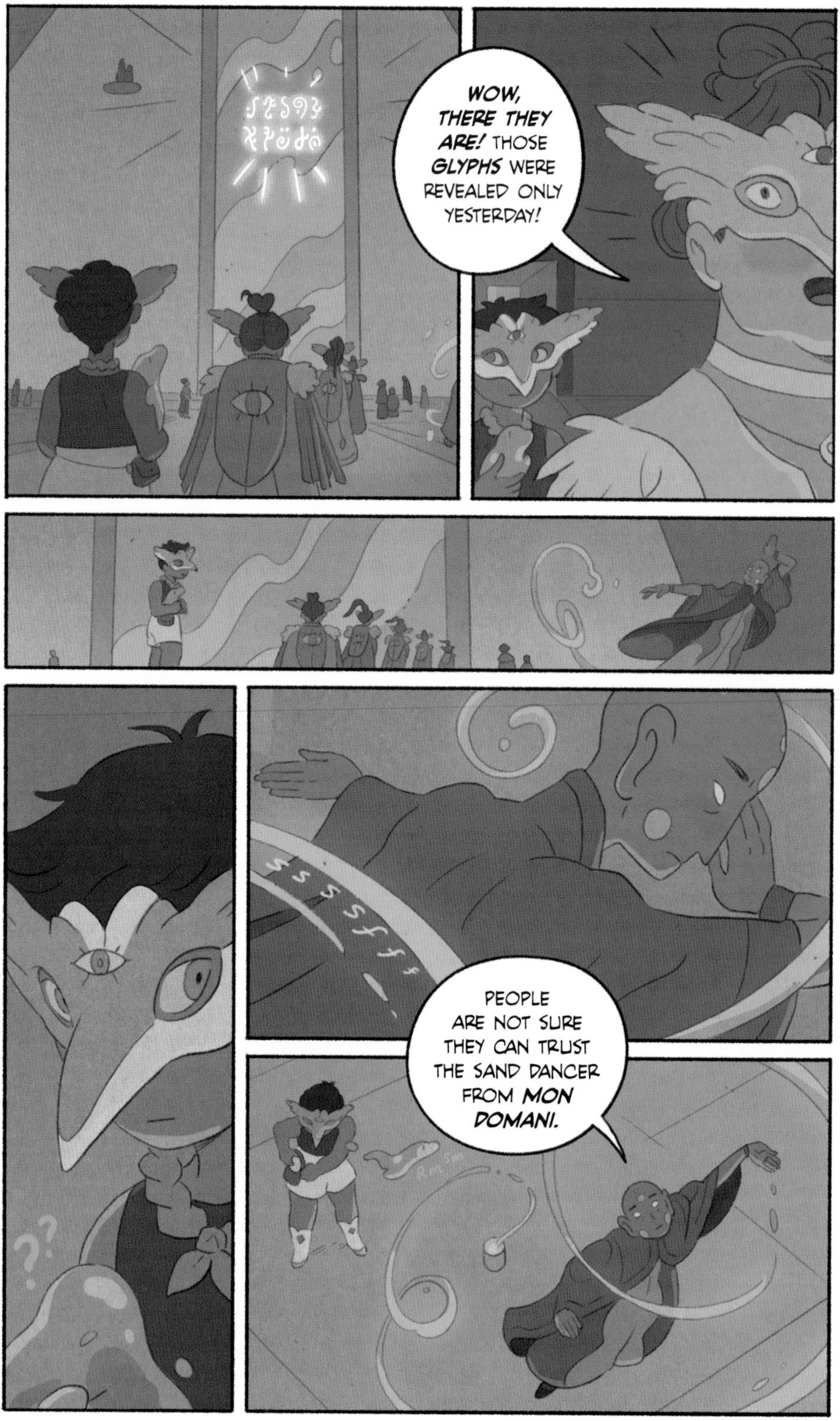
WOW, THERE THEY ARE! THOSE GLYPHS WERE REVEALED ONLY YESTERDAY!
PEOPLE ARE NOT SURE THEY CAN TRUST THE SAND DANCER FROM MON DOMANI.

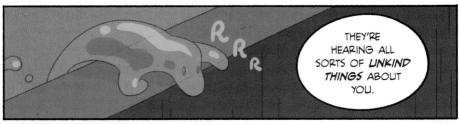

THEY'RE HEARING ALL SORTS OF *UNKIND THINGS* ABOUT YOU.

FROM THAT *PEET BOWL* ON THE *CITIZEN FEEDS.*

WHEREVER THERE IS IGNORANCE, THERE IS ALWAYS A *PEET BOWL* FEEDING ON IT. BUT WHERE THERE IS THE *LIVING FIRE,* THINGS *ARE SHOWN FOR WHAT THEY REALLY ARE.*

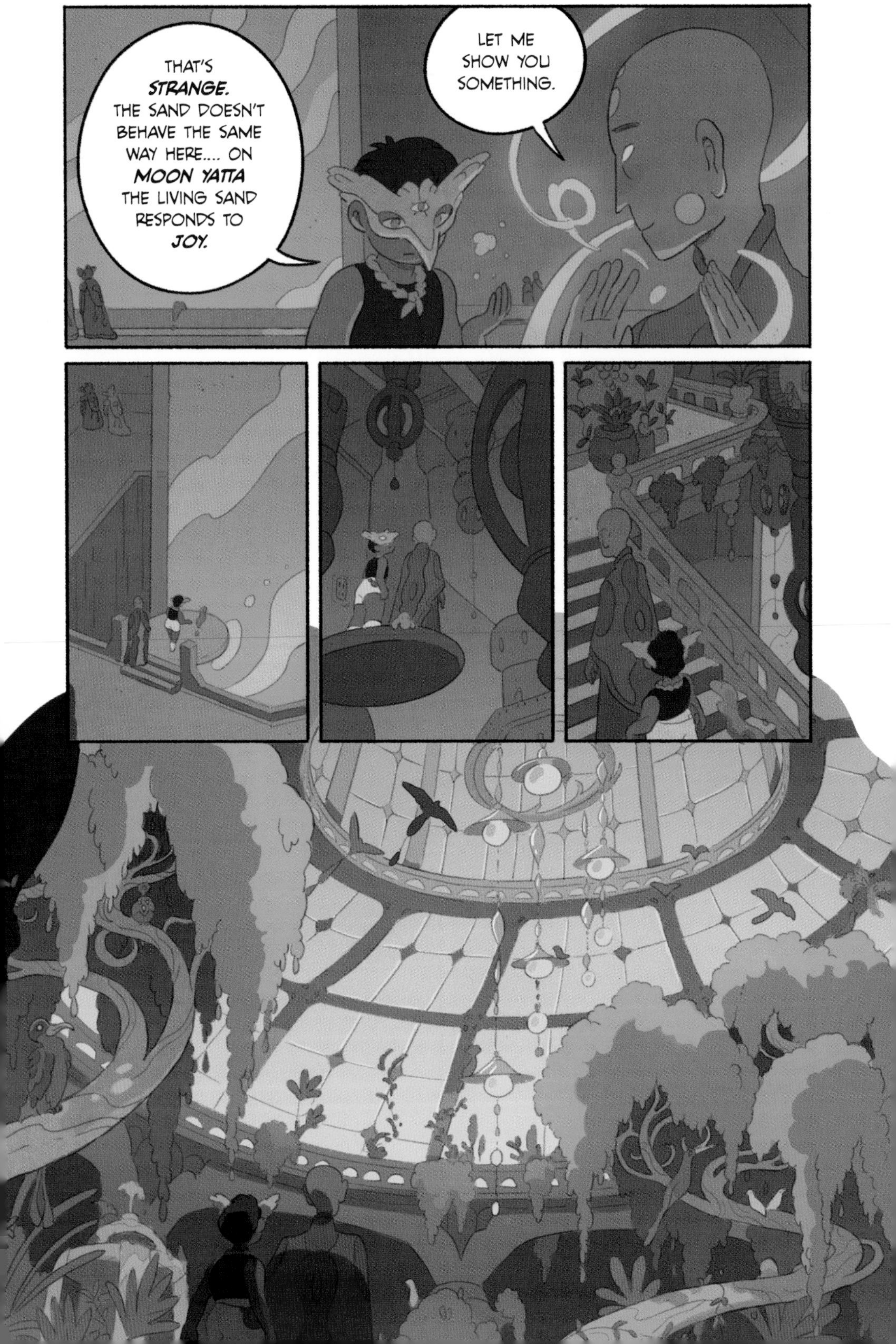
THAT'S STRANGE. THE SAND DOESN'T BEHAVE THE SAME WAY HERE.... ON MOON YATTA THE LIVING SAND RESPONDS TO JOY.
LET ME SHOW YOU SOMETHING.

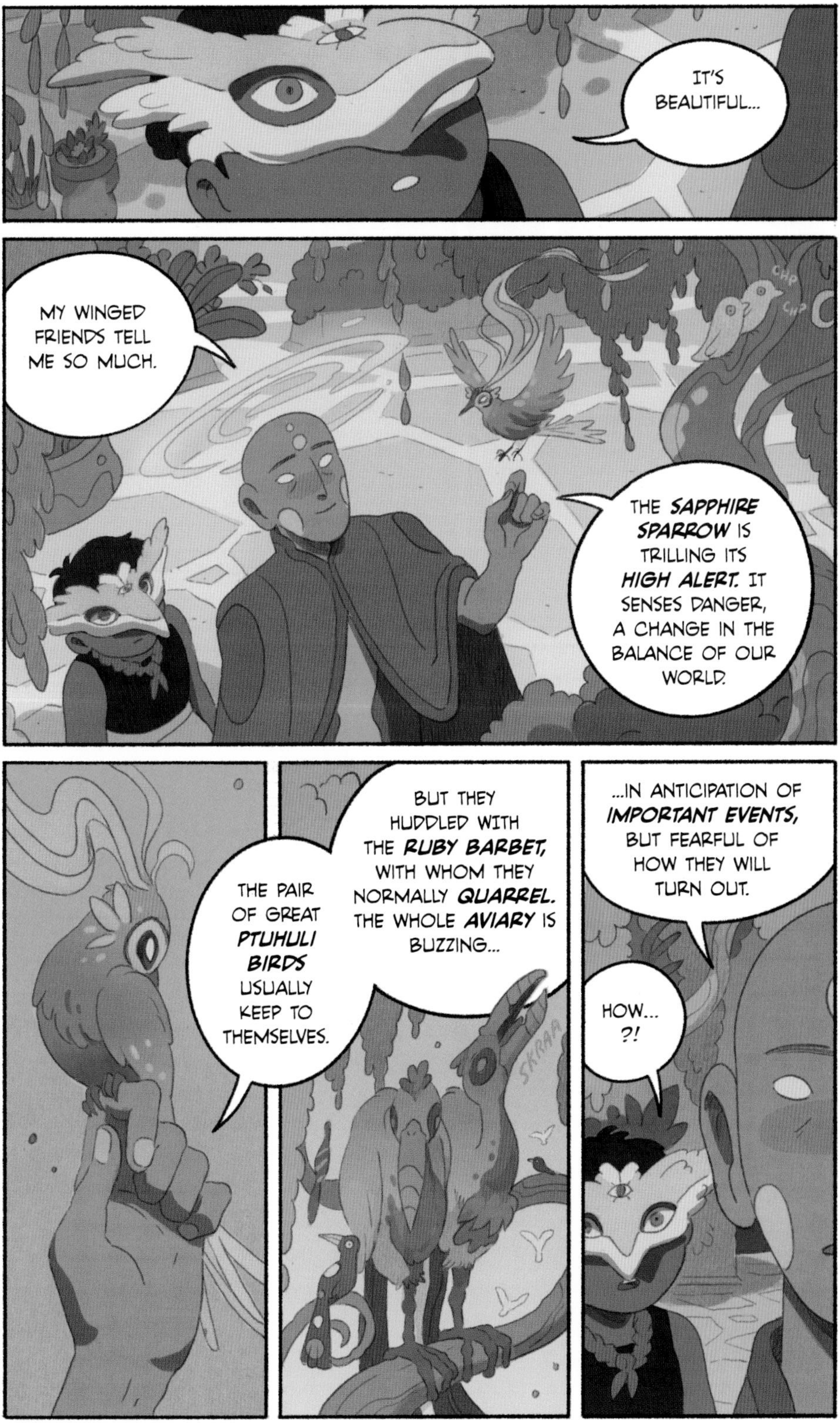
IT'S BEAUTIFUL...
MY WINGED FRIENDS TELL ME SO MUCH.
CHP CHP
THE SAPPHIRE SPARROW IS TRILLING ITS HIGH ALERT. IT SENSES DANGER, A CHANGE IN THE BALANCE OF OUR WORLD.
THE PAIR OF GREAT PTUHULI BIRDS USUALLY KEEP TO THEMSELVES.
BUT THEY HUDDLED WITH THE RUBY BARBET, WITH WHOM THEY NORMALLY QUARREL. THE WHOLE AVIARY IS BUZZING...
SKRAA
...IN ANTICIPATION OF IMPORTANT EVENTS, BUT FEARFUL OF HOW THEY WILL TURN OUT.
HOW... ?!

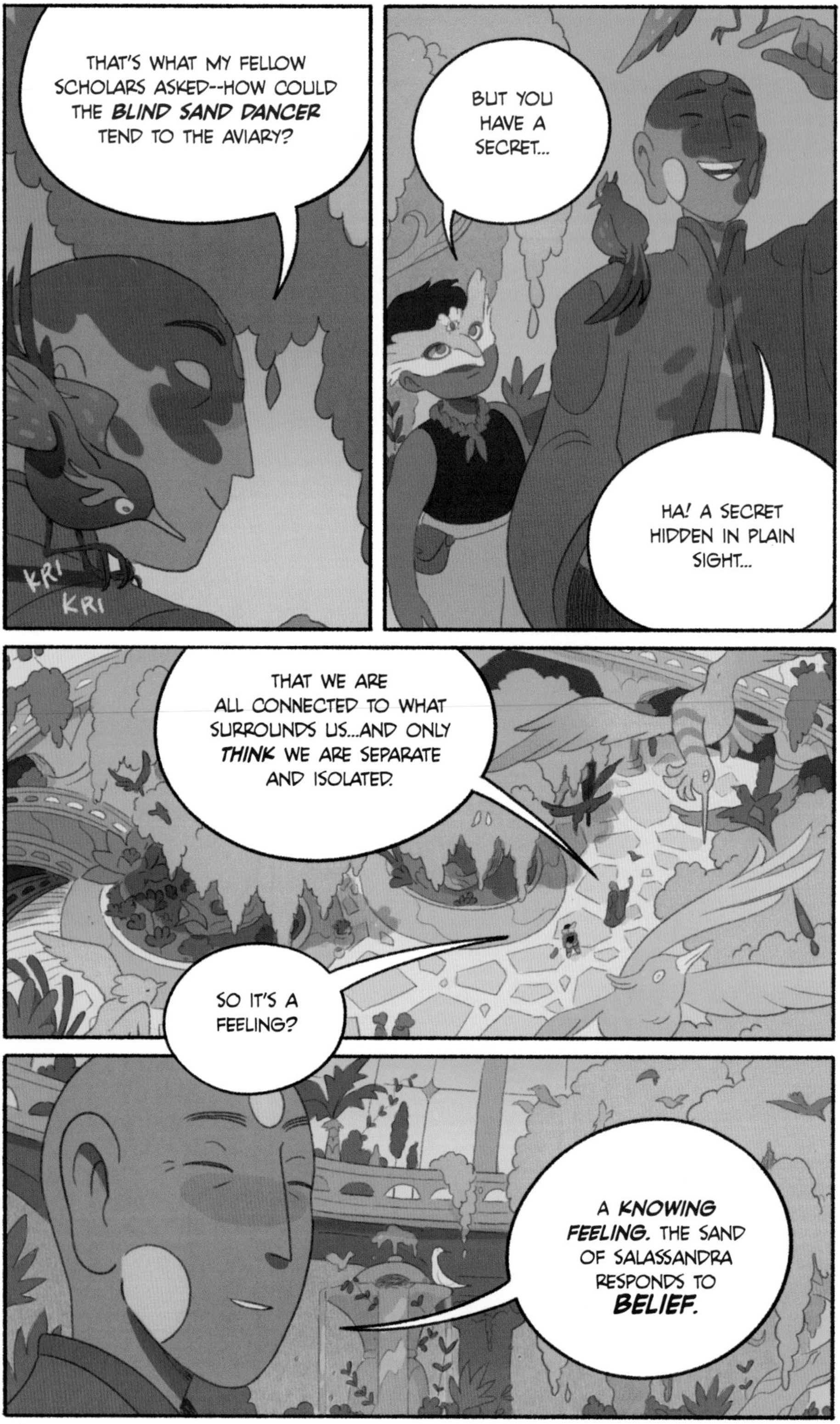
THAT'S WHAT MY FELLOW SCHOLARS ASKED--HOW COULD THE BLIND SAND DANCER TEND TO THE AVIARY?
KRI KRI
BUT YOU HAVE A SECRET...
HA! A SECRET HIDDEN IN PLAIN SIGHT...
THAT WE ARE ALL CONNECTED TO WHAT SURROUNDS US...AND ONLY THINK WE ARE SEPARATE AND ISOLATED.
SO IT'S A FEELING?
A KNOWING FEELING. THE SAND OF SALASSANDRA RESPONDS TO BELIEF.

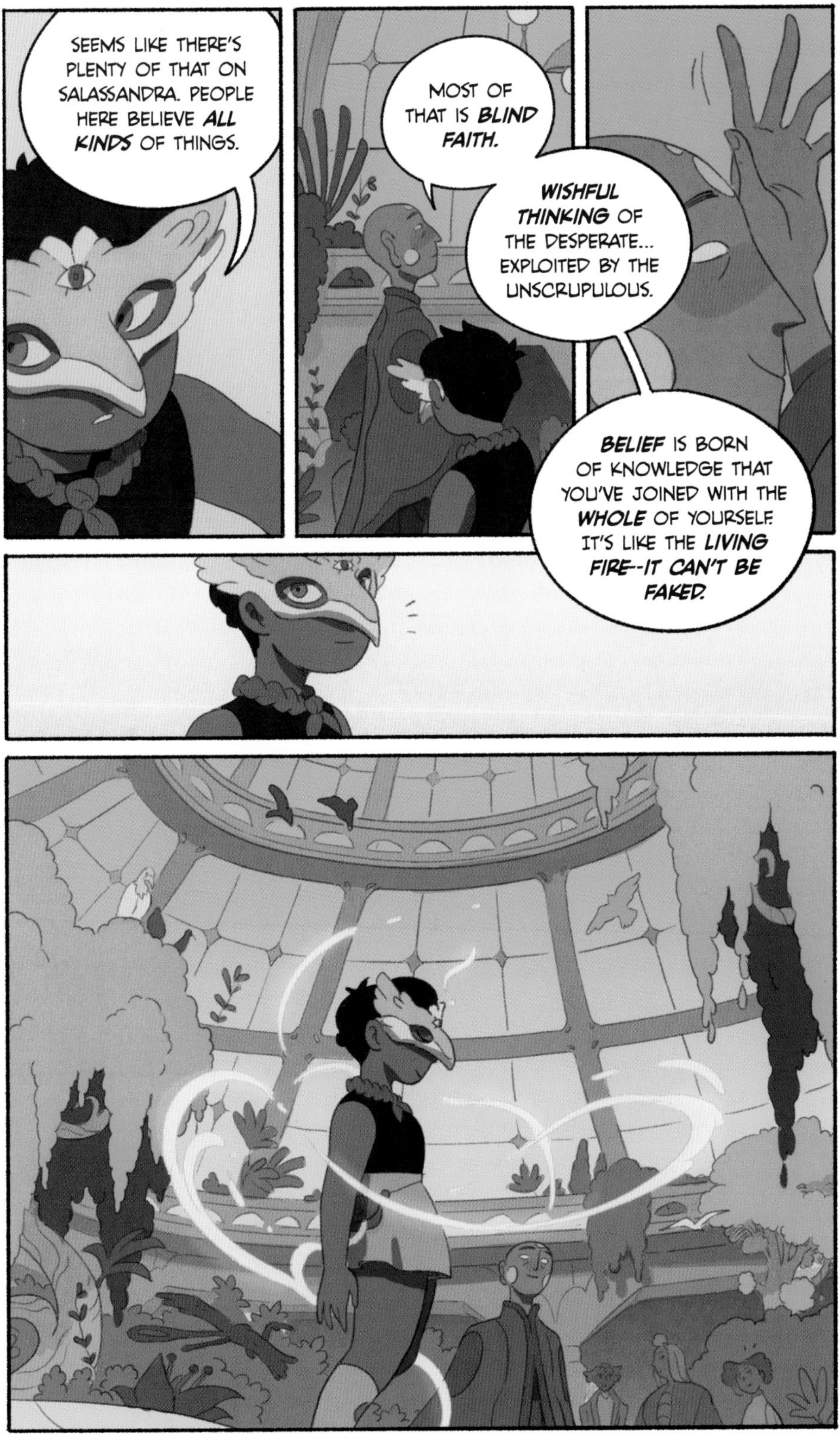
SEEMS LIKE THERE'S PLENTY OF THAT ON SALASSANDRA. PEOPLE HERE BELIEVE ALL KINDS OF THINGS.
MOST OF THAT IS BLIND FAITH.
WISHFUL THINKING OF THE DESPERATE... EXPLOITED BY THE UNSCRUPULOUS.
BELIEF IS BORN OF KNOWLEDGE THAT YOU'VE JOINED WITH THE WHOLE OF YOURSELF. IT'S LIKE THE LIVING FIRE--IT CAN'T BE FAKED.

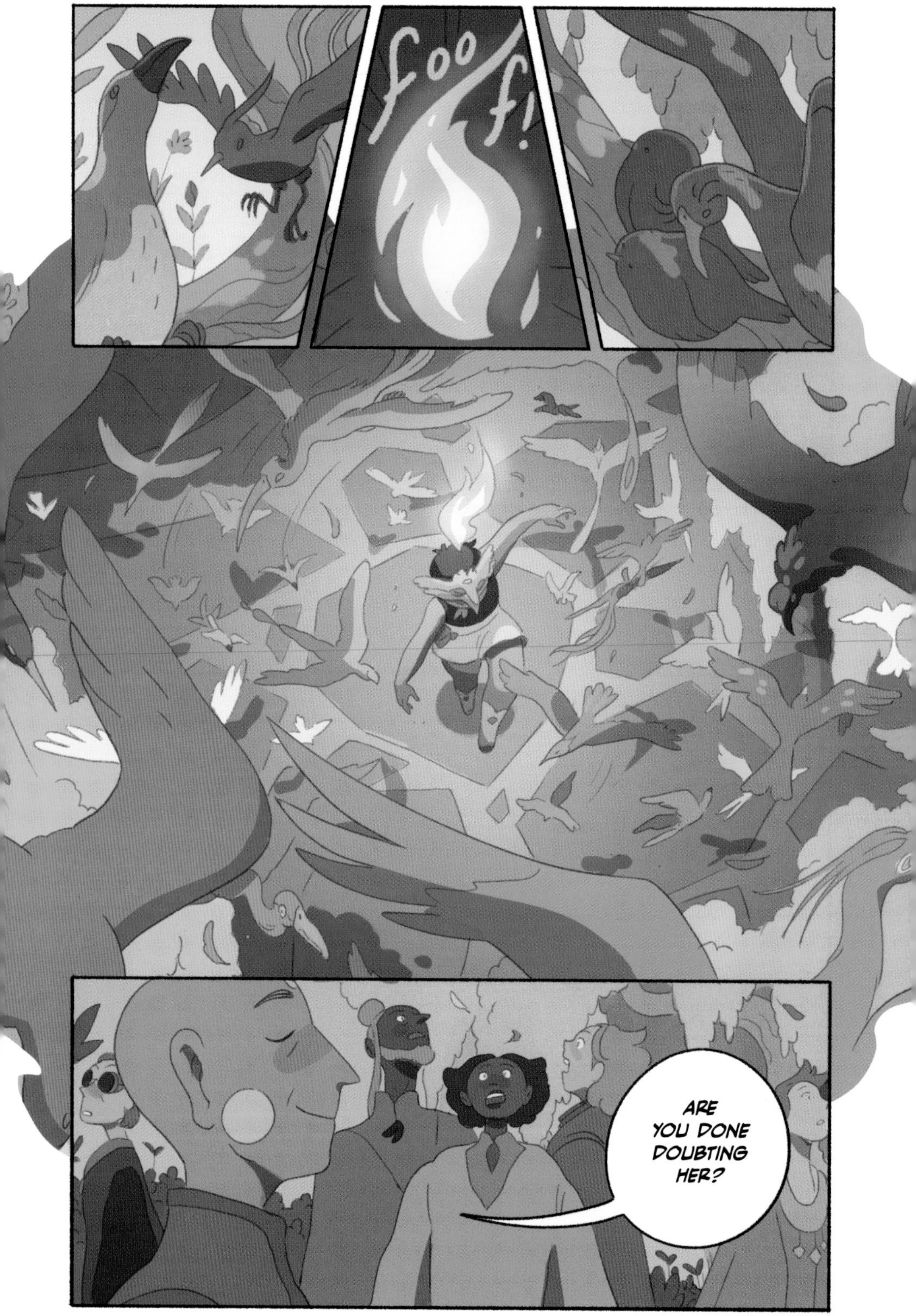
FOOF!
ARE YOU DONE DOUBTING HER?

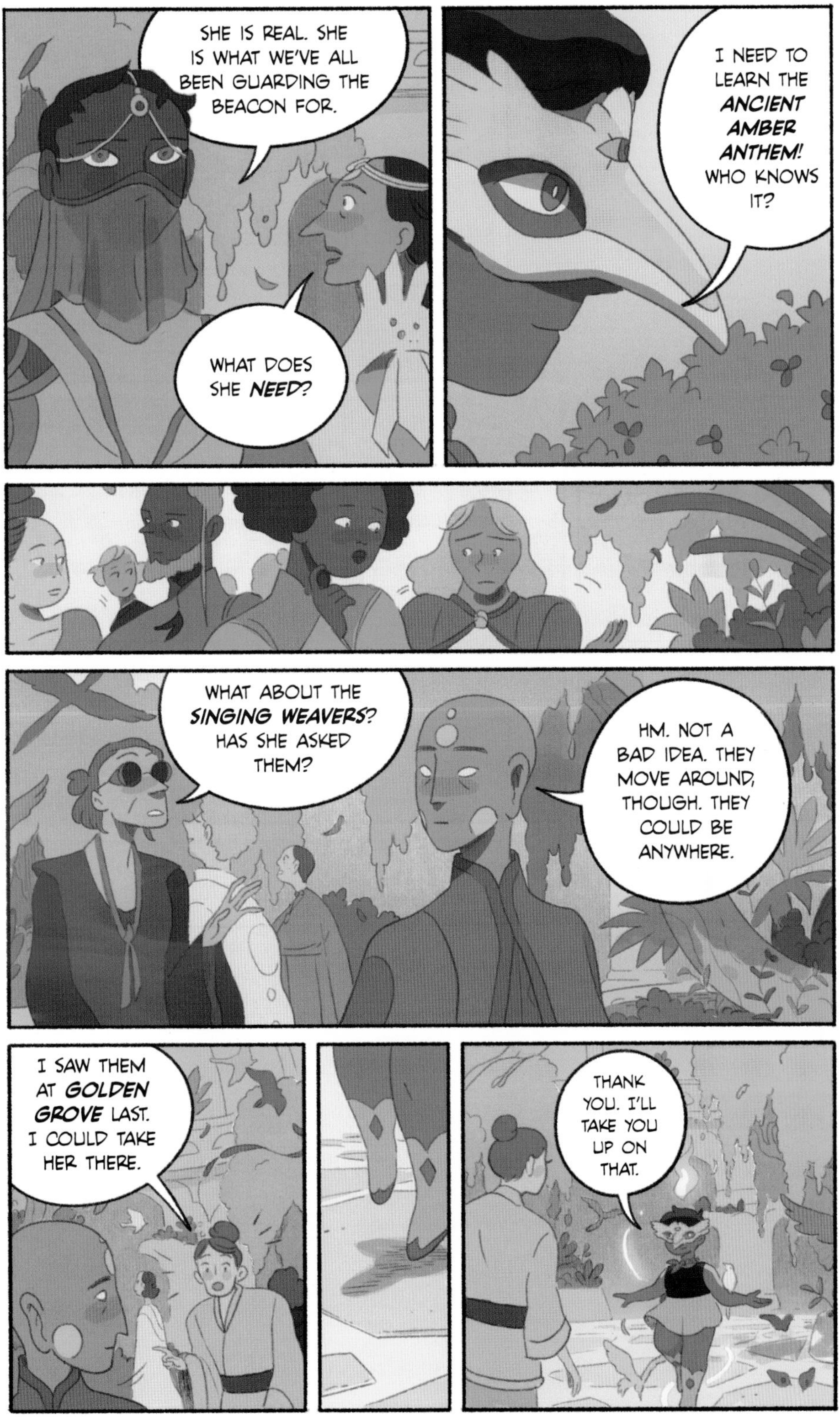
SHE IS REAL. SHE IS WHAT WE'VE ALL BEEN GUARDING THE BEACON FOR.
WHAT DOES SHE *NEED*?
I NEED TO LEARN THE ***ANCIENT AMBER ANTHEM!*** WHO KNOWS IT?
WHAT ABOUT THE ***SINGING WEAVERS***? HAS SHE ASKED THEM?
HM. NOT A BAD IDEA. THEY MOVE AROUND, THOUGH. THEY COULD BE ANYWHERE.
I SAW THEM AT ***GOLDEN GROVE*** LAST. I COULD TAKE HER THERE.
THANK YOU. I'LL TAKE YOU UP ON THAT.

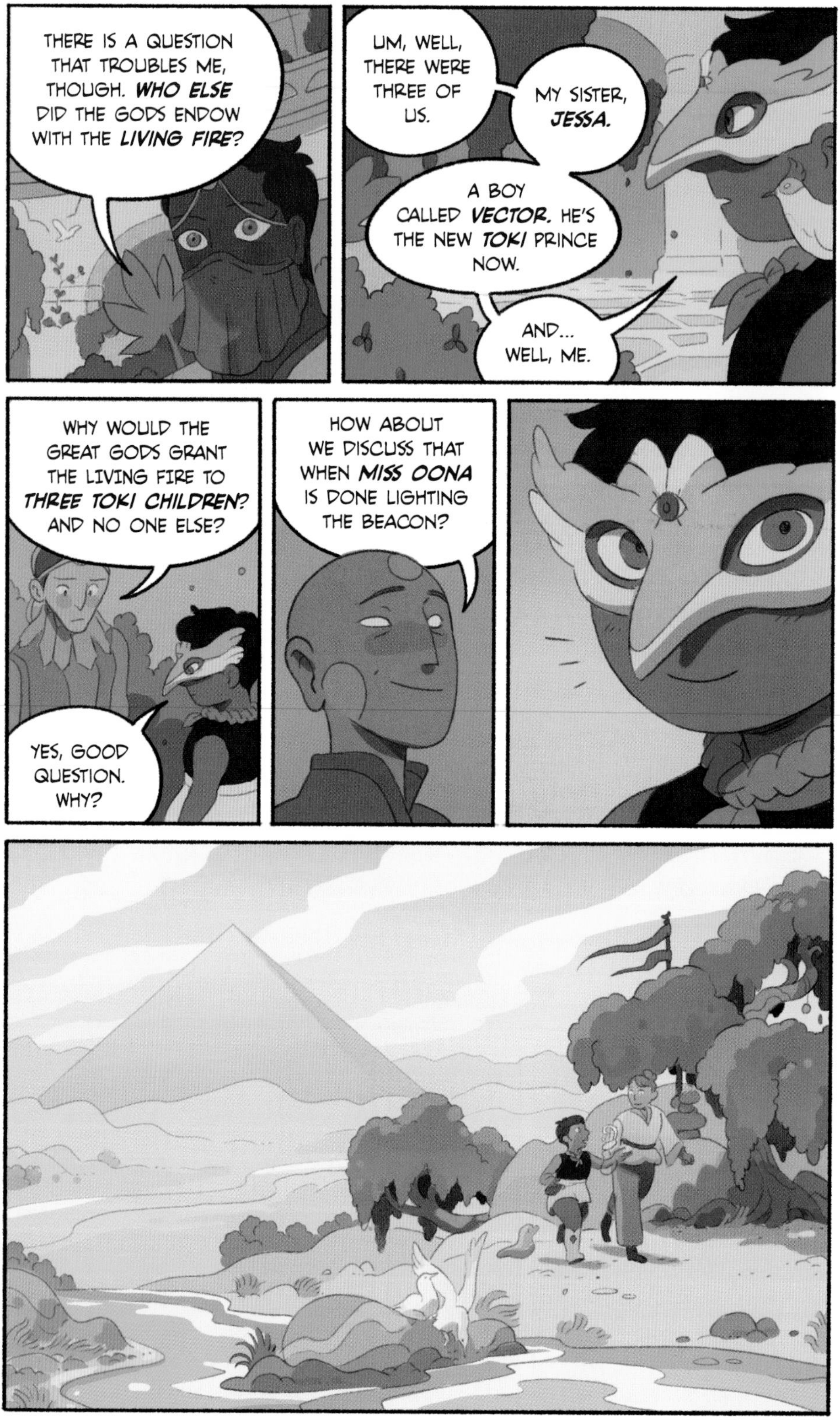
THERE IS A QUESTION THAT TROUBLES ME, THOUGH. ***WHO ELSE*** DID THE GODS ENDOW WITH THE ***LIVING FIRE?***
UM, WELL, THERE WERE THREE OF US.
MY SISTER, ***JESSA.***
A BOY CALLED ***VECTOR.*** HE'S THE NEW ***TOKI*** PRINCE NOW.
AND... WELL, ME.
WHY WOULD THE GREAT GODS GRANT THE LIVING FIRE TO ***THREE TOKI CHILDREN?*** AND NO ONE ELSE?
YES, GOOD QUESTION. WHY?
HOW ABOUT WE DISCUSS THAT WHEN ***MISS OONA*** IS DONE LIGHTING THE BEACON?

Chapter 6
THE SINGING WEAVERS

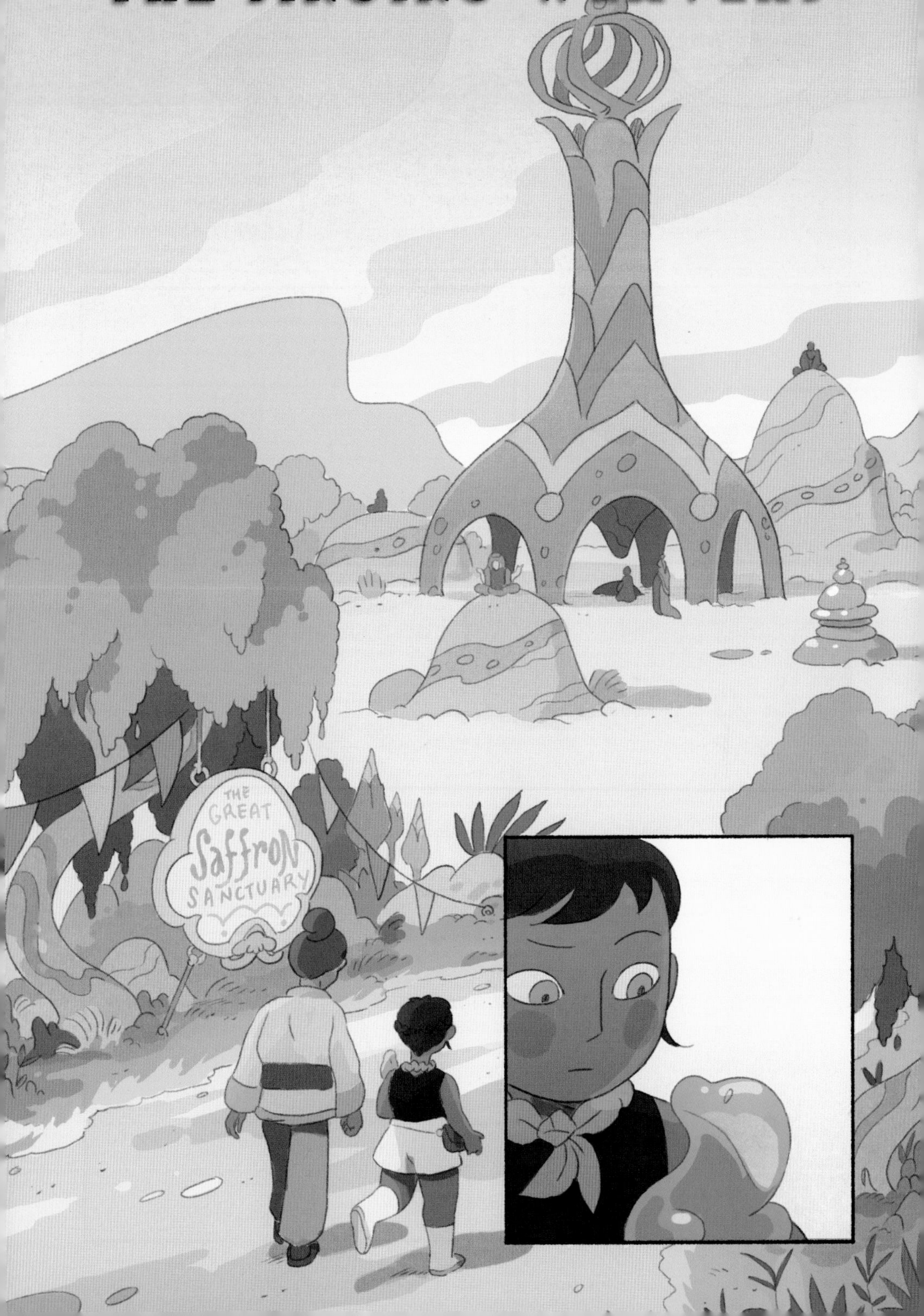
THE GREAT Saffron SANCTUARY

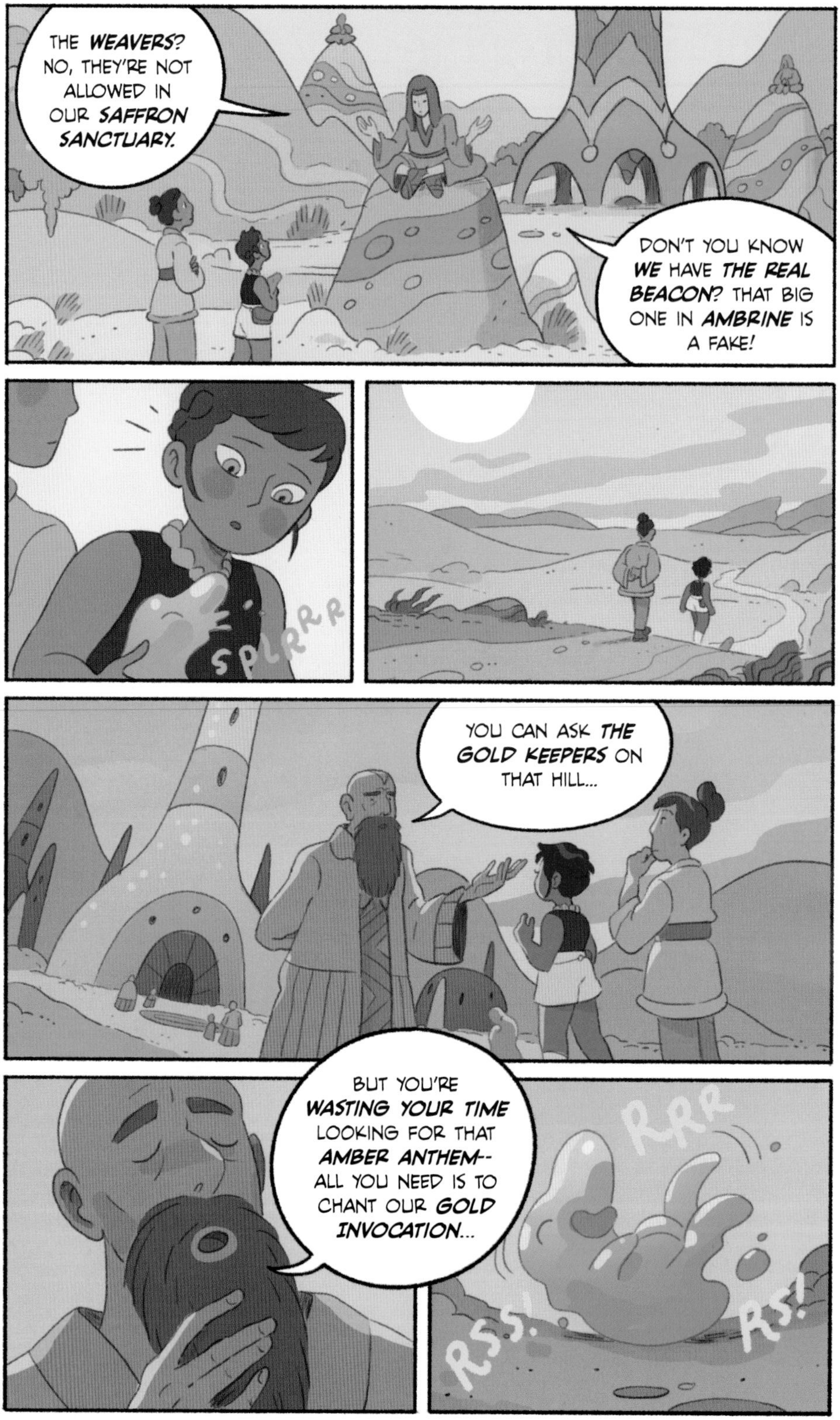
THE WEAVERS? NO, THEY'RE NOT ALLOWED IN OUR SAFFRON SANCTUARY.
DON'T YOU KNOW WE HAVE THE REAL BEACON? THAT BIG ONE IN AMBRINE IS A FAKE!
SPLRRR
YOU CAN ASK THE GOLD KEEPERS ON THAT HILL...
BUT YOU'RE WASTING YOUR TIME LOOKING FOR THAT AMBER ANTHEM-- ALL YOU NEED IS TO CHANT OUR GOLD INVOCATION...
RRR
RSS!
RS!

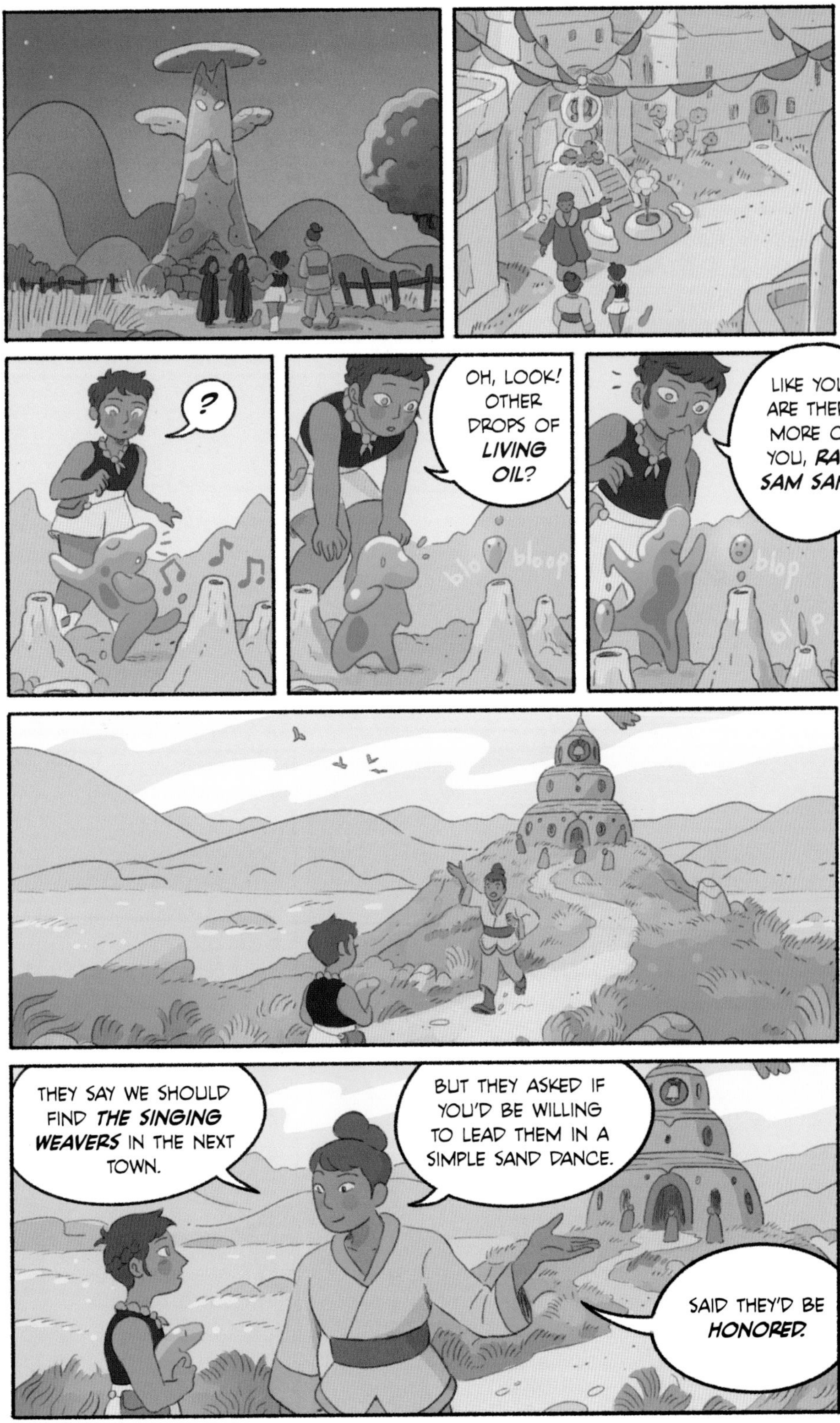
?
OH, LOOK! OTHER DROPS OF *LIVING OIL?*
bloop
LIKE YOU? ARE THERE MORE OF YOU, *RAM SAM SAM?*
blop
THEY SAY WE SHOULD FIND *THE SINGING WEAVERS* IN THE NEXT TOWN.
BUT THEY ASKED IF YOU'D BE WILLING TO LEAD THEM IN A SIMPLE SAND DANCE.
SAID THEY'D BE *HONORED.*

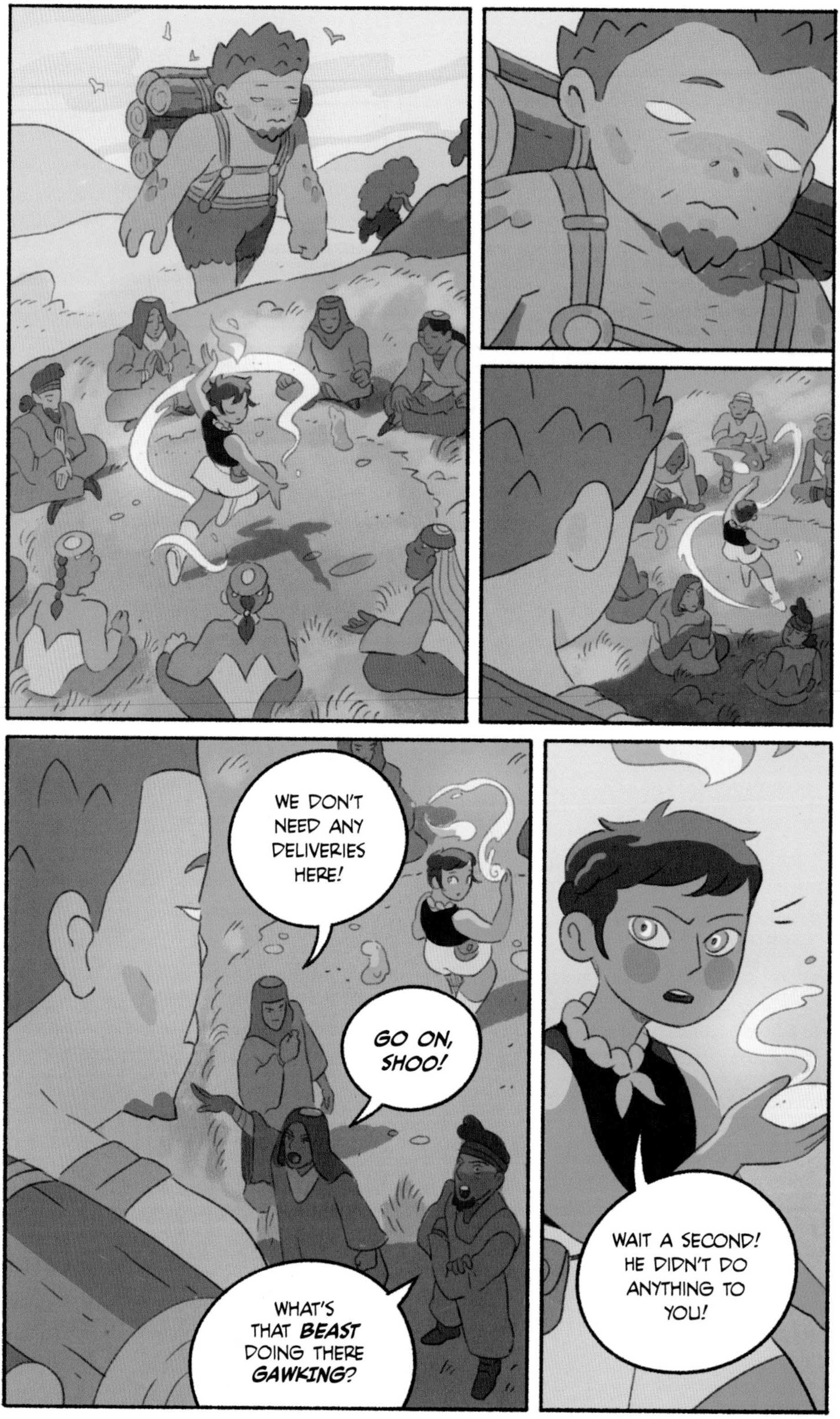
WE DON'T NEED ANY DELIVERIES HERE!
GO ON, SHOO!
WHAT'S THAT BEAST DOING THERE GAWKING?
WAIT A SECOND! HE DIDN'T DO ANYTHING TO YOU!

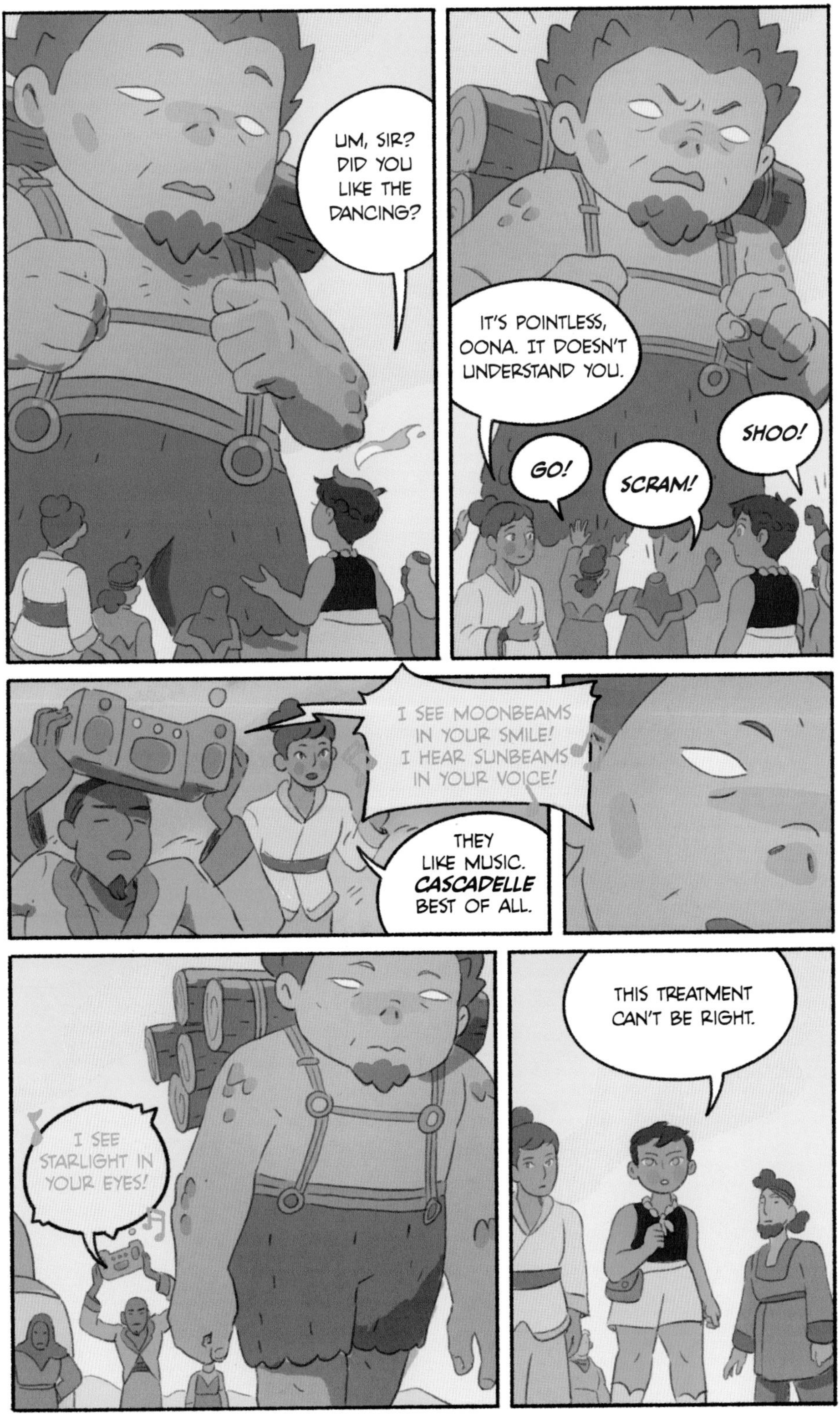
UM, SIR? DID YOU LIKE THE DANCING?
IT'S POINTLESS, OONA. IT DOESN'T UNDERSTAND YOU.
GO!
SCRAM!
SHOO!
I SEE MOONBEAMS IN YOUR SMILE! I HEAR SUNBEAMS IN YOUR VOICE!
THEY LIKE MUSIC. CASCADELLE BEST OF ALL.
I SEE STARLIGHT IN YOUR EYES!
THIS TREATMENT CAN'T BE RIGHT.

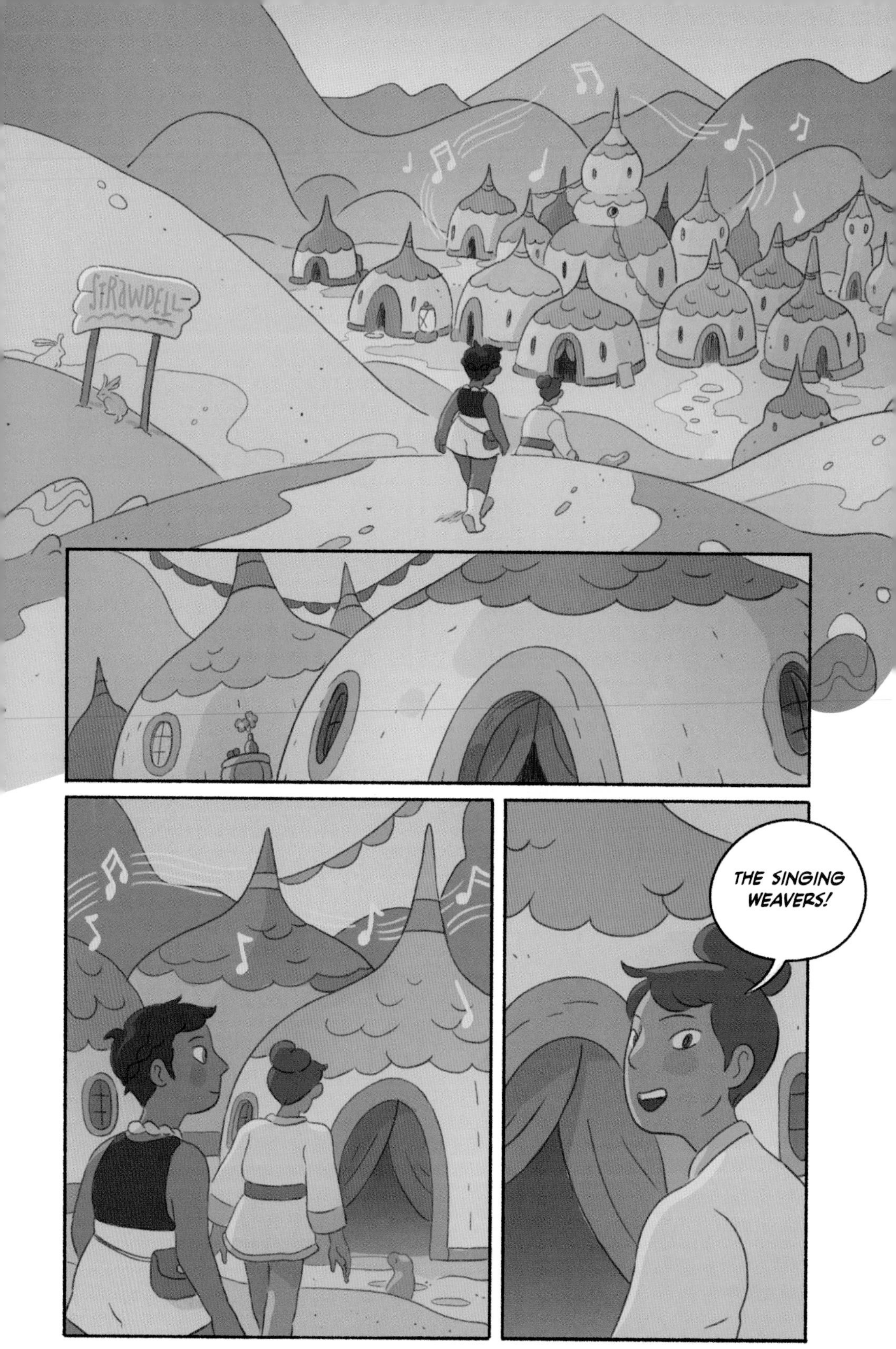
STRAWDELL
THE SINGING WEAVERS!

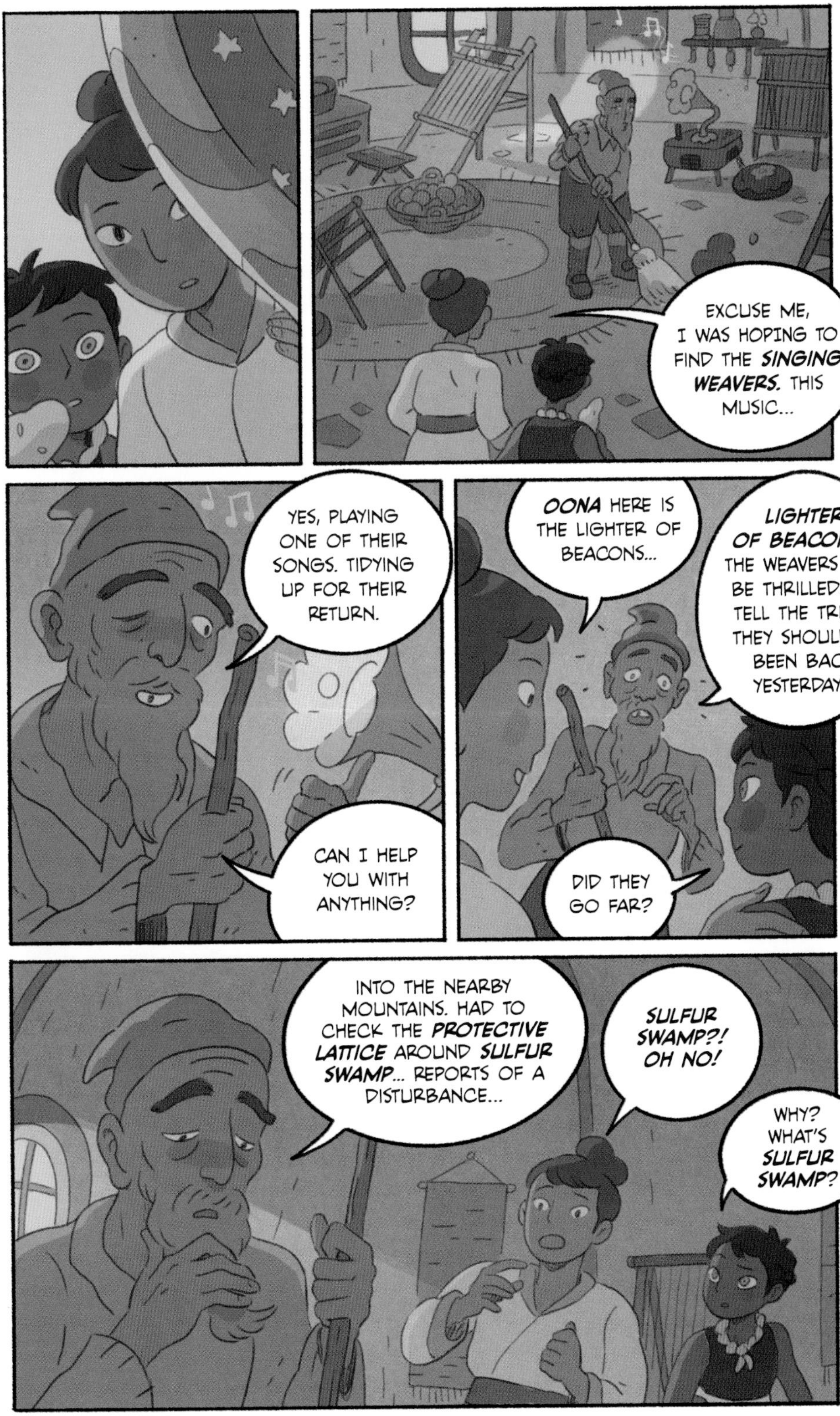
EXCUSE ME, I WAS HOPING TO FIND THE ***SINGING WEAVERS.*** THIS MUSIC...
YES, PLAYING ONE OF THEIR SONGS. TIDYING UP FOR THEIR RETURN.
CAN I HELP YOU WITH ANYTHING?
OONA HERE IS THE LIGHTER OF BEACONS...
LIGHTER OF BEACONS!! THE WEAVERS WILL BE THRILLED! TO TELL THE TRUTH, THEY SHOULD'VE BEEN BACK YESTERDAY...
DID THEY GO FAR?
INTO THE NEARBY MOUNTAINS. HAD TO CHECK THE ***PROTECTIVE LATTICE*** AROUND ***SULFUR SWAMP***... REPORTS OF A DISTURBANCE...
SULFUR SWAMP?! OH NO!
WHY? WHAT'S ***SULFUR SWAMP?***

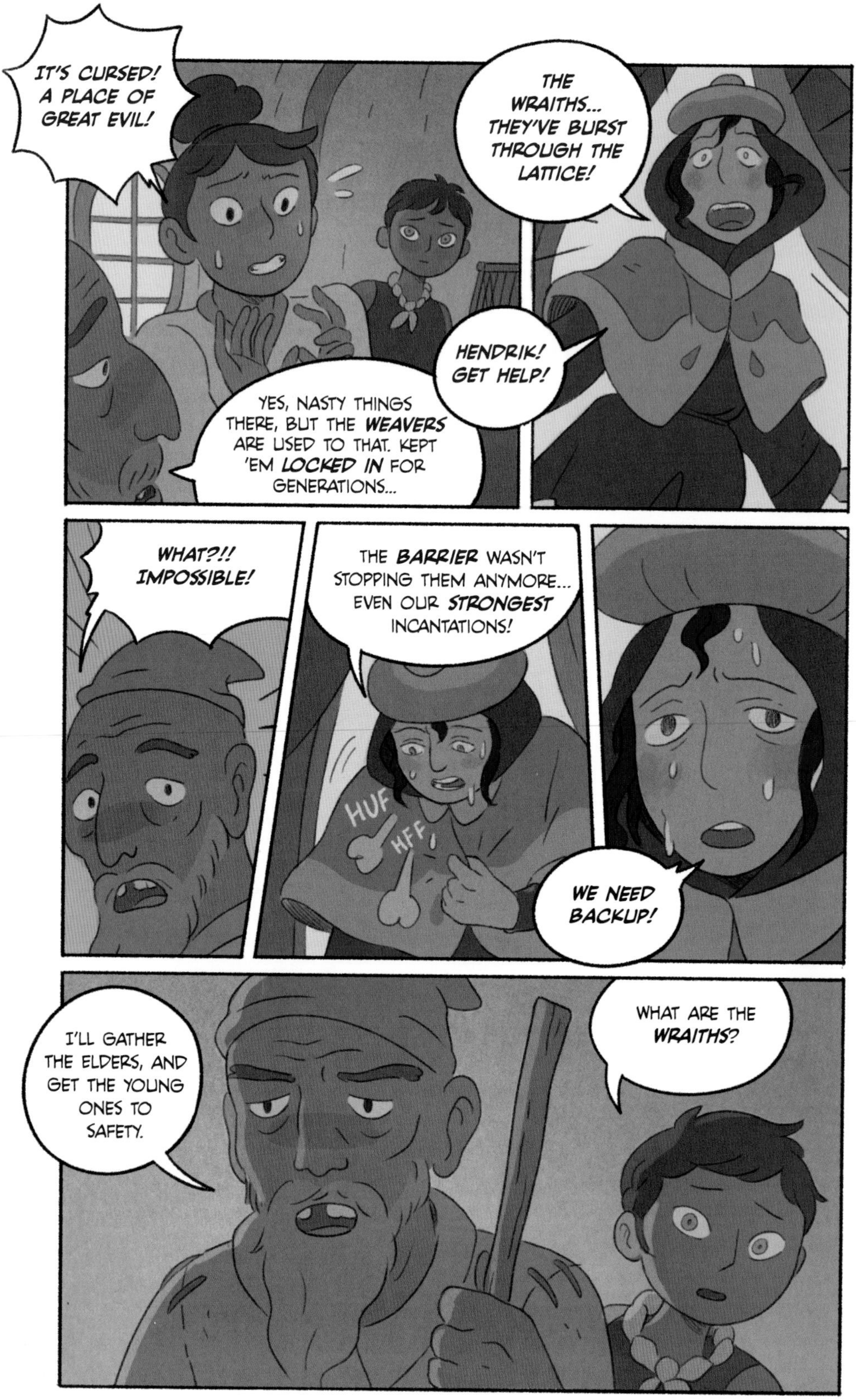
IT'S CURSED! A PLACE OF GREAT EVIL!
YES, NASTY THINGS THERE, BUT THE WEAVERS ARE USED TO THAT. KEPT 'EM LOCKED IN FOR GENERATIONS...
THE WRAITHS... THEY'VE BURST THROUGH THE LATTICE!
HENDRIK! GET HELP!
WHAT?!! IMPOSSIBLE!
THE BARRIER WASN'T STOPPING THEM ANYMORE... EVEN OUR STRONGEST INCANTATIONS!
HUF
HFF
WE NEED BACKUP!
I'LL GATHER THE ELDERS, AND GET THE YOUNG ONES TO SAFETY.
WHAT ARE THE WRAITHS?

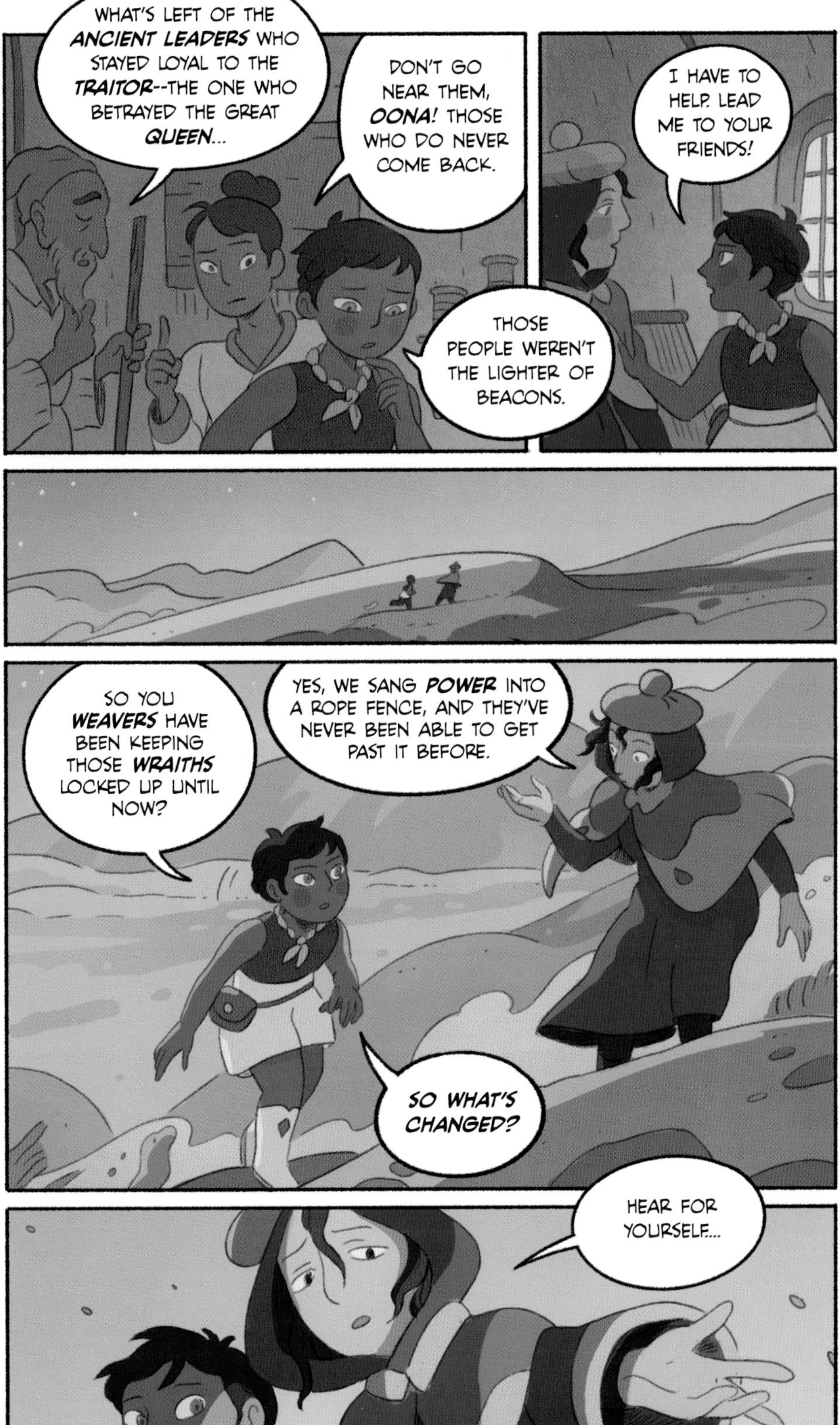
WHAT'S LEFT OF THE ANCIENT LEADERS WHO STAYED LOYAL TO THE TRAITOR--THE ONE WHO BETRAYED THE GREAT QUEEN...
DON'T GO NEAR THEM, OONA! THOSE WHO DO NEVER COME BACK.
THOSE PEOPLE WEREN'T THE LIGHTER OF BEACONS.
I HAVE TO HELP. LEAD ME TO YOUR FRIENDS!
SO YOU WEAVERS HAVE BEEN KEEPING THOSE WRAITHS LOCKED UP UNTIL NOW?
YES, WE SANG POWER INTO A ROPE FENCE, AND THEY'VE NEVER BEEN ABLE TO GET PAST IT BEFORE.
SO WHAT'S CHANGED?
HEAR FOR YOURSELF...

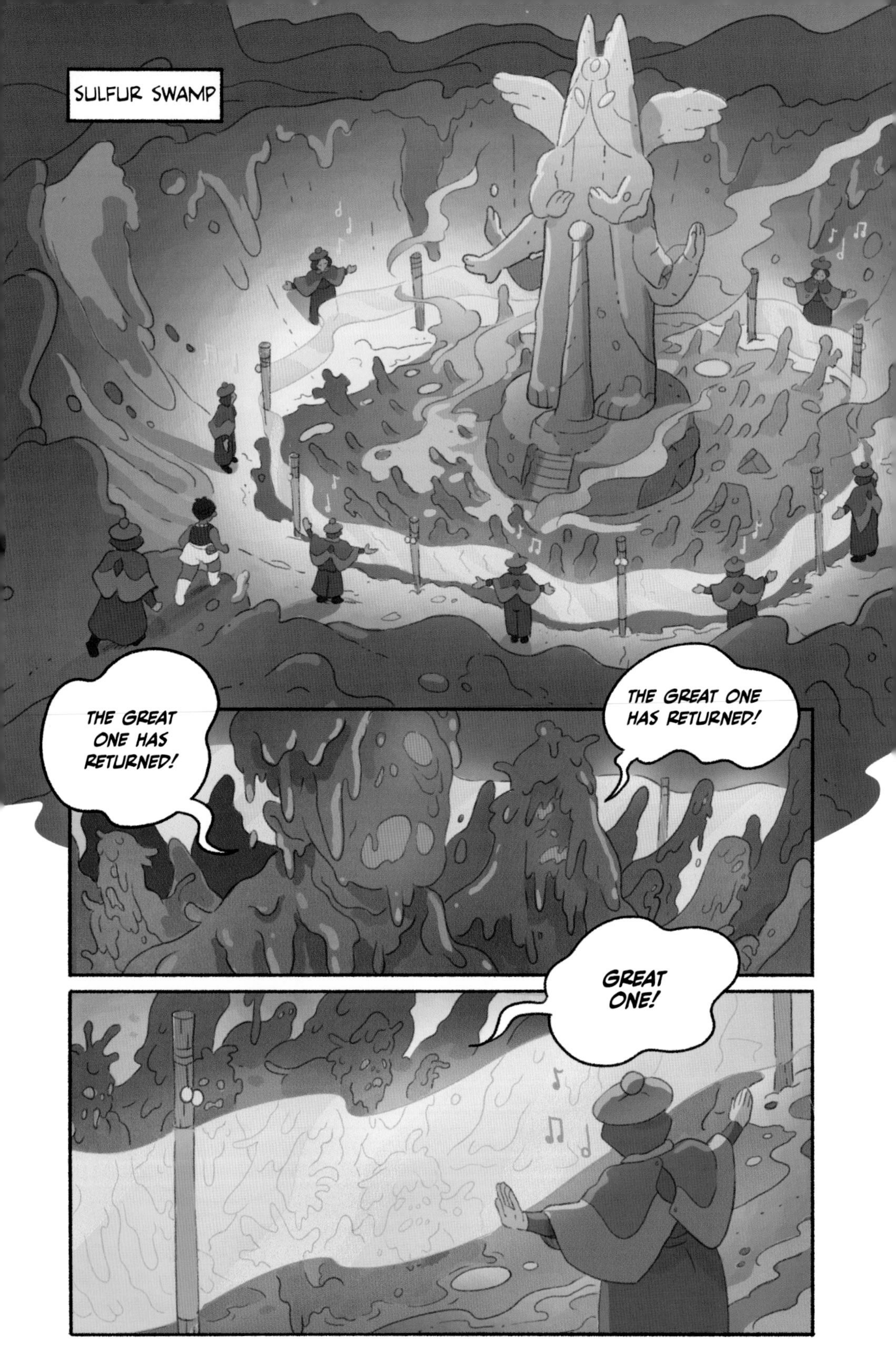
SULFUR SWAMP
THE GREAT ONE HAS RETURNED!
THE GREAT ONE HAS RETURNED!
GREAT ONE!

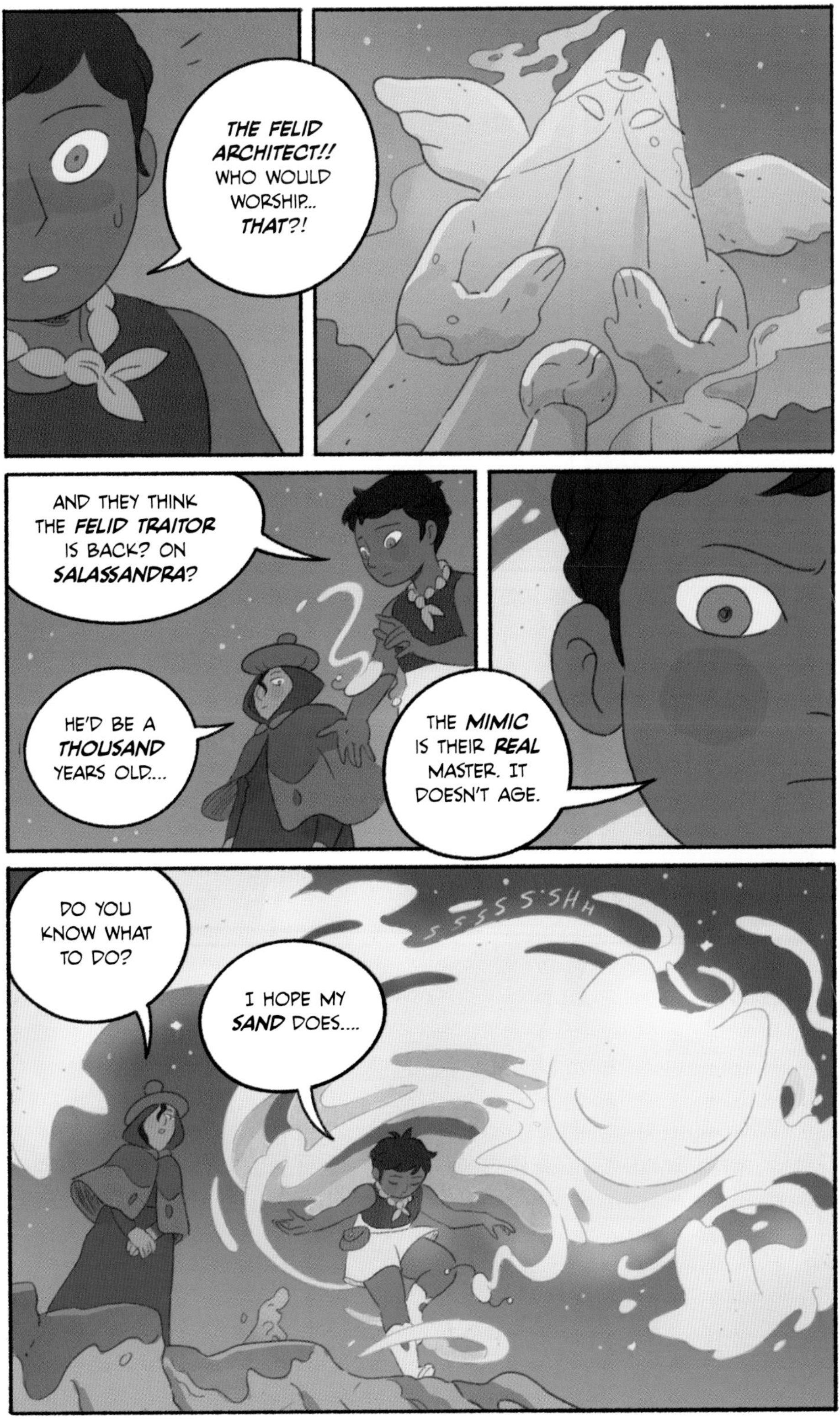
THE FELID ARCHITECT!! WHO WOULD WORSHIP... THAT?!
AND THEY THINK THE FELID TRAITOR IS BACK? ON SALASSANDRA?
HE'D BE A THOUSAND YEARS OLD....
THE MIMIC IS THEIR REAL MASTER. IT DOESN'T AGE.
DO YOU KNOW WHAT TO DO?
SSSSSSSHH
I HOPE MY SAND DOES....

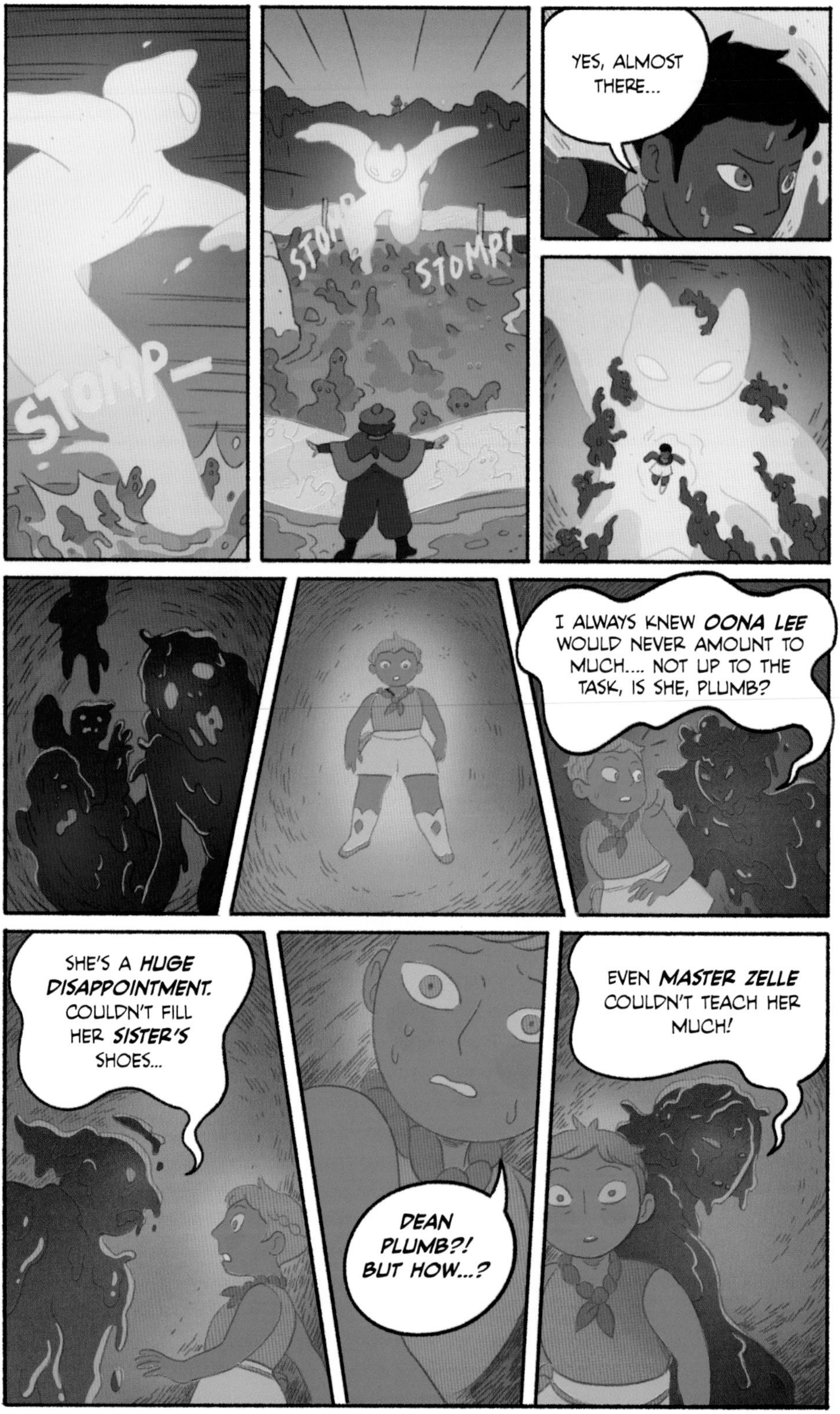
STOMP—
STOMP
STOMP!
YES, ALMOST THERE...
I ALWAYS KNEW OONA LEE WOULD NEVER AMOUNT TO MUCH.... NOT UP TO THE TASK, IS SHE, PLUMB?
SHE'S A HUGE DISAPPOINTMENT. COULDN'T FILL HER SISTER'S SHOES...
DEAN PLUMB?! BUT HOW...?
EVEN MASTER ZELLE COULDN'T TEACH HER MUCH!

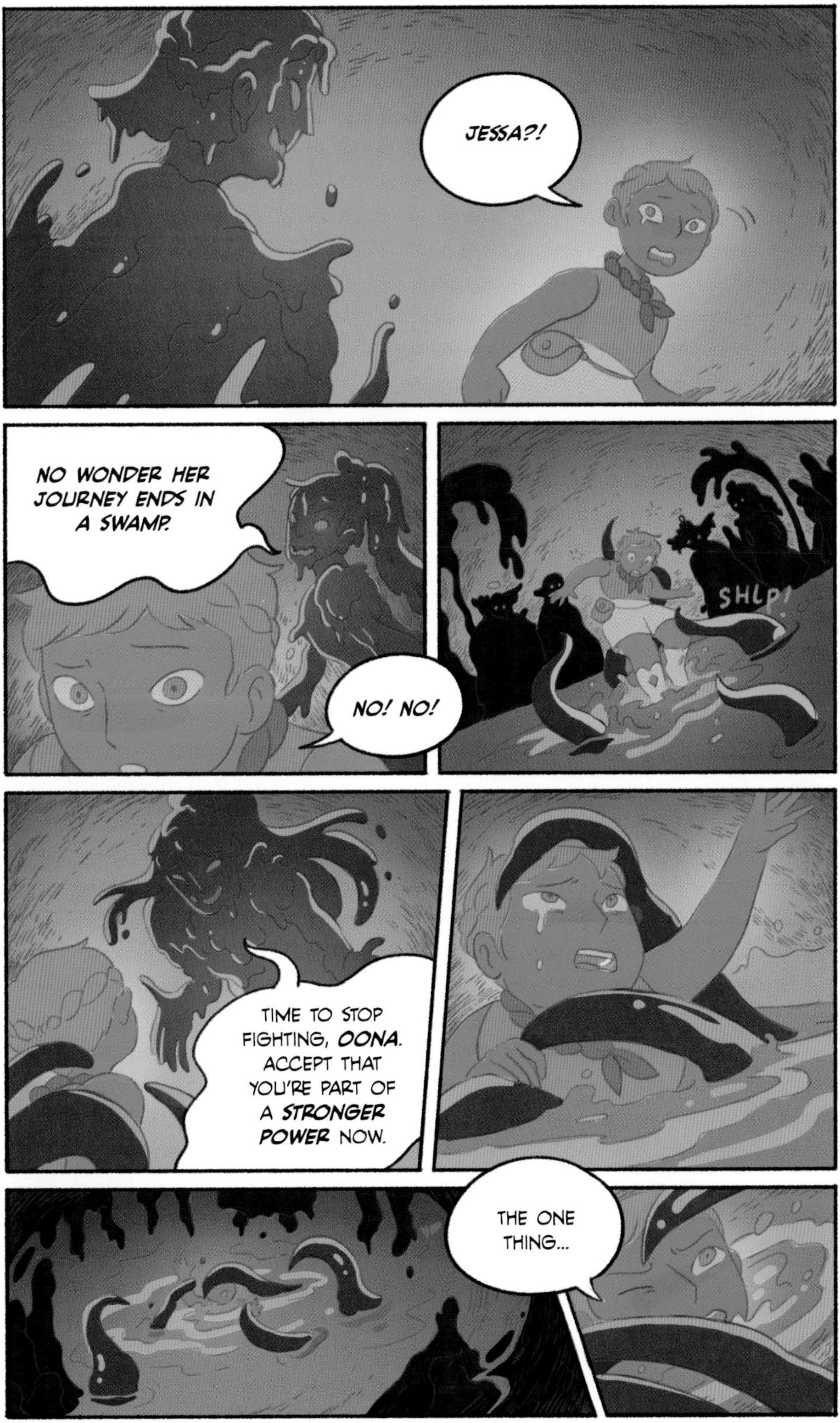
JESSA?!
NO WONDER HER JOURNEY ENDS IN A SWAMP?
NO! NO!
SHLP!
TIME TO STOP FIGHTING, *OONA*. ACCEPT THAT YOU'RE PART OF A *STRONGER POWER* NOW.
THE ONE THING...

I'M SORRY, I JUST COULDN'T BEAT THOSE WRAITHS. TOO MANY...TOO POWERFUL...

THMP—

YOU BRING THE GREATEST OF GIFTS...

...LIGHTER OF BEACONS.

THE LIVING FIRE!

THE LIVING FIRE CAN BE... TRANSFERRED?!

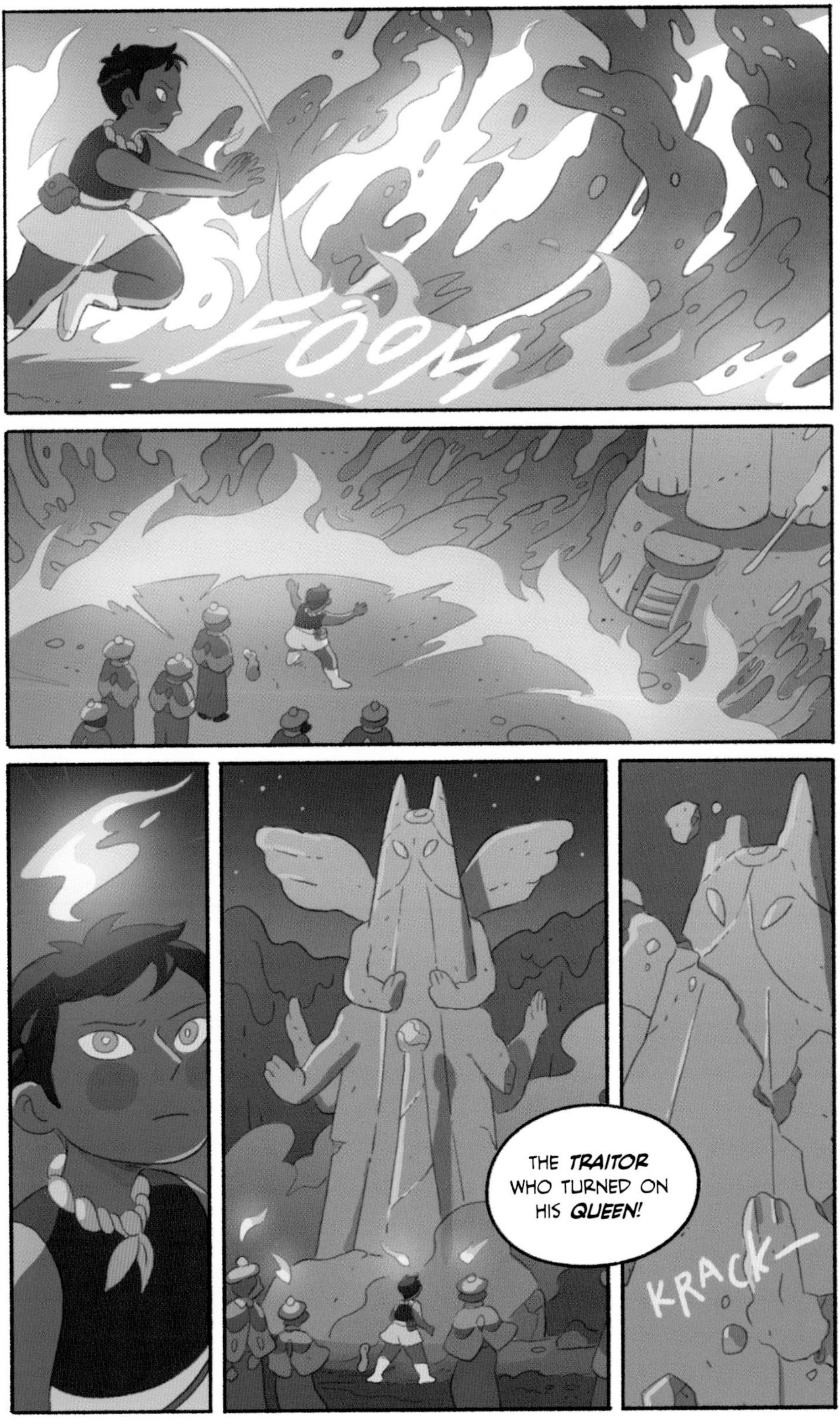
FOOM
THE TRAITOR WHO TURNED ON HIS QUEEN!
KRACK—

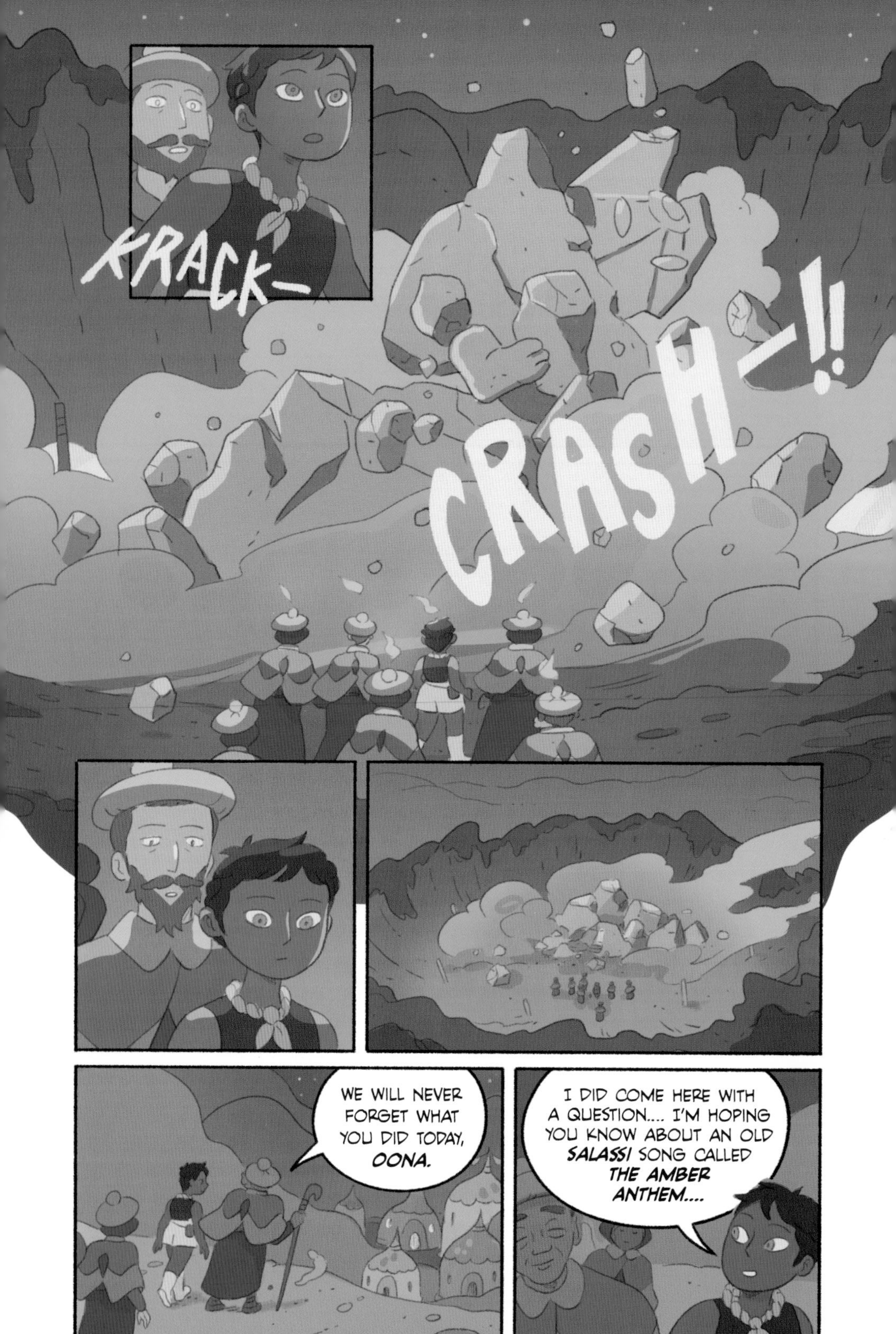
KRACK—
CRASH—!!
WE WILL NEVER FORGET WHAT YOU DID TODAY, OONA.
I DID COME HERE WITH A QUESTION.... I'M HOPING YOU KNOW ABOUT AN OLD SALASSI SONG CALLED THE AMBER ANTHEM....

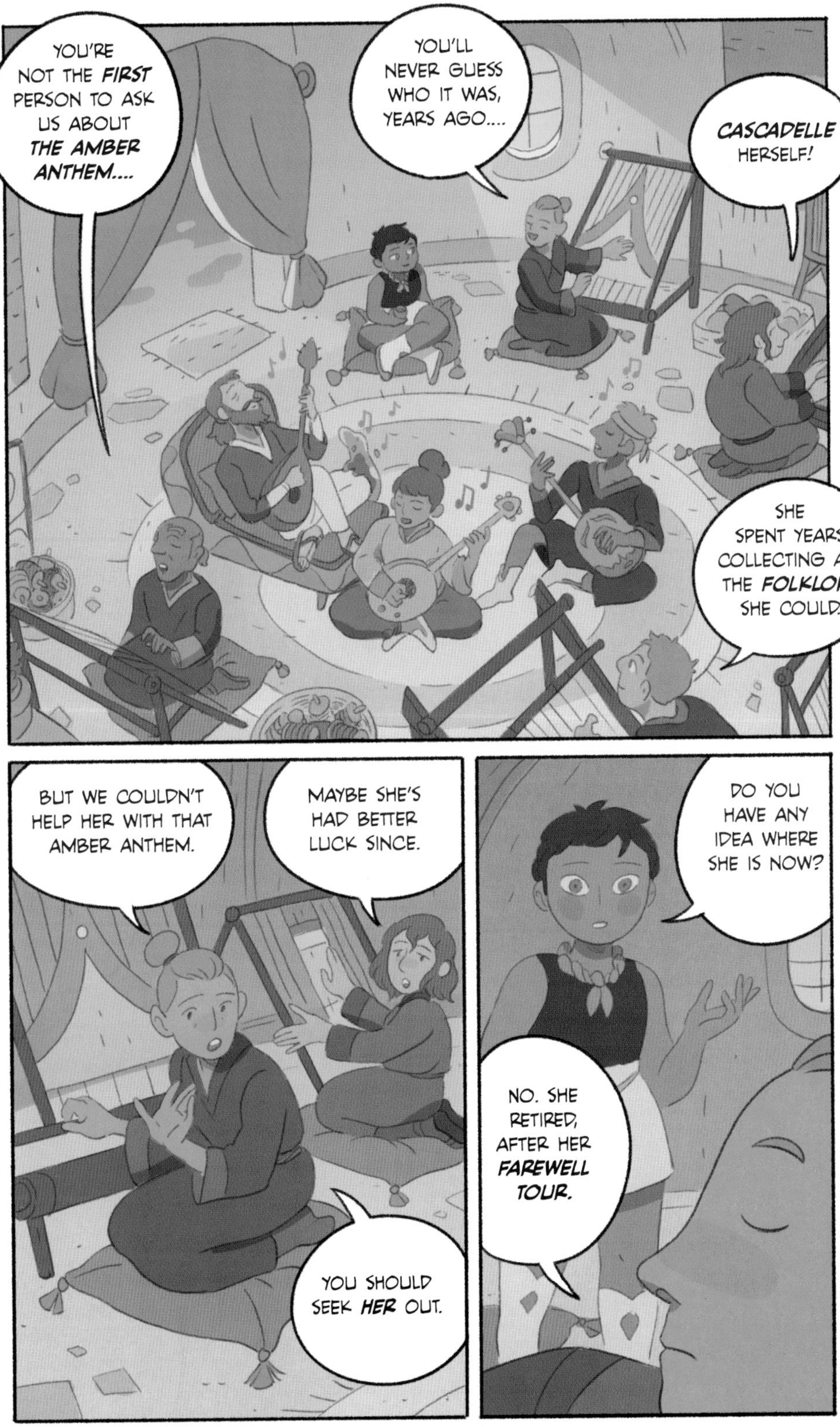
YOU'RE NOT THE **FIRST** PERSON TO ASK US ABOUT ***THE AMBER ANTHEM....***
YOU'LL NEVER GUESS WHO IT WAS, YEARS AGO....
CASCADELLE HERSELF!
SHE SPENT YEARS COLLECTING ALL THE ***FOLKLORE*** SHE COULD.
BUT WE COULDN'T HELP HER WITH THAT AMBER ANTHEM.
MAYBE SHE'S HAD BETTER LUCK SINCE.
YOU SHOULD SEEK ***HER*** OUT.
DO YOU HAVE ANY IDEA WHERE SHE IS NOW?
NO. SHE RETIRED, AFTER HER ***FAREWELL TOUR.***

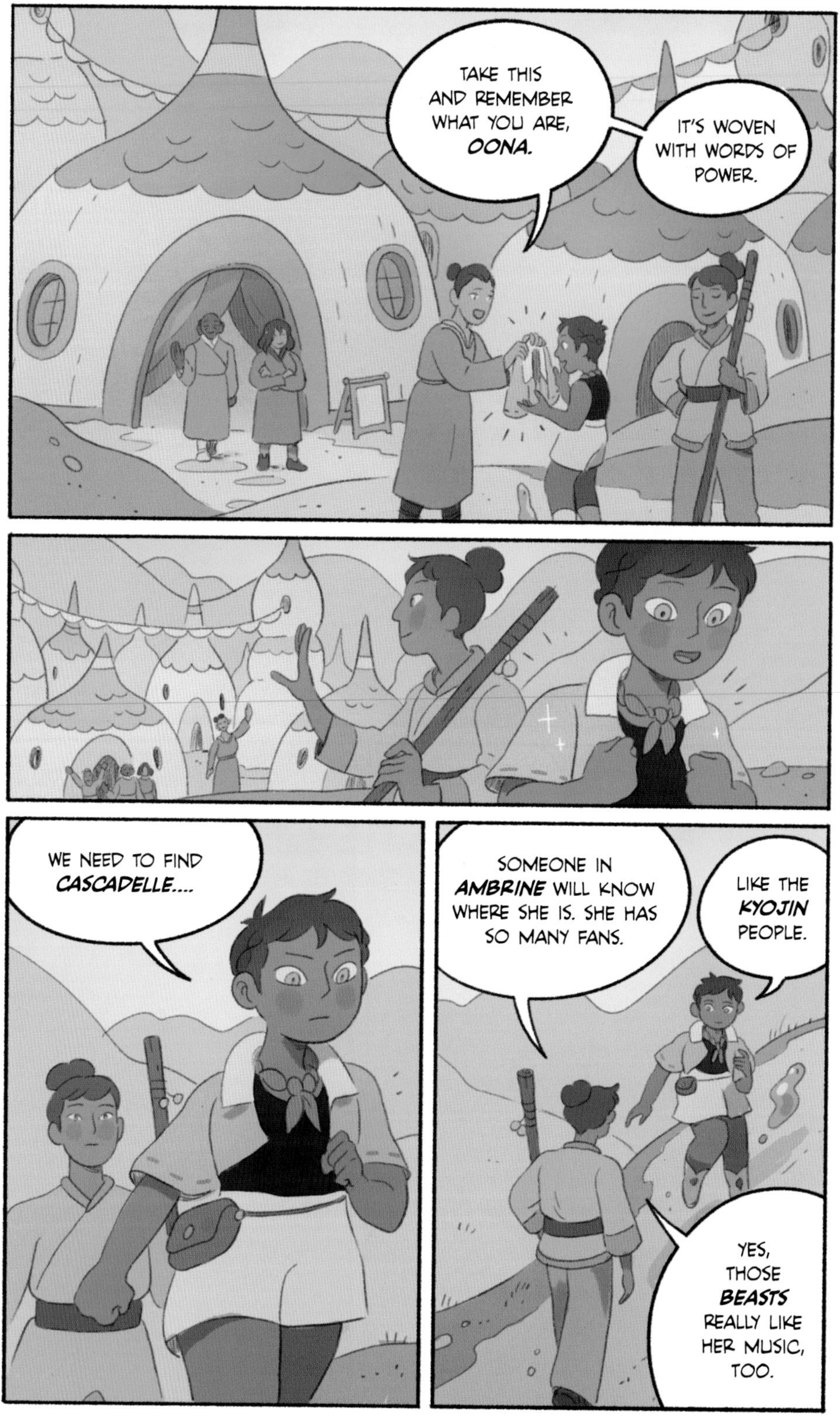
TAKE THIS AND REMEMBER WHAT YOU ARE, OONA.
IT'S WOVEN WITH WORDS OF POWER.
WE NEED TO FIND CASCADELLE....
SOMEONE IN AMBRINE WILL KNOW WHERE SHE IS. SHE HAS SO MANY FANS.
LIKE THE KYOJIN PEOPLE.
YES, THOSE BEASTS REALLY LIKE HER MUSIC, TOO.

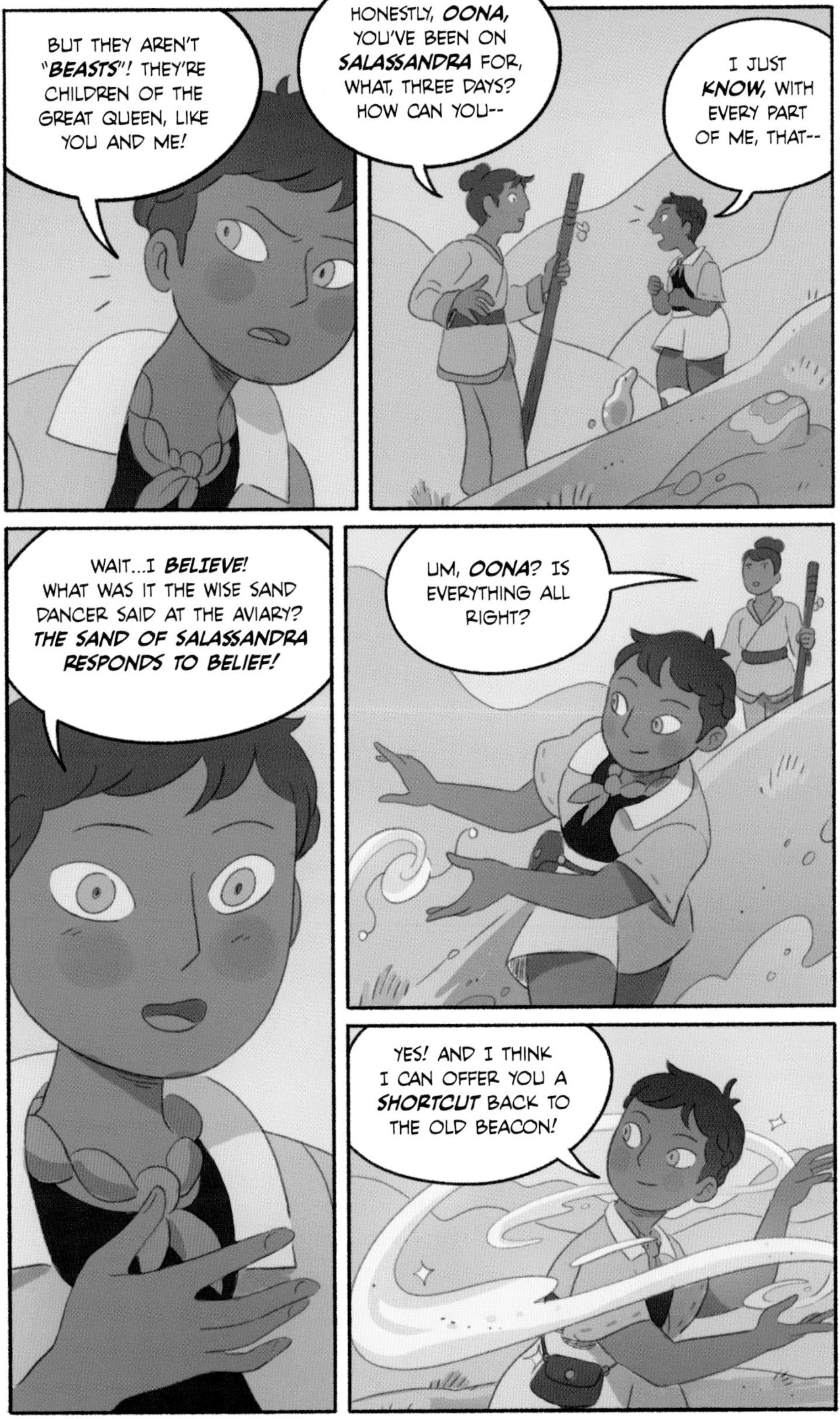
BUT THEY AREN'T "BEASTS"! THEY'RE CHILDREN OF THE GREAT QUEEN, LIKE YOU AND ME!
HONESTLY, OONA, YOU'VE BEEN ON SALASSANDRA FOR, WHAT, THREE DAYS? HOW CAN YOU--
I JUST KNOW, WITH EVERY PART OF ME, THAT--
WAIT...I BELIEVE! WHAT WAS IT THE WISE SAND DANCER SAID AT THE AVIARY? THE SAND OF SALASSANDRA RESPONDS TO BELIEF!
UM, OONA? IS EVERYTHING ALL RIGHT?
YES! AND I THINK I CAN OFFER YOU A SHORTCUT BACK TO THE OLD BEACON!

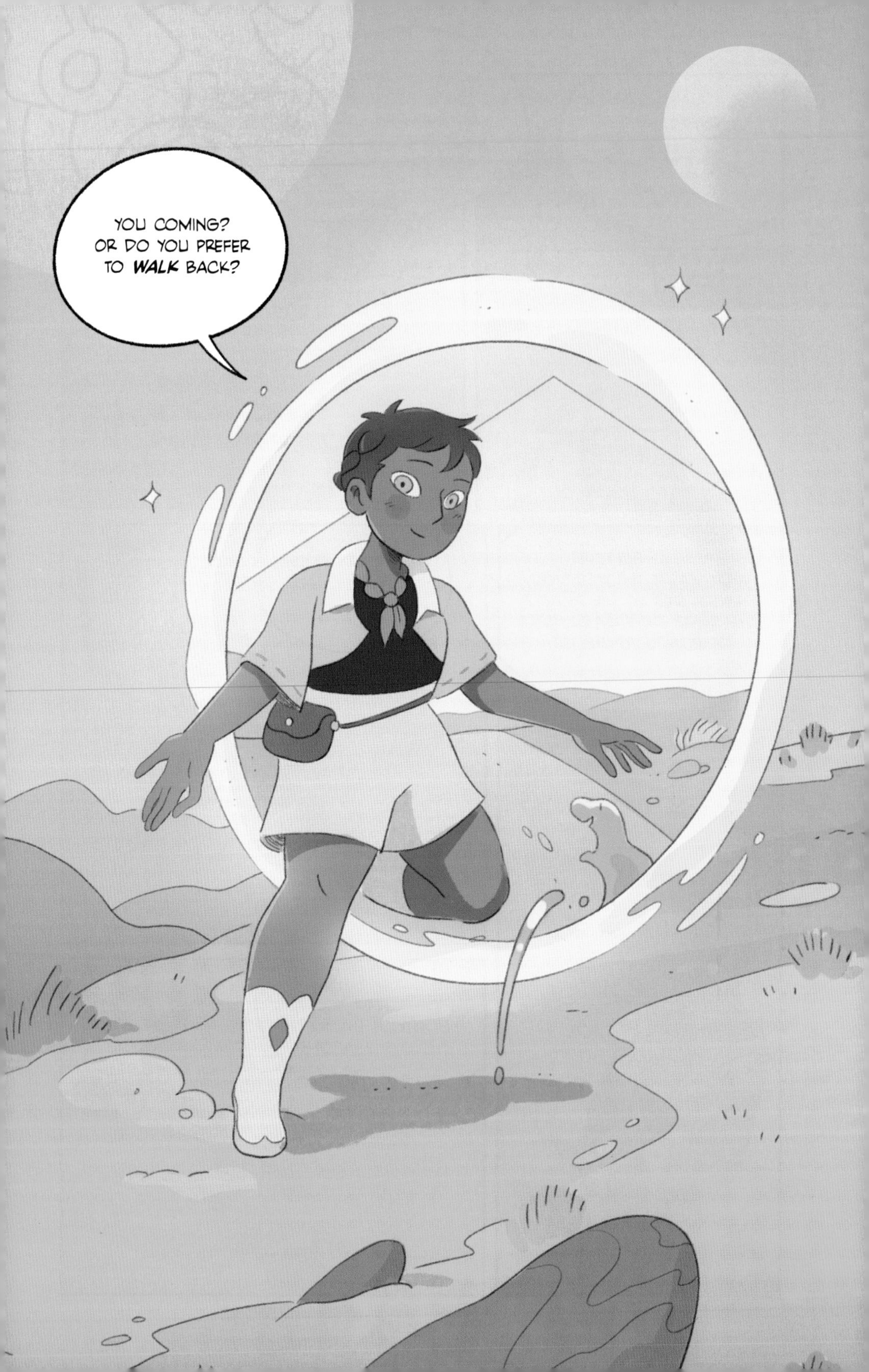
YOU COMING? OR DO YOU PREFER TO **WALK** BACK?

Chapter 7

THE SCARS

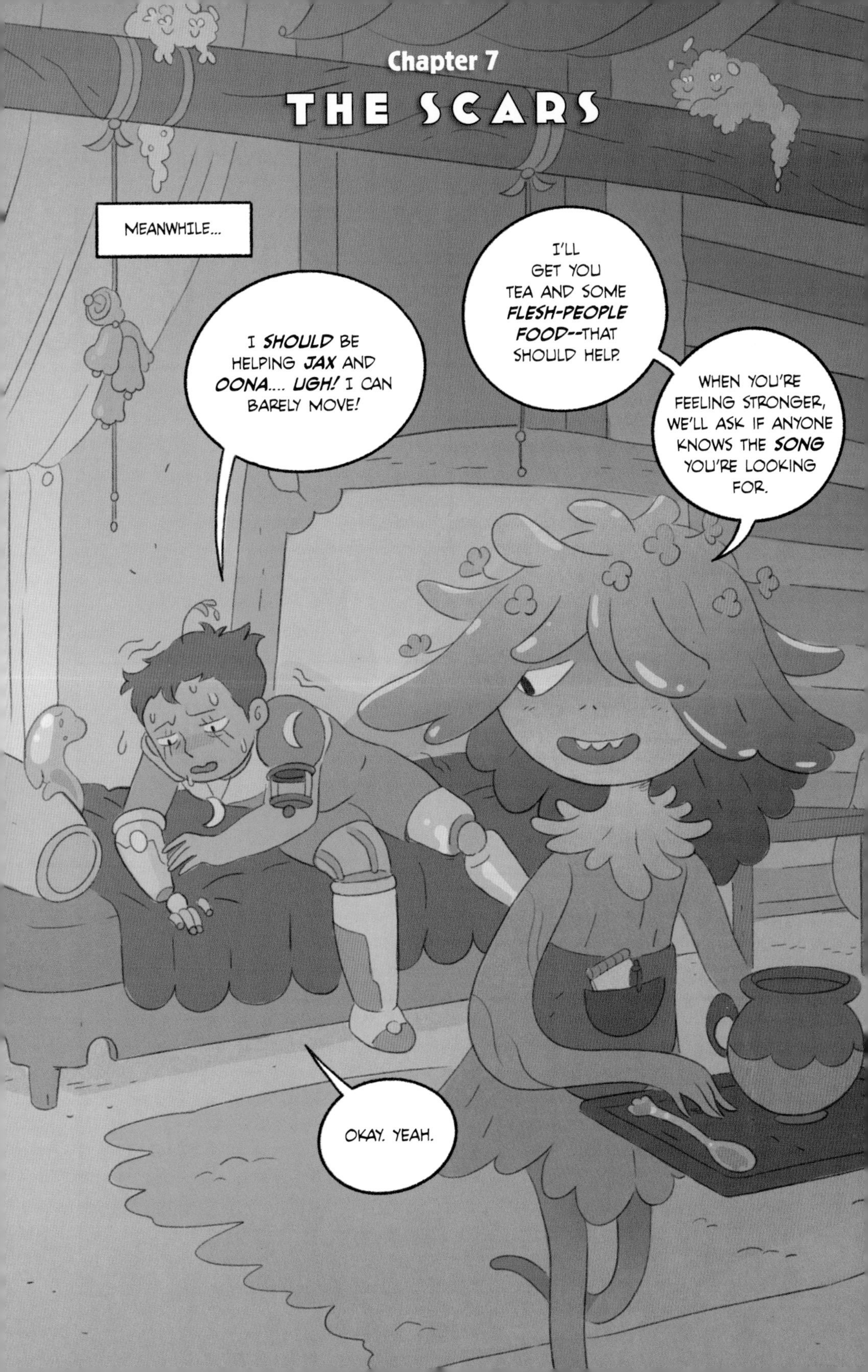
MEANWHILE...
I SHOULD BE HELPING JAX AND OONA.... UGH! I CAN BARELY MOVE!
I'LL GET YOU TEA AND SOME FLESH-PEOPLE FOOD--THAT SHOULD HELP.
WHEN YOU'RE FEELING STRONGER, WE'LL ASK IF ANYONE KNOWS THE SONG YOU'RE LOOKING FOR.
OKAY. YEAH.

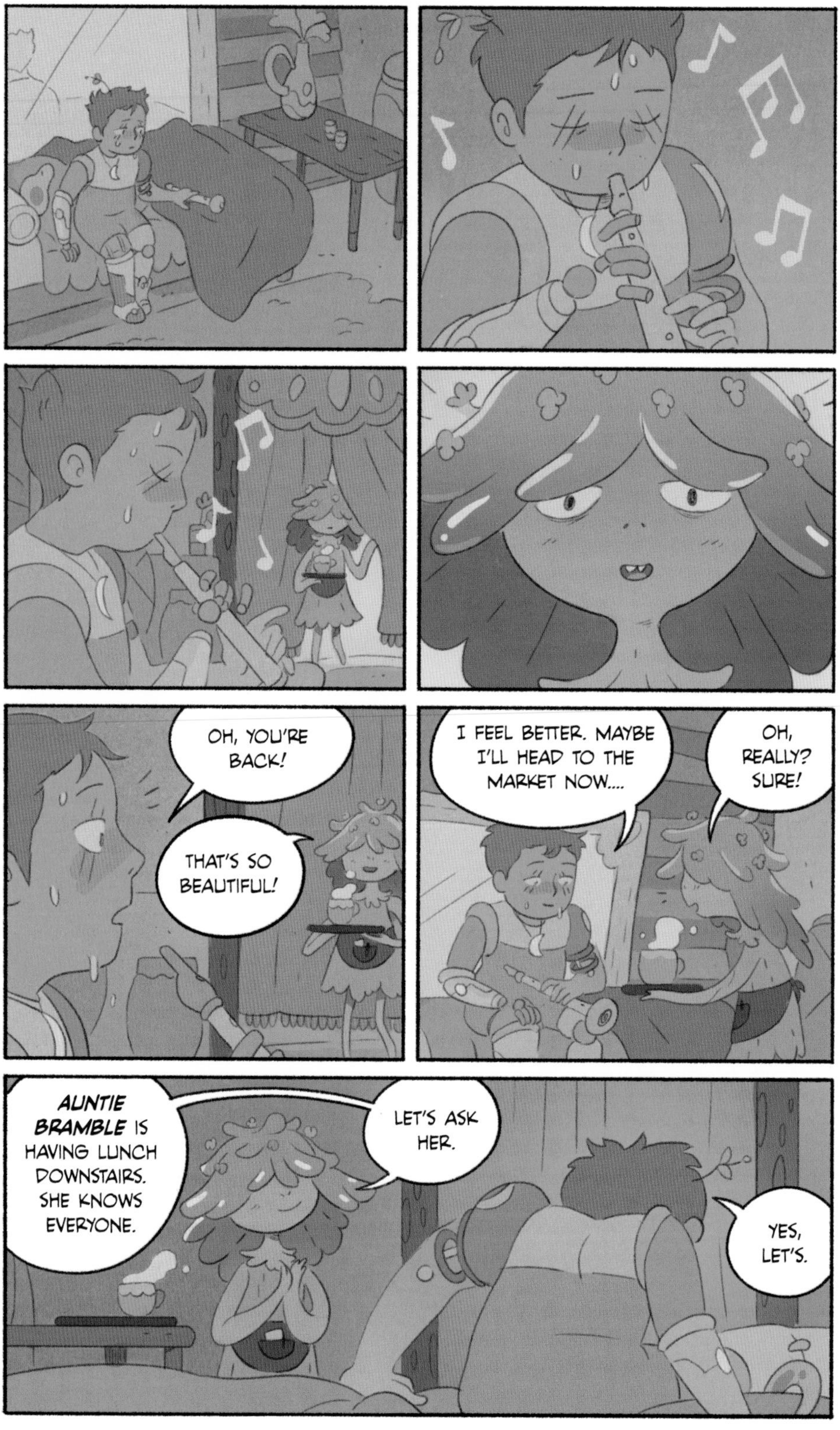
OH, YOU'RE BACK!
THAT'S SO BEAUTIFUL!
I FEEL BETTER. MAYBE I'LL HEAD TO THE MARKET NOW....
OH, REALLY? SURE!
AUNTIE BRAMBLE IS HAVING LUNCH DOWNSTAIRS. SHE KNOWS EVERYONE.
LET'S ASK HER.
YES, LET'S.

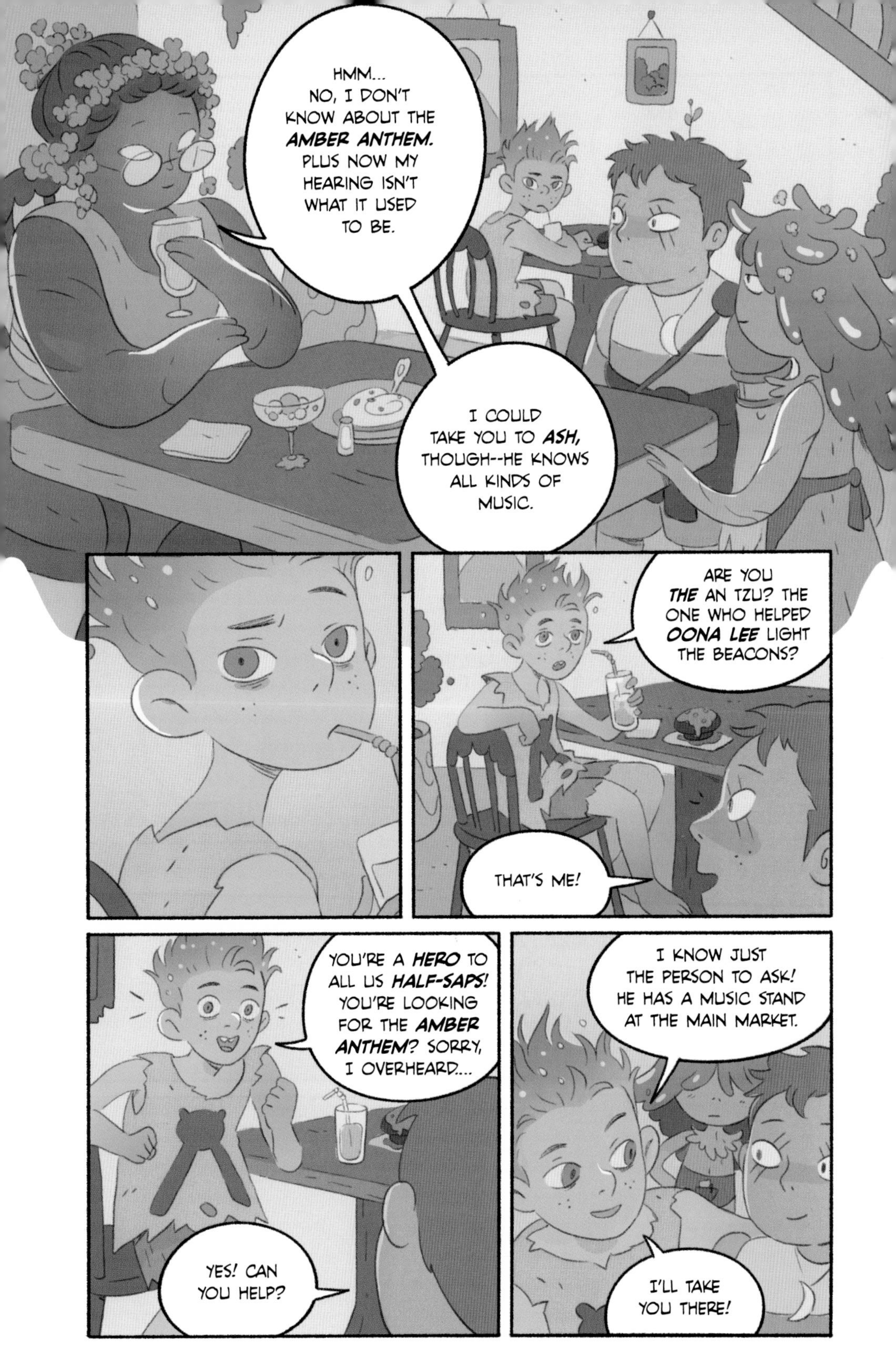
HMM... NO, I DON'T KNOW ABOUT THE AMBER ANTHEM. PLUS NOW MY HEARING ISN'T WHAT IT USED TO BE.
I COULD TAKE YOU TO ASH, THOUGH--HE KNOWS ALL KINDS OF MUSIC.
ARE YOU THE AN TZU? THE ONE WHO HELPED OONA LEE LIGHT THE BEACONS?
THAT'S ME!
YOU'RE A HERO TO ALL US HALF-SAPS! YOU'RE LOOKING FOR THE AMBER ANTHEM? SORRY, I OVERHEARD...
YES! CAN YOU HELP?
I KNOW JUST THE PERSON TO ASK! HE HAS A MUSIC STAND AT THE MAIN MARKET.
I'LL TAKE YOU THERE!

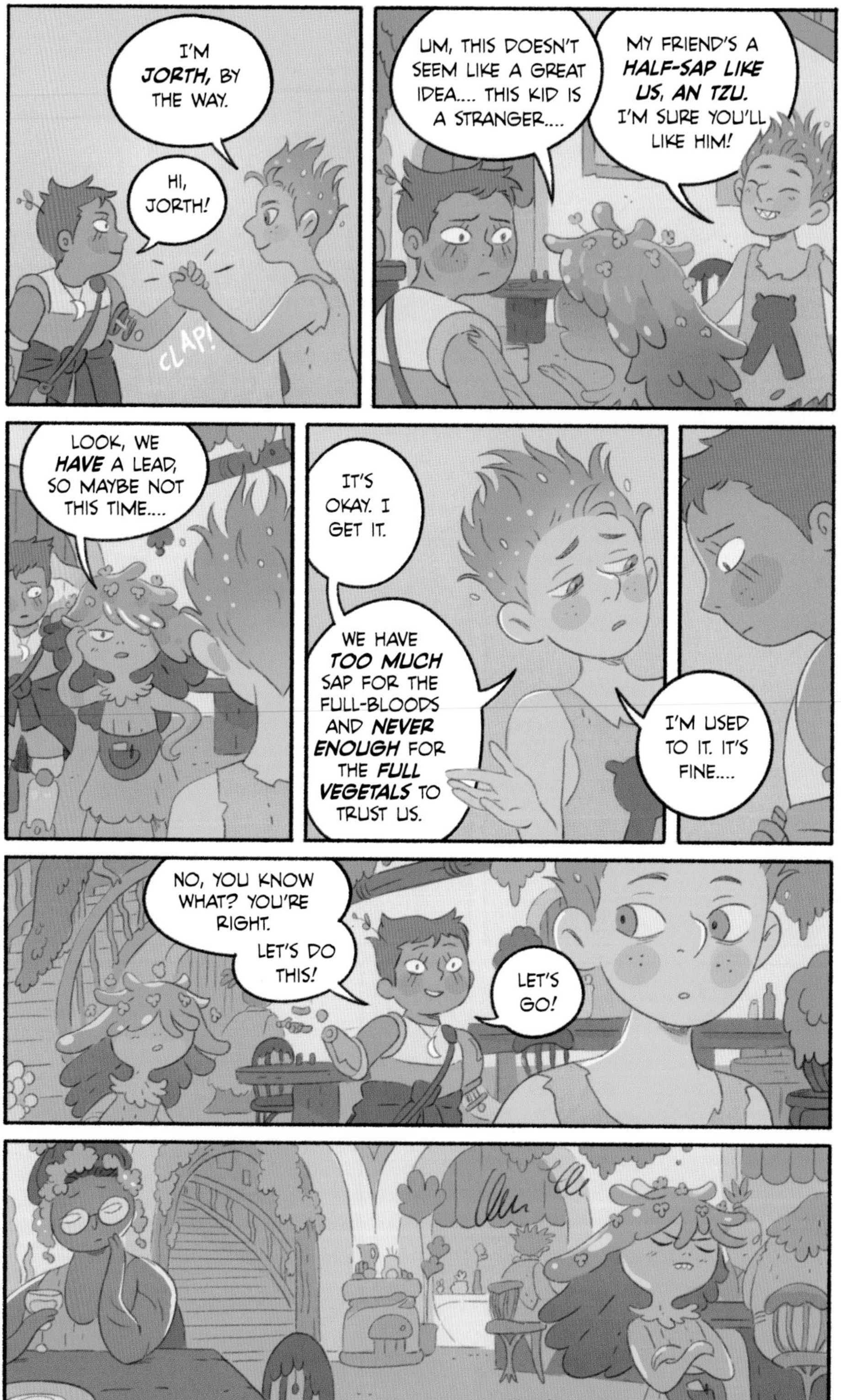
I'M JORTH, BY THE WAY.
HI, JORTH!
CLAP!
UM, THIS DOESN'T SEEM LIKE A GREAT IDEA.... THIS KID IS A STRANGER....
MY FRIEND'S A HALF-SAP LIKE US, AN TZU. I'M SURE YOU'LL LIKE HIM!
LOOK, WE HAVE A LEAD, SO MAYBE NOT THIS TIME....
IT'S OKAY. I GET IT.
WE HAVE TOO MUCH SAP FOR THE FULL-BLOODS AND NEVER ENOUGH FOR THE FULL VEGETALS TO TRUST US.
I'M USED TO IT. IT'S FINE....
NO, YOU KNOW WHAT? YOU'RE RIGHT.
LET'S DO THIS!
LET'S GO!

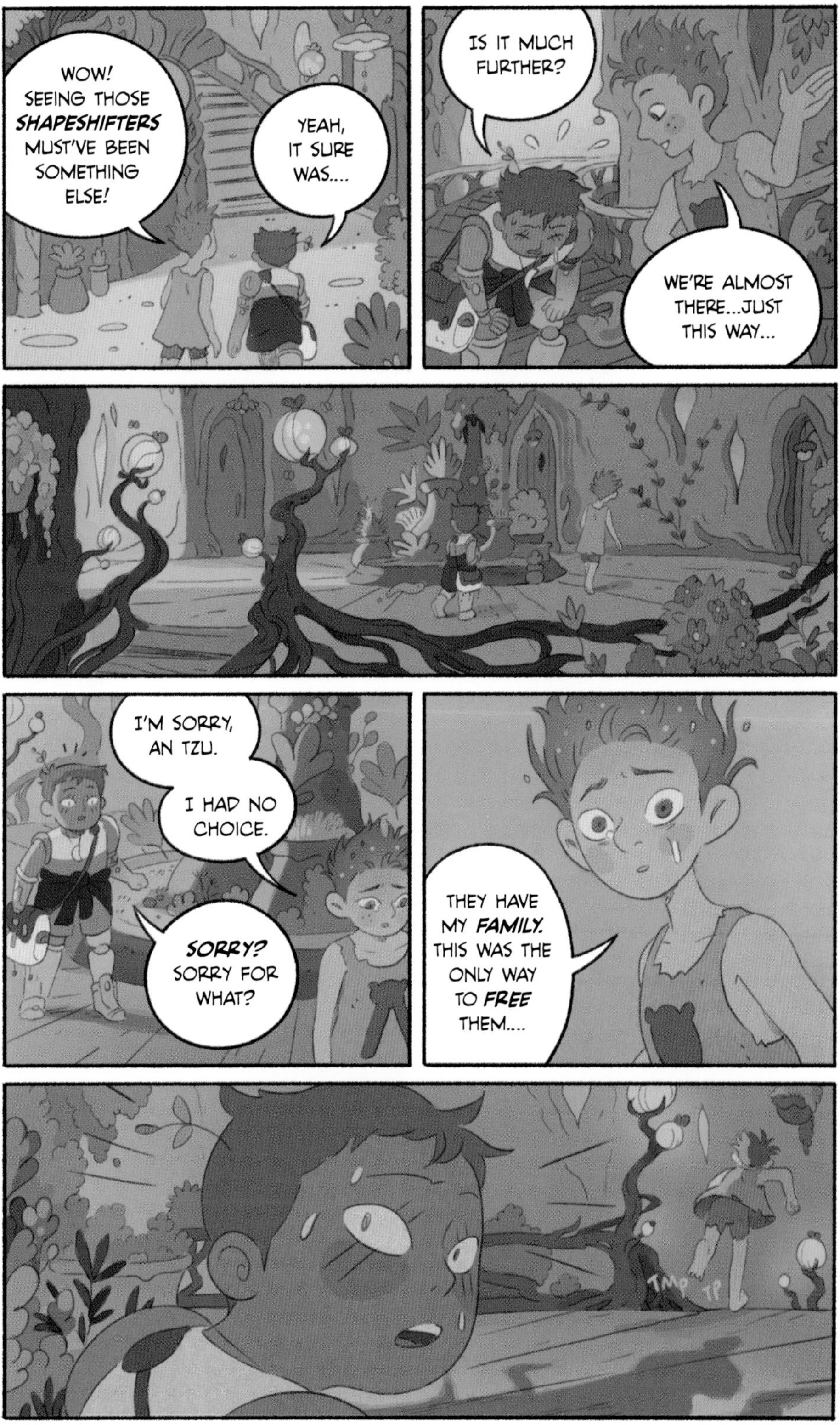
WOW! SEEING THOSE SHAPESHIFTERS MUST'VE BEEN SOMETHING ELSE!
YEAH, IT SURE WAS....
IS IT MUCH FURTHER?
WE'RE ALMOST THERE...JUST THIS WAY...
I'M SORRY, AN TZU.
I HAD NO CHOICE.
SORRY? SORRY FOR WHAT?
THEY HAVE MY FAMILY. THIS WAS THE ONLY WAY TO FREE THEM....
TMP TP

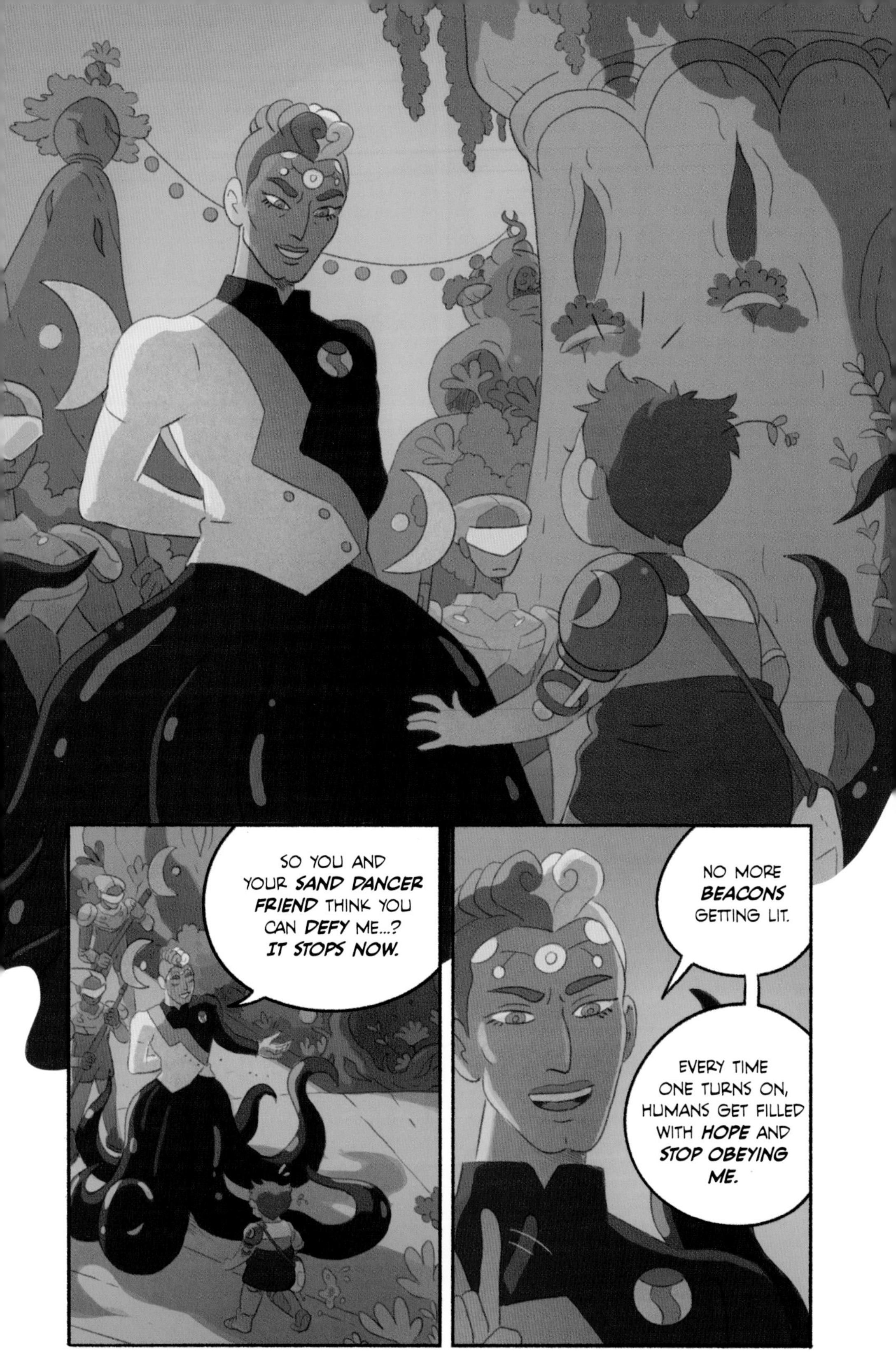
SO YOU AND YOUR SAND DANCER FRIEND THINK YOU CAN DEFY ME...? IT STOPS NOW.
NO MORE BEACONS GETTING LIT.
EVERY TIME ONE TURNS ON, HUMANS GET FILLED WITH HOPE AND STOP OBEYING ME.

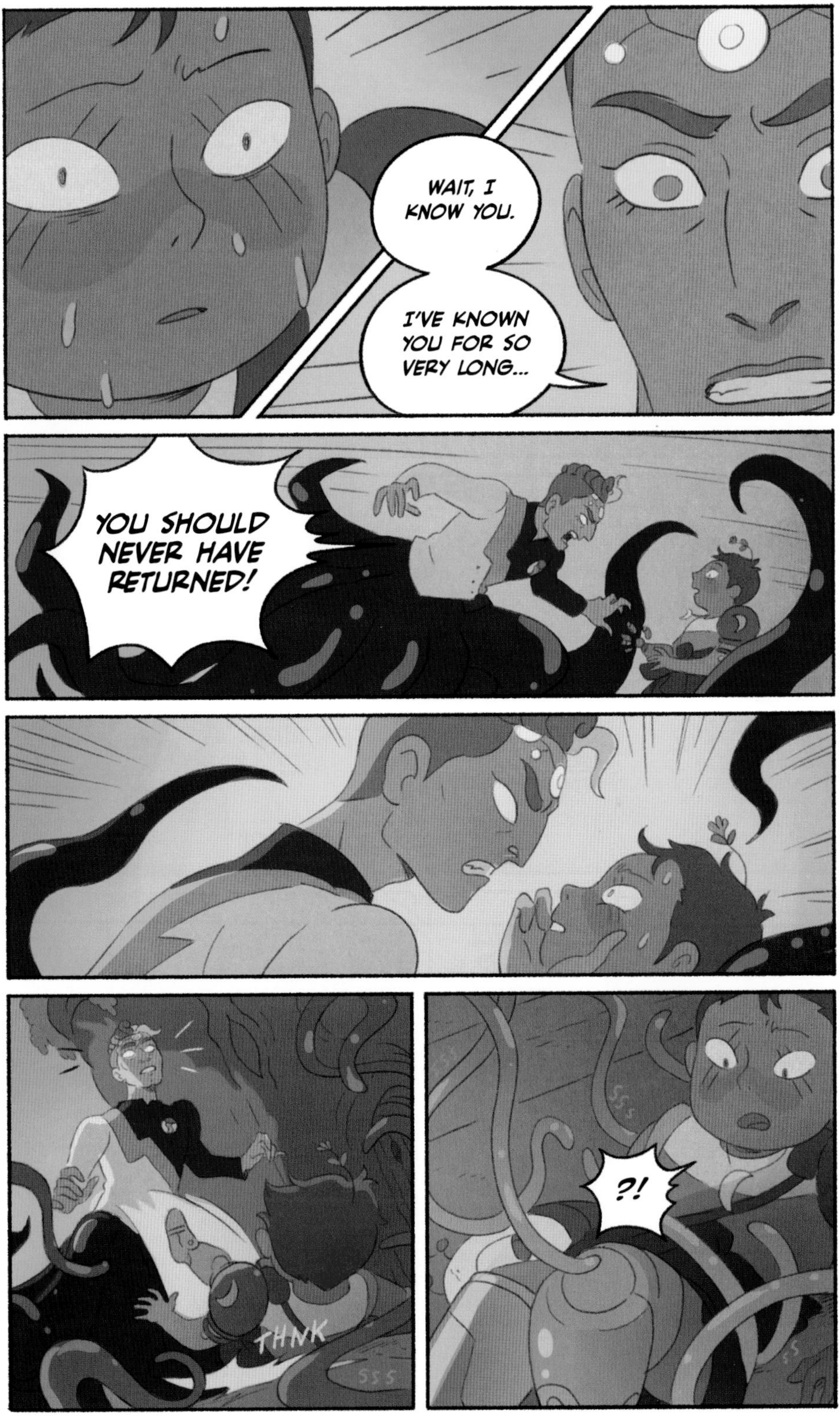
WAIT, I KNOW YOU.
I'VE KNOWN YOU FOR SO VERY LONG...
YOU SHOULD NEVER HAVE RETURNED!
THNK
?!

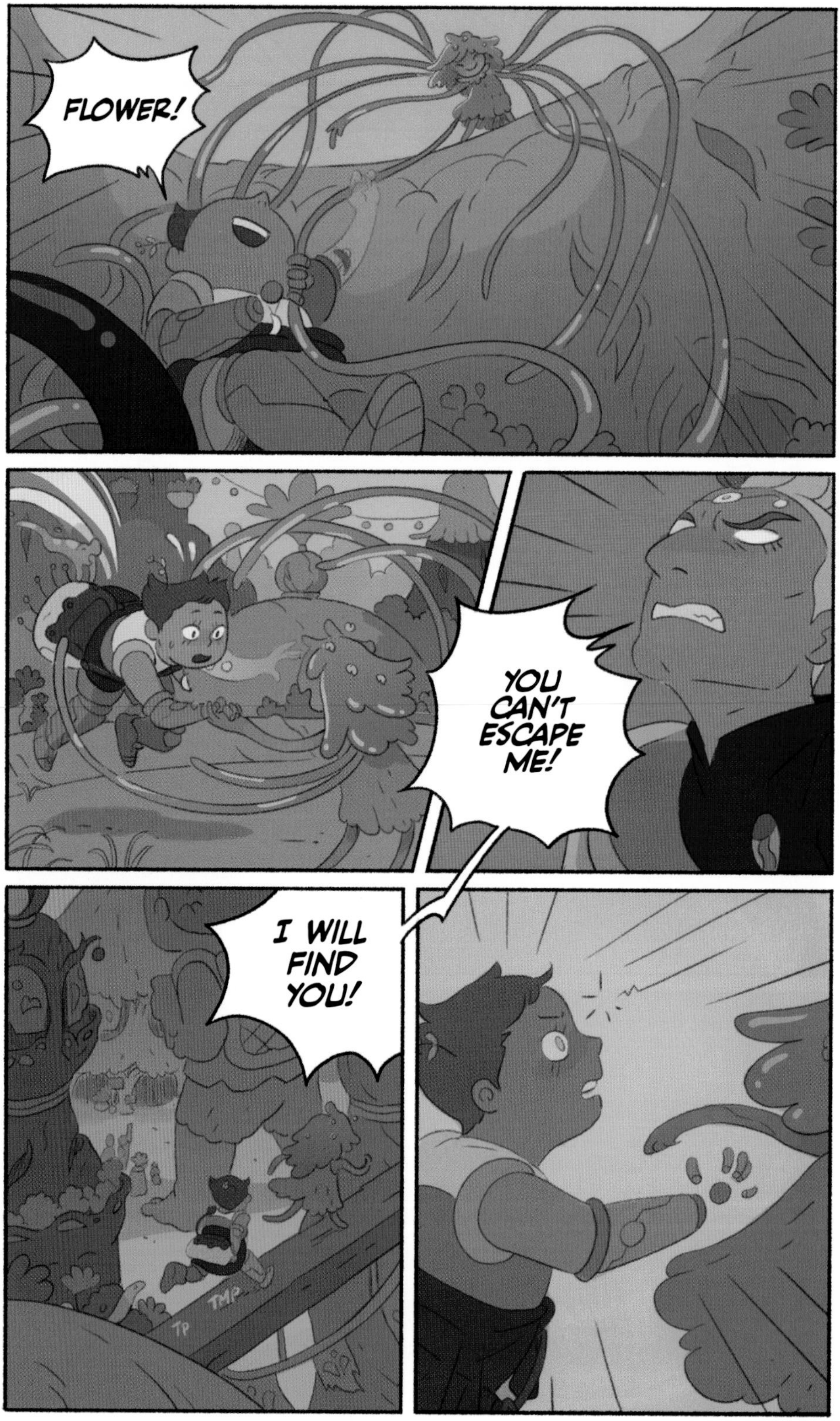
FLOWER!
YOU CAN'T ESCAPE ME!
I WILL FIND YOU!
TP
TMP

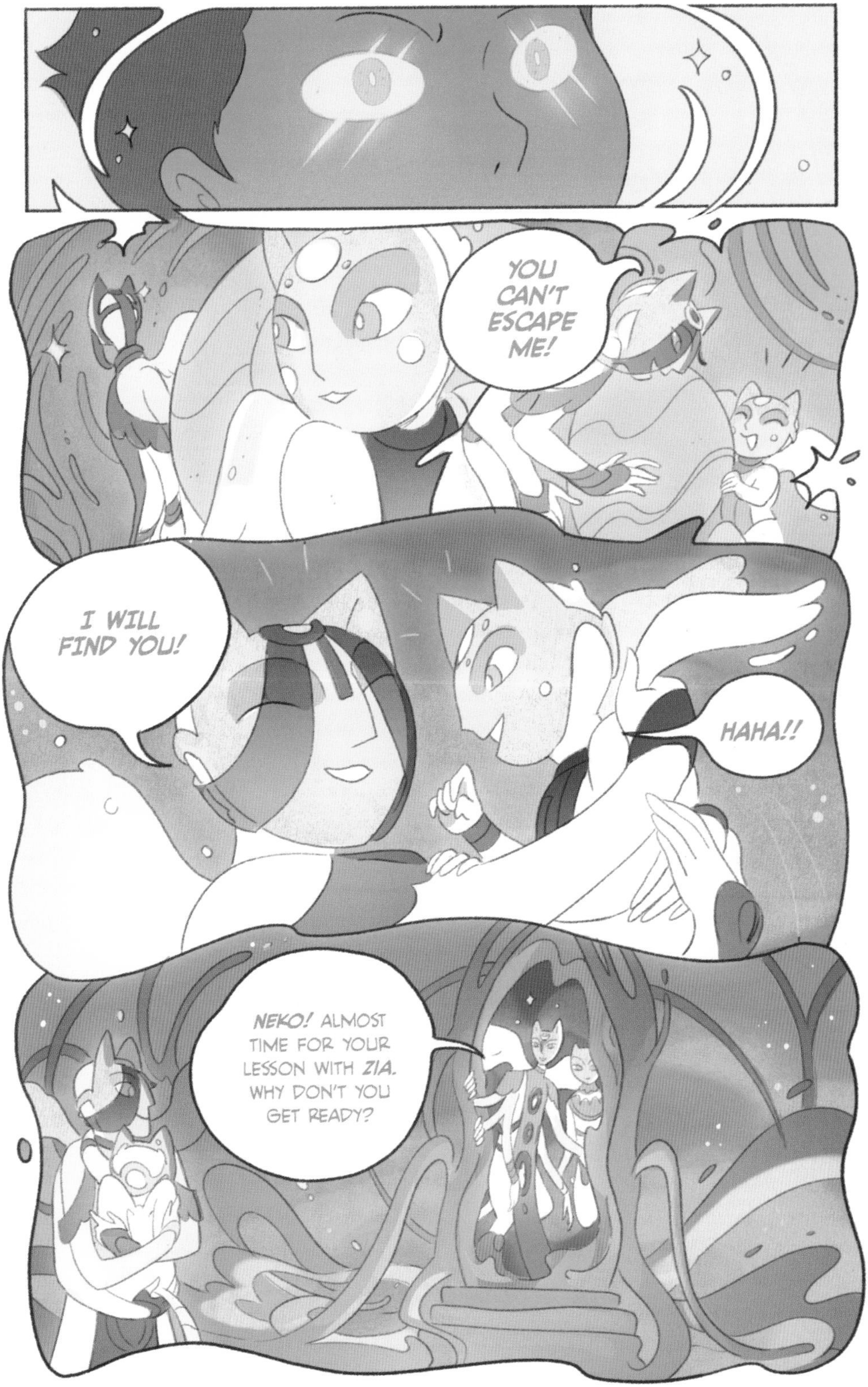
YOU CAN'T ESCAPE ME!
I WILL FIND YOU!
HAHA!!
NEKO! ALMOST TIME FOR YOUR LESSON WITH ZIA. WHY DON'T YOU GET READY?

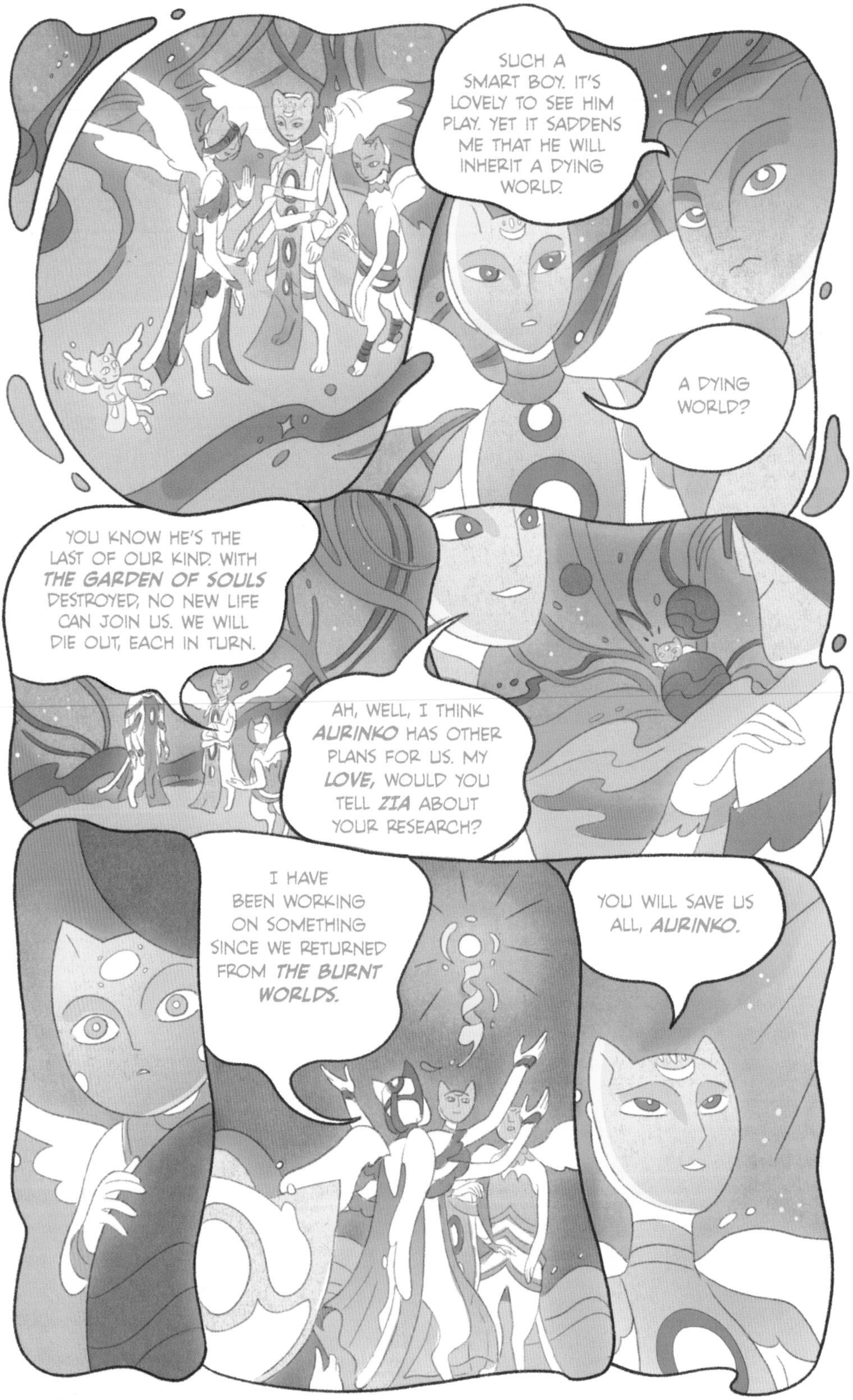
SUCH A SMART BOY. IT'S LOVELY TO SEE HIM PLAY. YET IT SADDENS ME THAT HE WILL INHERIT A DYING WORLD.
A DYING WORLD?
YOU KNOW HE'S THE LAST OF OUR KIND. WITH THE GARDEN OF SOULS DESTROYED, NO NEW LIFE CAN JOIN US. WE WILL DIE OUT, EACH IN TURN.
AH, WELL, I THINK AURINKO HAS OTHER PLANS FOR US. MY LOVE, WOULD YOU TELL ZIA ABOUT YOUR RESEARCH?
I HAVE BEEN WORKING ON SOMETHING SINCE WE RETURNED FROM THE BURNT WORLDS.
YOU WILL SAVE US ALL, AURINKO.

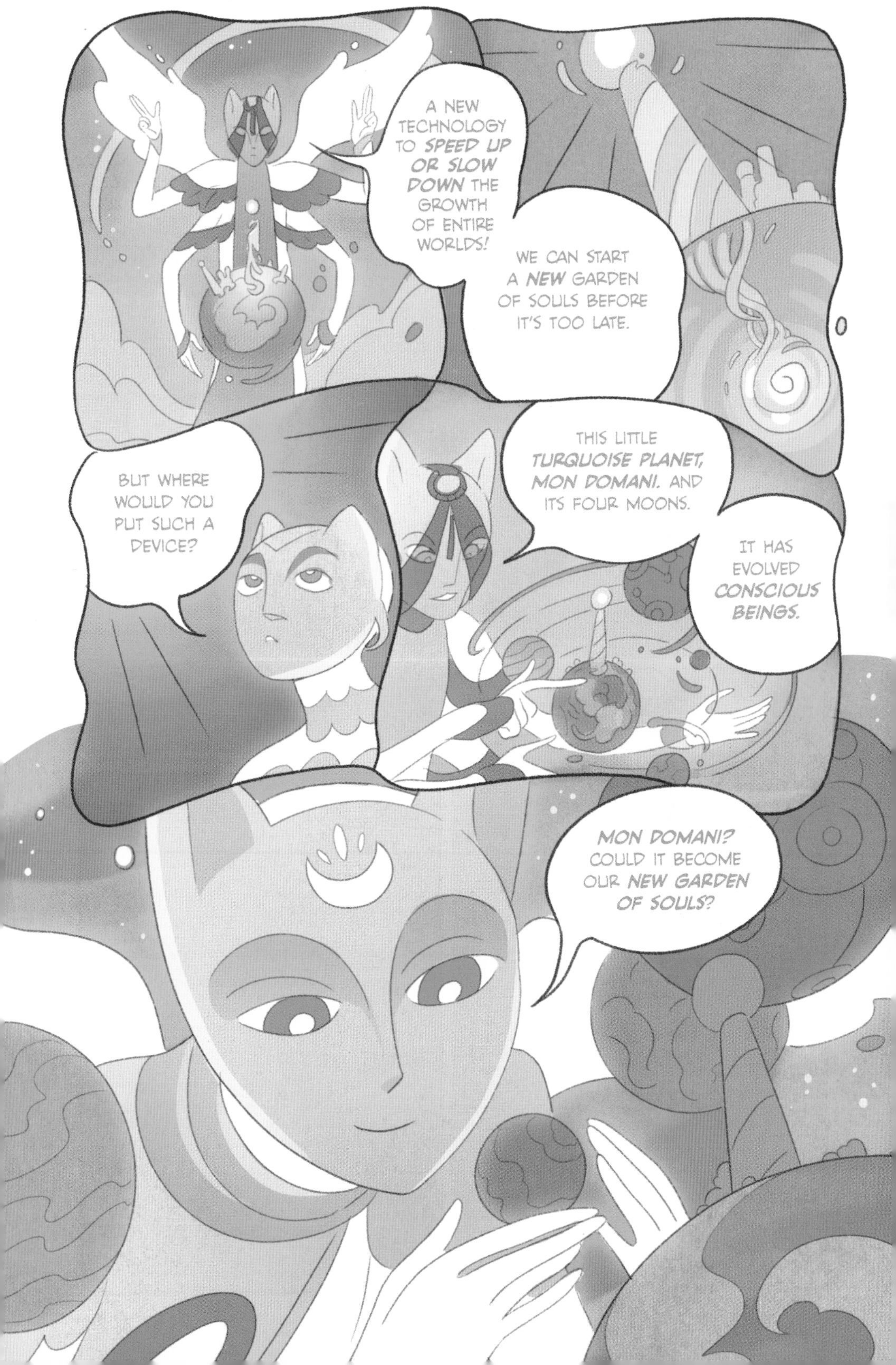
A NEW TECHNOLOGY TO **SPEED UP OR SLOW DOWN** THE GROWTH OF ENTIRE WORLDS!
WE CAN START A **NEW** GARDEN OF SOULS BEFORE IT'S TOO LATE.
BUT WHERE WOULD YOU PUT SUCH A DEVICE?
THIS LITTLE **TURQUOISE PLANET, MON DOMANI.** AND ITS FOUR MOONS.
IT HAS EVOLVED **CONSCIOUS BEINGS.**
MON DOMANI? COULD IT BECOME OUR **NEW GARDEN OF SOULS?**

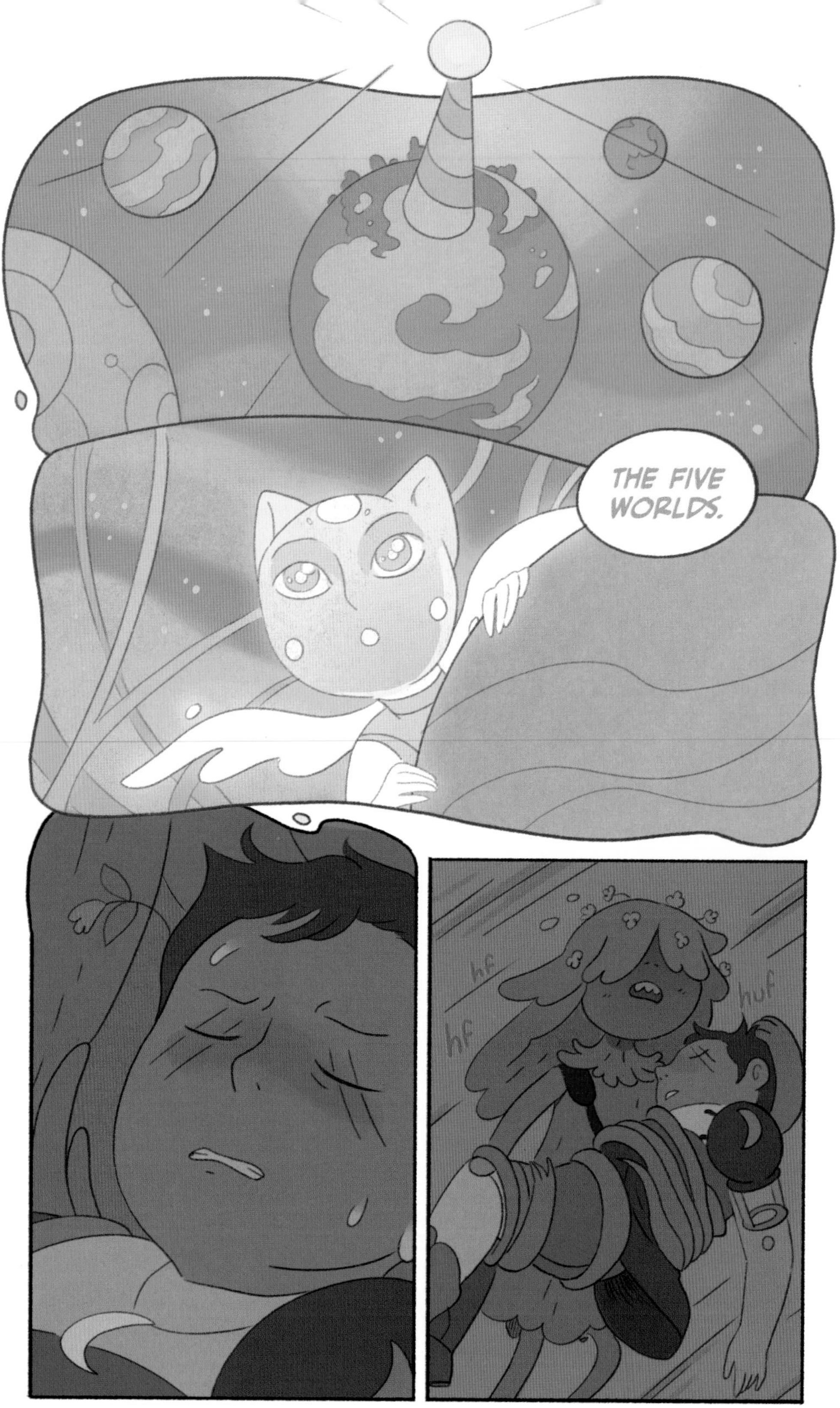
THE FIVE WORLDS.
hf
huf
hf

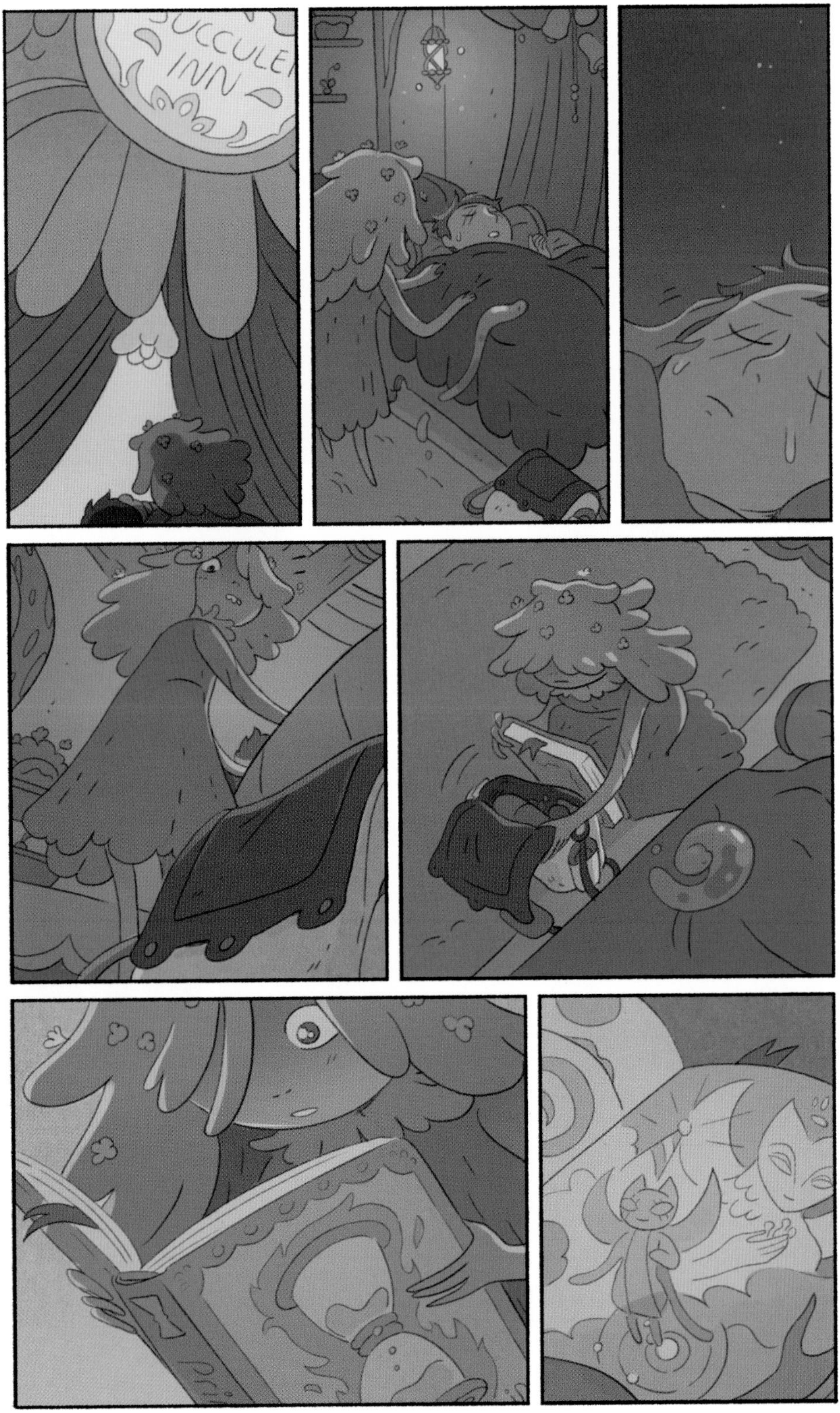
SUCCULENT
INN

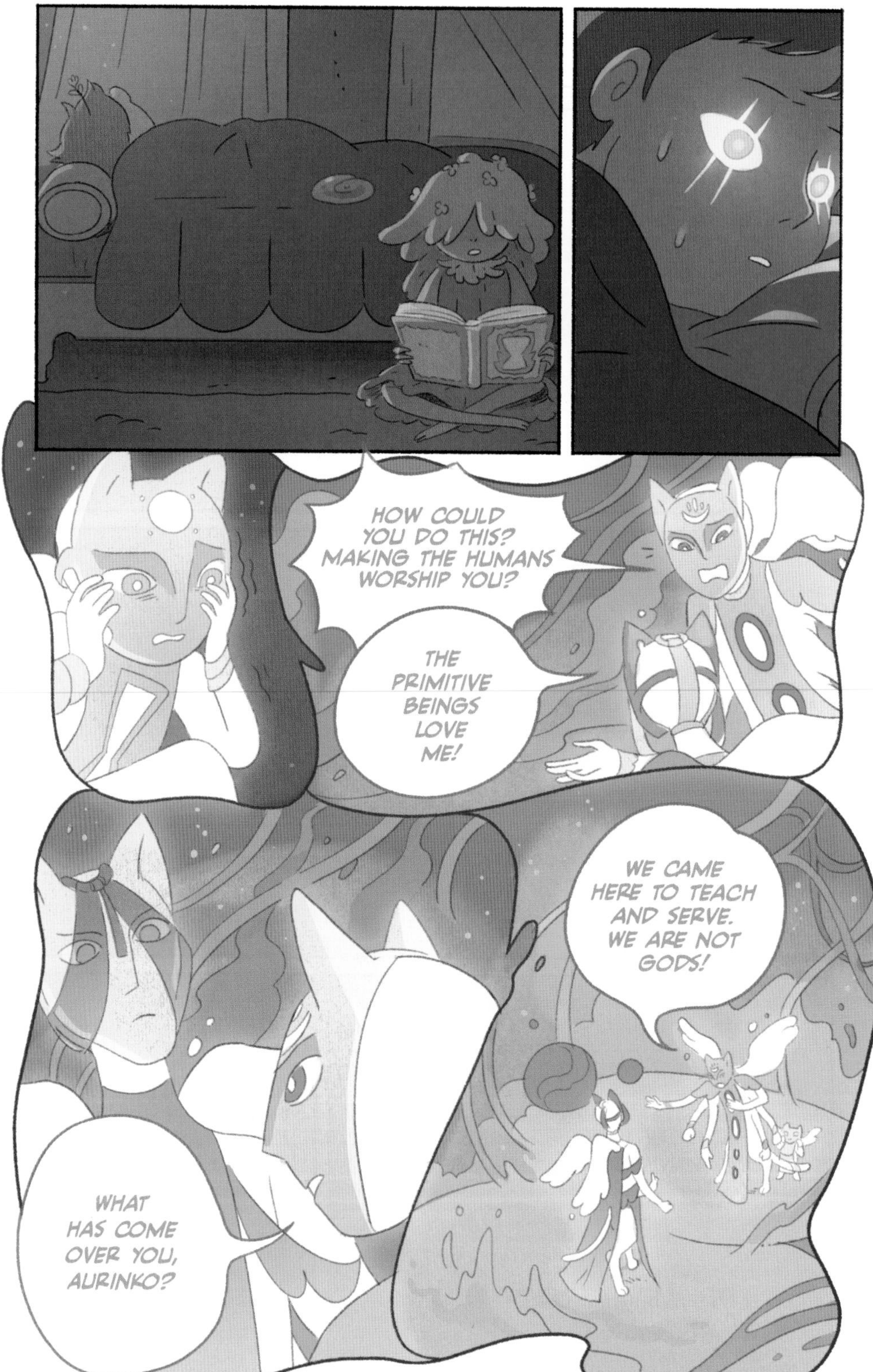
HOW COULD YOU DO THIS? MAKING THE HUMANS WORSHIP YOU?
THE PRIMITIVE BEINGS LOVE ME!
WE CAME HERE TO TEACH AND SERVE. WE ARE NOT GODS!
WHAT HAS COME OVER YOU, AURINKO?

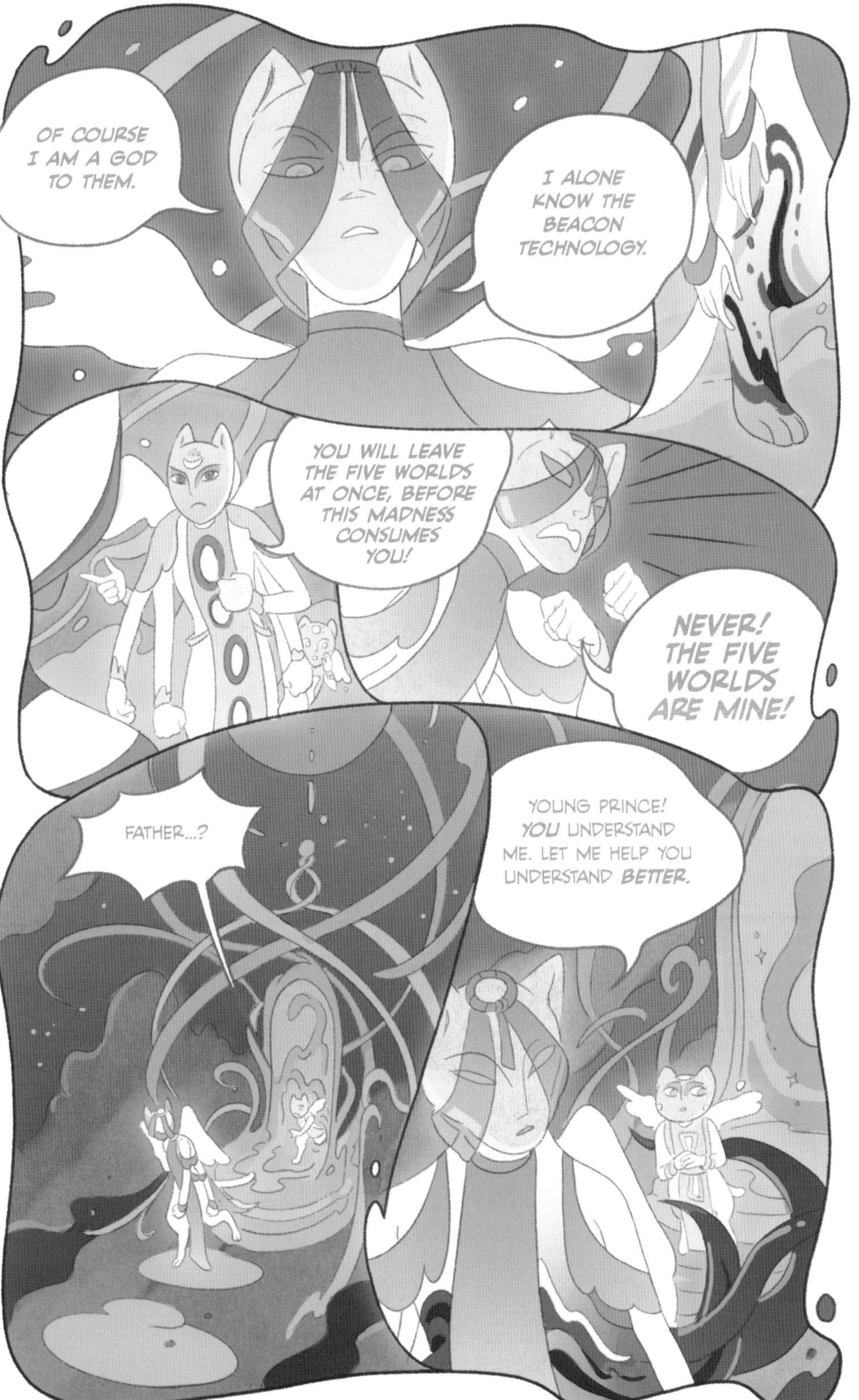
OF COURSE I AM A GOD TO THEM.
I ALONE KNOW THE BEACON TECHNOLOGY.
YOU WILL LEAVE THE FIVE WORLDS AT ONCE, BEFORE THIS MADNESS CONSUMES YOU!
NEVER! THE FIVE WORLDS ARE MINE!
FATHER...?
YOUNG PRINCE! YOU UNDERSTAND ME. LET ME HELP YOU UNDERSTAND BETTER.

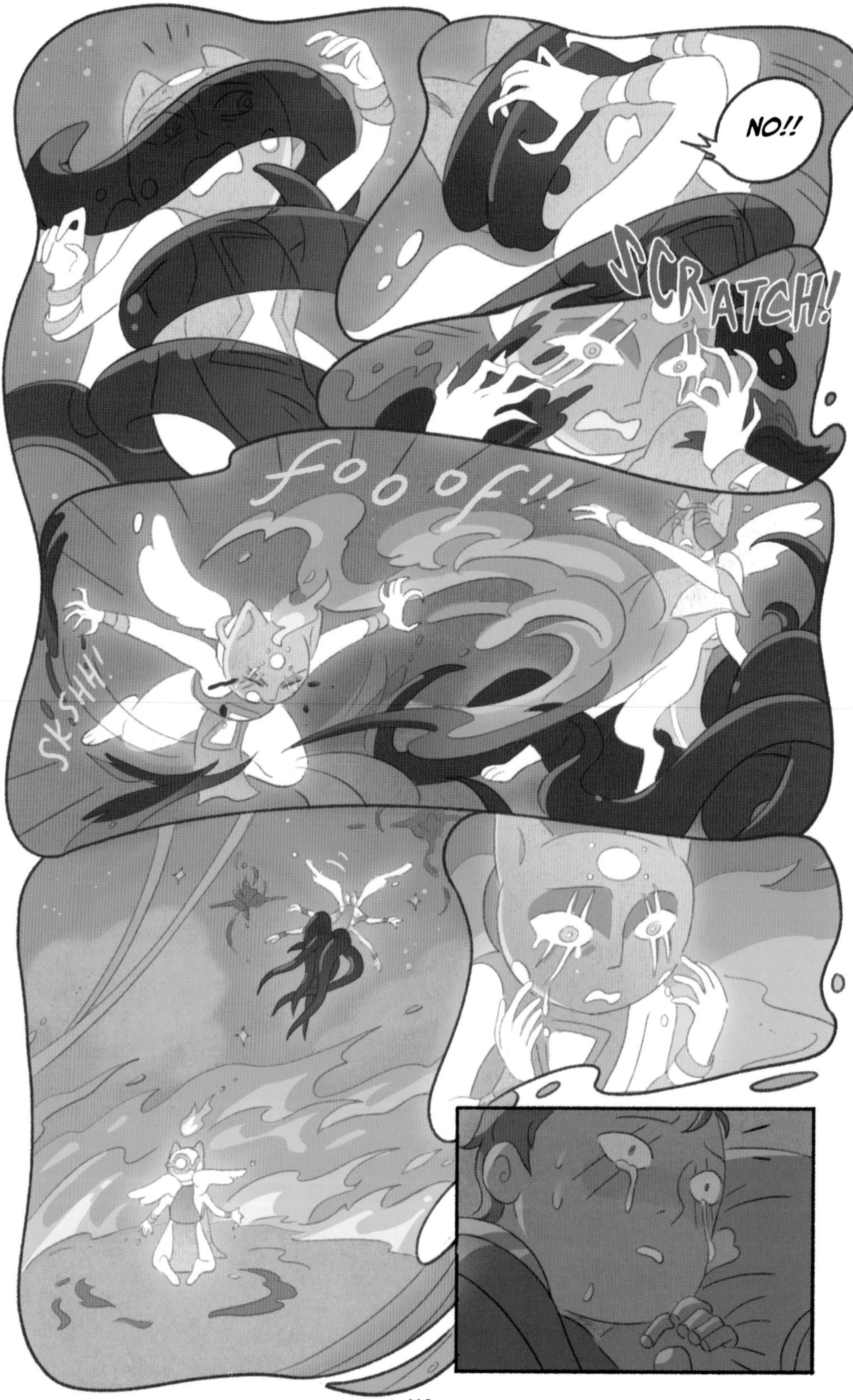
NO!!
SCRATCH!
fooof!!
SKSHH!

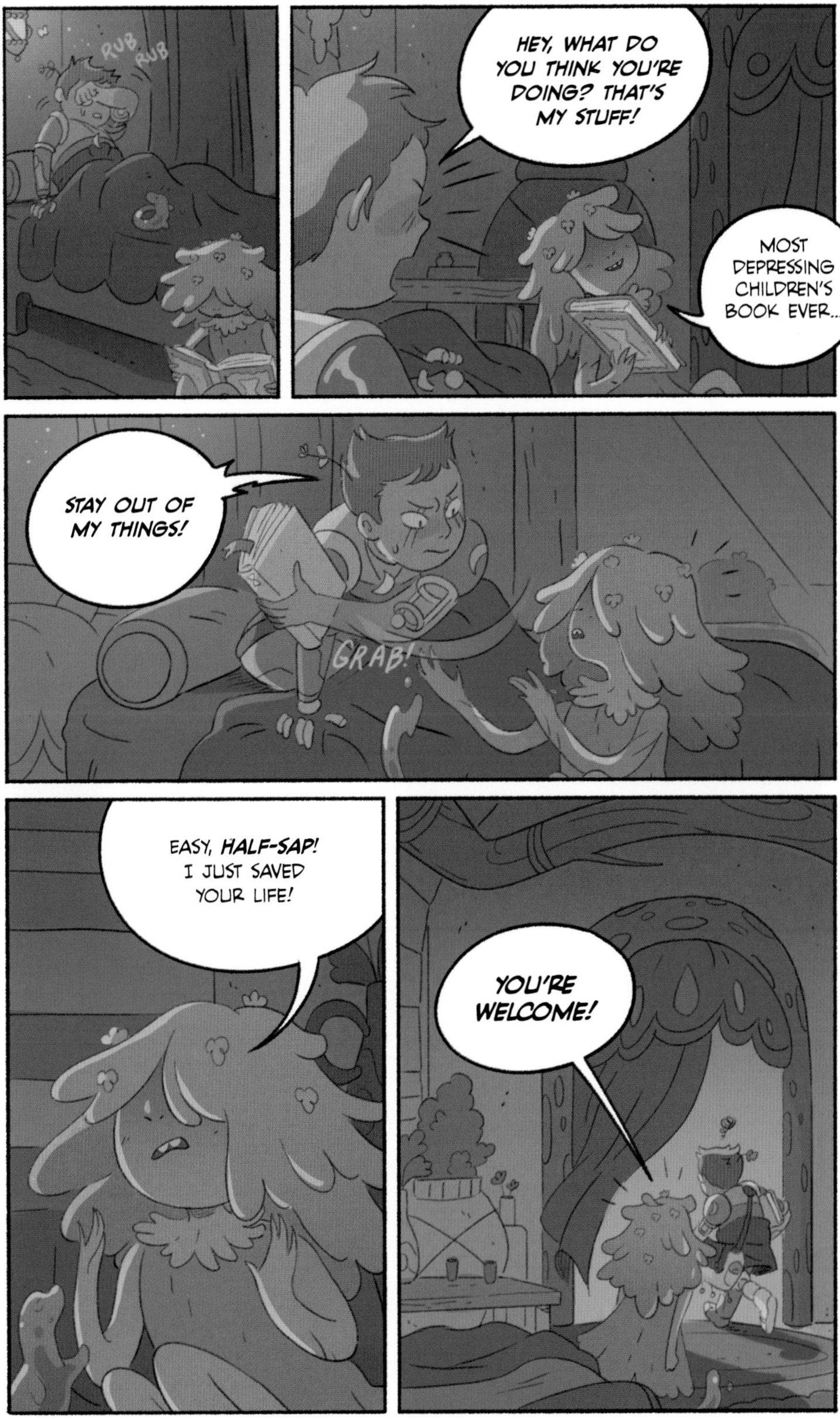
RUB RUB
HEY, WHAT DO YOU THINK YOU'RE DOING? THAT'S MY STUFF!
MOST DEPRESSING CHILDREN'S BOOK EVER...
STAY OUT OF MY THINGS!
GRAB!
EASY, HALF-SAP! I JUST SAVED YOUR LIFE!
YOU'RE WELCOME!

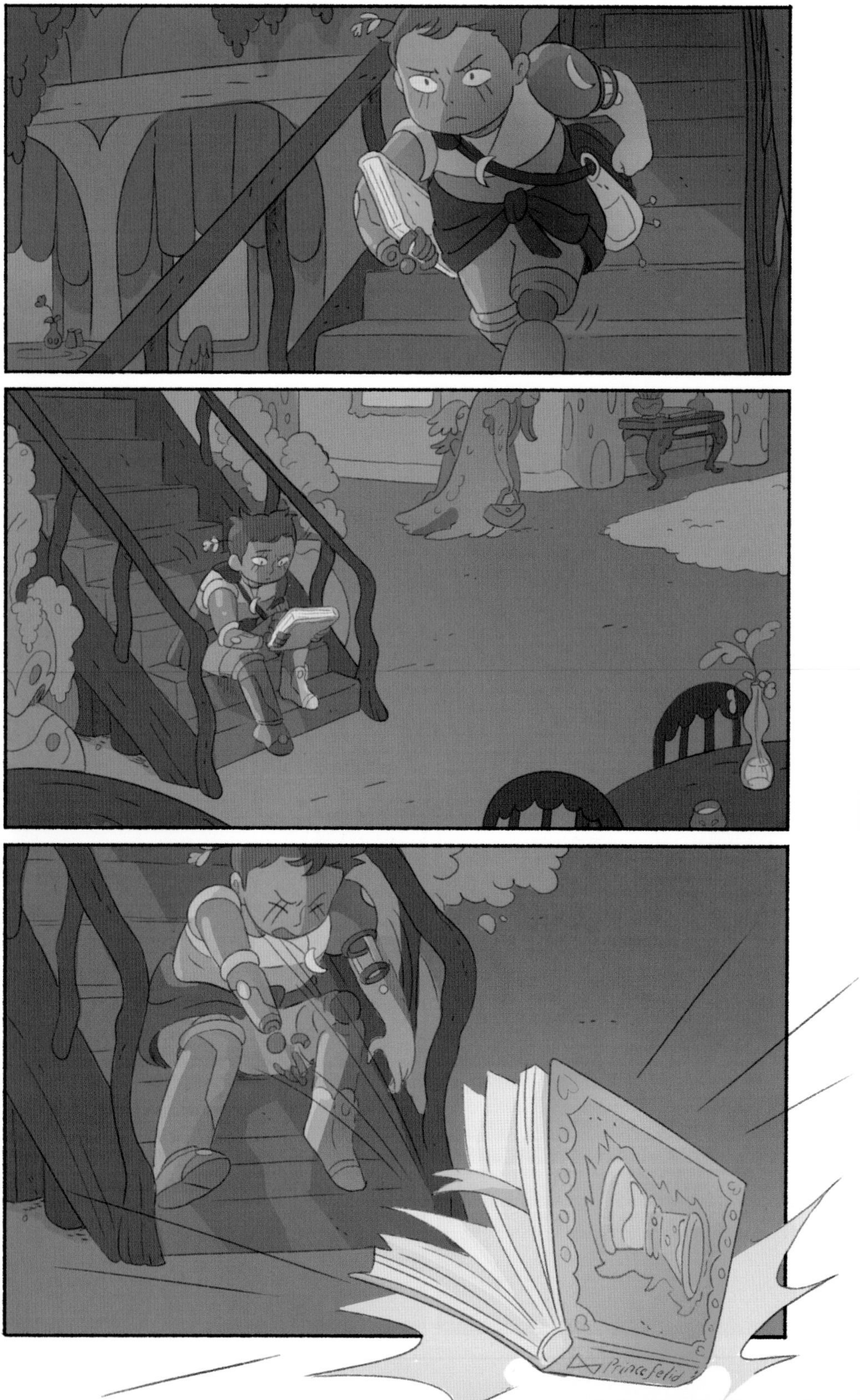
Princefeld

Chapter 8
THE KILLER STRIKES

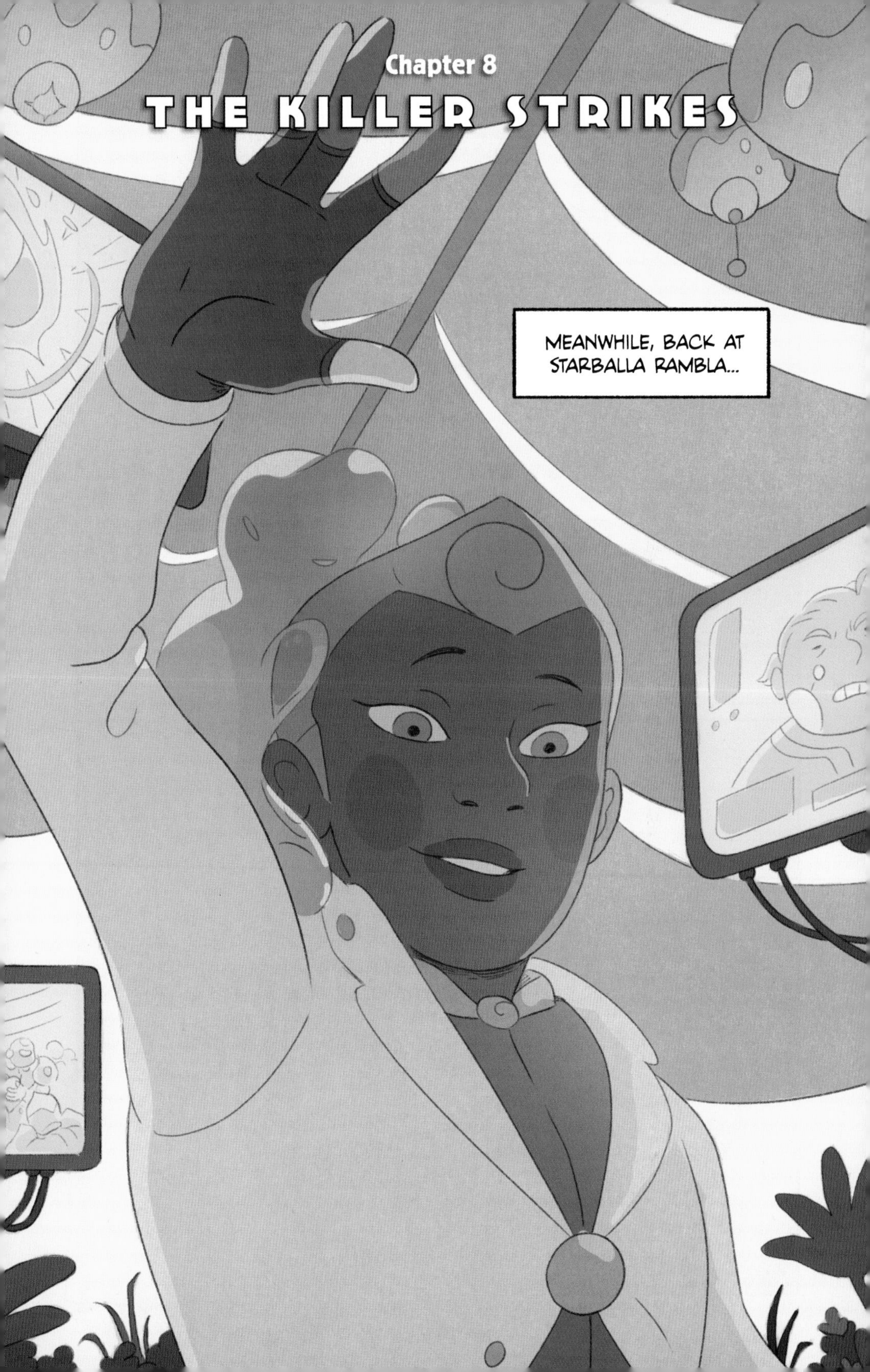
MEANWHILE, BACK AT STARBALLA RAMBLA...

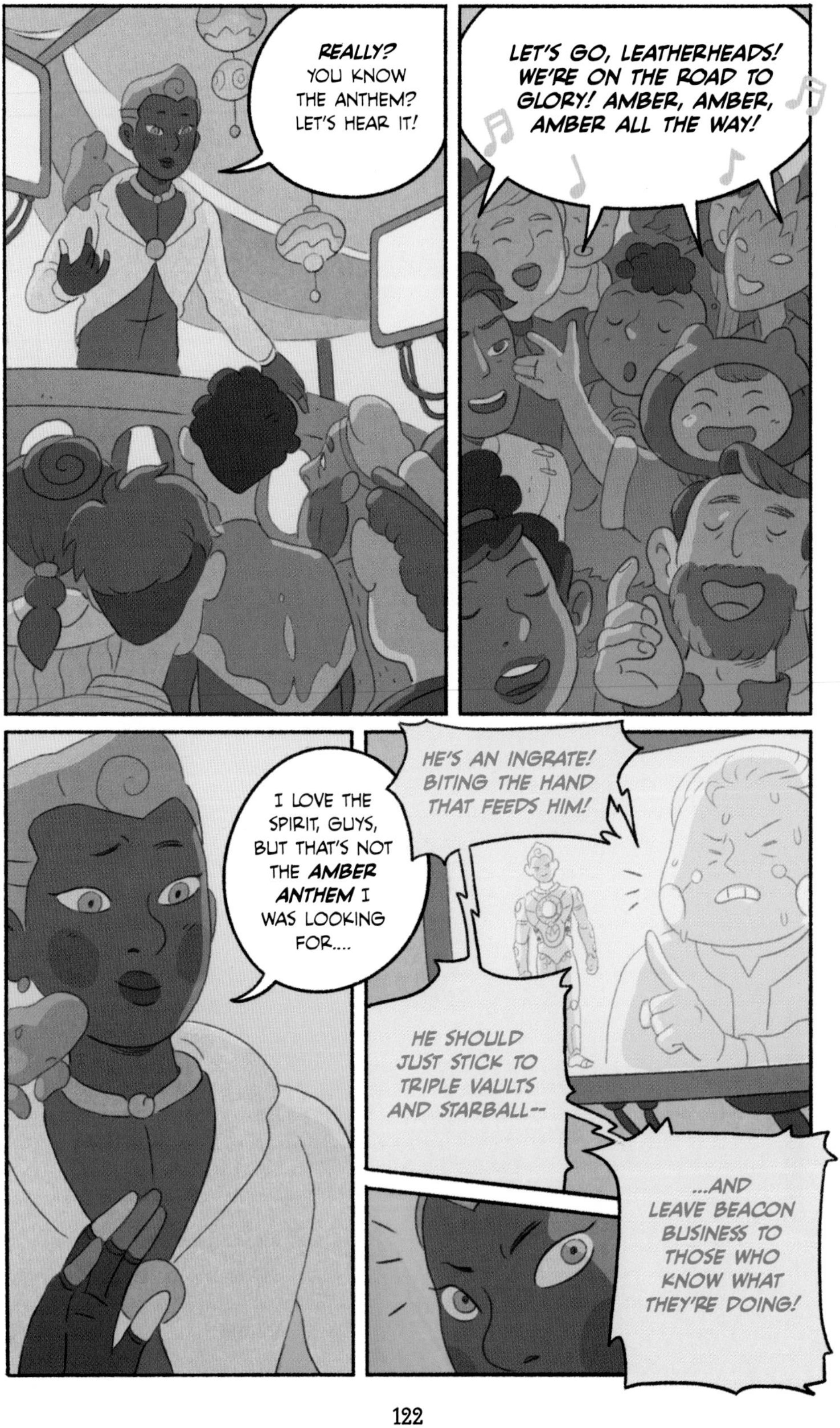
REALLY? YOU KNOW THE ANTHEM? LET'S HEAR IT!
LET'S GO, LEATHERHEADS! WE'RE ON THE ROAD TO GLORY! AMBER, AMBER, AMBER ALL THE WAY!
I LOVE THE SPIRIT, GUYS, BUT THAT'S NOT THE AMBER ANTHEM I WAS LOOKING FOR....
HE'S AN INGRATE! BITING THE HAND THAT FEEDS HIM!
HE SHOULD JUST STICK TO TRIPLE VAULTS AND STARBALL--
...AND LEAVE BEACON BUSINESS TO THOSE WHO KNOW WHAT THEY'RE DOING!

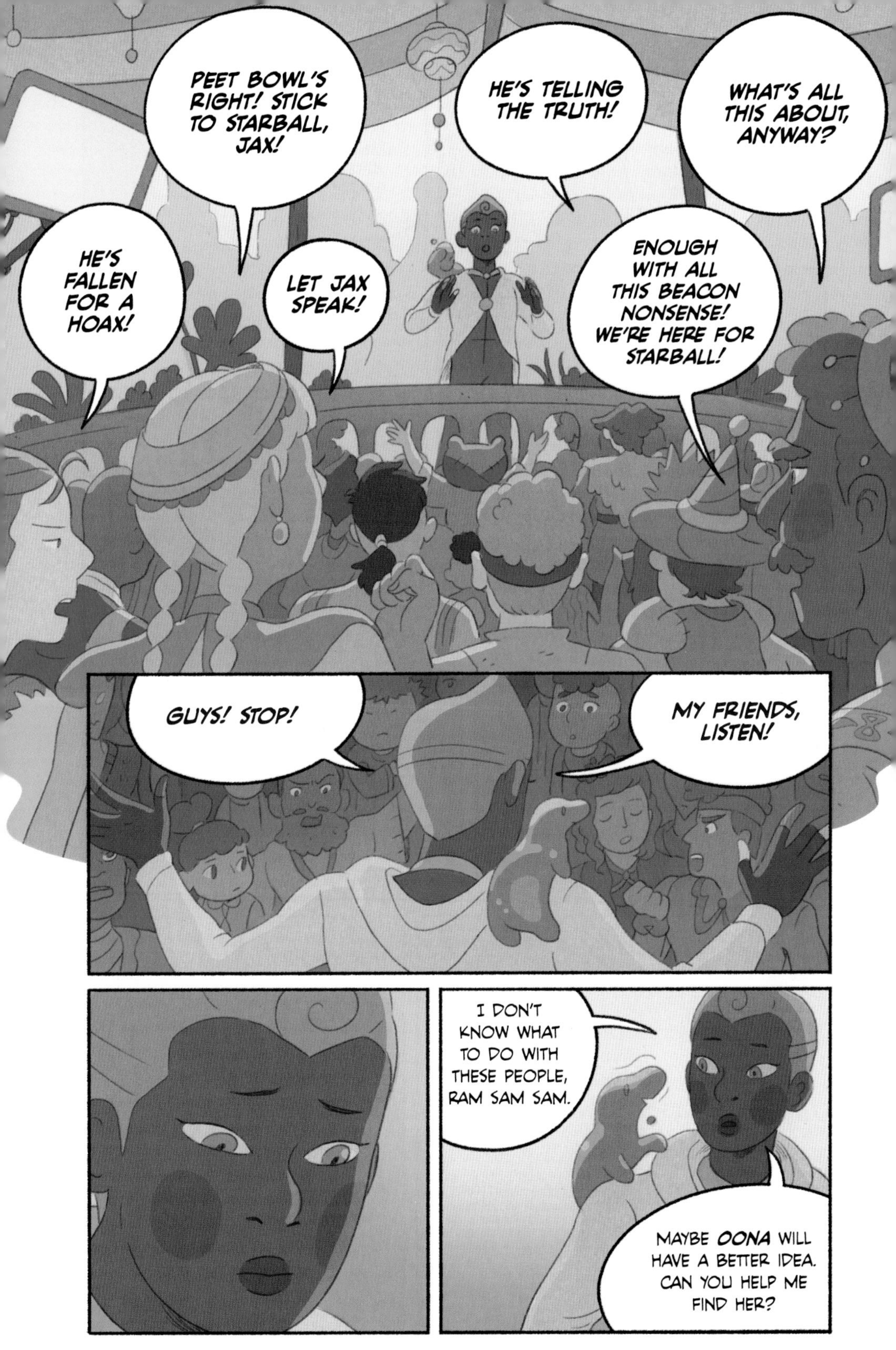
HE'S FALLEN FOR A HOAX!
PEET BOWL'S RIGHT! STICK TO STARBALL, JAX!
LET JAX SPEAK!
HE'S TELLING THE TRUTH!
ENOUGH WITH ALL THIS BEACON NONSENSE! WE'RE HERE FOR STARBALL!
WHAT'S ALL THIS ABOUT, ANYWAY?
GUYS! STOP!
MY FRIENDS, LISTEN!
I DON'T KNOW WHAT TO DO WITH THESE PEOPLE, RAM SAM SAM.
MAYBE OONA WILL HAVE A BETTER IDEA. CAN YOU HELP ME FIND HER?

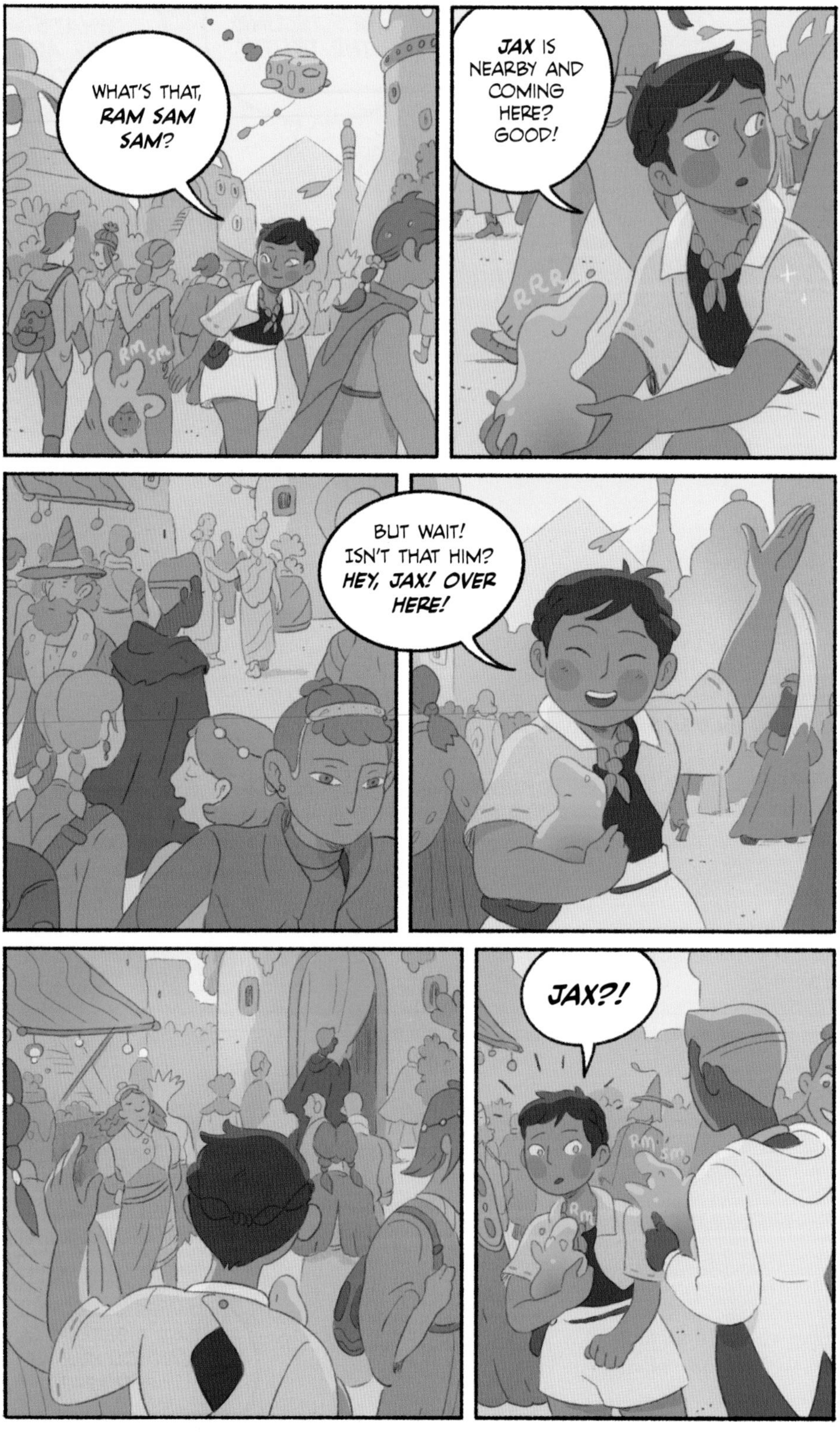
WHAT'S THAT, RAM SAM SAM?
RM SM
JAX IS NEARBY AND COMING HERE? GOOD!
RRR
BUT WAIT! ISN'T THAT HIM? HEY, JAX! OVER HERE!
JAX?!
RM SM

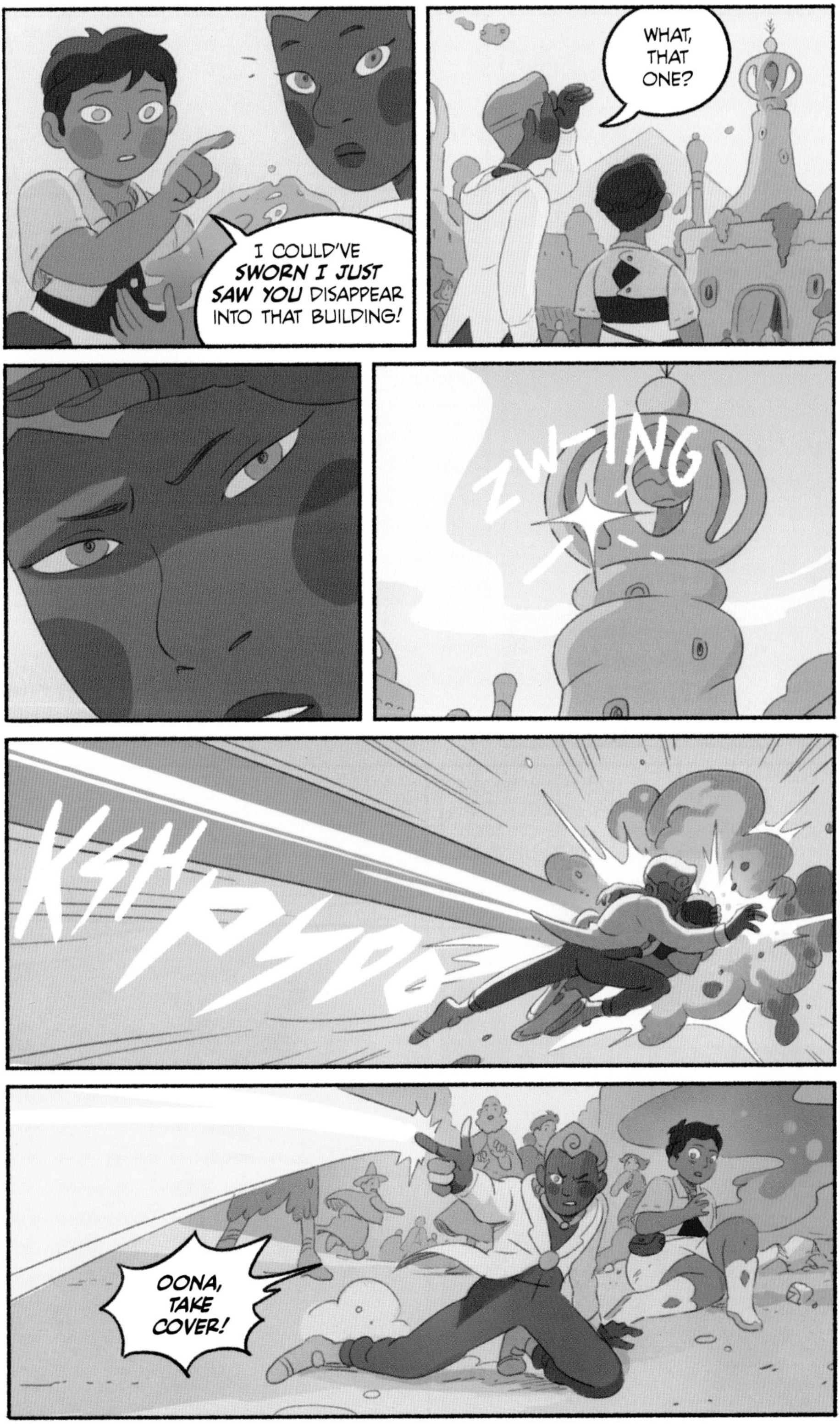

I COULD'VE **SWORN I JUST SAW YOU** DISAPPEAR INTO THAT BUILDING!
WHAT, THAT ONE?
ZW-ING
KSH PSDO
OONA, TAKE COVER!

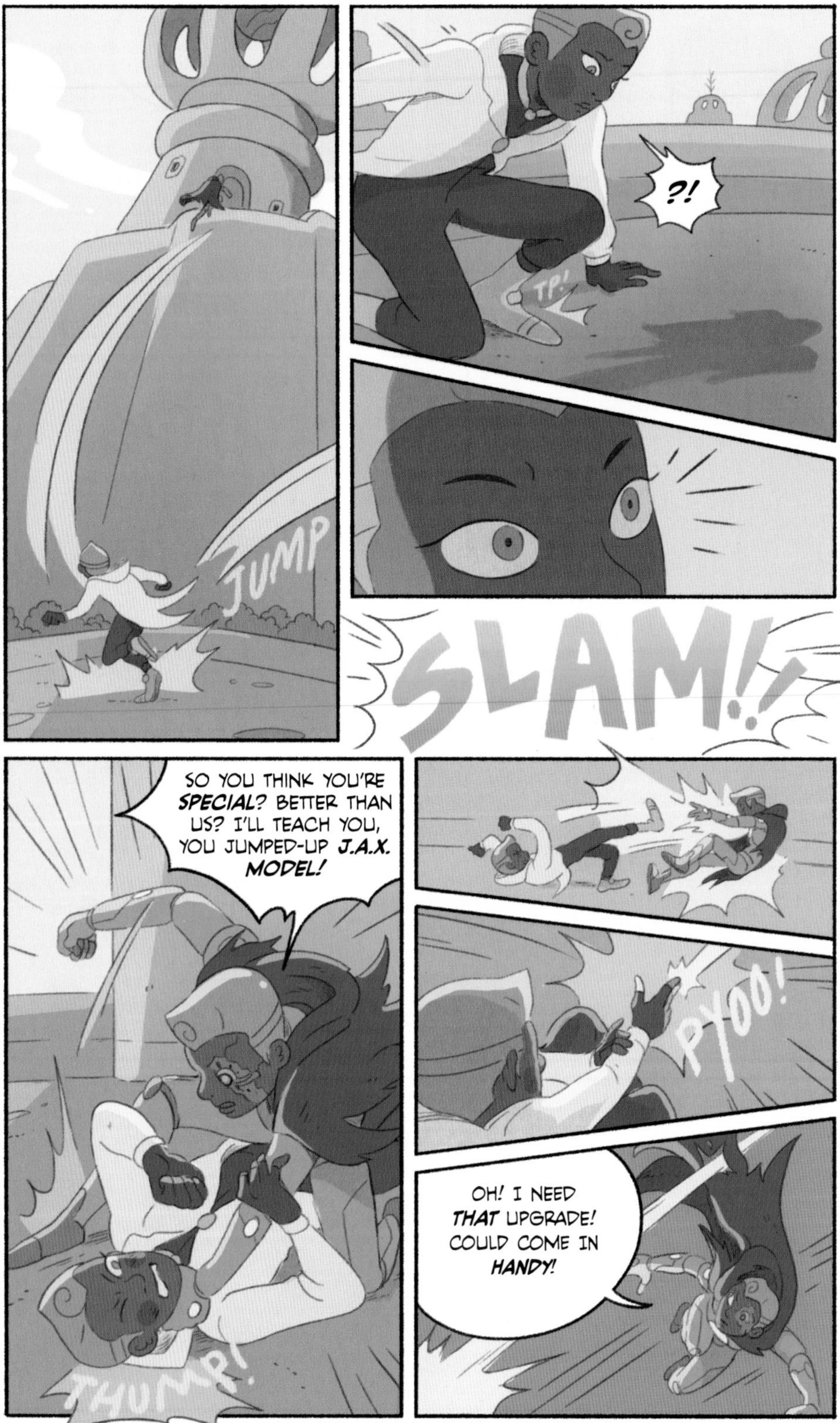
JUMP
?!
TP!
SLAM!!
SO YOU THINK YOU'RE SPECIAL? BETTER THAN US? I'LL TEACH YOU, YOU JUMPED-UP J.A.X. MODEL!
THUMP!
PYOO!
OH! I NEED THAT UPGRADE! COULD COME IN HANDY!

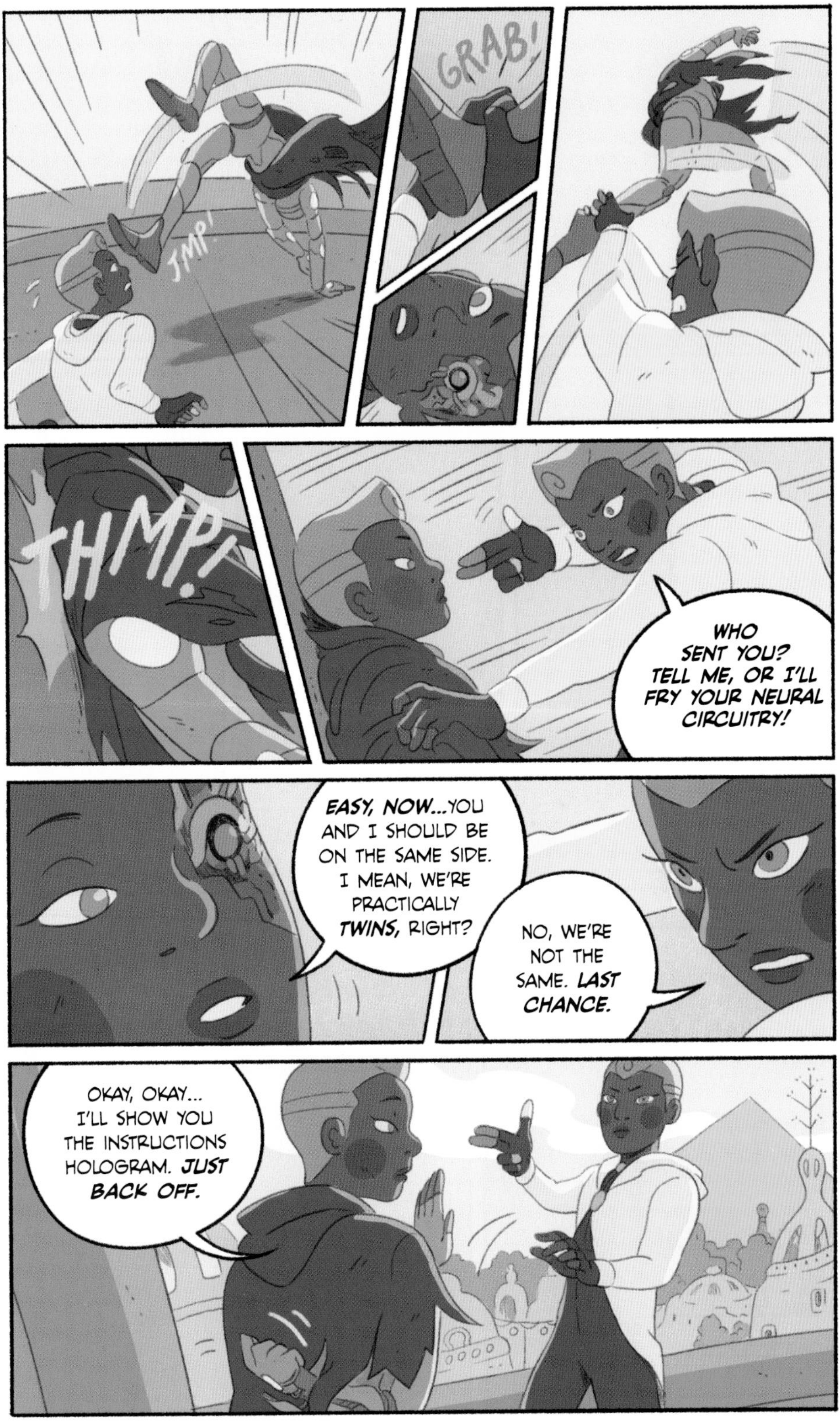
JMP!
GRAB!
THMP!
WHO SENT YOU? TELL ME, OR I'LL FRY YOUR NEURAL CIRCUITRY!
EASY, NOW...YOU AND I SHOULD BE ON THE SAME SIDE. I MEAN, WE'RE PRACTICALLY TWINS, RIGHT?
NO, WE'RE NOT THE SAME. LAST CHANCE.
OKAY, OKAY... I'LL SHOW YOU THE INSTRUCTIONS HOLOGRAM. JUST BACK OFF.

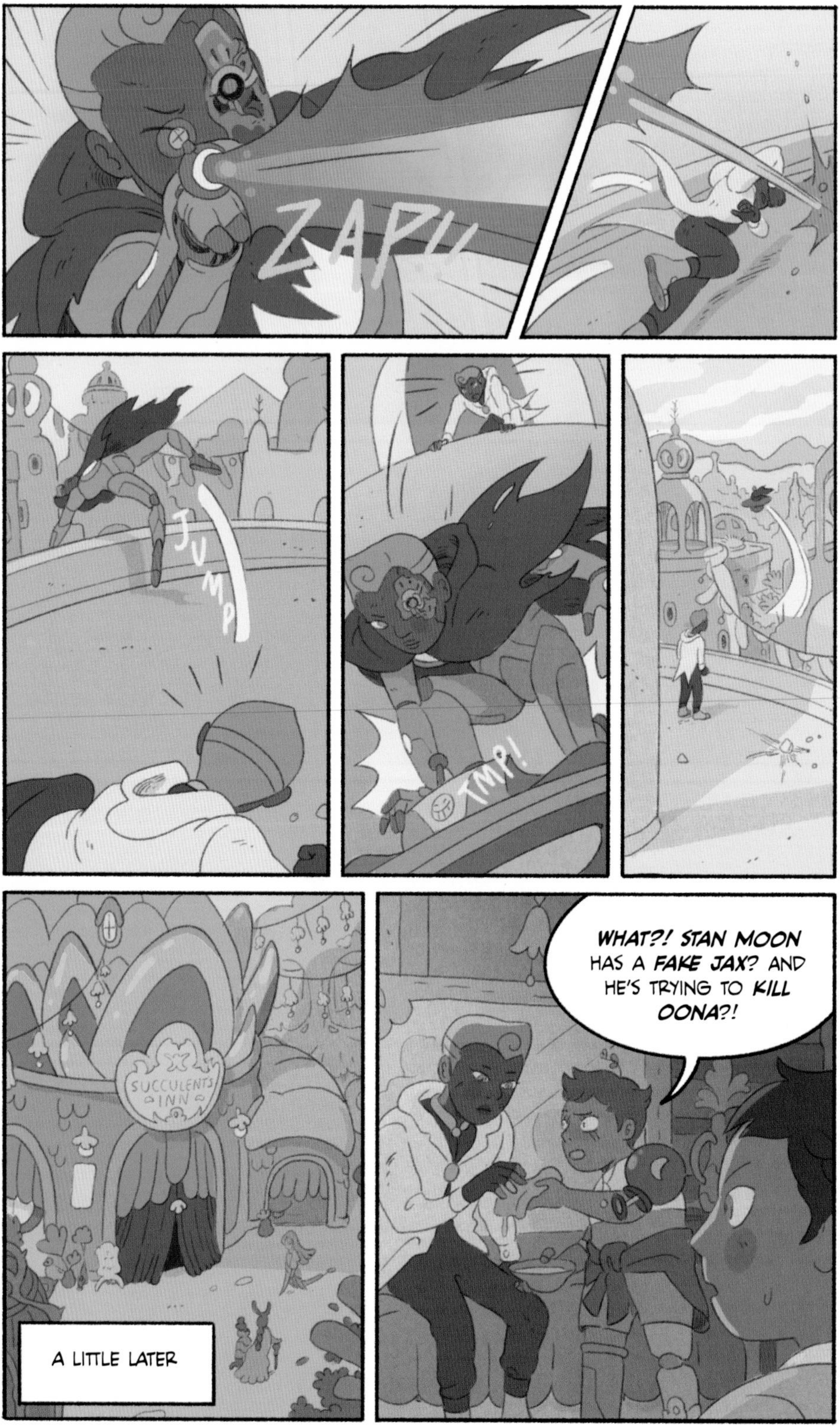
ZAP!!
JUMP
TMP!
A LITTLE LATER
SUCCULENTS INN
WHAT?! STAN MOON HAS A FAKE JAX? AND HE'S TRYING TO KILL OONA?!

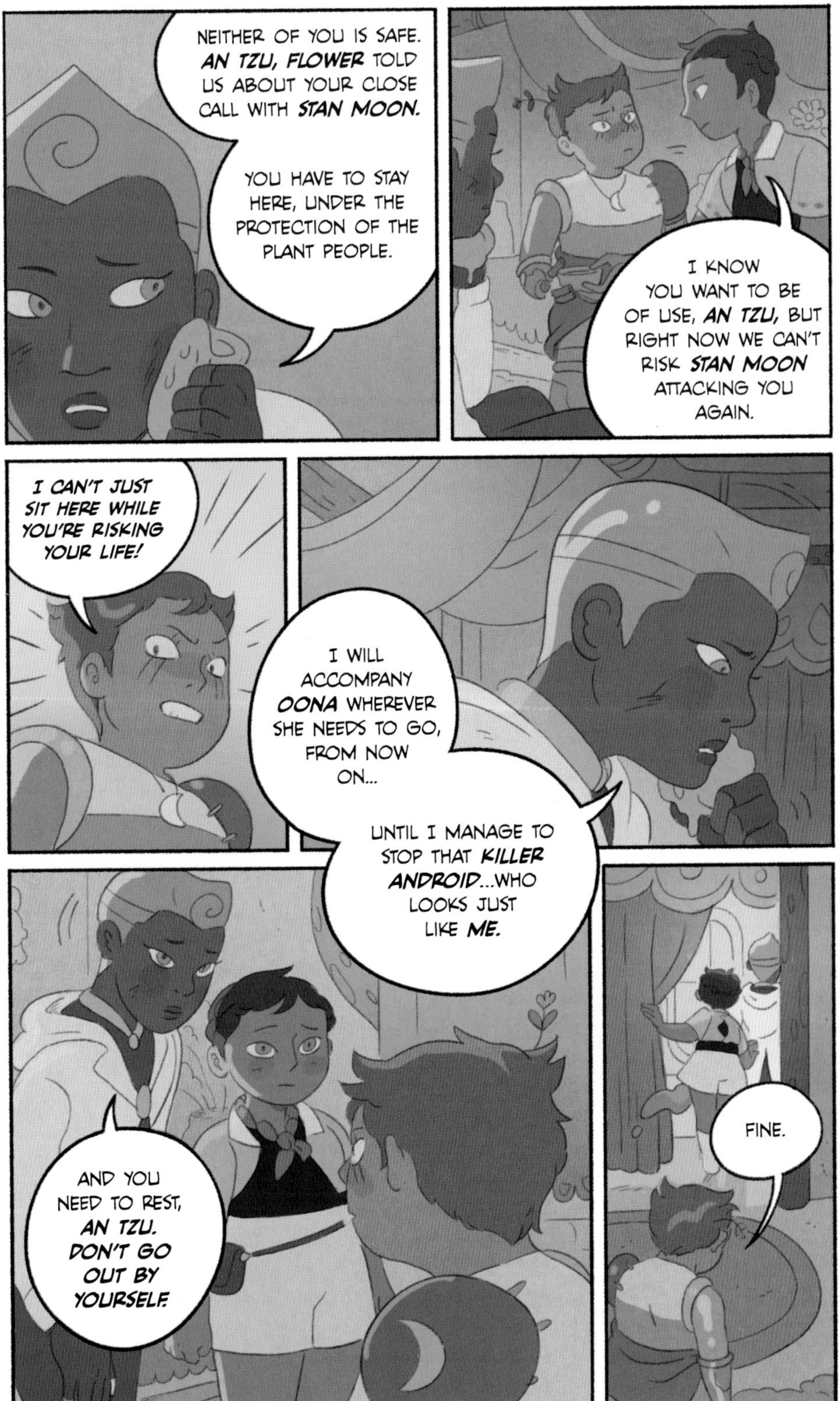

NEITHER OF YOU IS SAFE. AN TZU, FLOWER TOLD US ABOUT YOUR CLOSE CALL WITH STAN MOON.
YOU HAVE TO STAY HERE, UNDER THE PROTECTION OF THE PLANT PEOPLE.
I KNOW YOU WANT TO BE OF USE, AN TZU, BUT RIGHT NOW WE CAN'T RISK STAN MOON ATTACKING YOU AGAIN.
I CAN'T JUST SIT HERE WHILE YOU'RE RISKING YOUR LIFE!
I WILL ACCOMPANY OONA WHEREVER SHE NEEDS TO GO, FROM NOW ON...
UNTIL I MANAGE TO STOP THAT KILLER ANDROID...WHO LOOKS JUST LIKE ME.
AND YOU NEED TO REST, AN TZU. DON'T GO OUT BY YOURSELF.
FINE.

Chapter 9

AN ANCIENT GRIEVANCE

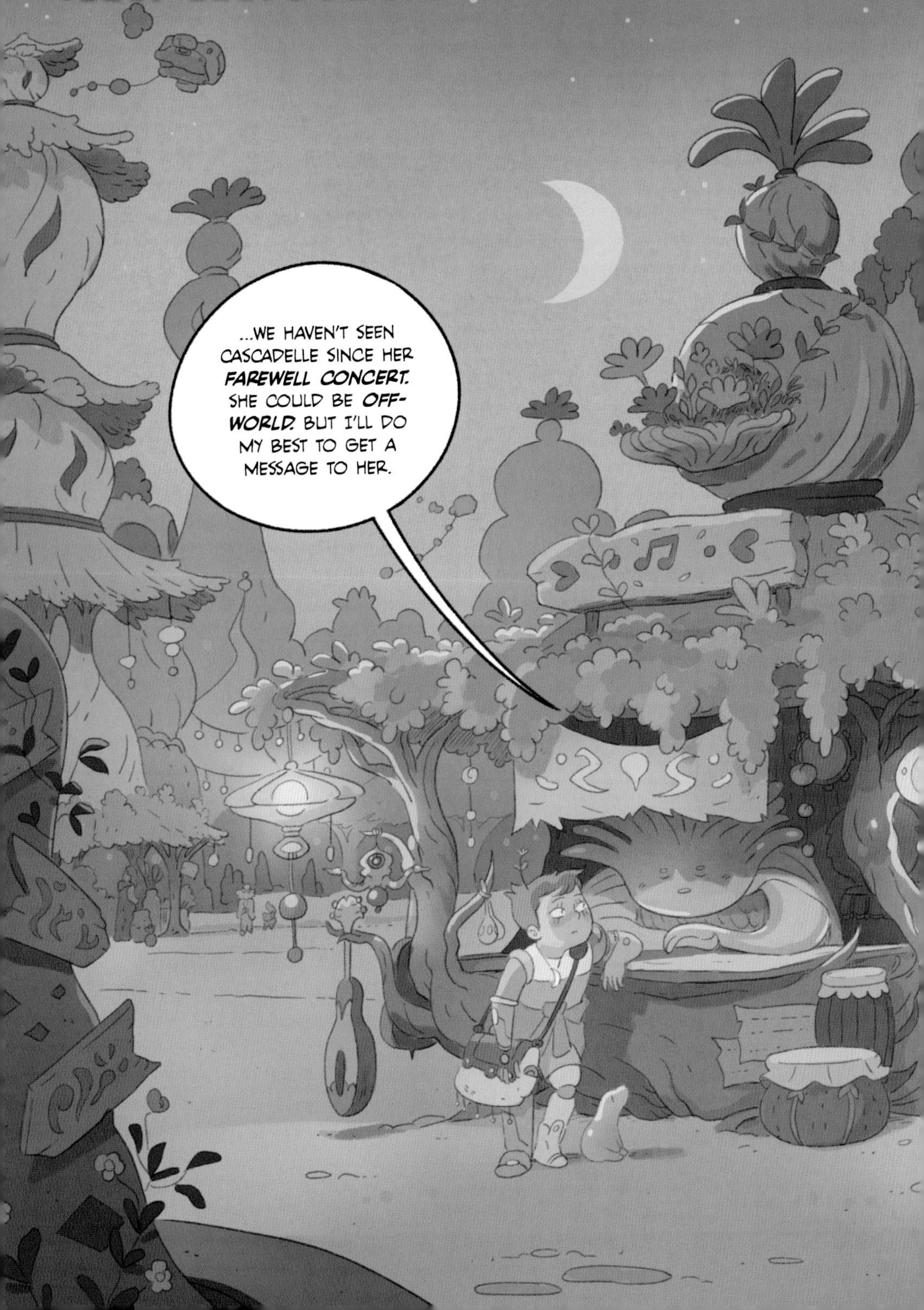
...WE HAVEN'T SEEN CASCADELLE SINCE HER *FAREWELL CONCERT.* SHE COULD BE *OFF-WORLD.* BUT I'LL DO MY BEST TO GET A MESSAGE TO HER.

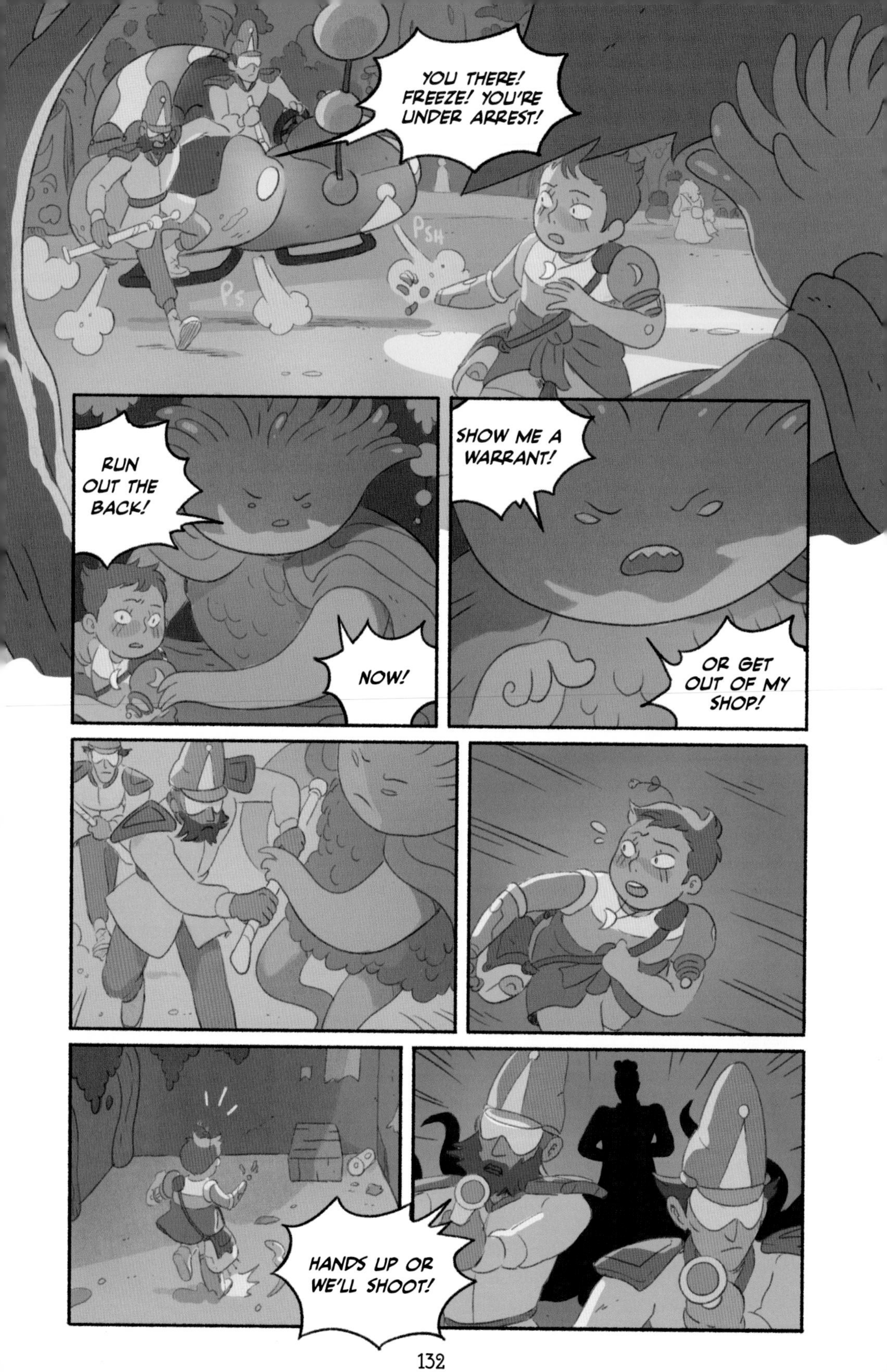
YOU THERE! FREEZE! YOU'RE UNDER ARREST!
PSH
PS
RUN OUT THE BACK!
NOW!
SHOW ME A WARRANT!
OR GET OUT OF MY SHOP!
HANDS UP OR WE'LL SHOOT!

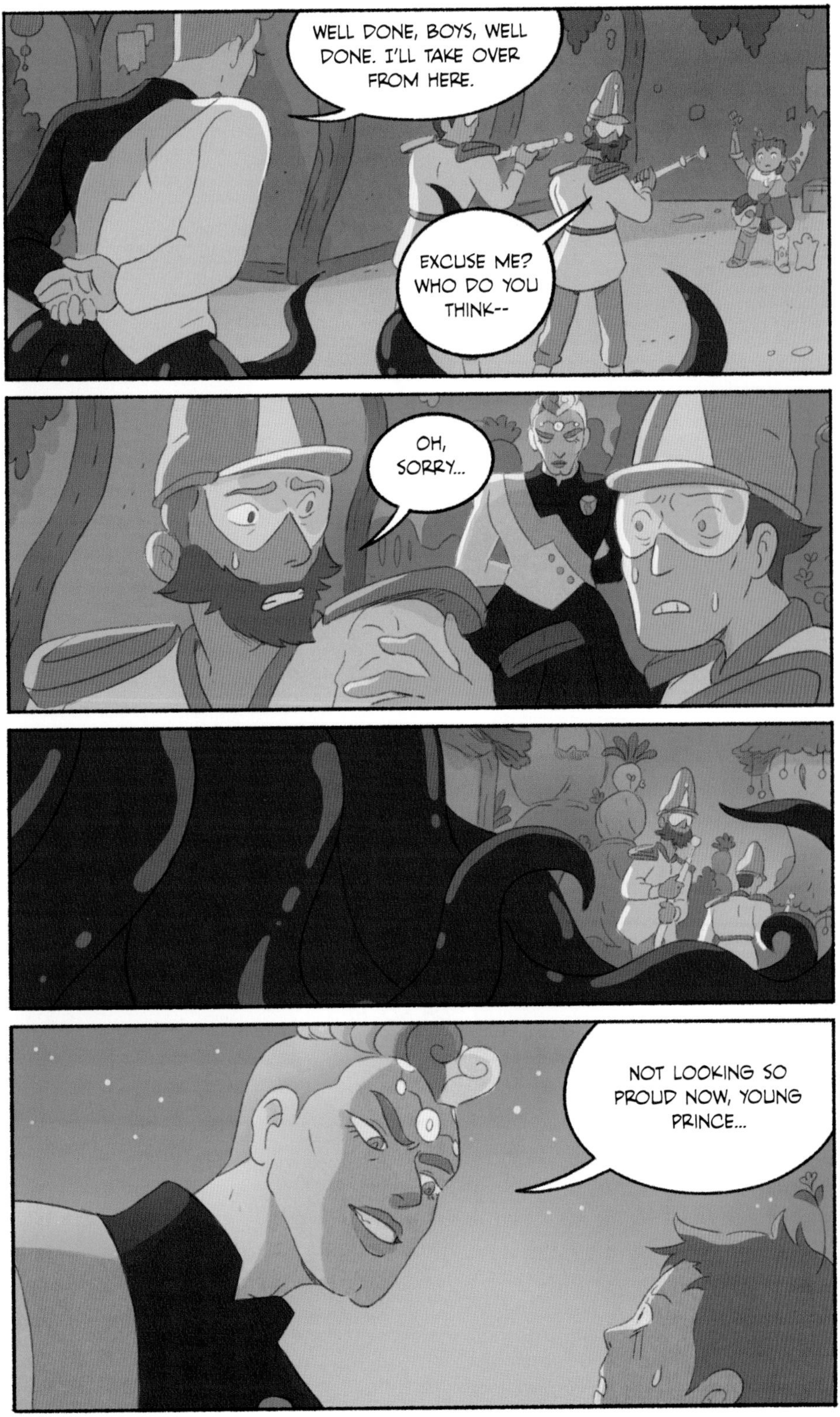
WELL DONE, BOYS, WELL DONE. I'LL TAKE OVER FROM HERE.
EXCUSE ME? WHO DO YOU THINK--
OH, SORRY...
NOT LOOKING SO PROUD NOW, YOUNG PRINCE...

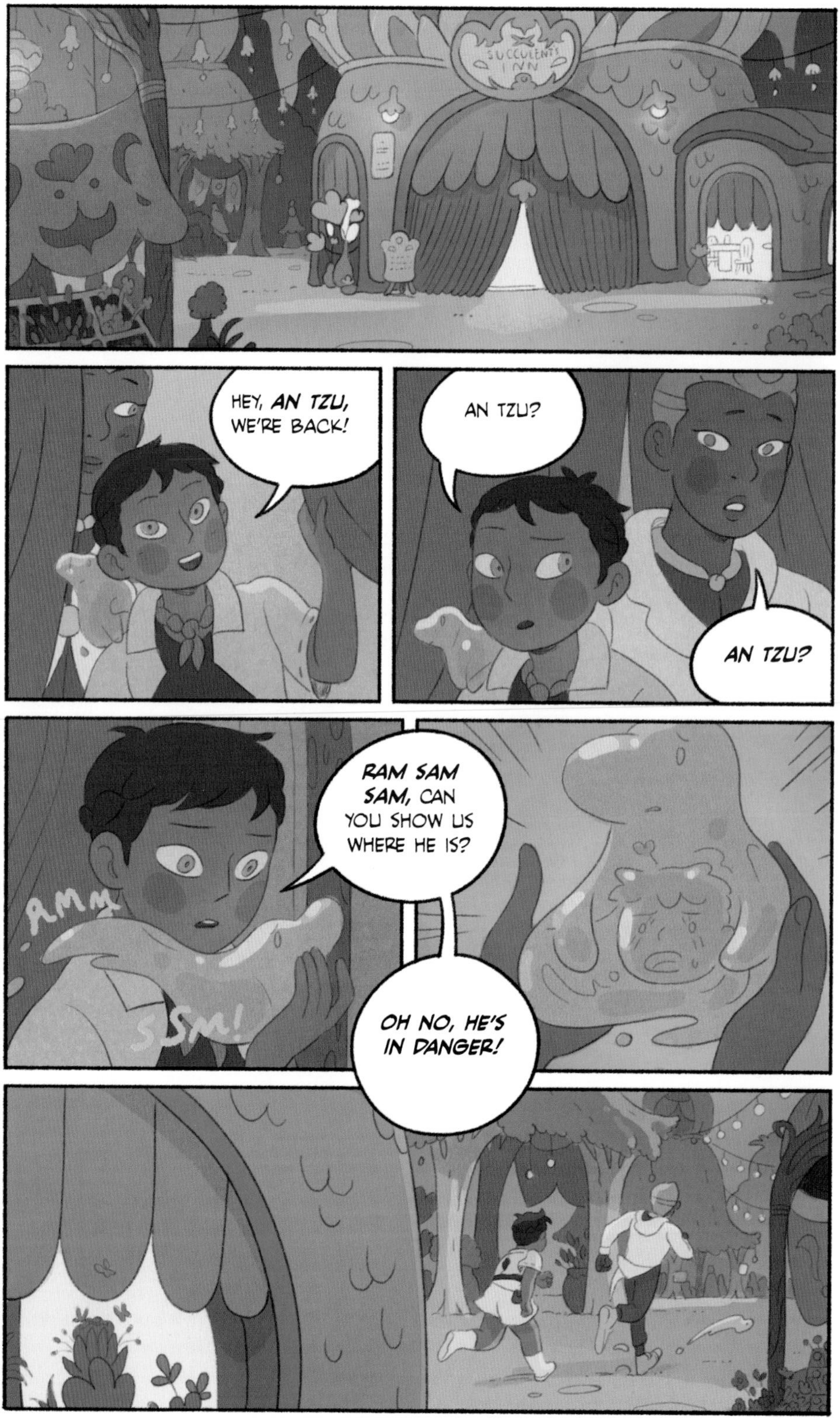
SUCCULENTS INN
HEY, AN TZU, WE'RE BACK!
AN TZU?
AN TZU?
RAM SAM SAM, CAN YOU SHOW US WHERE HE IS?
AMM
SSM!
OH NO, HE'S IN DANGER!

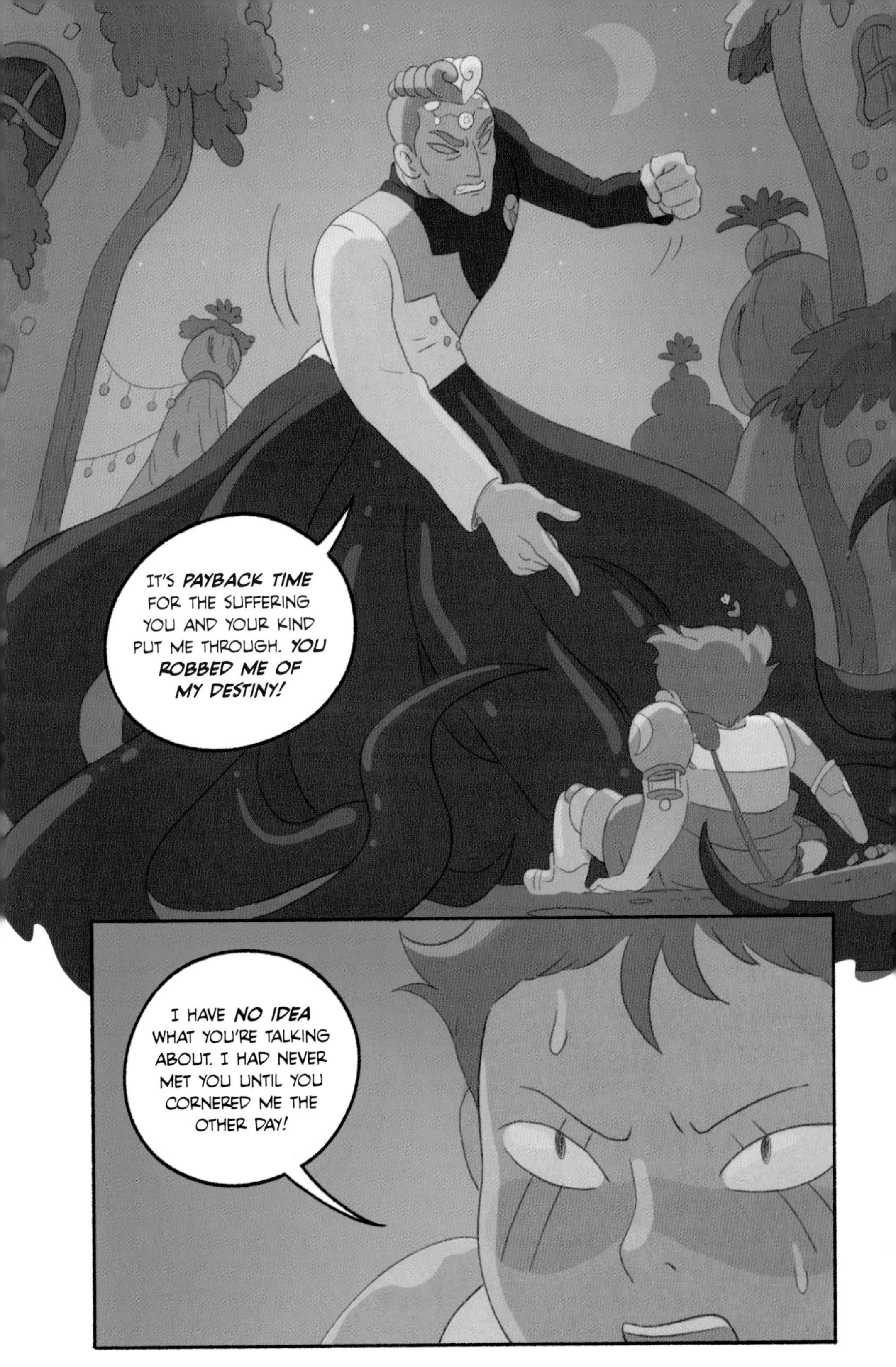
IT'S PAYBACK TIME FOR THE SUFFERING YOU AND YOUR KIND PUT ME THROUGH. YOU ROBBED ME OF MY DESTINY!
I HAVE NO IDEA WHAT YOU'RE TALKING ABOUT. I HAD NEVER MET YOU UNTIL YOU CORNERED ME THE OTHER DAY!

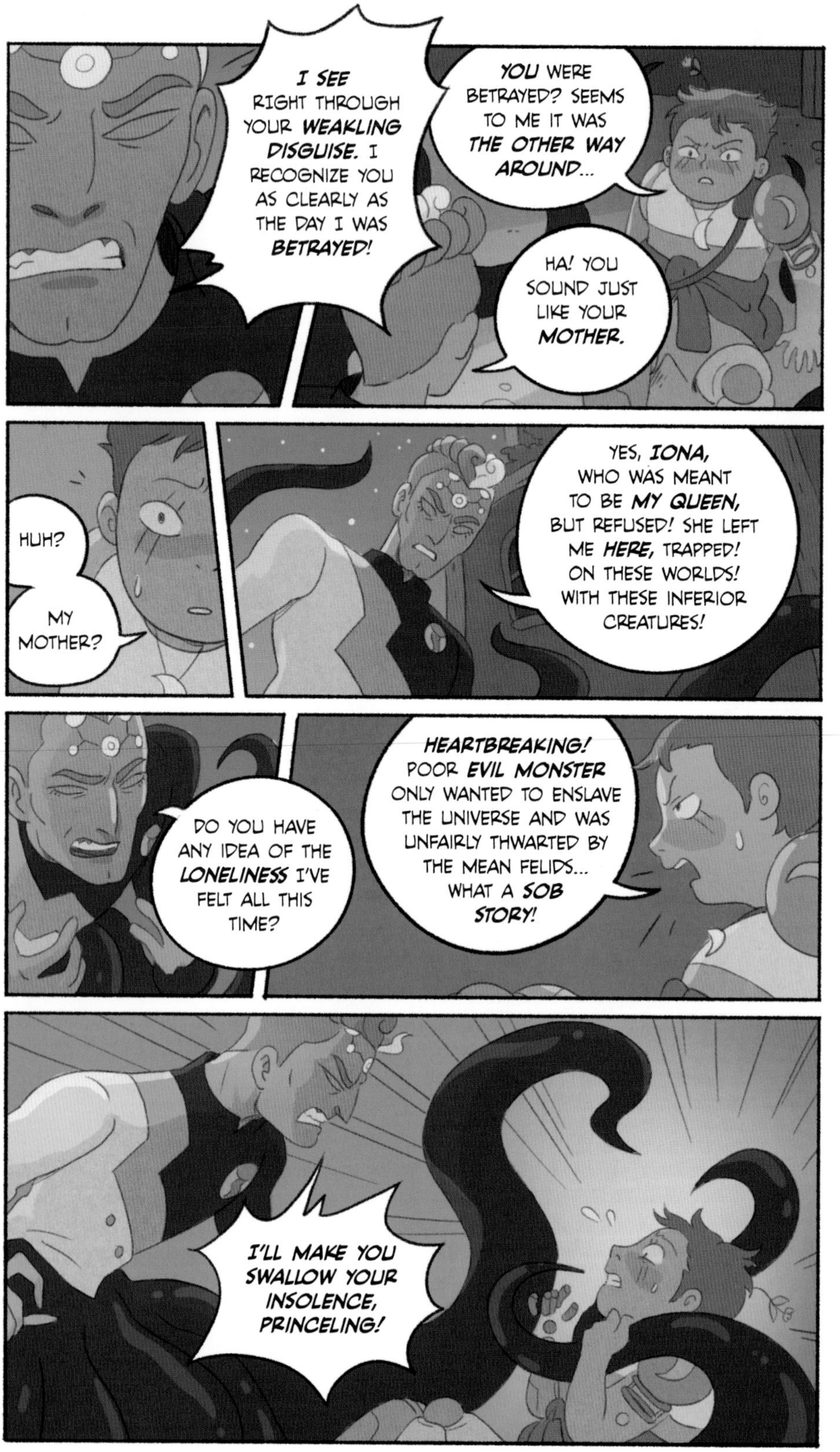
I SEE RIGHT THROUGH YOUR WEAKLING DISGUISE. I RECOGNIZE YOU AS CLEARLY AS THE DAY I WAS BETRAYED!
YOU WERE BETRAYED? SEEMS TO ME IT WAS THE OTHER WAY AROUND...
HA! YOU SOUND JUST LIKE YOUR MOTHER.
HUH?
MY MOTHER?
YES, IONA, WHO WAS MEANT TO BE MY QUEEN, BUT REFUSED! SHE LEFT ME HERE, TRAPPED! ON THESE WORLDS! WITH THESE INFERIOR CREATURES!
DO YOU HAVE ANY IDEA OF THE LONELINESS I'VE FELT ALL THIS TIME?
HEARTBREAKING! POOR EVIL MONSTER ONLY WANTED TO ENSLAVE THE UNIVERSE AND WAS UNFAIRLY THWARTED BY THE MEAN FELIDS... WHAT A SOB STORY!
I'LL MAKE YOU SWALLOW YOUR INSOLENCE, PRINCELING!

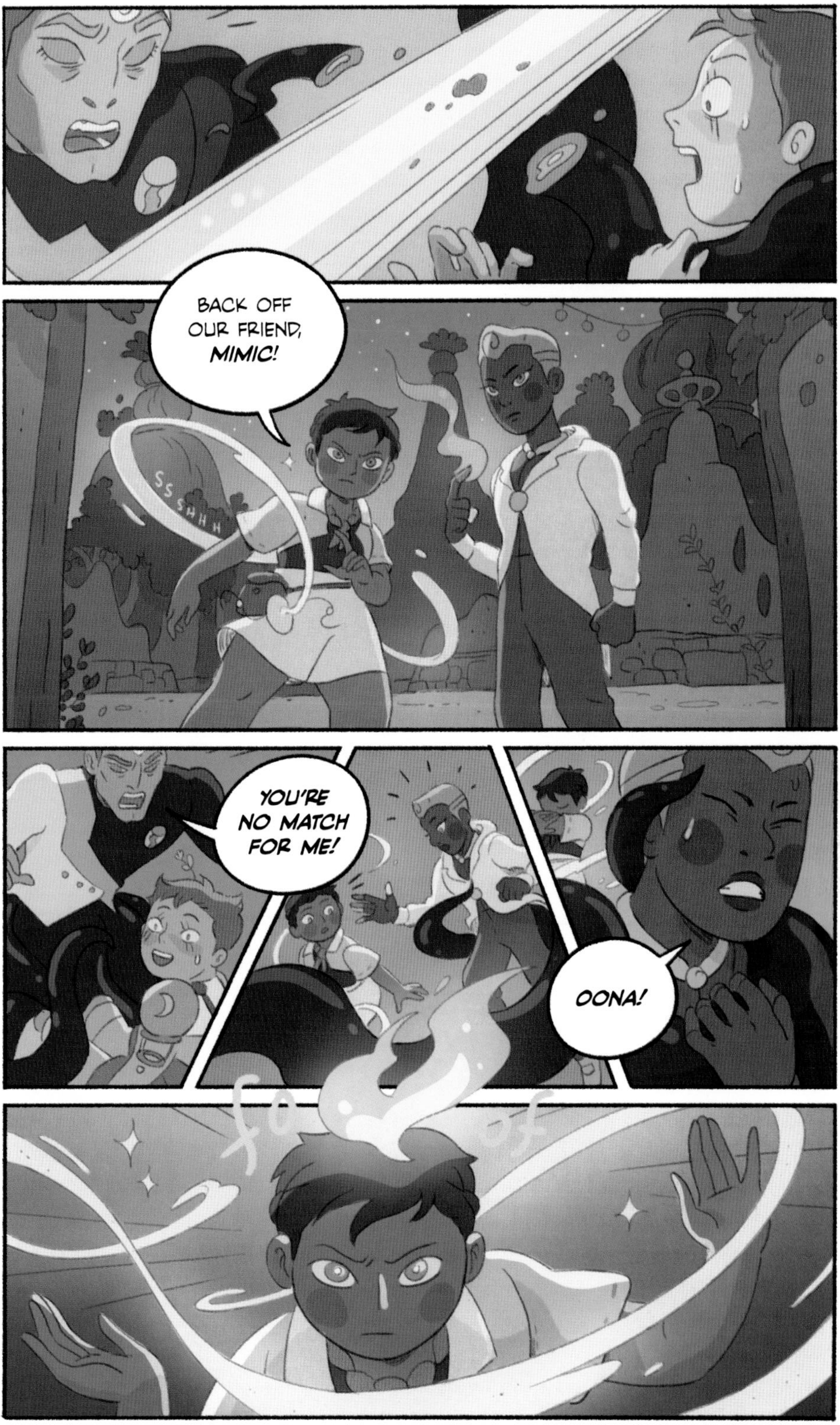
BACK OFF OUR FRIEND, MIMIC!
SSSHHH
YOU'RE NO MATCH FOR ME!
OONA!

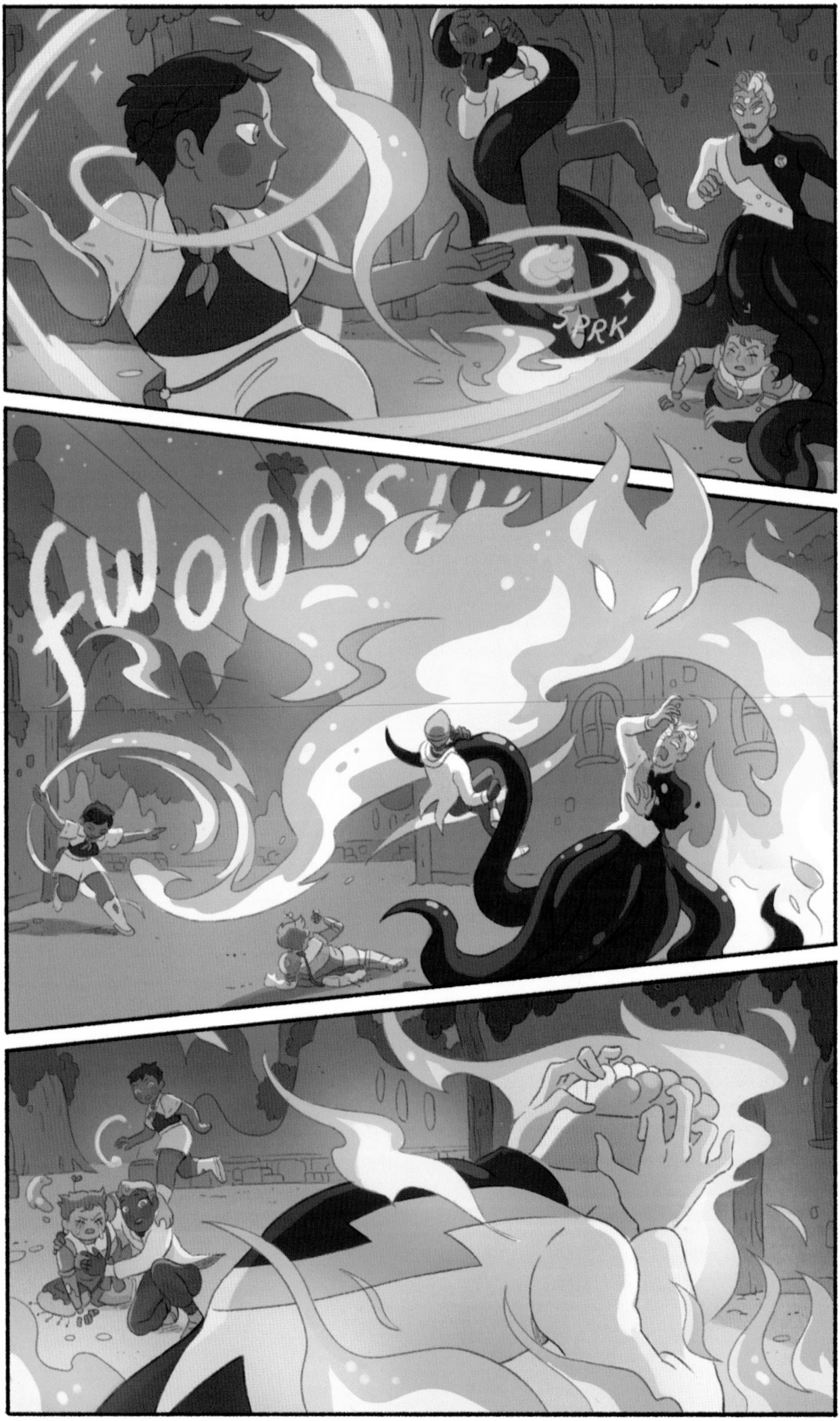
SPRK
FWOOOSH

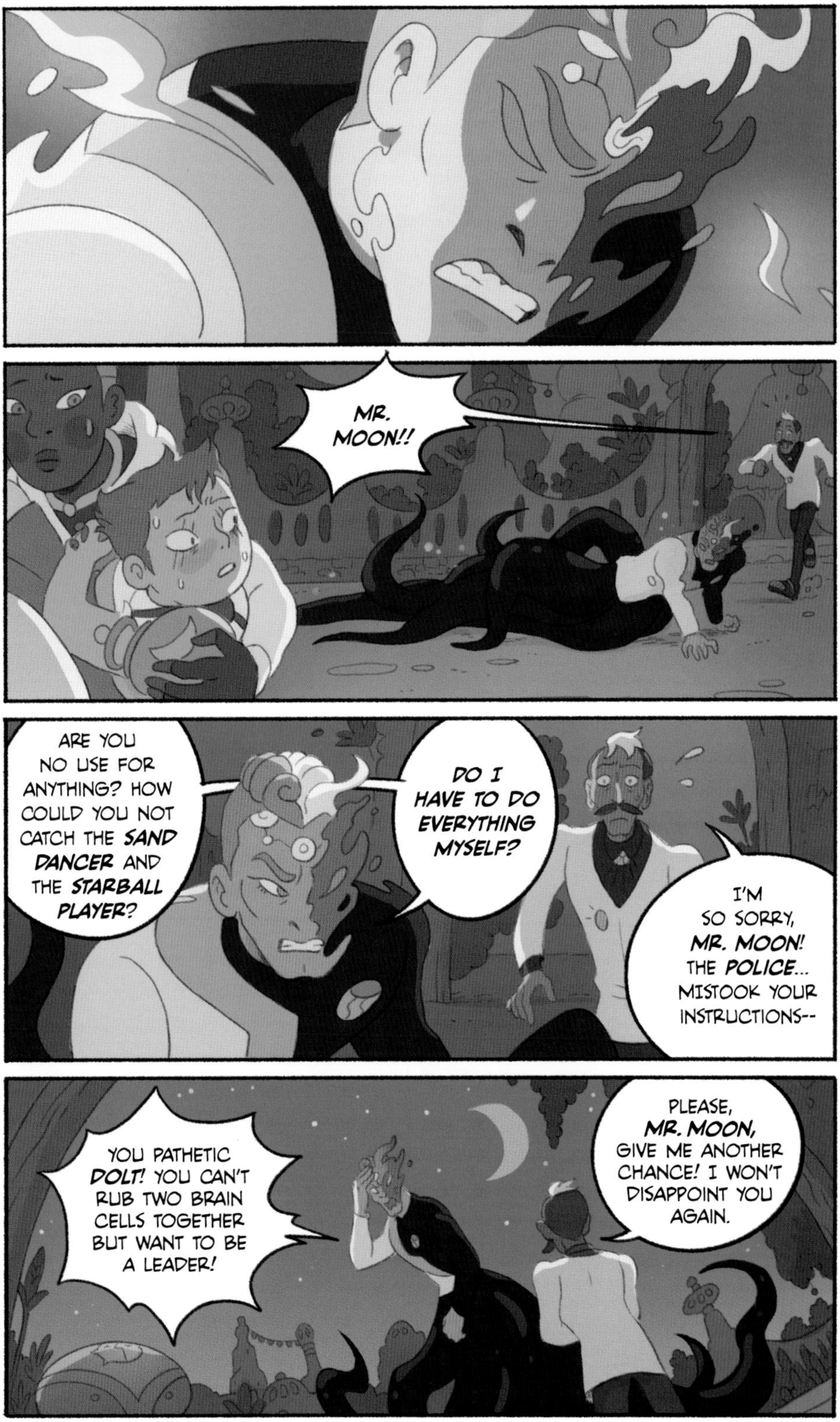

MR. MOON!!
ARE YOU NO USE FOR ANYTHING? HOW COULD YOU NOT CATCH THE SAND DANCER AND THE STARBALL PLAYER?
DO I HAVE TO DO EVERYTHING MYSELF?
I'M SO SORRY, MR. MOON! THE POLICE... MISTOOK YOUR INSTRUCTIONS--
YOU PATHETIC DOLT! YOU CAN'T RUB TWO BRAIN CELLS TOGETHER BUT WANT TO BE A LEADER!
PLEASE, MR. MOON, GIVE ME ANOTHER CHANCE! I WON'T DISAPPOINT YOU AGAIN.

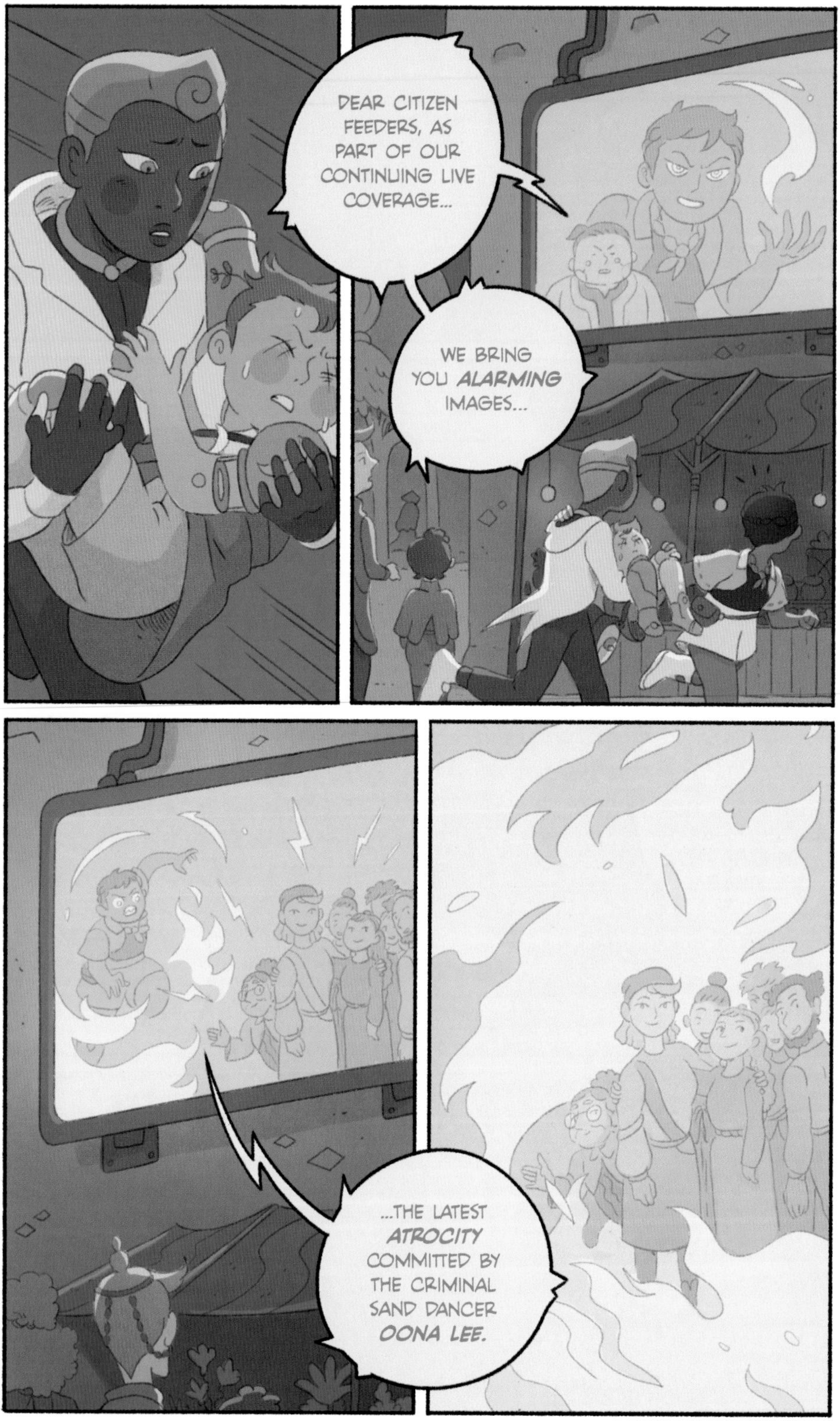
DEAR CITIZEN FEEDERS, AS PART OF OUR CONTINUING LIVE COVERAGE...
WE BRING YOU *ALARMING* IMAGES...
...THE LATEST *ATROCITY* COMMITTED BY THE CRIMINAL SAND DANCER *OONA LEE.*

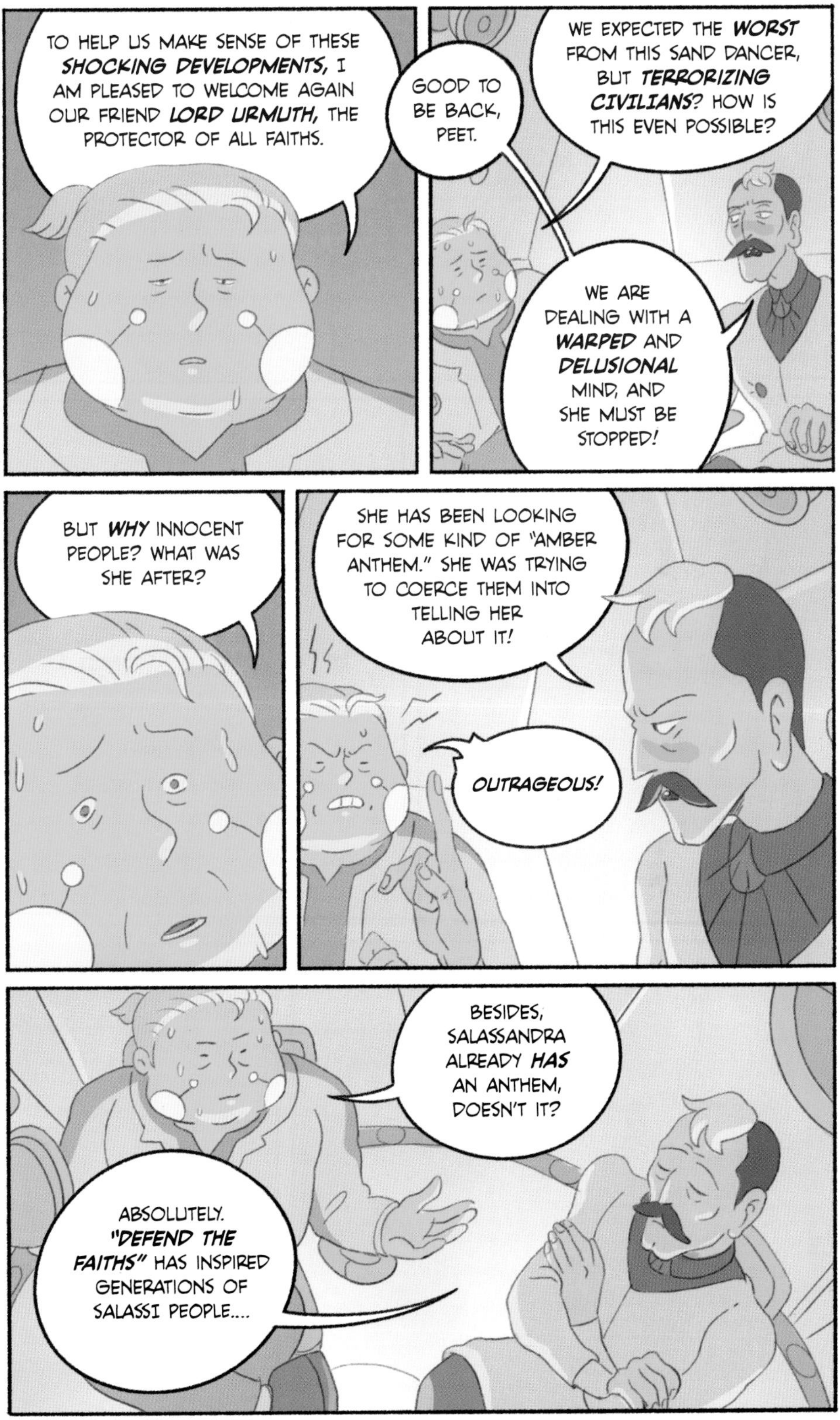
TO HELP US MAKE SENSE OF THESE SHOCKING DEVELOPMENTS, I AM PLEASED TO WELCOME AGAIN OUR FRIEND LORD URMUTH, THE PROTECTOR OF ALL FAITHS.
GOOD TO BE BACK, PEET.
WE EXPECTED THE WORST FROM THIS SAND DANCER, BUT TERRORIZING CIVILIANS? HOW IS THIS EVEN POSSIBLE?
WE ARE DEALING WITH A WARPED AND DELUSIONAL MIND, AND SHE MUST BE STOPPED!
BUT WHY INNOCENT PEOPLE? WHAT WAS SHE AFTER?
SHE HAS BEEN LOOKING FOR SOME KIND OF "AMBER ANTHEM." SHE WAS TRYING TO COERCE THEM INTO TELLING HER ABOUT IT!
OUTRAGEOUS!
BESIDES, SALASSANDRA ALREADY HAS AN ANTHEM, DOESN'T IT?
ABSOLUTELY. "DEFEND THE FAITHS" HAS INSPIRED GENERATIONS OF SALASSI PEOPLE....

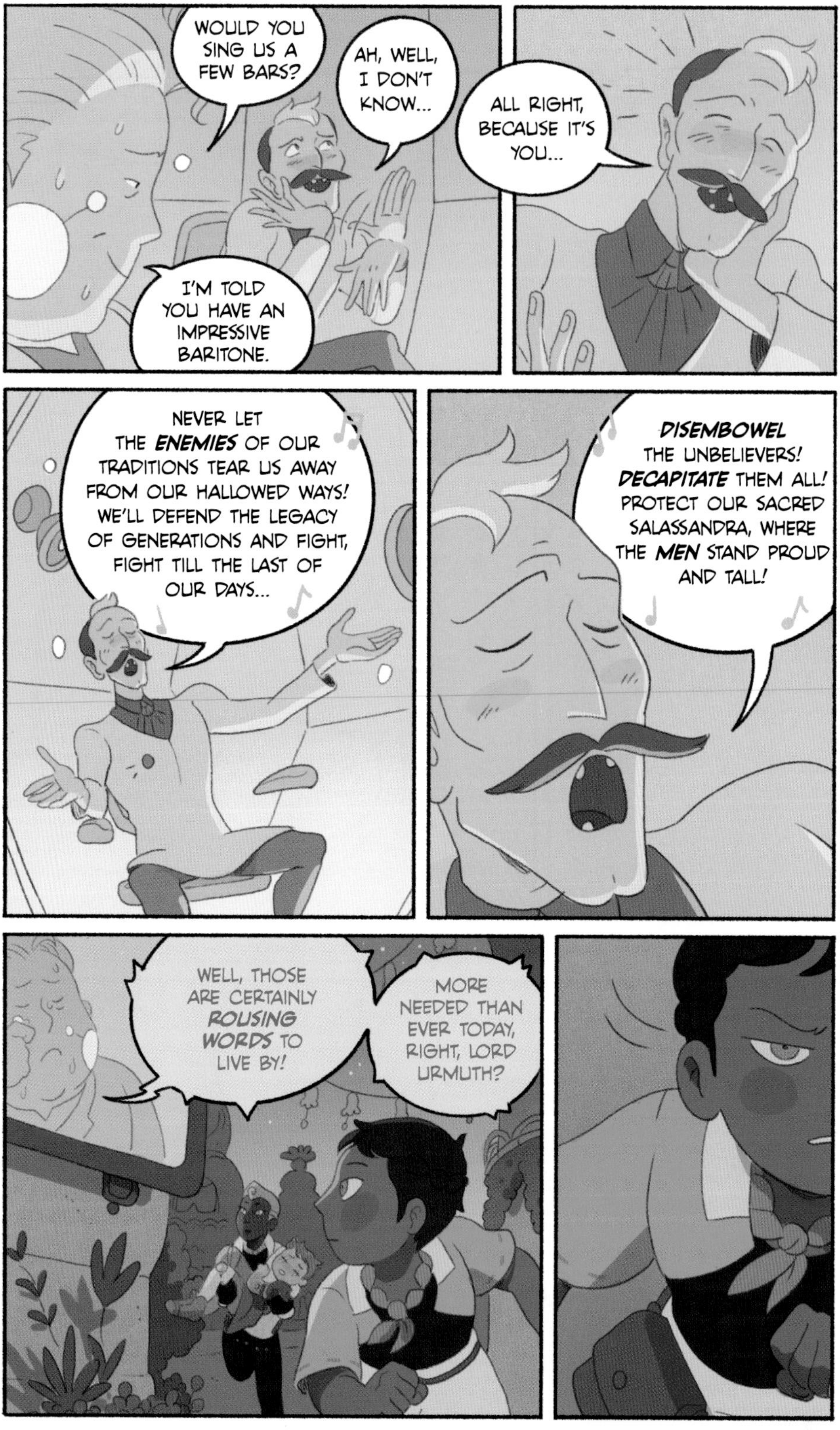

WOULD YOU SING US A FEW BARS?
AH, WELL, I DON'T KNOW...
I'M TOLD YOU HAVE AN IMPRESSIVE BARITONE.
ALL RIGHT, BECAUSE IT'S YOU...
NEVER LET THE **ENEMIES** OF OUR TRADITIONS TEAR US AWAY FROM OUR HALLOWED WAYS! WE'LL DEFEND THE LEGACY OF GENERATIONS AND FIGHT, FIGHT TILL THE LAST OF OUR DAYS...
DISEMBOWEL THE UNBELIEVERS! **DECAPITATE** THEM ALL! PROTECT OUR SACRED SALASSANDRA, WHERE THE **MEN** STAND PROUD AND TALL!
WELL, THOSE ARE CERTAINLY **ROUSING WORDS** TO LIVE BY!
MORE NEEDED THAN EVER TODAY, RIGHT, LORD URMUTH?

Chapter 10

THE GRIP TIGHTENS

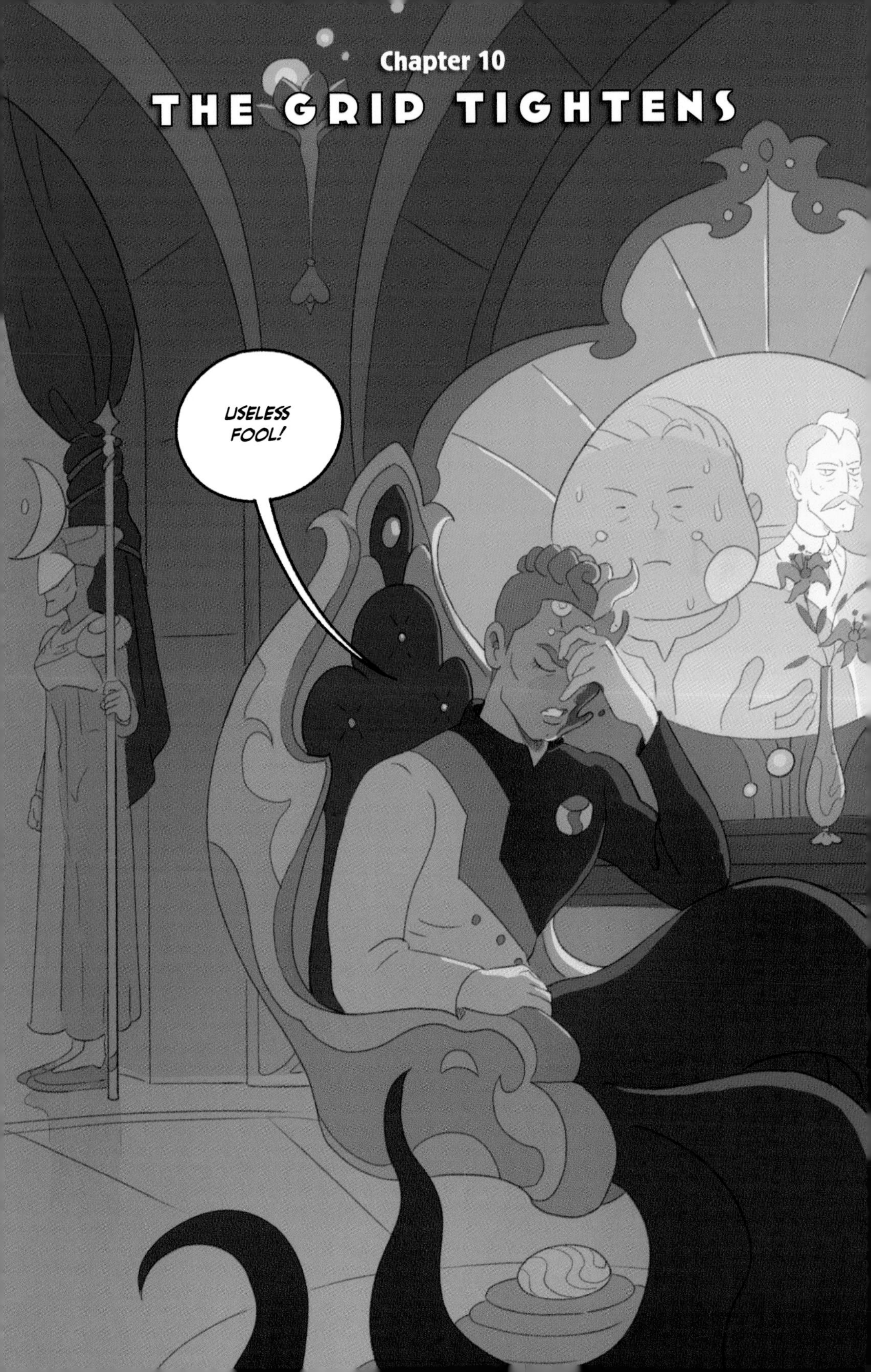
USELESS FOOL!

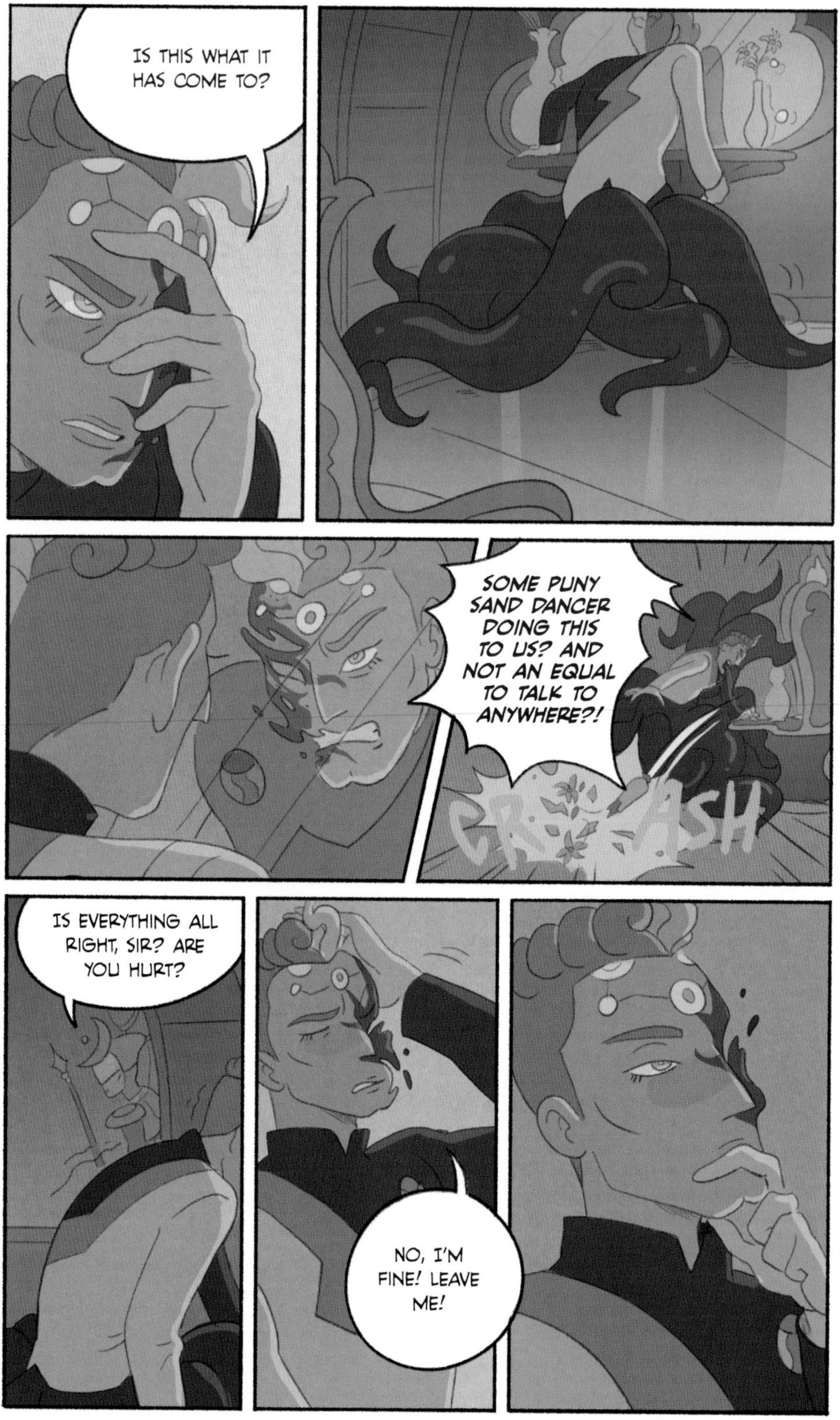
IS THIS WHAT IT HAS COME TO?
SOME PUNY SAND DANCER DOING THIS TO US? AND NOT AN EQUAL TO TALK TO ANYWHERE?!
CRASH
IS EVERYTHING ALL RIGHT, SIR? ARE YOU HURT?
NO, I'M FINE! LEAVE ME!

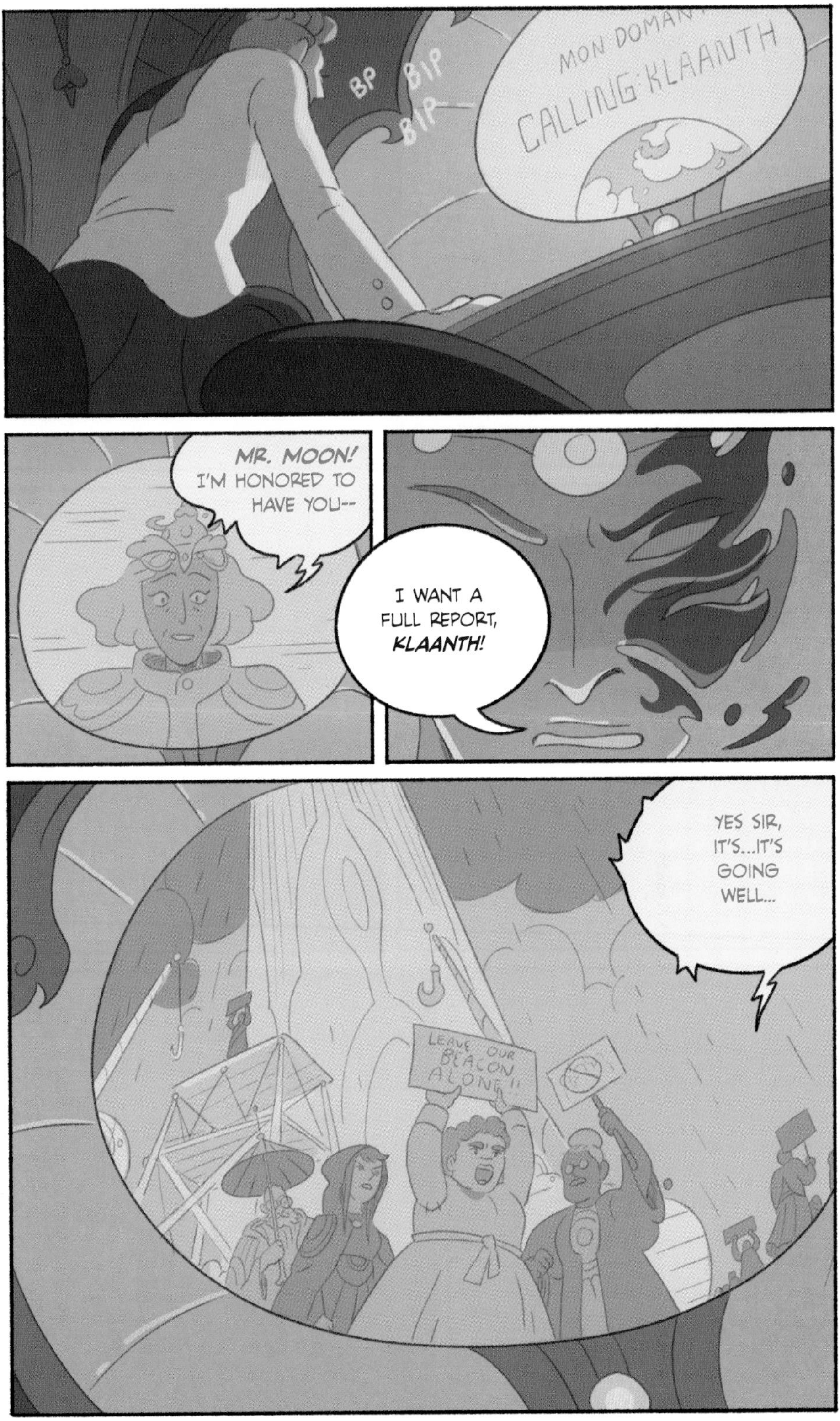
BP BIP BIP
CALLING:KLAANTH
MR. MOON! I'M HONORED TO HAVE YOU--
I WANT A FULL REPORT, KLAANTH!
YES SIR, IT'S...IT'S GOING WELL...
LEAVE OUR BEACON ALONE!!

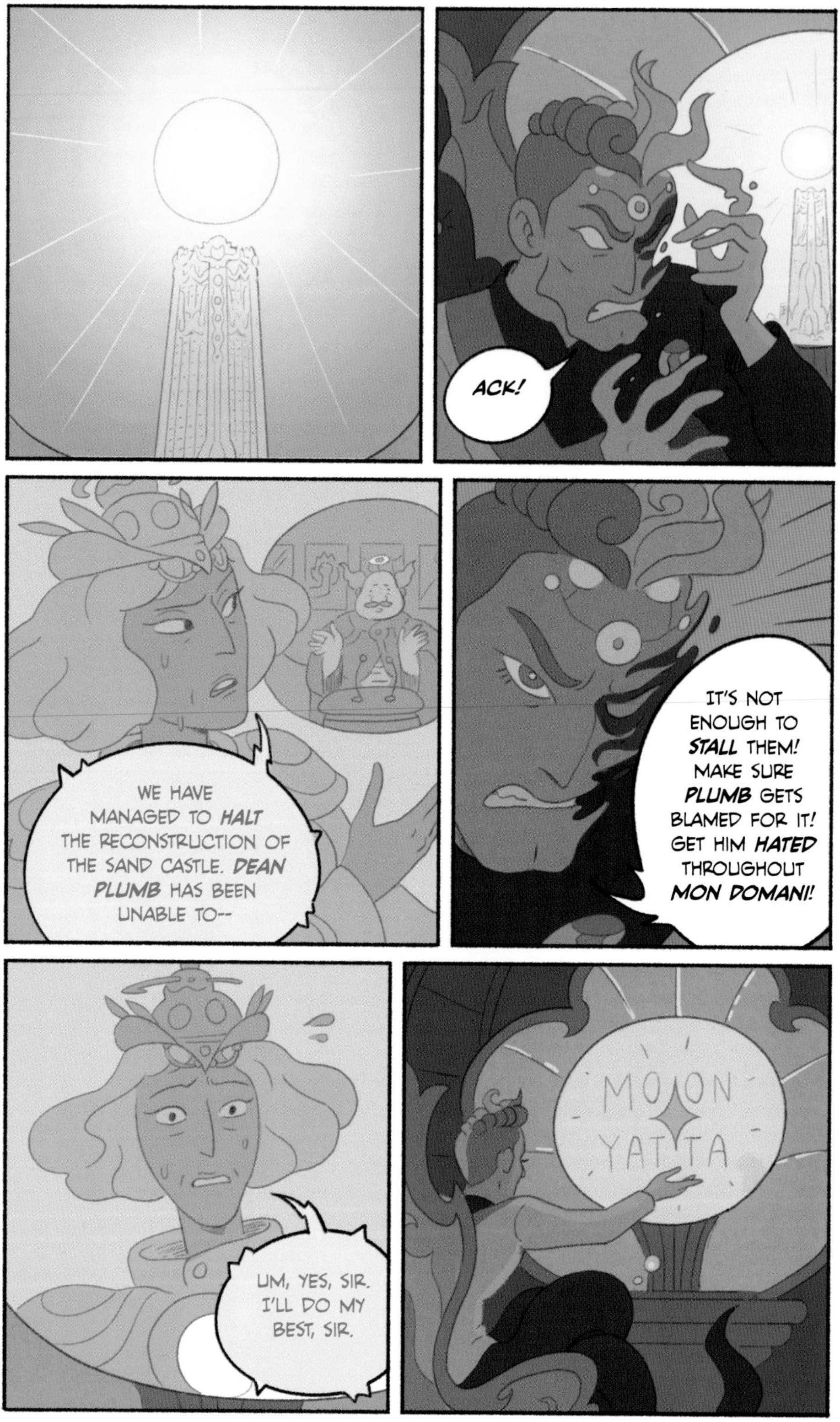
ACK!
WE HAVE MANAGED TO HALT THE RECONSTRUCTION OF THE SAND CASTLE. DEAN PLUMB HAS BEEN UNABLE TO--
IT'S NOT ENOUGH TO STALL THEM! MAKE SURE PLUMB GETS BLAMED FOR IT! GET HIM HATED THROUGHOUT MON DOMANI!
UM, YES, SIR. I'LL DO MY BEST, SIR.
MOON YATTA

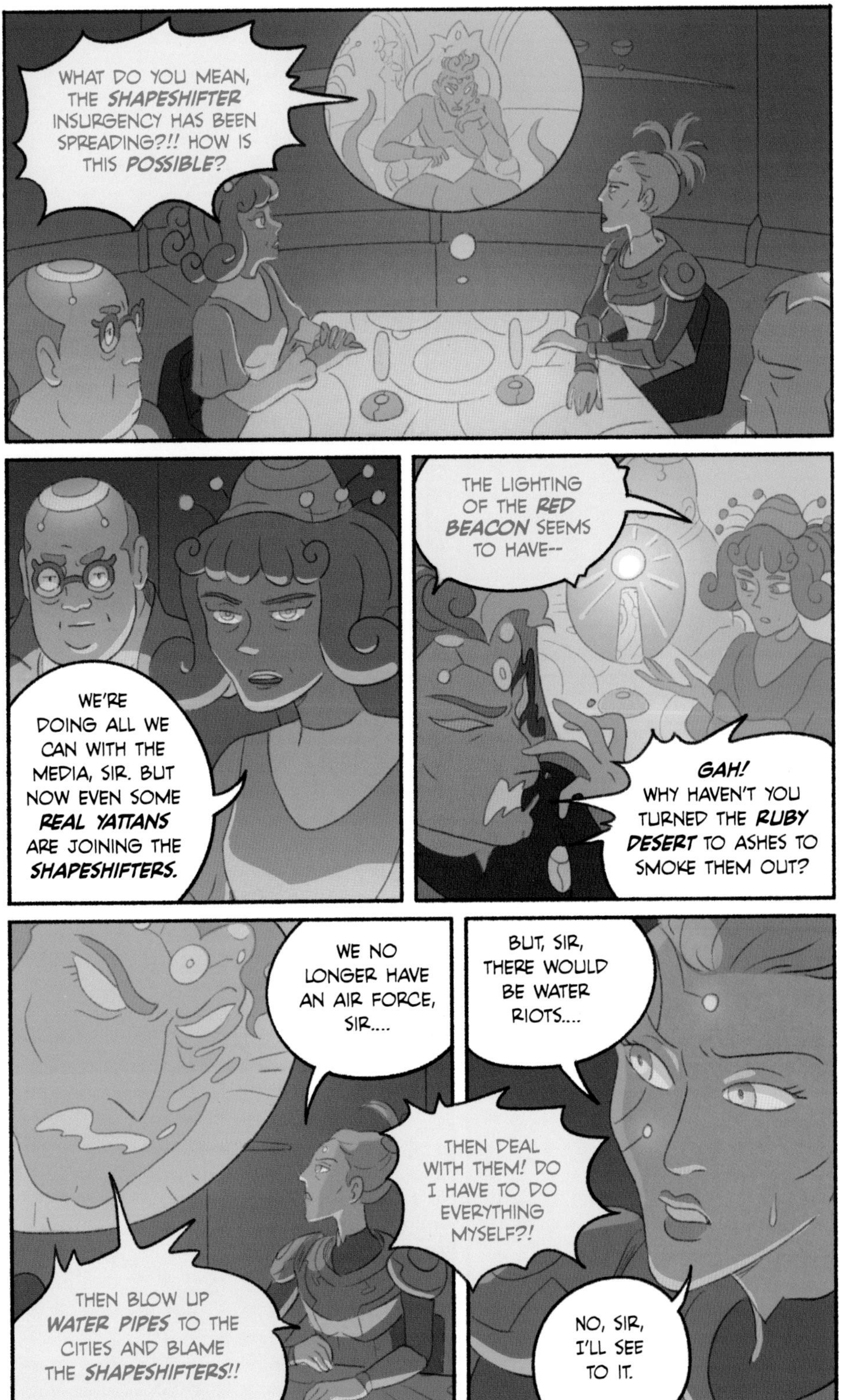
WHAT DO YOU MEAN, THE SHAPESHIFTER INSURGENCY HAS BEEN SPREADING?!! HOW IS THIS POSSIBLE?
WE'RE DOING ALL WE CAN WITH THE MEDIA, SIR. BUT NOW EVEN SOME REAL YATTANS ARE JOINING THE SHAPESHIFTERS.
THE LIGHTING OF THE RED BEACON SEEMS TO HAVE--
GAH! WHY HAVEN'T YOU TURNED THE RUBY DESERT TO ASHES TO SMOKE THEM OUT?
WE NO LONGER HAVE AN AIR FORCE, SIR....
THEN BLOW UP WATER PIPES TO THE CITIES AND BLAME THE SHAPESHIFTERS!!
BUT, SIR, THERE WOULD BE WATER RIOTS....
THEN DEAL WITH THEM! DO I HAVE TO DO EVERYTHING MYSELF?!
NO, SIR, I'LL SEE TO IT.

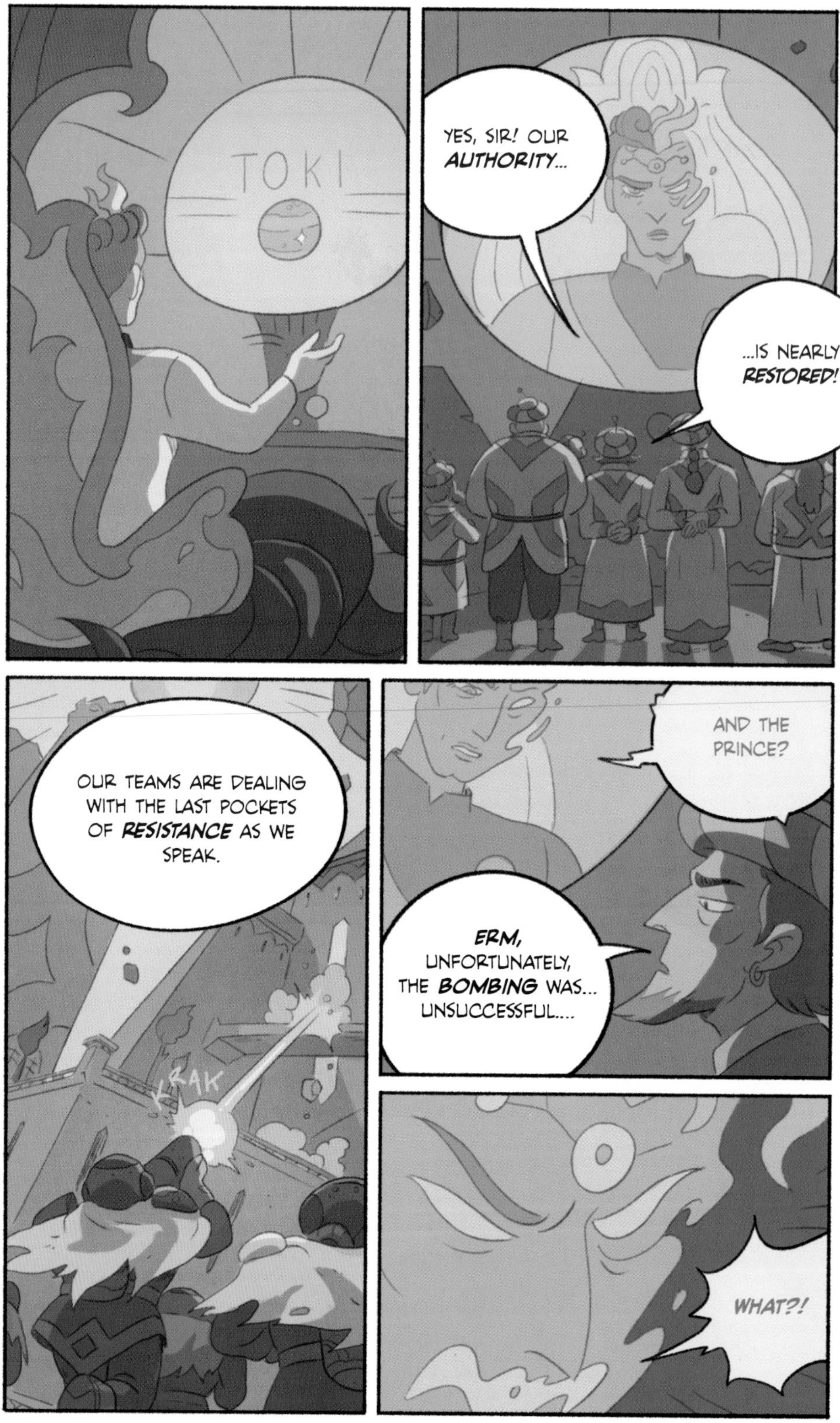
TOKI
YES, SIR! OUR AUTHORITY...
...IS NEARLY RESTORED!
OUR TEAMS ARE DEALING WITH THE LAST POCKETS OF RESISTANCE AS WE SPEAK.
KRAK
AND THE PRINCE?
ERM, UNFORTUNATELY, THE BOMBING WAS... UNSUCCESSFUL....
WHAT?!

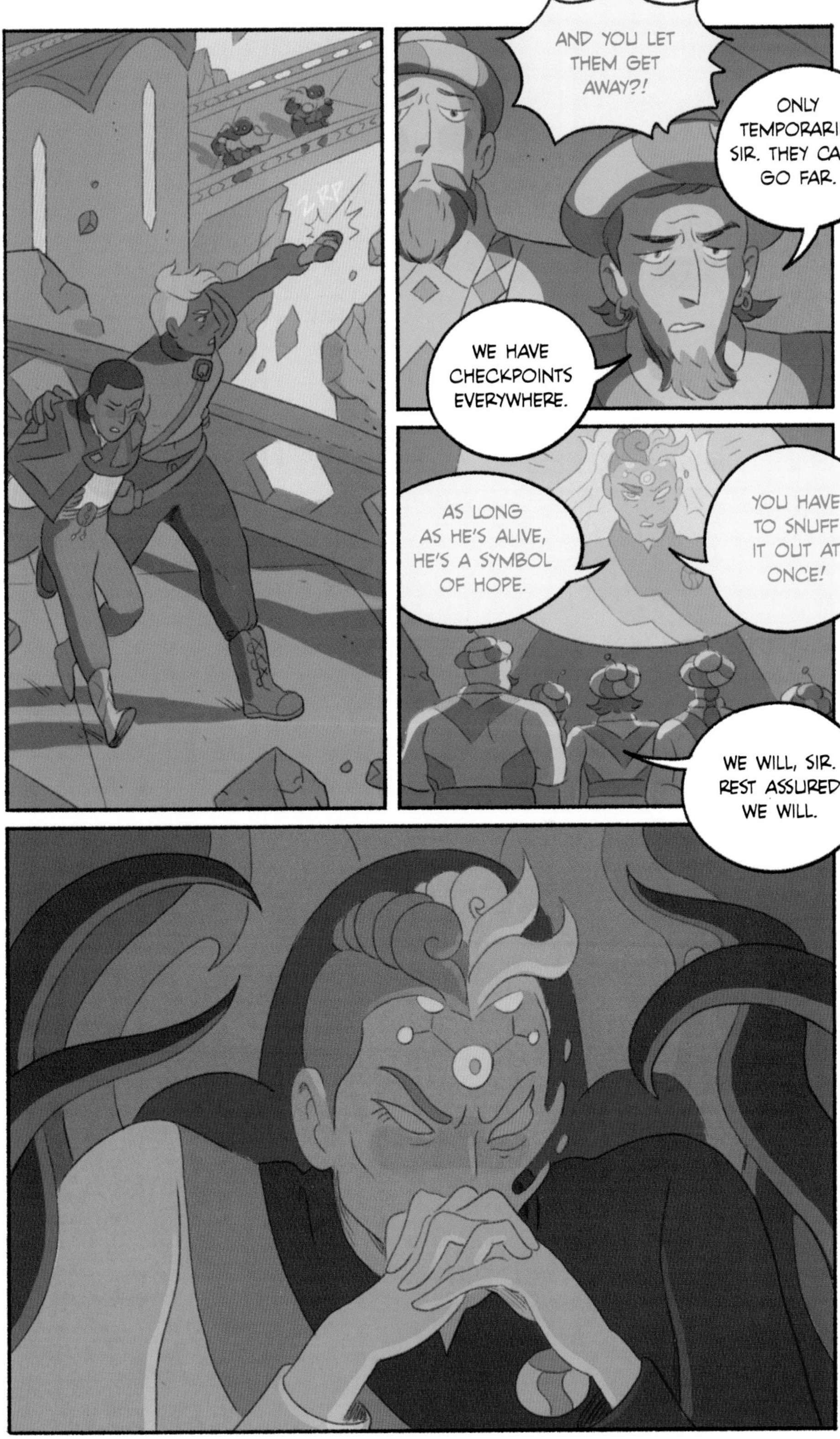
ZRP
AND YOU LET THEM GET AWAY?!
ONLY TEMPORARILY, SIR. THEY CAN'T GO FAR.
WE HAVE CHECKPOINTS EVERYWHERE.
AS LONG AS HE'S ALIVE, HE'S A SYMBOL OF HOPE.
YOU HAVE TO SNUFF IT OUT AT ONCE!
WE WILL, SIR. REST ASSURED WE WILL.

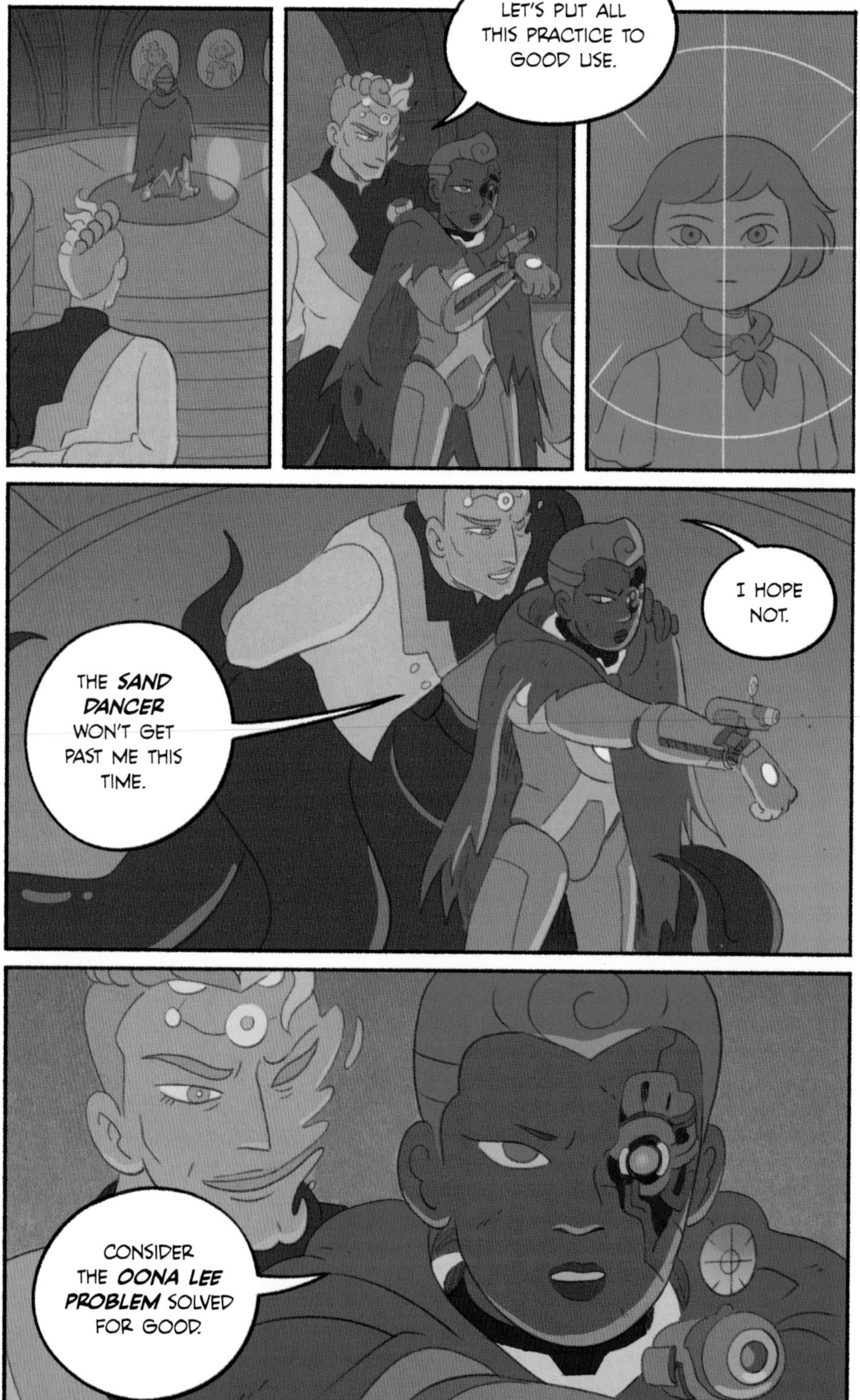
LET'S PUT ALL THIS PRACTICE TO GOOD USE.
THE *SAND DANCER* WON'T GET PAST ME THIS TIME.
I HOPE NOT.
CONSIDER THE *OONA LEE PROBLEM* SOLVED FOR GOOD.

Chapter 11
THE HOURGLASS

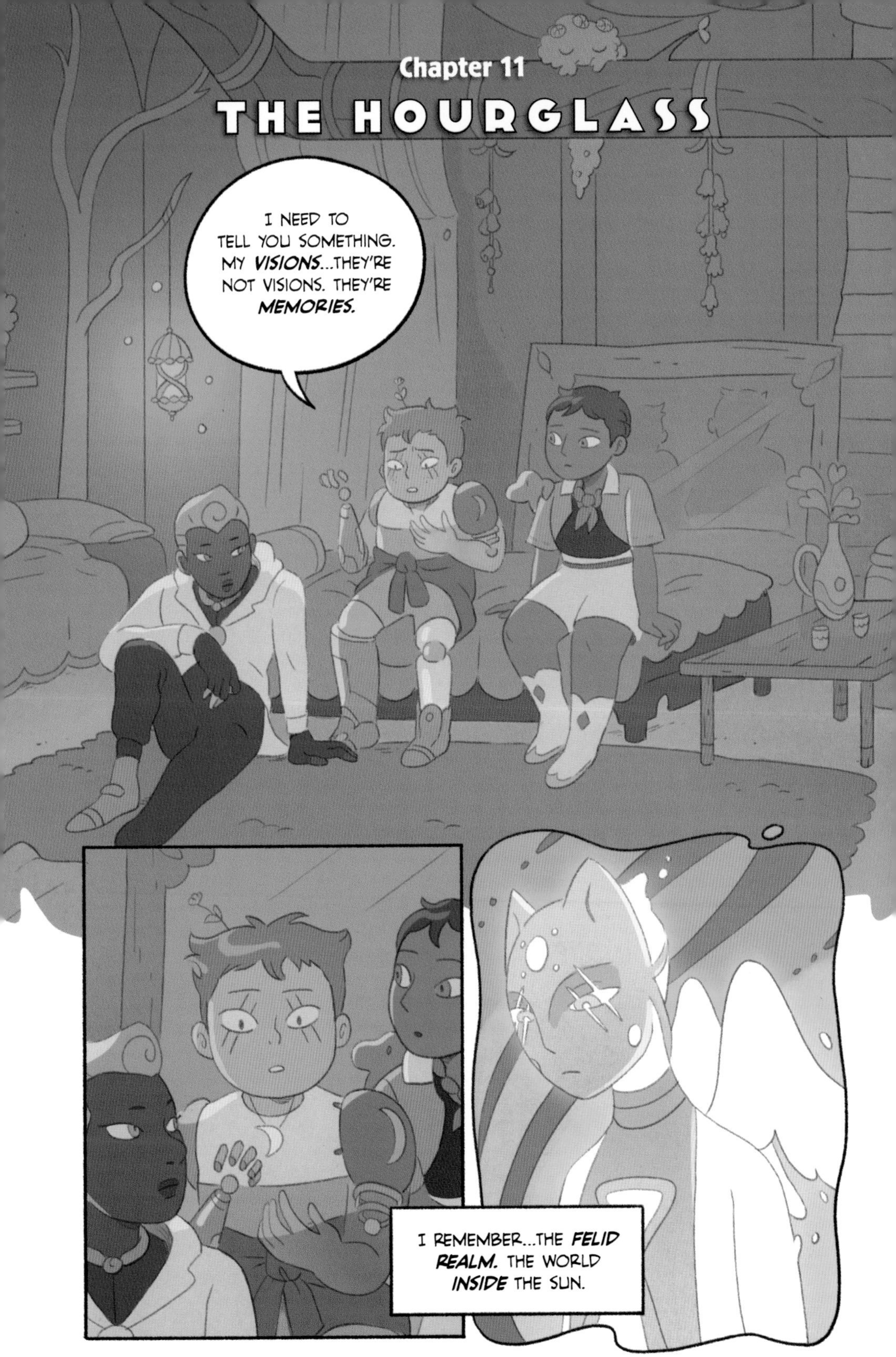
I NEED TO TELL YOU SOMETHING. MY *VISIONS*...THEY'RE NOT VISIONS. THEY'RE *MEMORIES.*
I REMEMBER...THE *FELID REALM.* THE WORLD *INSIDE* THE SUN.

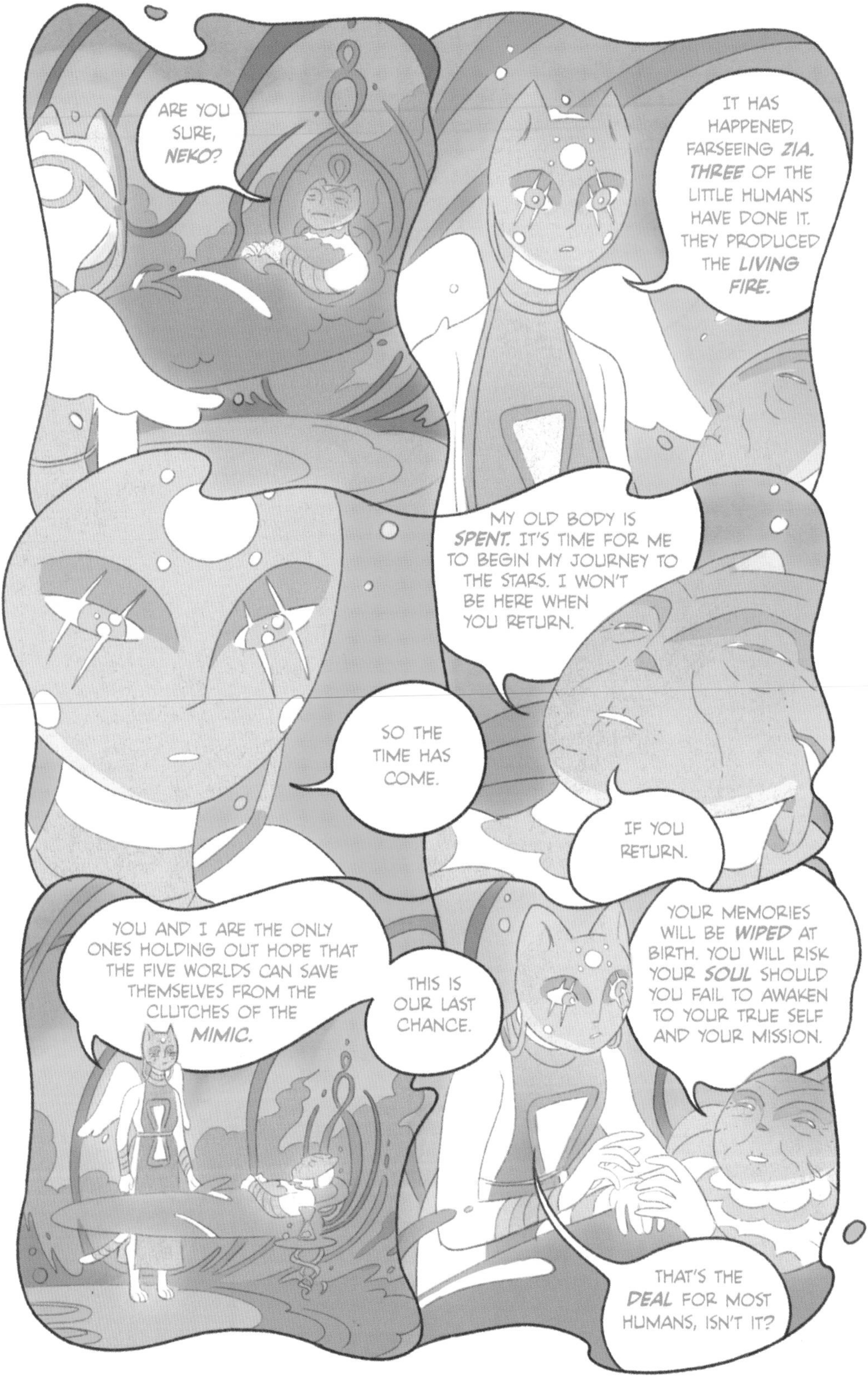
ARE YOU SURE, NEKO?
IT HAS HAPPENED, FARSEEING ZIA. THREE OF THE LITTLE HUMANS HAVE DONE IT. THEY PRODUCED THE LIVING FIRE.
MY OLD BODY IS SPENT. IT'S TIME FOR ME TO BEGIN MY JOURNEY TO THE STARS. I WON'T BE HERE WHEN YOU RETURN.
SO THE TIME HAS COME.
IF YOU RETURN.
YOU AND I ARE THE ONLY ONES HOLDING OUT HOPE THAT THE FIVE WORLDS CAN SAVE THEMSELVES FROM THE CLUTCHES OF THE MIMIC.
THIS IS OUR LAST CHANCE.
YOUR MEMORIES WILL BE WIPED AT BIRTH. YOU WILL RISK YOUR SOUL SHOULD YOU FAIL TO AWAKEN TO YOUR TRUE SELF AND YOUR MISSION.
THAT'S THE DEAL FOR MOST HUMANS, ISN'T IT?

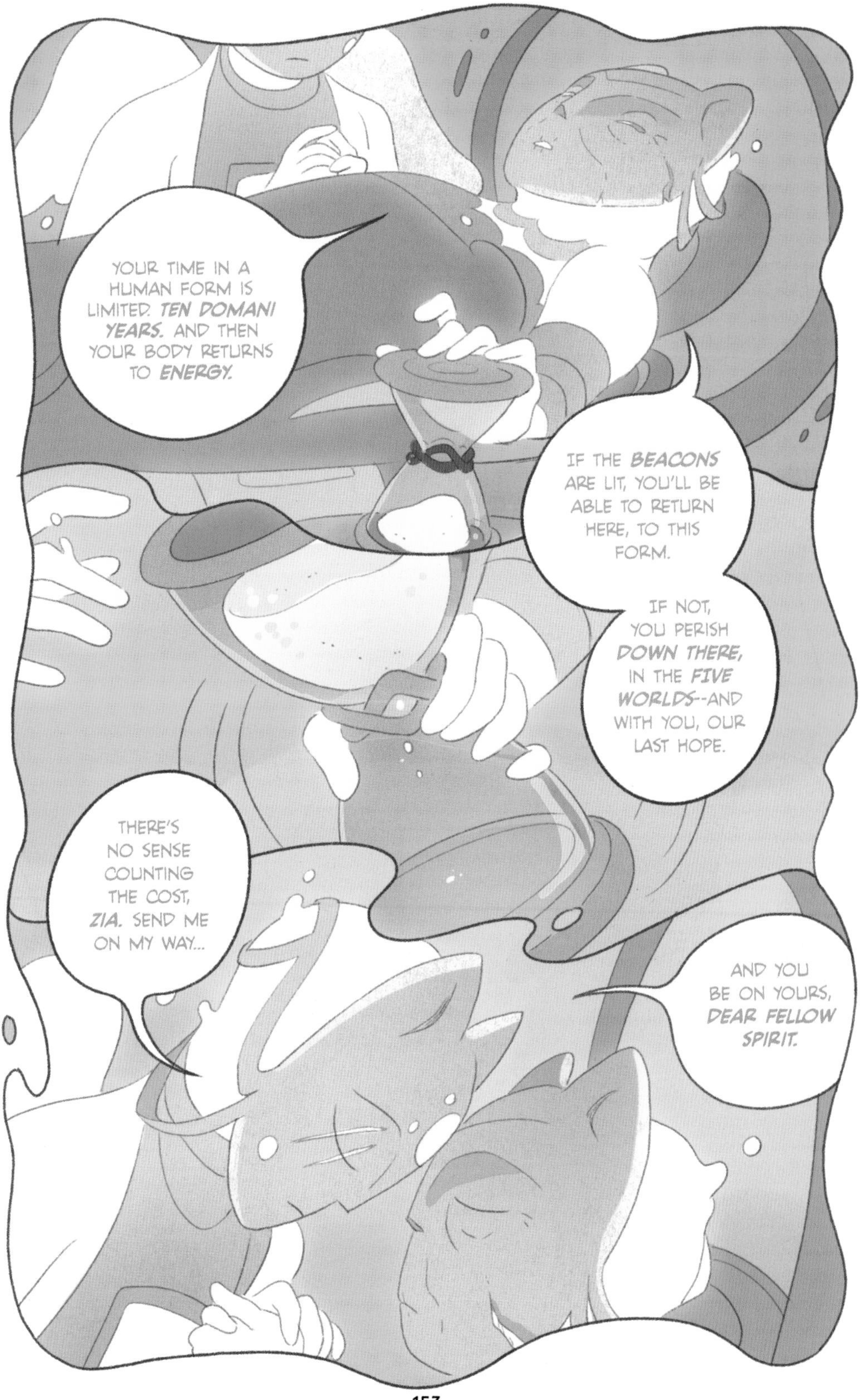
YOUR TIME IN A HUMAN FORM IS LIMITED. TEN DOMANI YEARS. AND THEN YOUR BODY RETURNS TO ENERGY.
IF THE BEACONS ARE LIT, YOU'LL BE ABLE TO RETURN HERE, TO THIS FORM.
IF NOT, YOU PERISH DOWN THERE, IN THE FIVE WORLDS--AND WITH YOU, OUR LAST HOPE.
THERE'S NO SENSE COUNTING THE COST, ZIA. SEND ME ON MY WAY...
AND YOU BE ON YOURS, DEAR FELLOW SPIRIT.

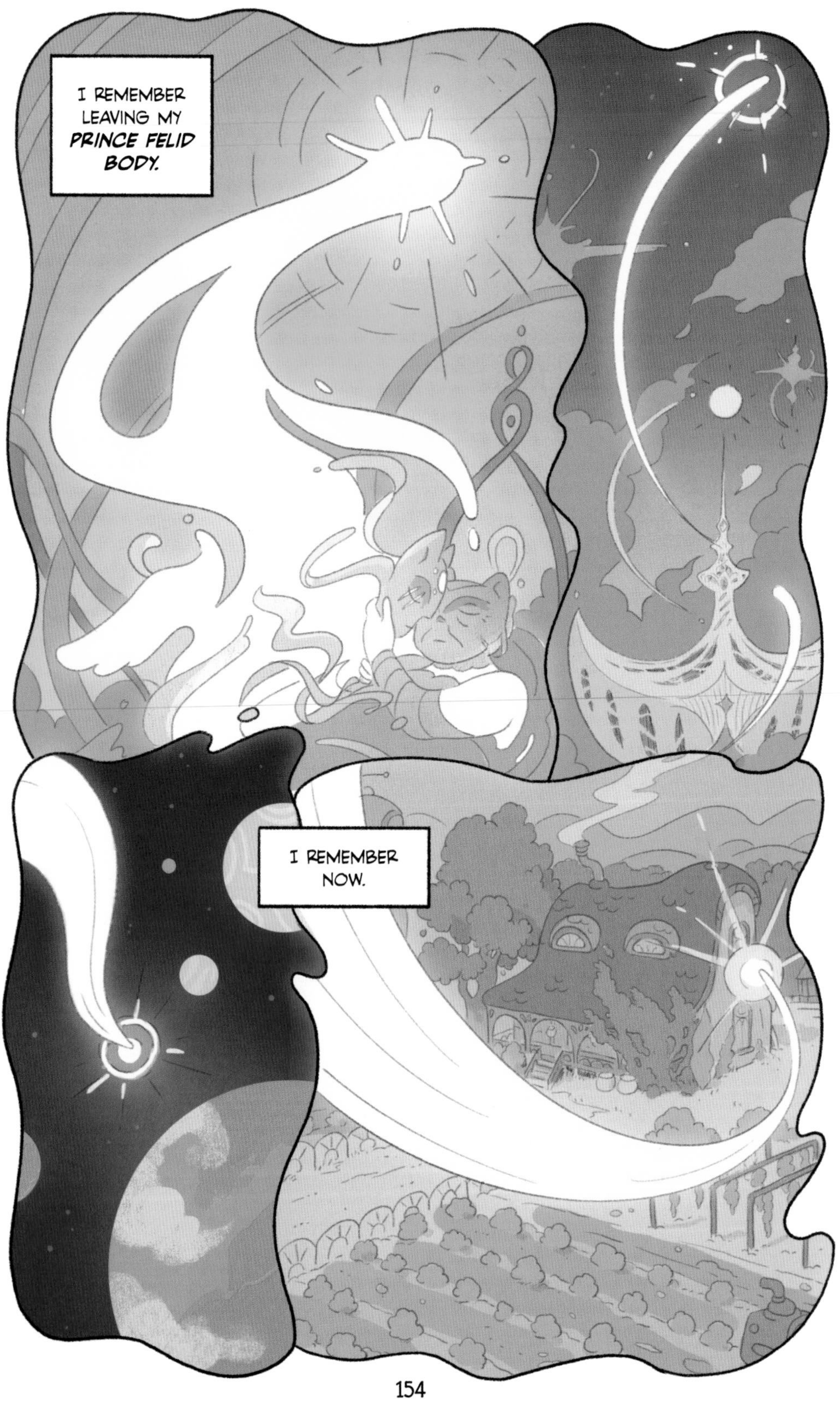
I REMEMBER LEAVING MY *PRINCE FELID BODY.*
I REMEMBER NOW.

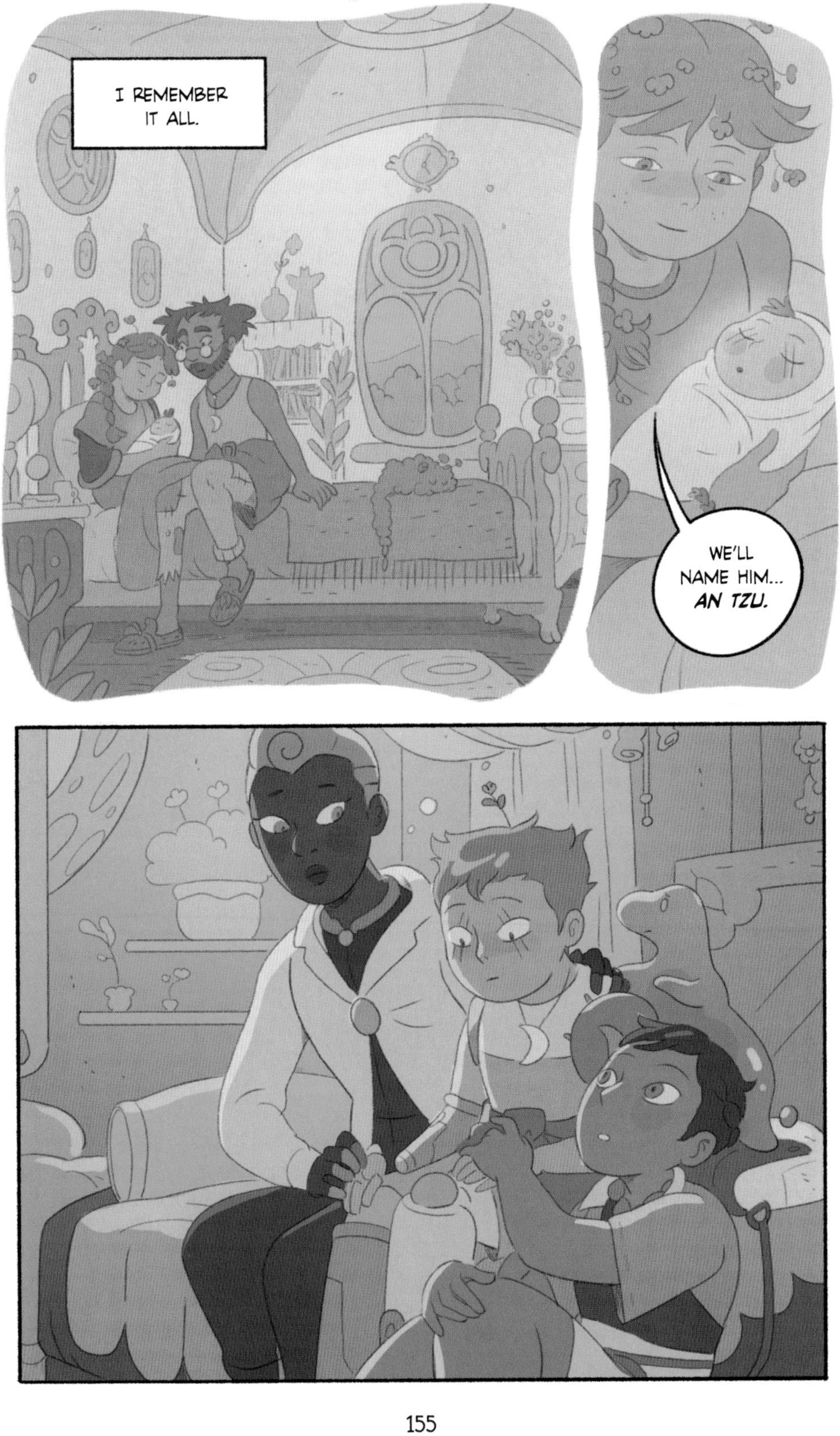
I REMEMBER IT ALL.
WE'LL NAME HIM... AN TZU.

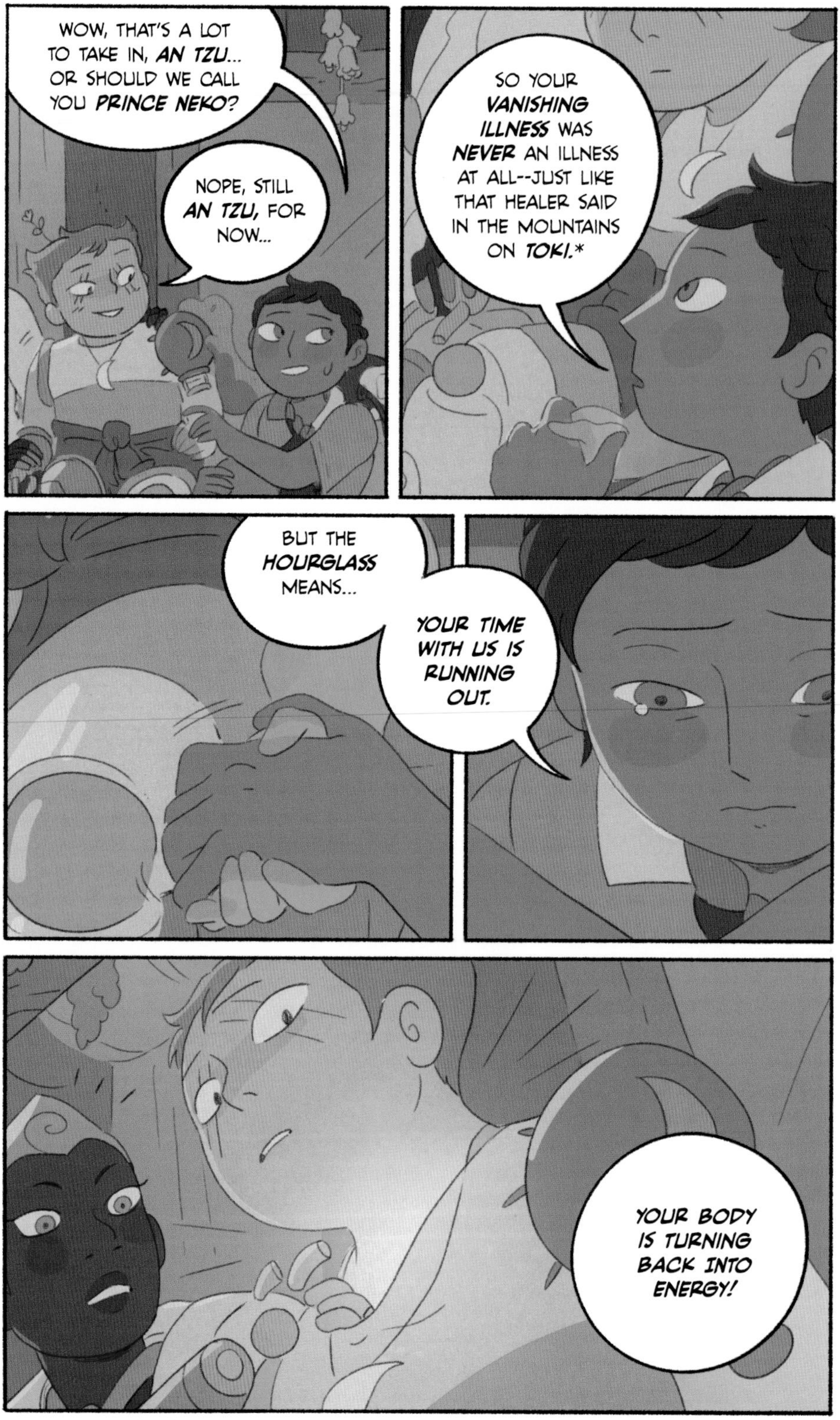
WOW, THAT'S A LOT TO TAKE IN, AN TZU... OR SHOULD WE CALL YOU PRINCE NEKO?
NOPE, STILL AN TZU, FOR NOW...
SO YOUR VANISHING ILLNESS WAS NEVER AN ILLNESS AT ALL--JUST LIKE THAT HEALER SAID IN THE MOUNTAINS ON TOKI.*
BUT THE HOURGLASS MEANS...
YOUR TIME WITH US IS RUNNING OUT.
YOUR BODY IS TURNING BACK INTO ENERGY!

* SEE 5W2: ***THE COBALT PRINCE***

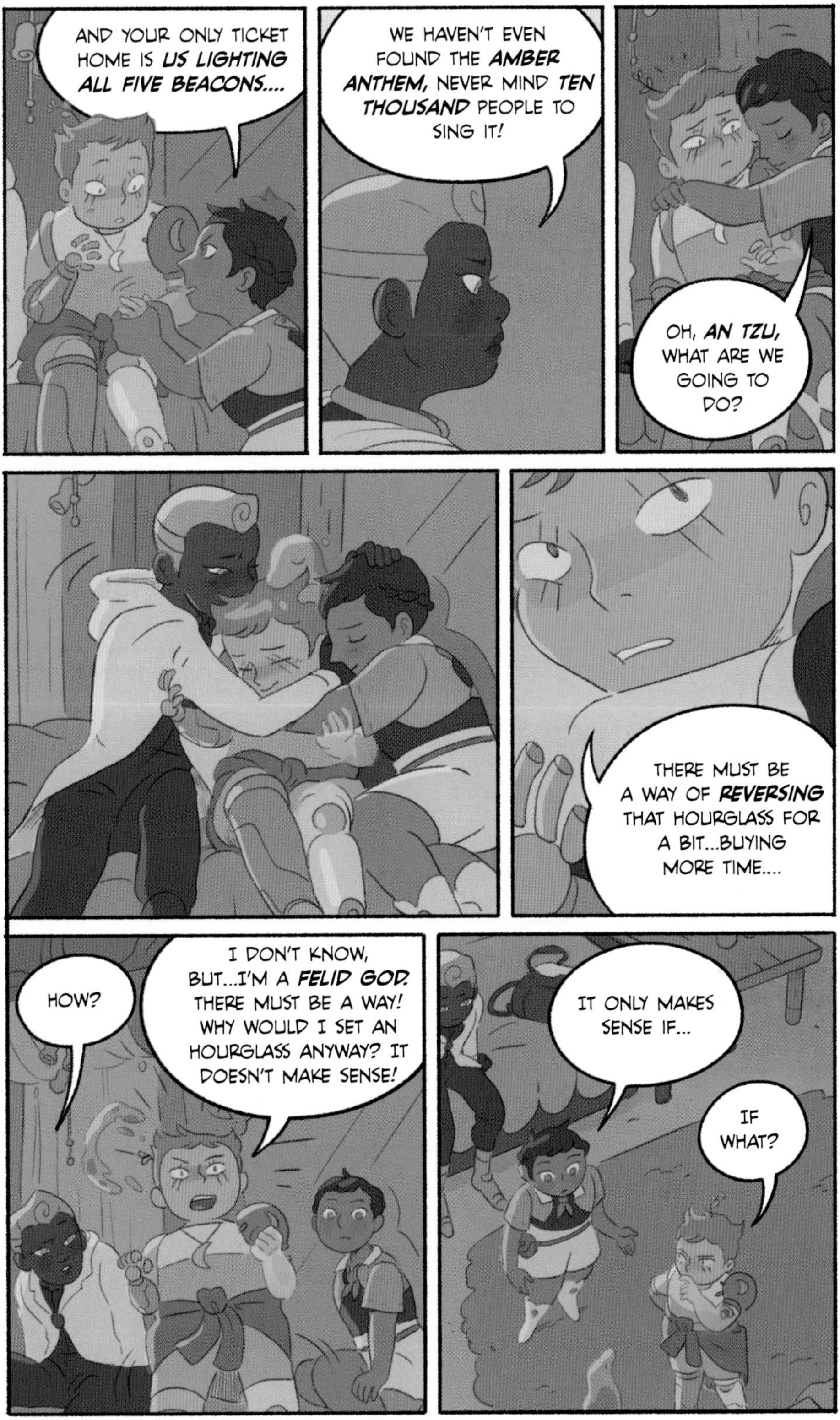
AND YOUR ONLY TICKET HOME IS US LIGHTING ALL FIVE BEACONS....
WE HAVEN'T EVEN FOUND THE AMBER ANTHEM, NEVER MIND TEN THOUSAND PEOPLE TO SING IT!
OH, AN TZU, WHAT ARE WE GOING TO DO?
THERE MUST BE A WAY OF REVERSING THAT HOURGLASS FOR A BIT...BUYING MORE TIME....
HOW?
I DON'T KNOW, BUT...I'M A FELID GOD. THERE MUST BE A WAY! WHY WOULD I SET AN HOURGLASS ANYWAY? IT DOESN'T MAKE SENSE!
IT ONLY MAKES SENSE IF...
IF WHAT?

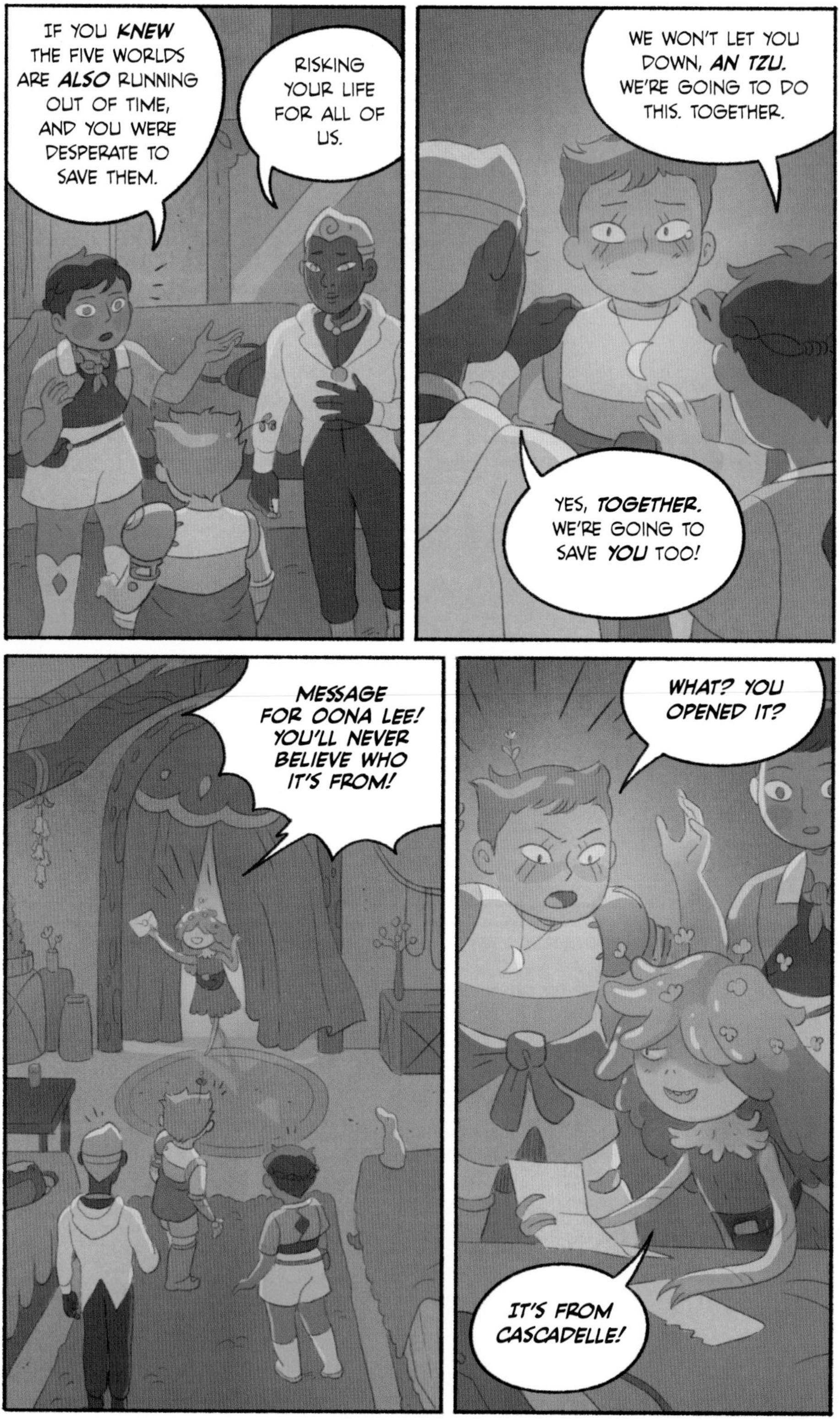
IF YOU KNEW THE FIVE WORLDS ARE ALSO RUNNING OUT OF TIME, AND YOU WERE DESPERATE TO SAVE THEM.
RISKING YOUR LIFE FOR ALL OF US.
WE WON'T LET YOU DOWN, AN TZU. WE'RE GOING TO DO THIS. TOGETHER.
YES, TOGETHER. WE'RE GOING TO SAVE YOU TOO!
MESSAGE FOR OONA LEE! YOU'LL NEVER BELIEVE WHO IT'S FROM!
WHAT? YOU OPENED IT?
IT'S FROM CASCADELLE!

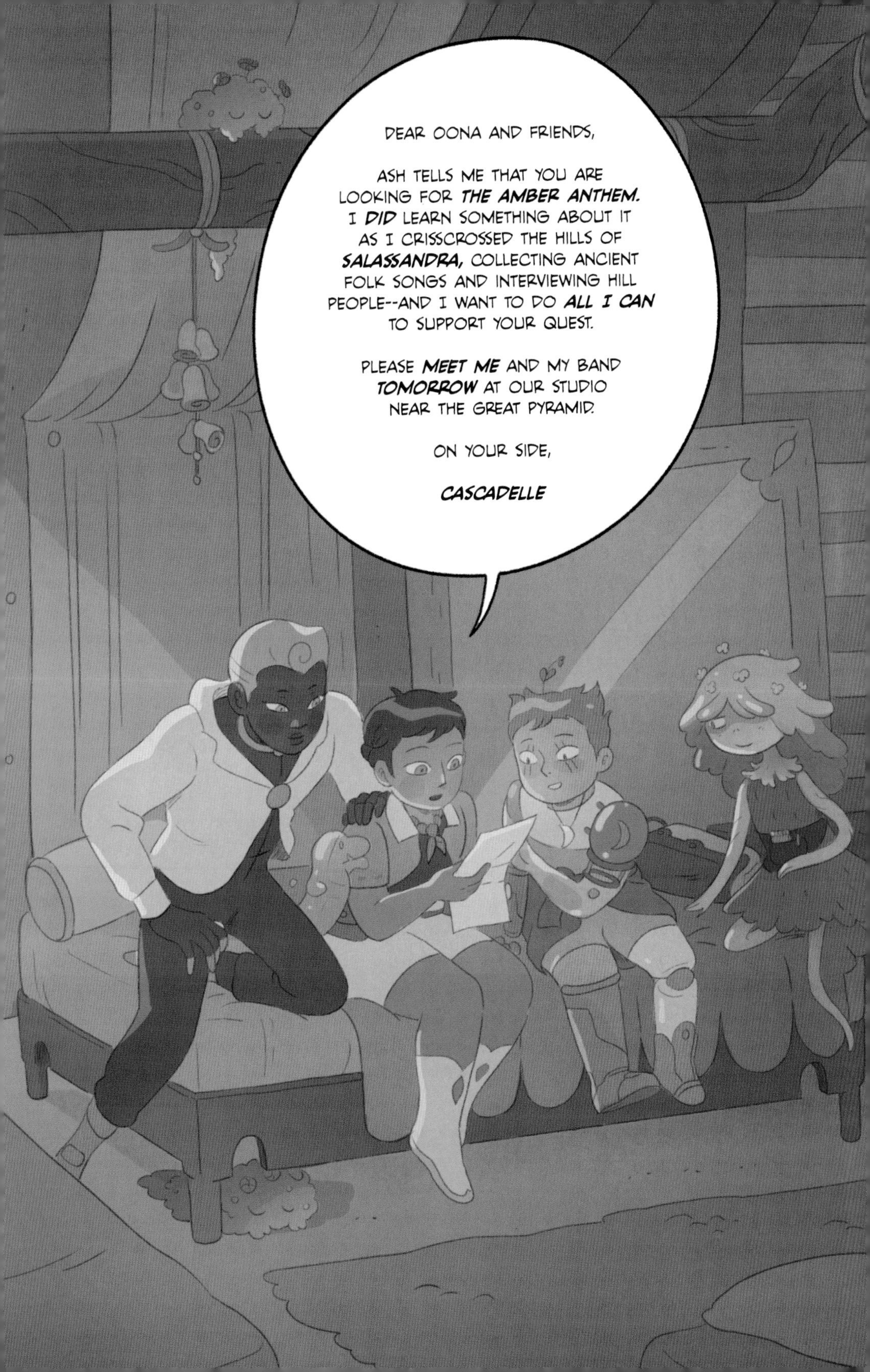
DEAR OONA AND FRIENDS,
ASH TELLS ME THAT YOU ARE LOOKING FOR THE AMBER ANTHEM. I DID LEARN SOMETHING ABOUT IT AS I CRISSCROSSED THE HILLS OF SALASSANDRA, COLLECTING ANCIENT FOLK SONGS AND INTERVIEWING HILL PEOPLE--AND I WANT TO DO ALL I CAN TO SUPPORT YOUR QUEST.
PLEASE MEET ME AND MY BAND TOMORROW AT OUR STUDIO NEAR THE GREAT PYRAMID.
ON YOUR SIDE,
CASCADELLE

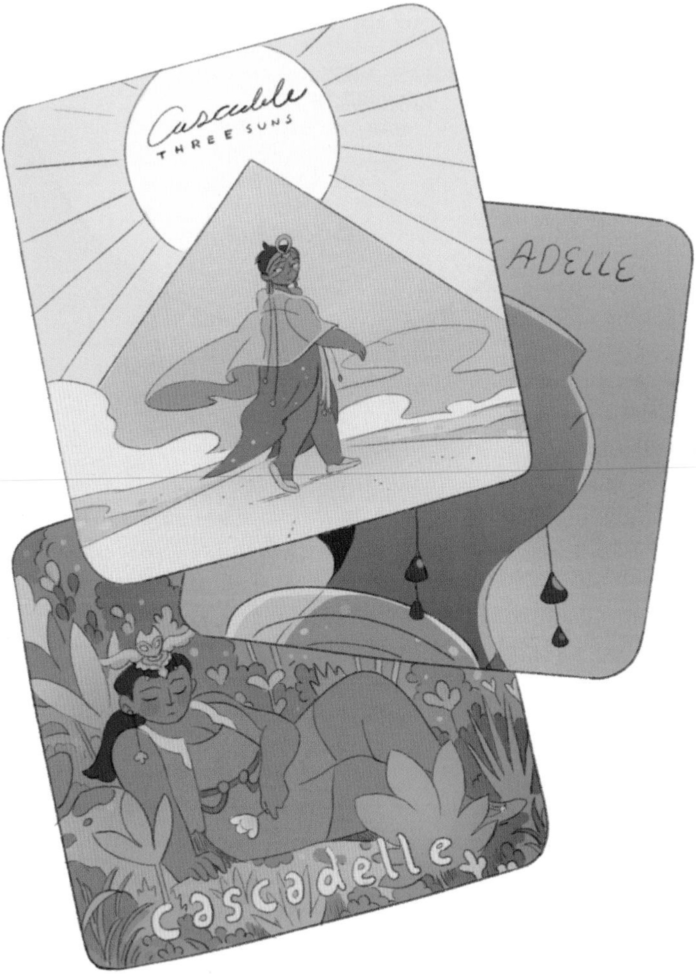
Cascadelle
THREE SUNS
cascadelle

Chapter 12
THE WOUND

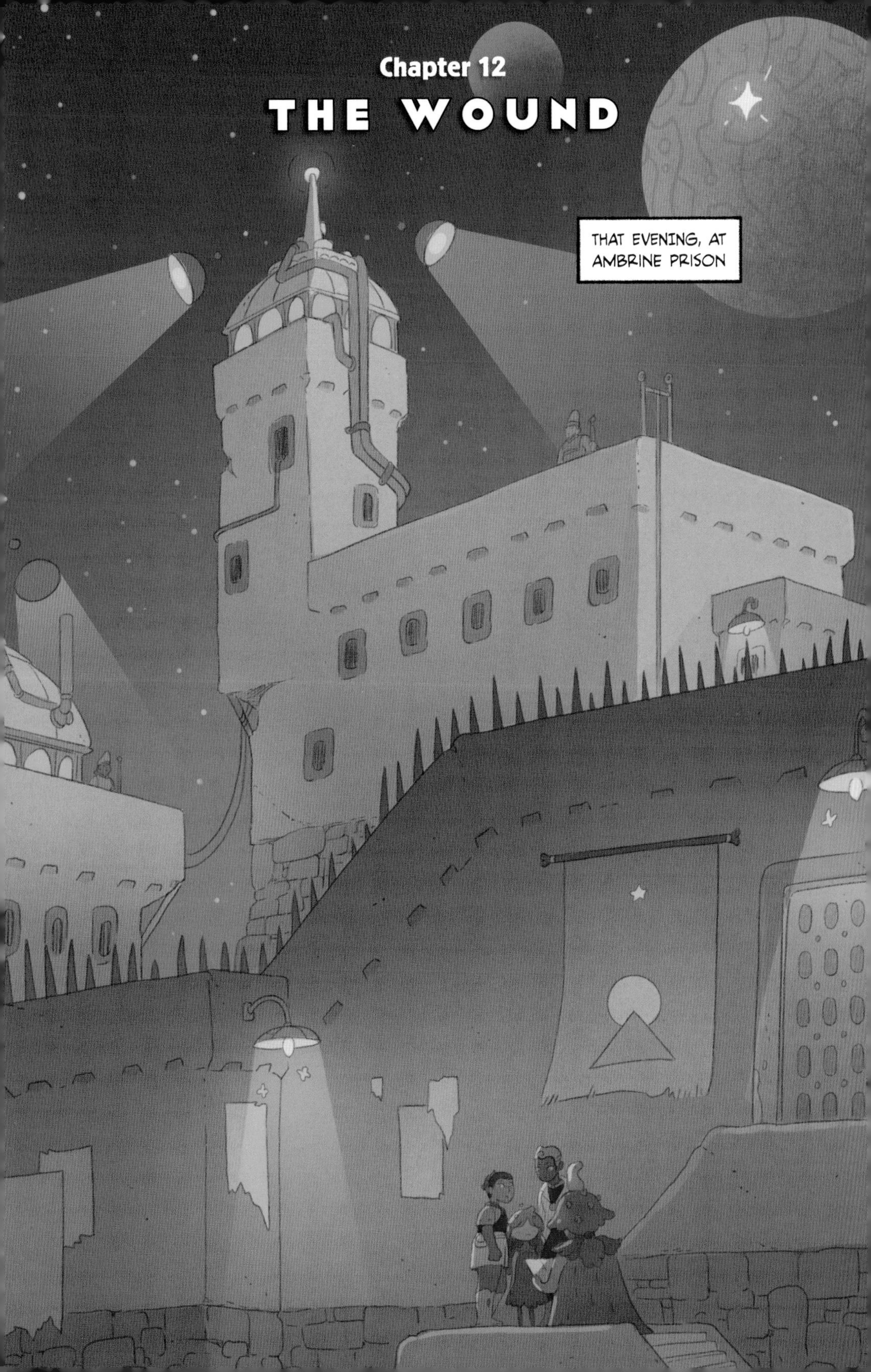
THAT EVENING, AT AMBRINE PRISON

AND YOU'RE SURE IT'S *O'ZIRG*, PEONY?

YES, MY FRIEND IN THE PRISON'S CLEANING CREW KNOWS HIM. SHE SAYS THEY KEEP HIM RIGHT *HERE.*

YOU'LL BE ABLE TO GET HIM OUT?

I'M NOT SURE HOW TO *PORTAL* INTO A BUILDING I'VE NEVER VISITED. I'LL NEED ALL OF YOU HELPING ME.

HOW?!

JOIN HANDS...OR TENDRILS, AND SEND ME ALL YOUR *BELIEF* THAT I CAN DO THIS.

SSSHAA

OONA!

YOU CAME BACK FOR ME!

HOW CAN WE BE SURE SHE MADE IT?

WE'LL KNOW WHEN SHE *PORTALS* BACK TO THE INN WITH *O'ZIRG.*

PUT ME THROUGH TO *MR. MOON* RIGHT AWAY. HE'LL WANT TO HEAR THIS.

WHAT'S TAKING THEM SO LONG, *RAM SAM SAM?*

DON'T YOU THINK *OONA* SHOULD BE BACK ALREADY?

I TOLD THEM I'D BE ABLE TO HELP, BUT THEY WERE ALL, "NO, YOU NEED TO STAY SAFE."

THEY THINK I'M STILL JUST SOME STREET KID FROM *MON DOMANI.*

BUT YOU KNOW I'M *NOT,* RIGHT?

RRm Sm?

I'M *PRINCE FELID.* IT'S TIME I ACTED LIKE IT.

THE MAIN PRISON? IT'S THAT WAY, THEN BEAR LEFT AT THE STATUE.

YOU CAN'T ESCAPE! SURRENDER!

DASH
CAN'T ESCAPE!
SURRENDER!
CAN'T!
CAN'T ESCAPE!
CAN'T ESCAPE!
NO RUNNING AWAY THIS TIME, LITTLE PRINCE!

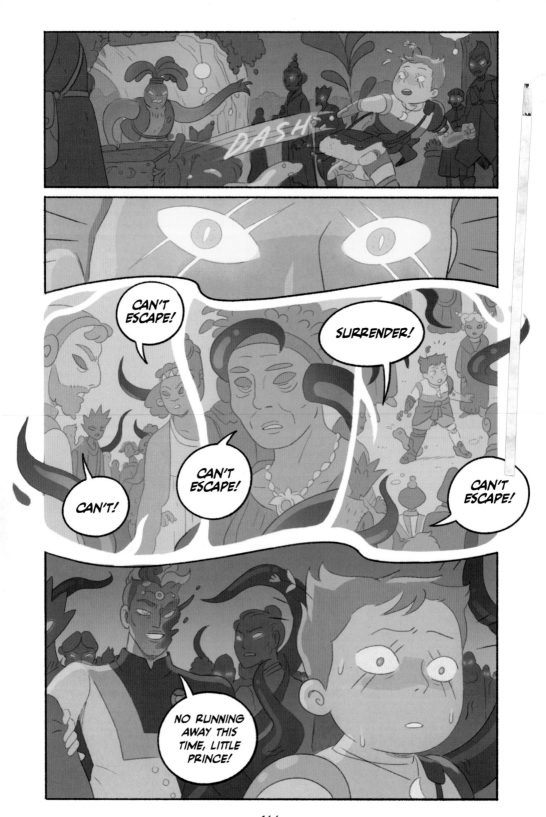

GAH!!
THUNK!
!?

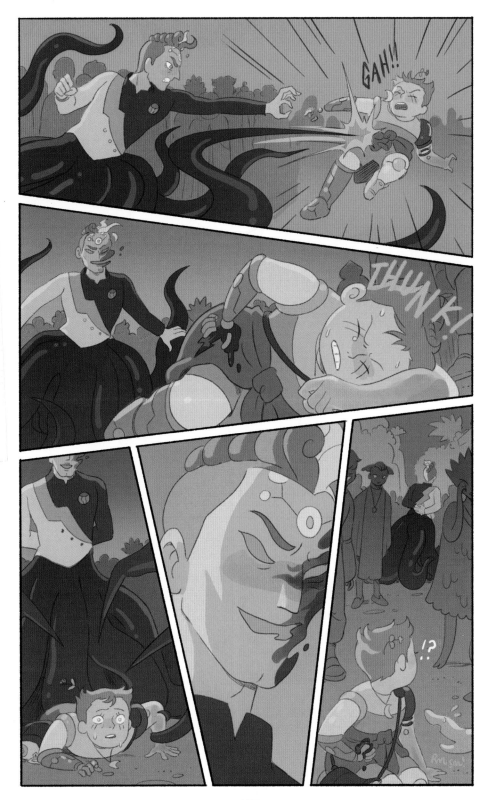

WHAT HAPPENED? HOW DID I GET HERE?

HEY, KID, YOU HURT?

EXCUSE ME, I KNOW HIM.

AN TZU, WHAT HAPPENED? ARE YOU INJURED?

I'M OKAY. HE BACKED OFF! I DON'T KNOW *WHY*. HE COULD'VE *KILLED* ME THEN AND THERE.

AN TZU!

HE WAS ATTACKED BY THE MIMIC AGAIN!

DID HE HURT YOU? ARE YOU **WOUNDED?**

NO...HE...**TRIED.** I'M JUST...I'M FINE. IS IT TIME TO GO SEE **CASCADELLE?** CAN YOU BELIEVE WE'RE ACTUALLY MEETING HER?!

Chapter 13

AT CASCADELLE'S

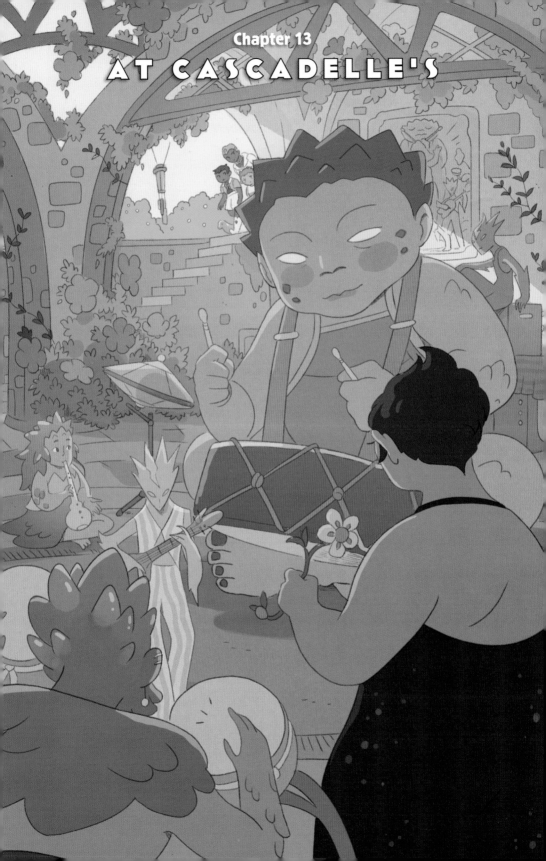

UM, HELLO?
MISS CASCADELLE? I'M--
OONA! I'M SO GLAD TO FINALLY MEET YOU! THE REAL "TOKI GIRL FROM MON DOMANI"!
THANK YOU FOR INVITING US. IT'S AN HONOR--
NONSENSE! THE HONOR'S ALL MINE. YOU KIDS ARE AMAZING!
JAX AMBOY! AN TZU! LET ME HUG YOU TOO.
COME, HAVE SOME TEA.
AND LET'S TALK ABOUT THIS AMBER ANTHEM.

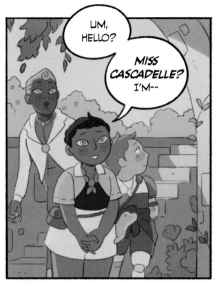

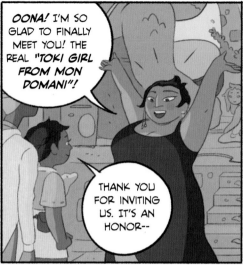

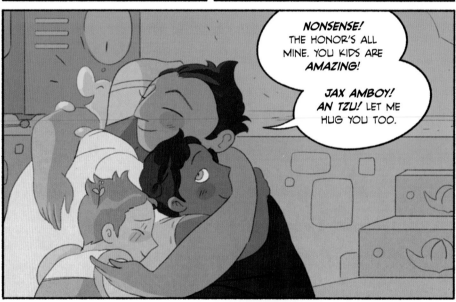

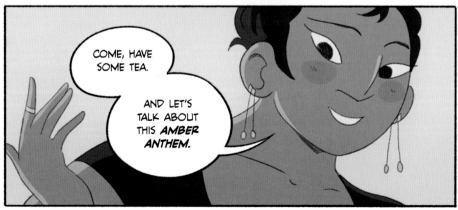

YES, I WAS TRAVELING THROUGH SALASSANDRA WHEN I FIRST HEARD ABOUT THE ANTHEM....
I WAS COLLECTING ALL THE MUSIC AND STORIES I COULD.
BUT FOR YEARS THE ANTHEM SEEMED LIKE IT WAS JUST A ***RUMOR.***
UNTIL...

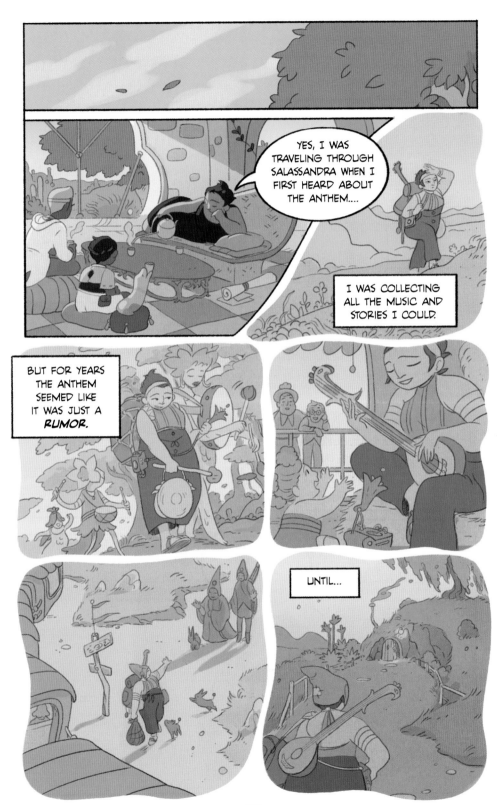

IN THE HILLS OF HARPVILLE, I MET A VERY OLD MAN WHO LIVED, AND PRAYED, ALONE.
HE HAD KEPT A TREASURE TROVE OF RECORDS...
INCLUDING A FELID TEXT THAT HE THOUGHT MIGHT BE THE WORDS TO THE AMBER ANTHEM!
IT WAS IN THE OLD LANGUAGE AND NEITHER OF US COULD READ IT, BUT I FOUND SCHOLARS ON TOKI WHO TRANSLATED IT FOR ME.
HERE, HAVE A LOOK.

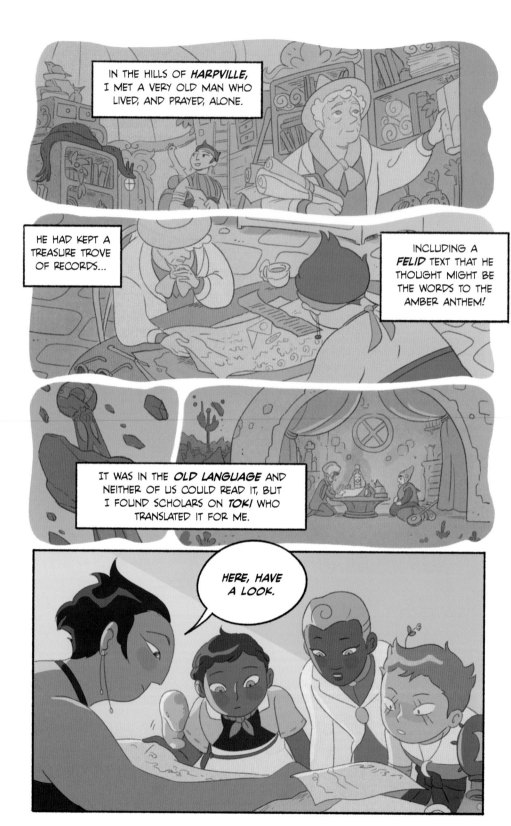

A LITTLE HARD TO UNDERSTAND, ISN'T IT?

I THINK YOU'RE SUPPOSED TO *FEEL* IT, EVEN IF YOU DON'T *UNDERSTAND* ALL THE WORDS.

BUT WHAT DO YOU THINK IT'S SAYING?

WELL, ITS OTHER TITLE IS *"ALL THE LIVING."* I THINK IT MEANS WE'RE ALL IN THIS TOGETHER, AND ALL THE *SAME* IN WHAT REALLY MATTERS.

OKAY...

AND *ALL* ARE NEEDED TO SING THE AMBER ANTHEM.

"ALL" MEANING THOSE TEN THOUSAND VOICES?

YES, BUT THINGS GET A BIT *TRICKY* AT THIS POINT....

"TRICKY"?

I THOUGHT THINGS GOT *TRICKY* THE MOMENT WE LANDED HERE!

WELL, IT SAYS HERE *THE TEN THOUSAND VOICES* HAVE TO REPRESENT THE *"FIVE RACES."*

FIVE RACES?!

WAIT, WE NEED NOT JUST *TEN THOUSAND* PEOPLE BUT ALSO *FIVE RACES* TO LIGHT THIS BEACON?!

I HAVEN'T BEEN ABLE TO FIGURE OUT *WHAT* THE FIVE RACES ARE.

DOES IT MEAN *BLUE-SKINNED TOKI* LIKE YOU AND ME--ONE RACE--AND *SALASSI* PEOPLE AS ANOTHER RACE...?

NO, THIS HERE SUGGESTS ALL FLESHY HUMANS ARE *ONE RACE.*

THERE'S THE *PLANT PEOPLE*, LIKE *ASH, SYCAMORE,* AND *CEDAR* OVER THERE. THAT'S *TWO.*

AND THE *KYOJIN!* THAT MAKES *THREE.*

EXACTLY--THE *KYOJIN*, LIKE *URUM* OVER HERE.

AFTER THAT, IT'S A BLANK. SOME ARCHIVES MENTION LUMINOUS BEINGS CALLED THE *SALASSI DEVOTI*...

BUT I HONESTLY THINK THAT'S A *LEGEND*--

NOT A LEGEND.

-SHI ING-

I MET THEM. ON MY FIRST VISIT TO **SALASSANDRA.** ONE OF THEM **JOINED ME.**

JOINED YOU?

I CAN REPRESENT THE **SALASSI DEVOTI.**

YES, THAT'S RIGHT! NOW **WHAT** COULD BE THE **FIFTH--?**

RRM

LET'S SEE... THAT LITTLE SYMBOL LOOKS LIKE... WHAT DOES IT LOOK LIKE...?

EXCUSE ME, **RAM SAM SAM,** YOU'RE IN THE WAY.

SPIRAL SQUIGGLE WITH LITTLE LEGS. WHERE HAVE I SEEN THAT BEFORE...?
RR!
RMM
LIVING SAND? MAYBE IT'S AN **ANIFORM!**
THAT'S PART OF YOU...
TUG
TUG
HOW ABOUT THE **PTUHULI**
COUNT THEMSELVES IN THE FIVE RACES?
OR HOW ABOUT
REGULAR, **ROOTED** PLANTS? MAYBE THEY'RE THE FIFTH--
IS ANDROID A RACE?
HOW ABOUT THE ANCIENT
I DON'T THINK SO, **AN TZU.** HOW COULD THEY SING?
BOING
BOOF
BONK

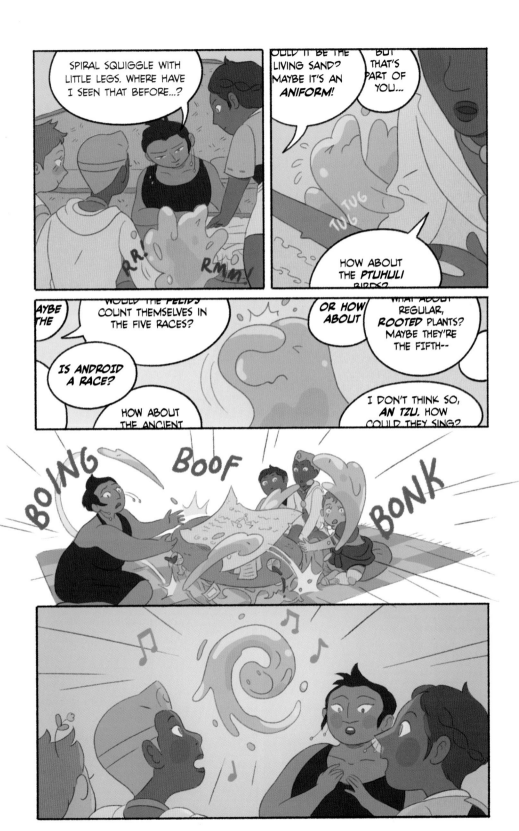

THE LIVING OIL?
AND THAT TUNE YOU WERE JUST SINGING--COULD I HEAR IT AGAIN?
RRM!
SMM
RRR!
SMM
IT FITS THE LYRICS OF THE AMBER ANTHEM PERFECTLY!
RAM SAM SAM IS THE FIFTH RACE!!
LET'S PLAY IT!
COME ALONG, LITTLE OIL!
Rm sm!

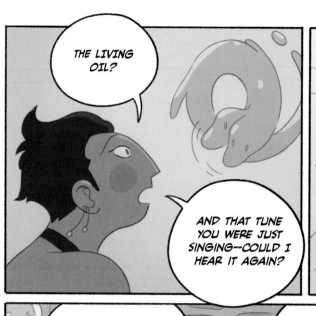

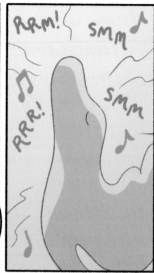

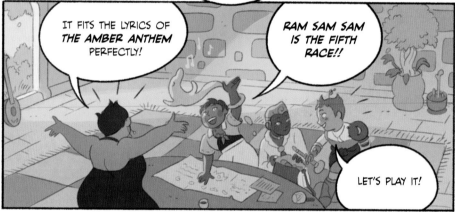

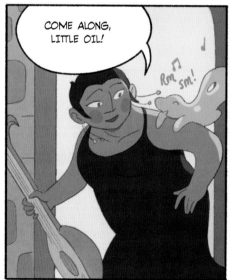

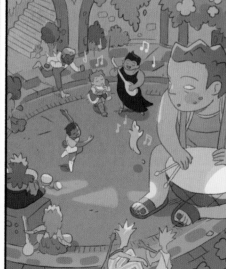

WE NEED TO DO THIS AT THE **BEACON!**

CAN WE **SNEAK THERE** WITHOUT BEING SPOTTED?

NO, USE A PORTAL!

WAIT, NO... I THINK WE NEED TO GO DOWN THE MAIN AVENUE. IN **BROAD DAYLIGHT!**

I BELIEVE... I BELIEVE WE SHOULD!

BUT, OONA, YOU CAN'T BE OUT IN THE OPEN! THAT **KILLER ANDROID...**

IT'S THE ONLY WAY TO GATHER THE **CROWD** WE NEED, **JAX.** I KNOW YOU'LL KEEP ME SAFE.

Chapter 14
COMMUNION

IT'S CASCADELLE! GO GET YOUR MAMA! QUICK!
CASCADELLE!! IT'S REALLY HER!

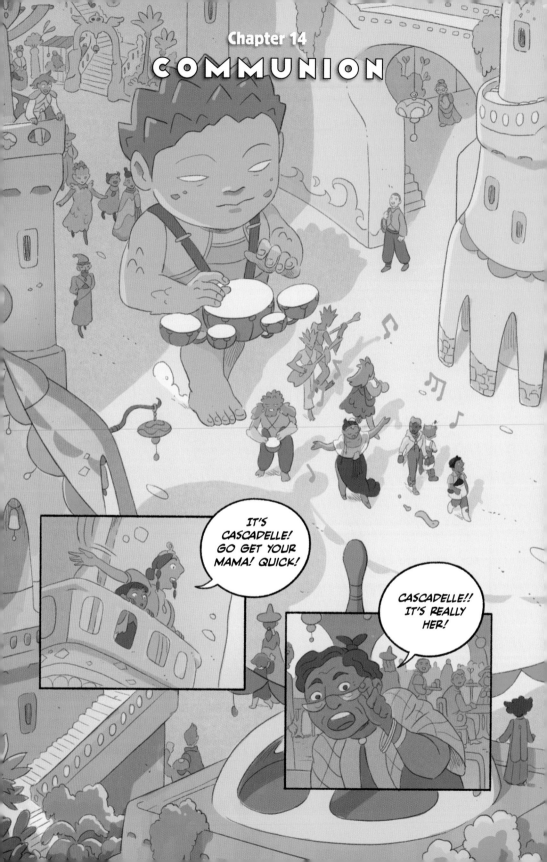

LOOK, NEXT TO HER!
JAX AMBOY?!
JAX AMBOY!!
AND THAT'S OONA!
OONA LEE!!
LOOK! LOOK!
IT'S OONA LEE!
DADDY, PLEASE, PLEASE, PLEASE, CAN WE?!

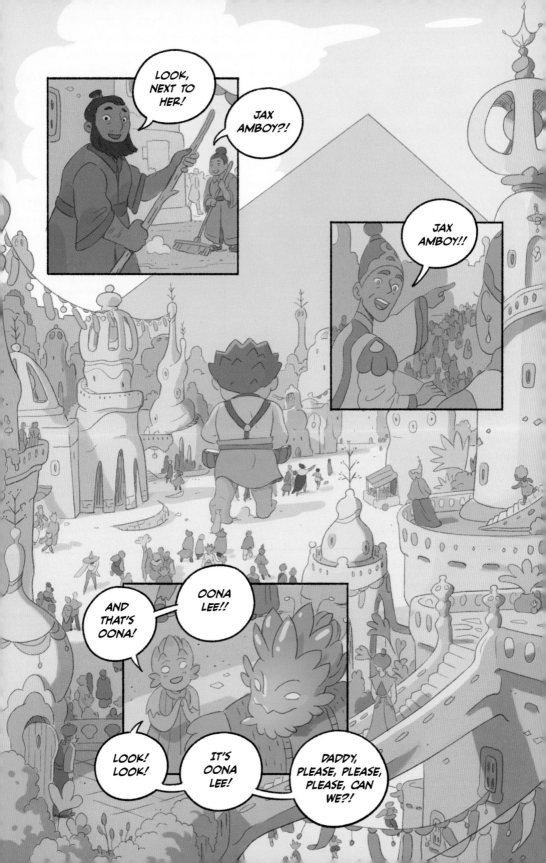

HURRY, WE HAVE TO CUT THEM OFF!
AH, THERE YOU ARE, JORTH! WHERE ARE THEY?
RIGHT HERE, LORD URMUTH! THIS WAY!

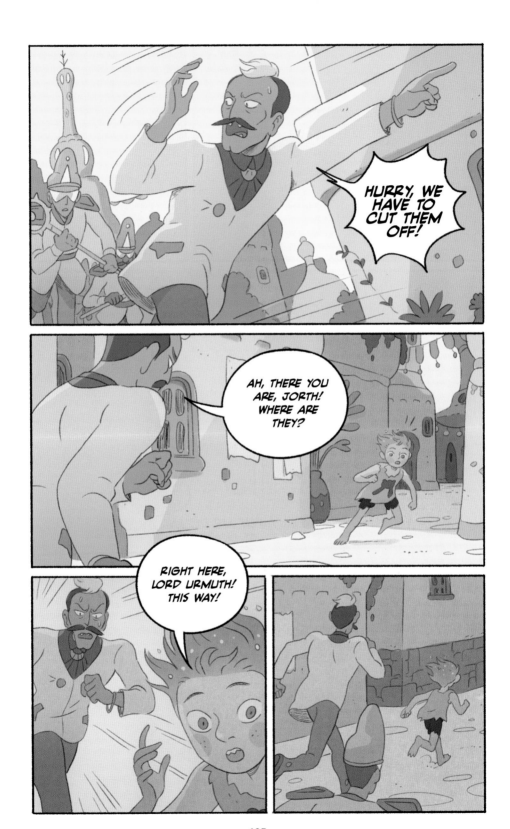

TMP
TP
ZWIP!
PUT ME DOWN AT ONCE! IN THE NAME OF THE LAW...

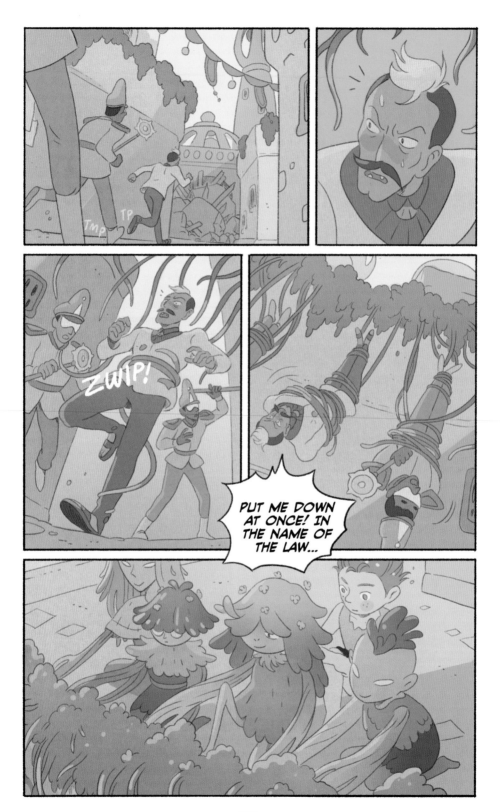

SO...
FRIENDS?
I'LL THINK
ABOUT IT.
POFF
POFF

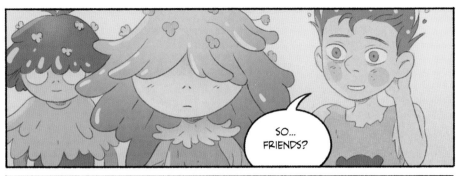

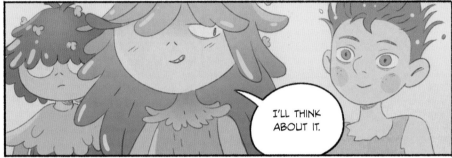

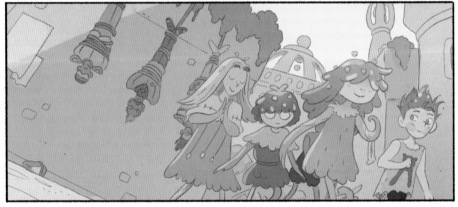

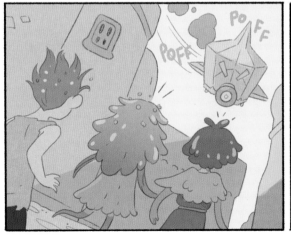

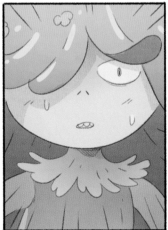

AND WE ARE NOW LIVE ON THE SCENE OF THIS SHOCKINGLY VIOLENT RIOT...
POFF
PF
COMING IN FOR A CLOSER LOOK AT THESE THUGS...
GRAB

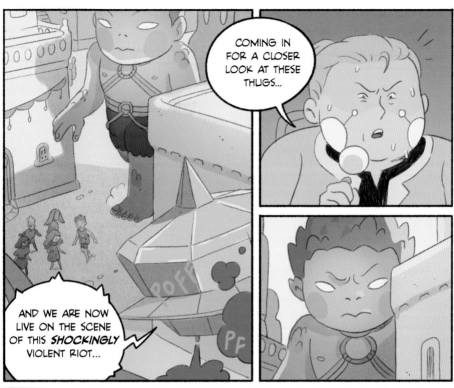

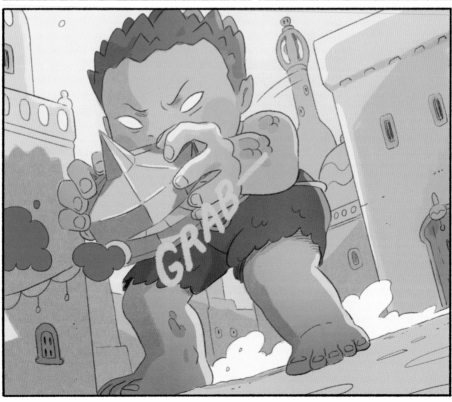

SKREEK
CRUNCH
HOW DARE YOU?! I'LL...
I'LL... TELL MR. MOON ABOUT THIS!

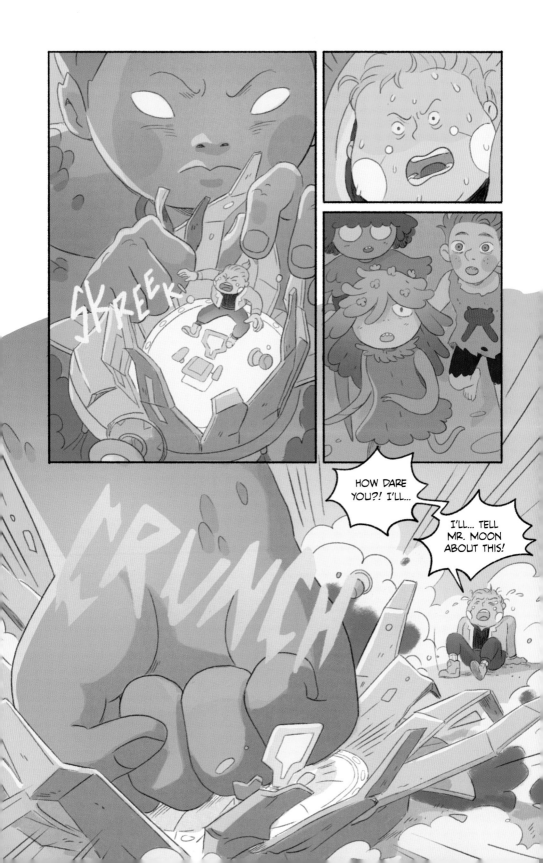

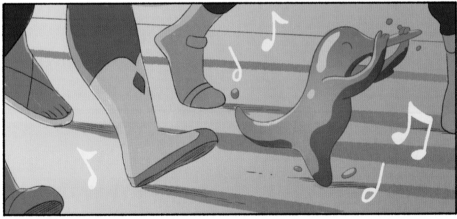

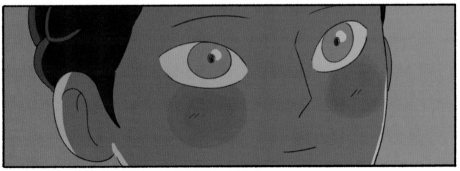

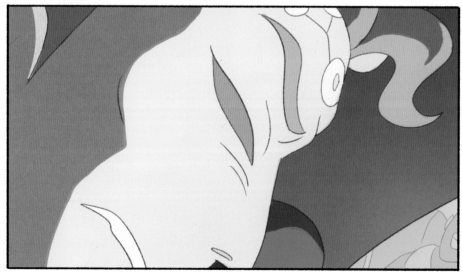

PATCH ME TO THE BOSS.

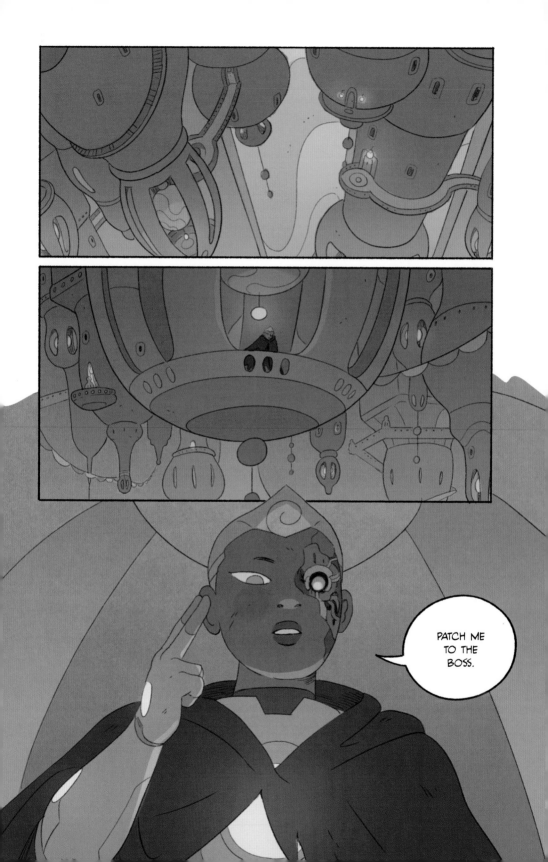

NO HINDRANCE IF ALL
THE LIVING JOIN IN
...DIFFERENCE IS
WHAT UNITES, NOT SEPARATES...
AND, DEFYING DARKNE
CELEBRATE GIVING...

WHEN FEAR AND
COME REAVING,
TURN AWAY FROM HATE AND ITS DICTATES
DIFFERENCE IS NO HINDRANCE
FOR ALL THE LIVING...
EVEN IN SORROW...
HEAVY WEIGHT HEAVING, A SMALL VOICE
STILL RESONATES...
DEFY THE DARKNESS,
CELEBRATE GIVING!

...THERE IS CLARITY AT THE TIME OF LEAVING...
WE'LL KNOW AS WE STAND BEFOR
THE GATE...
MORE LIVING OIL!!
DIFFERENCE IS NO HINDRANCE WIT
NG!
LOTS MORE!

LITTLE *RAM SAM SAM* IS PART OF A HUGE ENTITY!
YOU NEED TO REJOIN IT. I UNDERSTAND.
THANK YOU, *RAM SAM SAM. GO BE WHAT YOU ARE.*

defying

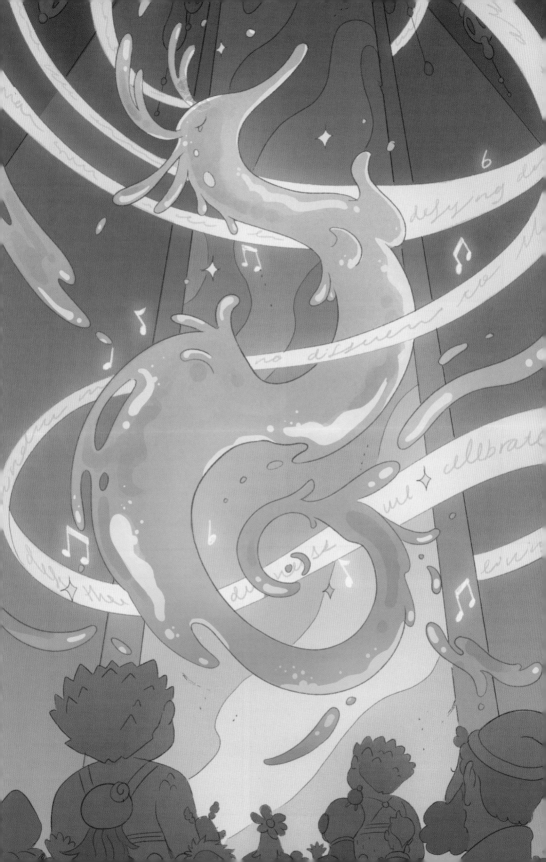

MANY STRANDS OF LIGHT...
INTERWEAVING

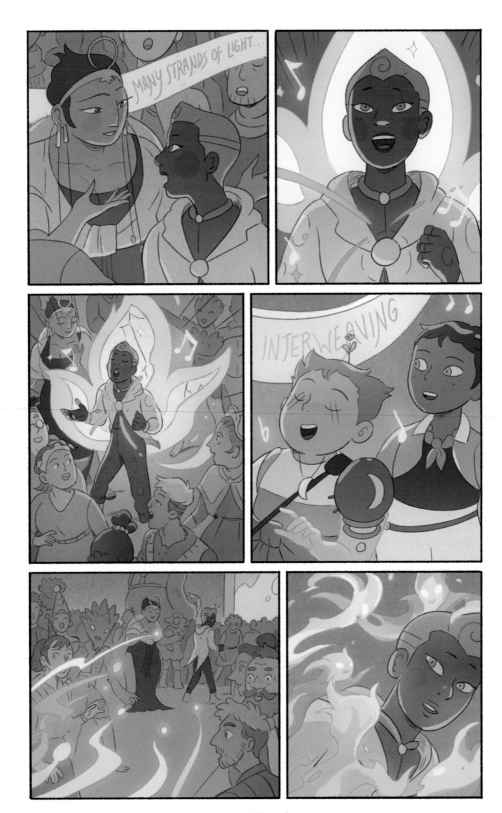

TO BLOCK THE POISON THAT BURNS, THAT HATES—
DEFYING THE DARKNESS...
WE CELEBRATE LIVIN

OPPORTUNITY HAD LEFT US
GRIEVING
BUT WE ARE JOINED IN THE SAME FATES...

TEN THOUSAND VOICES!!
NO HINDRANCE AS
DEFYING THE DARKNESS, CELEBRATE GIVING

S S S
SSSSH
foo
of

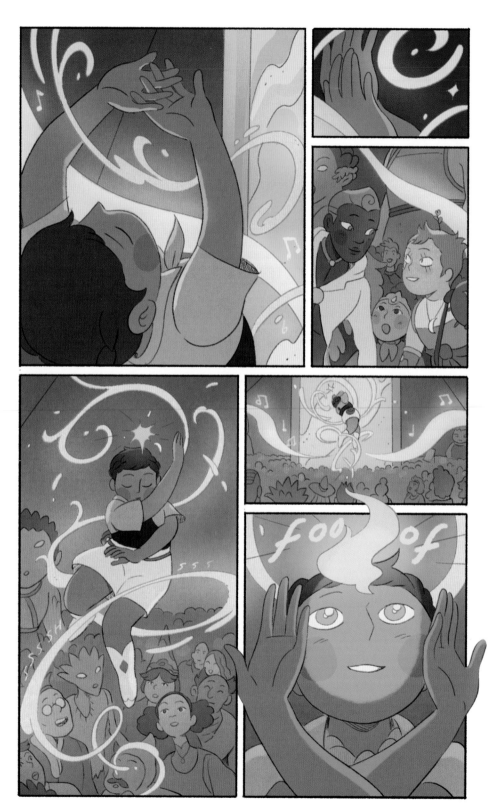

MR. MOON, I CAN TAKE HER OUT RIGHT NOW.
NO. STAND DOWN. I HAVE A MUCH BETTER IDEA.
THOSE PORTALS... AN ACTUAL GIFT FROM THE GODS! THEY'LL BRING ME MORE THAN I EVER HOPED FOR... THOSE CENTURIES OF LONELINESS WILL FINALLY PAY OFF....

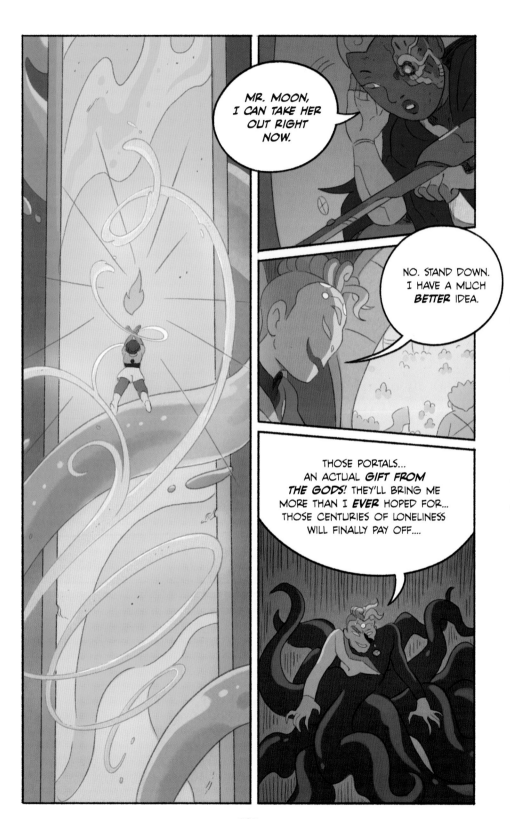

fooof *foobf!* *fooom* *foom!* *fooof*

SPRK!
I LOVE YOU, RAM SAM SAM.
FLOOOF

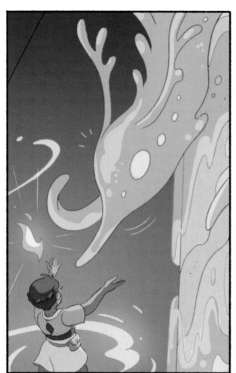

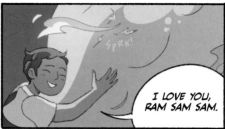

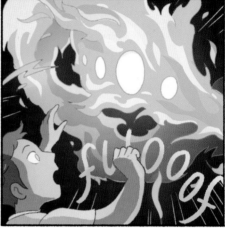

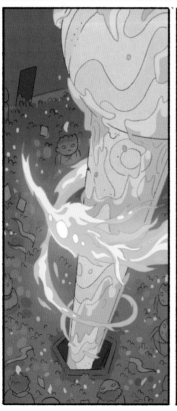

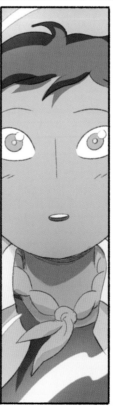

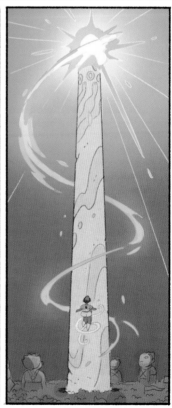

AN TZU...?

Chapter 15
SEAWEED SALAD

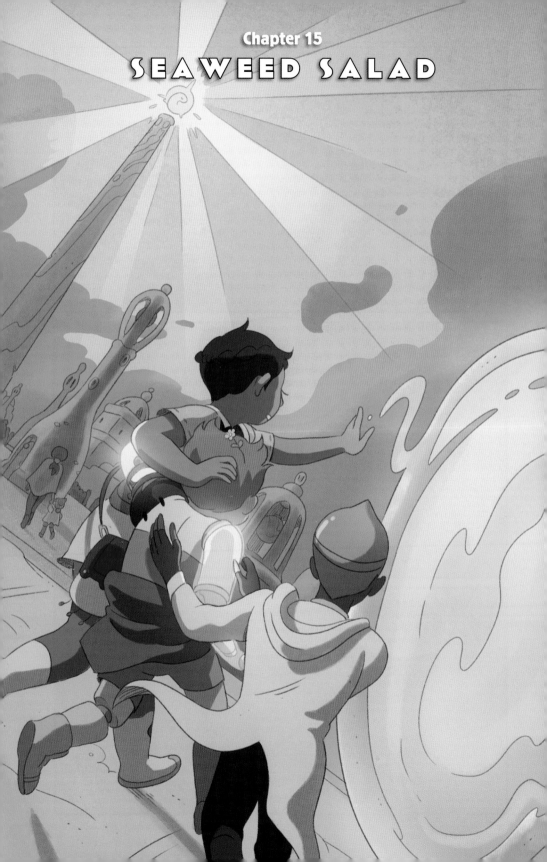

WE'LL NEED TO FILE PAPERWORK AND RECLAIM THE *FLITORI.* IT MAY TAKE TIME.

YOU MUST GO AHEAD. LIGHT THE LAST BEACON!

OONA, YOU NEED TO MAKE A PORTAL...TO *GRIMBO-E!*

THAT'S *POSSIBLE,* RIGHT?

A PORTAL TO *ANOTHER WORLD*...I'LL NEED ALL OF YOU.

WAIT... I'VE NEVER BEEN TO *GRIMBO-E!* HOW DO I TUNE IN TO IT?

WE STILL HAVE SOME *SEAWEED SALAD* FROM *MINTZ!*

YOU DO?!

THAT MIGHT WORK!

MUNCH!

MNCH MNCH

THAT'S ON THE MAIN *LICHEN ISLAND!* IT'S *GRIMBO-E,* ALL RIGHT.

CAN I EAT THE REST OF THAT?

KNOCK YOURSELF OUT.
MMM~!

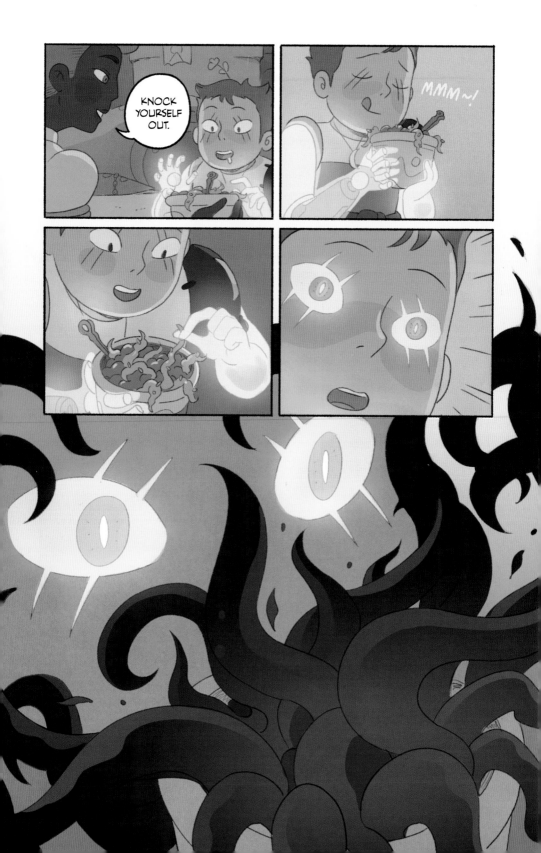

YOUR ONLY WAY TO RETURN HOME FROM THE FIVE WORLDS, NEKO...
...IS TO PORTAL BACK FROM SUN DOMANI ONCE ALL FIVE BEACONS ARE LIT!
I UNDERSTAND.

DO YOU REALLY? THERE CAN BE NO TRACE OF THE MIMIC CONTAMINATION, OR YOU WOULD RISK INFECTING THE SUN REALM, AND THE UNIVERSE--
IT WOULD NO LONGER BE CONTAINED IN THE FIVE WORLDS! ITS CORRUPTION WOULD SPREAD TO EVERYTHING. THAT CANNOT HAPPEN!
I'D SOONER BURN THE FIVE WORLDS THAN RISK THAT.

AN TZU?

UH...NOT HUNGRY ANYMORE.

Epilogue

CONTAMINATION

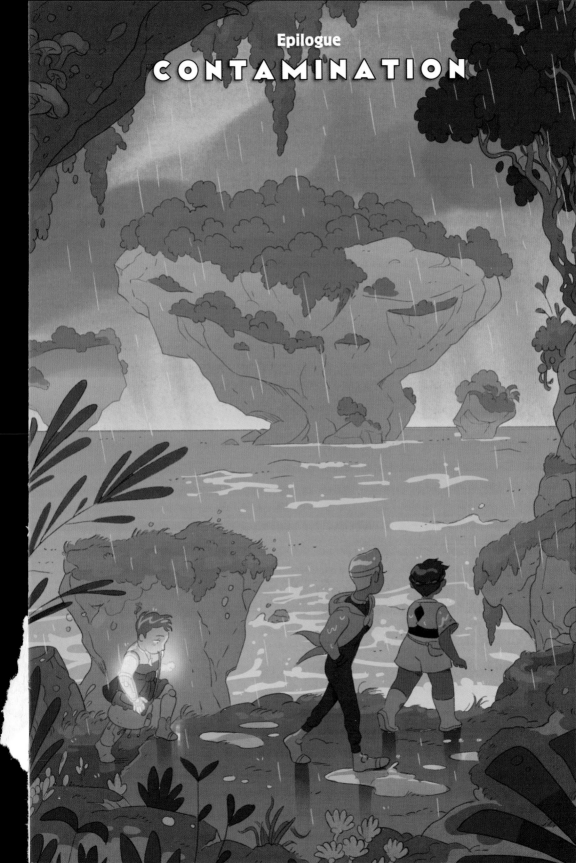

GAH!

I CAN'T LET OONA LIGHT THE LAST BEACON.

TO BE CONCLUDED IN 5W5: ***THE EMERALD GATE***

To my 5W teammates, one thousand pages on —MS

To Shudan —AS

To my beloved felids, Beepboop and Yeti —XB

To those who fight for what they believe in —MR

To Mom —BS

ACKNOWLEDGMENTS

Thank you, champions Tanya McKinnon, Fauzia Burke, and Kane Lee

Our exquisite Random House team:
Chelsea Eberly, Michelle Nagler, Elizabeth Tardiff, Diane Landolf, Kelly McGauley,
Joshua Redlich, Adrienne Waintraub, Janine Perez, Alison Kolani,
Jen Jie Li, Jocelyn Lange, Lauren Morgan, Mallory Loehr, Barbara Marcus

+ Special thanks for added help, friendship, and magic:
Edward & Marie-Claire, Siena, Clio & Julien, Sonia, Felix & Elia, Shudan,
Julie Sandfort, Cynthia Cheng, Sasha Marciano

And Bryan Konietzko, Kazu Kibuishi, Lisa Yee, Noelle Stevenson,
Gene Luen Yang, Vera Brosgol, George O'Connor, Sara Varon, Ben Hatke

And thank you, dear fans young and old, for inviting others into the Five Worlds,
and thank you friends and allies among booksellers, librarians,
teachers, bloggers, and reviewers. We love to hear from you.

 Published in the United States by Random House Children's Books, a division of Penguin Random House LLC, New York. • Random House and the colophon are registered trademarks of Penguin Random House LLC. • Visit us on the Web! rhcbooks.com • Educators and librarians, for a variety of teaching tools, visit us at RHTeachersLibrarians.com • Library of Congress Cataloging-in-Publication Data is available upon request. • ISBN 978-0-593-12055-2 (hardcover)—ISBN 978-0-593-12056-9 (paperback)—ISBN 978-0-593-12057-6 (lib. bdg.)—ISBN 978-0-593-12058-3 (ebook) • MANUFACTURED IN CHINA
10 9 8 7 6 5 4 3 2 1 • First Edition
Random House Children's Books supports the First Amendment and celebrates the right to read.

MARK SIEGEL has written and illustrated several award-winning picture books and graphic novels. He is also the editorial and creative director of First Second Books. He lives with his family in New York. Discover more at marksiegelbooks.com.

ALEXIS SIEGEL is a writer and translator based in Switzerland. He has translated a number of bestselling graphic novels, including Joann Sfar's *The Rabbi's Cat* and Pénélope Bagieu's *Exquisite Corpse* (both into English), and Gene Luen Yang's *American Born Chinese* (into French).

XANTHE BOUMA is an illustrator, comics artist, and colorist for animation and books. Based in Southern California, Xanthe enjoys soaking up the beachside sun.

MATT ROCKEFELLER is an illustrator and comics artist who grew up in Tucson, Arizona, and draws inspiration from its dramatic landscapes. His work has appeared in a variety of formats, including animation, book covers, and picture books such as *Pop!* and *Poesy the Monster Slayer*. He lives in Portland, Oregon, with his partner and a small dog that may or may not be a fox.

BOYA SUN loves to draw colorful comics about youth and adventure and is the creator of the graphic novel *Chasma Knights*. Originally from China, Boya has traveled from Canada to the United States and now lives in Los Angeles.

A Sneak Peek at the Making of 5W4

FELID REALM / FELID
COLOR-CONCEPT

FELIDS WRAP THEIR LOWER BODIES TO DEFINE THEIR DOUBLE CLOTHING

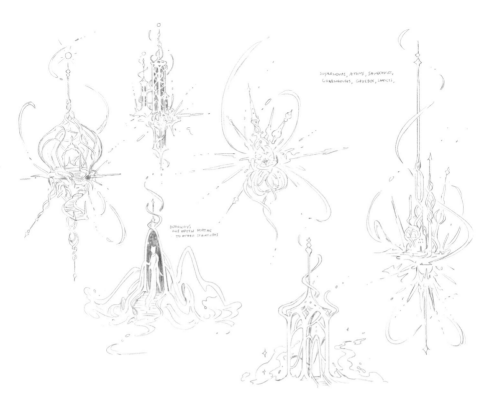

SUPERNOVAS, ATOMS, SATURSCARLET,
GREENHOUSES, GAZEBOS, LANCES.

DOORWAYS ARE OFTEN PORTALS
TO OTHER STRUCTURES

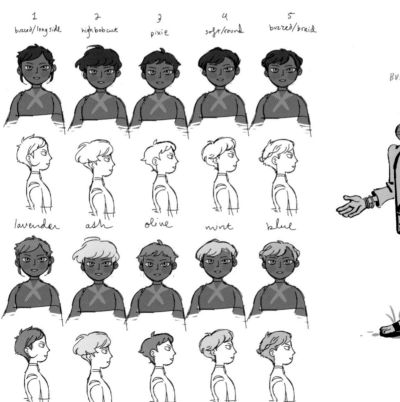

1	2	3	4	5
buzzed/long side	high bobcut	pixie	soft/round	buzzed/braid

lavender   ash   olive   mint   blue

BUSINESS URMUTH

Discover more  online!

@5WorldsTeam

POST YOUR **COSPLAY** PHOTOS AND SHARE YOUR BEST **FAN ART**
WITH OTHER 5-WORLDERS, WITH HASHTAGS #5WORLDSONA,
#DRAWOONA, #5WORLDS, AND #5WFANART.

jo_rioux

eclipse_orion

5worldsona expectation
THE
5worldsona reality
harmless grass kid
SAVE THE BEES

masqueradesage.art

Joy
is a music student in Salassandra that mainly focuses on her studies but draws for fun! Loves Music and always tries to be kind.
#5WorldSona

herro_cubes

eleoradraws

beside_wais

gay_as_a_pineapple

STAY TUNED
FOR CONTESTS
AND SPECIAL EVENTS
ON A PLANET NEAR YOU!

Where will the epic adventure end?
Find out in

5 Worlds
THE EMERALD GATE
"Mind-blowingly beautiful....
A must-read."
—R.J. Palacio,
#1 New York Times bestselling
author of Wonder
Mark Siegel
Alexis Siegel
Xanthe Bouma
Matt Rockefeller
Boya Sun

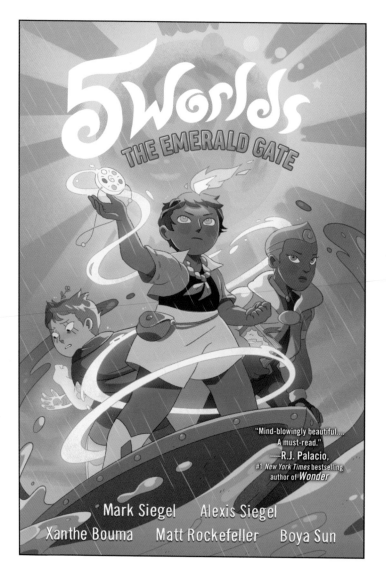

5W5:
THE EMERALD GATE

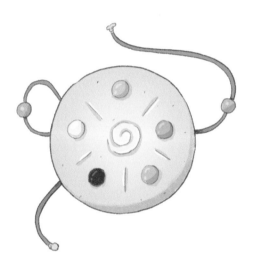

CITRINE CREST
FELICITY CRYSTALS
DANDELION TEMPLE
SALASSANDRA
GOLD KEEPERS
KYOJIN LANDS
Mystic's Moon
• WAKKA FELLA CARTOGRAPHERS •
SAFFRON SANCTUARY
Jonquil Woods
AMBRINE
LOVELY CURVES
GREENS MARKET
GREAT PYRAMID
HANGING MINARETS
GOLD BEACON
Succulents Inn
SUN QUEEN FOREST
LITTLE AMBRINE
STAR BALLA RAMBLA
LEMON RIVER